WHISKEY RIVER

Ralph Compton

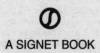

A SIGNET BOOK

SIGNET
Published by New American Library, a division of
Penguin Group (USA) Inc., 375 Hudson Street,
New York, New York 10014, USA
Penguin Group (Canada), 90 Eglinton Avenue East, Suite 700, Toronto,
Ontario M4P 2Y3, Canada (a division of Pearson Penguin Canada Inc.)
Penguin Books Ltd., 80 Strand, London WC2R 0RL, England
Penguin Ireland, 25 St. Stephen's Green, Dublin 2,
Ireland (a division of Penguin Books Ltd.)
Penguin Group (Australia), 250 Camberwell Road, Camberwell, Victoria 3124,
Australia (a division of Pearson Australia Group Pty. Ltd.)
Penguin Books India Pvt. Ltd., 11 Community Centre, Panchsheel Park,
New Delhi - 110 017, India
Penguin Group (NZ), 67 Apollo Drive, Rosedale, North Shore 0632,
New Zealand (a division of Pearson New Zealand Ltd.)
Penguin Books (South Africa) (Pty.) Ltd., 24 Sturdee Avenue,
Rosebank, Johannesburg 2196, South Africa

Penguin Books Ltd., Registered Offices:
80 Strand, London WC2R 0RL, England

First published by Signet, an imprint of New American Library,
a division of Penguin Group (USA) Inc.

First Printing, January 1999
First Printing (repackage RE), January 2011
10 9 8 7 6 5 4 3 2 1

A DEADLY CHOICE

"I *could* have you court-martialed for murder," Ferguson said. "Conviction calls for a mandatory death sentence."

"You speak as though there's some other choice," said Mark.

"Maybe there is. Have either of you ever heard of Wolf Estrello and his whiskey runners?"

Mark and Bill shook their heads, and Captain Ferguson continued.

"Rotgut whiskey is being brought by steamboat to Fort Smith," said Ferguson, "and wagoned from there to Estrello's stronghold in Indian Territory. This poison is being sold to the Kiowas and the Comanches. During the war, when we lacked the manpower to strike back, Estrello built a formidable empire, creating a haven for deserters from both sides of the conflict. Now we're ready to infiltrate Estrello's outfit and finish him once and for all."

"That's interesting," said Bill, "but it means nothing to us."

"Suppose there's a way the two of you can help destroy these whiskey runners, and in so doing, regain your freedom, your confiscated property, and full amnesty? Would it still mean nothing to you?"

"Great God almighty, what I wouldn't give for such a chance," Mark said.

This work is respectfully dedicated
to the memory
of my Texas friend, Tim Smith.
Vaya con Dios.

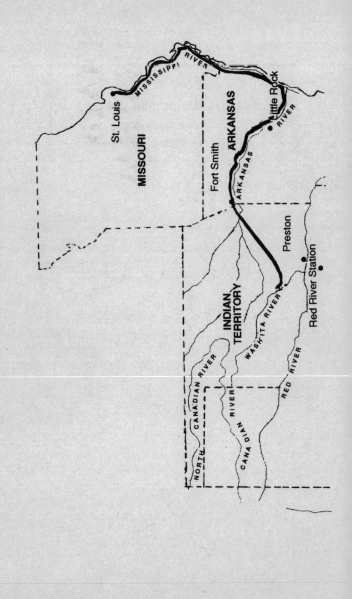

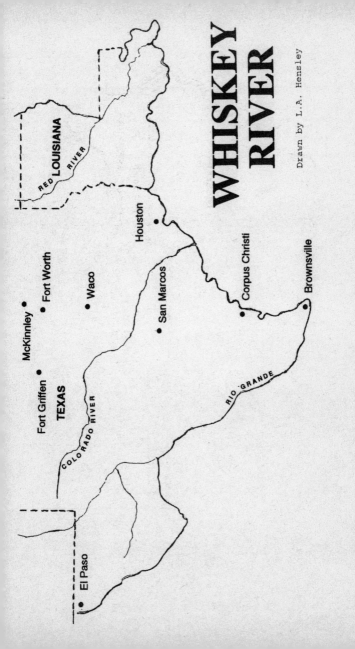

WHISKEY RIVER

Drawn by L.A. Hensley

CHARACTERS

The military at Waco: Lieutenant Henry
Sheriff at Waco: Rufe Elkins

The military at Fort Worth: Captain Ferguson, Lieutenant
Wanz, Sergeant Waymont, Corp. Tewksbury

Amanda and Betsy Miles: Twin sisters held captive by outlaws after their father was killed

Mark Rogers and Bill Harder: Young Texans forced by the
military to join the Wolf Estrello gang in an attempt to end
whiskey smuggling to the Indians

The Estrello gang:	
Wolf Estrello	Hugh Odell
Carl Long *	Bert Hamby
Lee Sullivan *	Alfonso Suggs
Vernon Clemans *	Snider Irvin
Todd Keithley *	Elgin Kendrick
Nick Ursino *	Burrel Hedgepith
Ed Stackler *	Ezra Shadley
Jules Hiram	Gid Patton
Walsh Tilden	Drew Wilder
	Chad Graves

(Estrello gang cont'd)

Skull Worsham	Dutch McCarty
Alonzo Bideno	Franklin Schorp
Waddy Jackman	Tull McLean
Blanco Cordier	Aldous Rains
Gabe Haddock	Saul Renato
Boyd DeWitt	Ike Jabez
Phelps Brice	

* Men who have sworn to break away from Estrello's gang

The Barton gang (Enemies of Estrello): Elizabeth Barton, Lefty Paschal, Hugh Sterns, French Loe, Whit Sumner, Will Macklin, Tobe Harve, Green Perryman

Second Barton gang (after Frank is killed): Elizabeth "Liz" Barton, Sim Bowdre, Kirk Epps, Tasby Winters, Wilson Soules, Weaver Upton, Blake McSween, Tally Weaver, Boyce Mann, Cordell Kazman, Burly Grimes, Duncan Trevino, Seldon Bagwell

Steamboat captains:
Boat #1, The *Aztec* (Captain Savage)
Boat #2, The *Goose* (Captain Lytle)
Boat #3, The *Midnight* (Captain Stock)
Boat #4, The *Star* (Captain Jenks)
Taylor Laird: Owner of illegal distillery in St. Louis
Burt Wills: Second in command to Laird
Captain Tyndall: Captain of Taylor Laird's steamboat

The Military in St. Louis: Captain Hailey, Sergeant Ember, Lieutenant Banyon
Dan Rowden: Sheriff of St. Louis county
Broken Nose: A renegade Indian
Otter Tail: Friend of Broken Nose
Buckshot Orr: A saloon owner in Fort Smith

Prologue

Waco, Texas. June 25, 1866.

After four long years they were coming home.

Mark Rogers and Bill Harder had much in common. While still young men, they had "learned cow" together in south Texas. When they were of age, they each had "proved up" on a half section of land, just north of Waco, on opposite banks of the Brazos River. The combined half sections were an ideal spread, with the Brazos providing abundant water. But when the war came and Texas seceded, Mark and Bill answered the call of the Confederacy, each just a few days shy of twenty-five. Now, after four long years of war, they neared Waco. They were self-conscious, for they were dressed in rags, which had once been the proud uniforms of the Confederacy. Neither man was armed, and for lack of saddles they rode mules bareback. Mark Rogers and Bill Harder were as gaunt as the animals they rode. When they rode in, Waco didn't *look* any different, but somehow, it felt all wrong. They reined up before Bradley's Mercantile. Ab Bradley had known them all their lives, and as they entered the store, he came limping to meet them.

"My soul and body," Ab said. "Mark Rogers and Bill Harder. I heard you was dead."

"There was times when we wished we were, Ab," said Mark. "Better that than rotting away in a Yankee prison."

"Yeah," Bill agreed. "All we have is these rags we're wearin', and two poor old mules as hungry as we are. The Yankees stomped hell out of us, took our guns, and sent us back with our tails between our legs. We heard soldiers would be comin' to put us under martial law until the Congress can decide what our punishment should be. Has any of 'em showed up?"

"They have," said Ab gravely. "There's already a full company of them in Austin. But that's not the problem. The problem is the newly appointed tax collectors. First thing they done was re-assess everybody's spreads, and them that couldn't pay lost everything. They started out takin' what belonged to those of you who went to war."

"The sons of bitches," Mark said. "We wasn't here. They've taken our spread?"

"Yours, and a dozen others, all up and down the Brazos," said Ab. "They're bein' held by men armed with scatterguns."

"By God," Bill said, "we'll organize the rest of the rightful owners and raise hell."

"I don't think so," said Ab. "Riley Wilkerson, Mike Duvall, and Ellis Van Horn tried to do exactly that. Without weapons, they attacked armed men and were shot down like stray dogs. The others that come back saw how it was, and left, traveling west. You can fight, but you can't win."

"Legalized murder, then," Mark said.

"That's what I'd call it," said Ab, "but I wouldn't say it too loud."

"Ab," said Bill, "we don't have a *peso* between us, and I don't know when we'll be able to pay you, but we need grub. Can you help us?"

"Some," Ab said cautiously. "The state's been up against

a blockade, and supply lines still ain't open. All I got is home-grown beef, beans, and bacon. No coffee, salt, or sugar."

"We'll accept whatever you can spare, and be thankful," said Mark.

"You don't aim to back off, then, do you?" Ab asked.

"Hell no," said Mark. "I don't know what we'll do, but by the Eternal, we'll be doing something."

"Just be careful, boys," Ab said.

"We're obliged to you for the warning," said Bill. "At least we won't be walking into it cold."

Ab filled two gunnysacks with supplies. Mark and Bill thanked the old man and left the store. Nobody paid any attention to the two riders as they rode south. Darkness was several hours away, and they rode into a stand of cotton-wood where there was a spring they remembered.

"Whatever bronc we have to ride," Mark said, "I'll feel better jumpin' on it with a full belly."

There was lush graze near the river, and the half-starved mules took advantage of it. Mark and Bill built a small fire over which they broiled bacon. Their meager meal finished, the angry duo set about making plans to reclaim their holdings.

"From what Ab told us," said Bill, "there shouldn't be more than two of these varmints with scatterguns guardin' our spread, and we'll likely find one of 'em holed up in my shack and the other in yours. We can take 'em one at a time and get our hands on them scatterguns."

"That'll bring the soldiers," Mark said. "We can't stand off the damn army with a pair of scatterguns. Besides, we were granted amnesty by signing pledges not to take up arms against the Union."

"Soldiers and amnesty be damned," said Bill. "Just because they beat us don't give 'em the right to move in and rob us blind while we're not here to defend what's ours. Soon as it's dark enough, I'm movin' in. You comin' with me?"

"I reckon," Mark said. "We'll likely light more fires than we can put out, but we can't just let them pick us clean. Hell, we'll do what we have to."

When darkness had fallen, they could see a distant light in the window or each of their shacks. They first approached Bill's spread, and in the dim light from a window, they saw the dark shadow of a horse tied outside the shack.

"You spook the horse," said Bill, "and I'll get him as he comes out the door."

Taking a handful of rocks, Mark began pelting the horse. It nickered, reared, and then nickered again. It had the desired effect. The door swung open, and the man with the scattergun started out. In an instant Bill had an arm around his throat and a death grip on the muzzle of the shotgun. He drove a knee into the man's groin, who, with a gasp of pain, released the shotgun. As he doubled up in agony, Bill seized the shotgun's stock and slammed it under the unfortunate man's chin.

"One of 'em down," said Bill with satisfaction.

"God almighty," Mark said, kneeling by the fallen man, "his neck's broke. He's dead."

"I didn't shoot him," said Bill, more shaken than he wanted to admit. "I promised that I wouldn't take up arms, and I didn't."

"We can't leave him here," Mark said. "What do you aim to do with him?"

"Leave him where he is for now," said Bill. "He ain't goin' nowhere. After we've took care of the varmint at your place, we'll dispose of the both of them where they'll never be found. Nobody can prove anything against us."

"Maybe you're right," Mark said. "We've gone too far to back out now."

Mark and Bill found a shallows and crossed the Brazos afoot, Mark carrying the confiscated shotgun.

"Give me the scattergun," said Bill. "If this one goes sour, I'll do the shootin'. So far, they got nothin' on you."

"No," Mark said. "This is my place. I won't have you takin' a rap for what I should have done. This time, you spook the horse, and I'll get the drop when the varmint comes bustin' out."

Bill began antagonizing the picketed horse, and the animal reacted predictably. But the animal's owner didn't come busting through the front door. He came around the corner of the house, and Bill threw himself facedown just in time to avoid a lethal blast from the scattergun. Like an echo, Mark fired, and the deadly charge caught the guard in the chest. He collapsed like a crumpled sack.

"My God," Bill said, "now we're into it."

"So we are," said Mark. "Would you feel better if I'd let him cut you in two with that cannon?"

"This is no time for damned foolishness," Bill said. "There's still a chance we can get out of this if we can stash this pair where they'll never be found, and we got to do it fast. There'll be rain before morning, and it'll cover our trail. Get a blanket from inside. We don't want blood all over this hombre's saddle when his horse shows up somewhere."

Riding their mules, they each led a horse with a dead man slung over the saddle. Far down the Brazos, they disposed of both dead men in a bog hole that overflowed from the river.

"A damned shame, lettin' these horses and saddles go, while we're ridin' a broke-down pair of old mules," said Mark.

"Hell of a lot easier than explaining to the law where we got the horses and saddles," Bill replied.

Just for a moment, the moon peeked from behind the gathering clouds, and turning, Mark looked back.

"What are you lookin' at?" Bill asked.

"Them horses," said Mark. "They're followin' us."

"Won't matter," Bill replied. "There'll be rain before daylight."

But the shotgun blasts had been heard at the old Duvall place, and by the time Mark and Bill returned to Bill's shack, they had unwanted company. While the pair still had the weapons they had taken from the dead men, they had no chance to use them. A cold voice from the darkness spoke.

"You're covered, and there's three of us. Drop the guns and step down."

Mark Rogers and Bill Harder had no choice. Dropping the shotguns, they slid off their mules.

"You got nothing on us," Bill said angrily. "These are our spreads, proved up before we went to war."

"And confiscated for nonpayment of taxes," said the hostile voice.

"What do you aim to do with us?" Mark asked.

"Turn you over to the military, come morning," said their antagonist. "We heard the shooting. Now you coyotes show up with a pair of shotguns and the horses followin' you that belonged to Pritchett and Wade. We don't know what you done with 'em, but there's enough evidence for the law to consider 'em dead."

"Yeah," said a second voice with an ugly laugh, "they'll be the first ex-Rebs to face up to a military firing squad."

The unfortunate duo was marched into Bill's cabin, where they were bound hand and foot. They were shoved roughly against a wall, where they slid down to uncomfortable sitting positions.

"My name's Crowder," said the most talkative of their trio of antagonists. "Gortner and Preemo will keep you company and see that you don't get any ideas. I'll telegraph the military at Austin, and there'll be soldiers here by tomorrow."

Waco, Texas. June 26, 1866.

The soldiers arrived in the late afternoon. There was a lieutenant, a sergeant, and two corporals. They stared for a moment at the two bound captives, and the officer spoke.

"I am Lieutenant Henry. Who are you men?"

"Mark Rogers."

"Bill Harder."

"As former Rebs, you signed amnesty oaths?"

"We did," said Bill grimly. "We was given no choice."

"From what I'm told, there's evidence the two of you are not only in violation of those oaths, but you have committed murder," Lieutenant Henry said. "You will be taken to jail in Waco until I've had time to investigate these charges. If evidence points to your guilt, the two of you will be taken to the stockade at Fort Worth for trial. Do you either of you have anything to say?"

"Plenty," said Mark, "but nothing that would help our cause. You might as well get on with your investigation."

This time, as Mark and Bill rode into Waco on their gaunt mules, they attracted plenty of attention, for they wore manacles on their wrists and were followed by a soldier escort. Standing in the door of his mercantile, old Ab sighed, his heart heavy for the two young men who had only wanted to claim what was rightly theirs. Reaching the jail, Mark and Bill had an unpleasant surprise. The "sheriff" was Rufe Elkins, a down-at-the-heels rancher nobody liked. Not only had Elkins not gone to war, but had been suspected of rustling the cattle of men who had. He seemed especially gratified, seeing Mark Rogers and Bill Harder in irons.

"I been expectin' them two," Elkins said with an evil grin. "I got cells just waitin' for 'em."

"I'm Lieutenant Henry," said the officer, not liking the man. "See to it they're issued decent clothing and are fed properly. For the several days they're likely to be here, I am holding you responsible for their well-being. Do you understand?"

"Yeah, I . . . yes, sir, I understand," said Elkins with considerably less enthusiasm. He was inclined to bully better men when he had the chance, but the cold eyes of Lieutenant Henry had taken his measure. Being a sheriff wasn't all that rewarding, but it paid better than his rawhide outfit, even with the cattle he was able to rustle. He said nothing to either of his prisoners as he locked them in a cell. Suppertime came. To the surprise of Mark and Bill, they were served a decent meal, including coffee.

"I reckon it all depends on which side of the war you was on, whether you get coffee or not," said Mark.

"I reckon," Bill replied.

"Haw, haw," said Elkins, who had been listening, "you two bastards was purely on the wrong side."

"You no-account son-of-a-bitch," said Bill. "It don't take guts to lay out in the brush and steal other men's cattle when they're away at war."

"Hidin' behind them soldiers, you got a big mouth, Harder," Elkins snarled. "Maybe when them soldiers has gone on their way, you'll find *me* behind you with a loaded Colt."

"If I do," said Bill grimly, "you'd better use it, or I'll take it away from you and put it where the sun don't shine."

Waco, Texas. June 29, 1866.

Lieutenant Henry didn't return for three days. When he did, his manner was grim, and he wasted no time confronting Rogers and Harder. When he stood before the barred door, Mark and Bill rose to their feet.

"We found the bodies," said Lieutenant Henry. "You're both under military arrest upon suspicion of murder. You'll be taken to Fort Worth for trial. Attorneys will be appointed to defend you. Meanwhile, anything you say may be held against you."

Mark and Bill said nothing. They sat down on their bunks, seeking to appear as calm as they could. They well knew that a murder conviction meant the firing squad. As they had expected, Sheriff Rufe Elkins looked for some sign of weakness in them, but he looked in vain.

"Sheriff," said Lieutenant Henry, "you will have the prisoners prepared to depart in the morning at 0800 hours. See that they are fed and that they're supplied with horses and saddles. The mounts and saddles will be returned."

"Yes, sir," Rufe Elkins said. "Will I be goin' along?"

"No," said Lieutenant Henry, "your services are not required."

Mark and Bill grinned in delight as Elkins tried vainly to play upon an importance he didn't possess. Ignoring him, Lieutenant Henry left immediately.

Bill laughed. "You'd better stick to stealing cows, Elkins. You just ain't impressive as a sheriff. Or a human being, for that matter."

"You mouthy bastards," said Elkins, "I'll ride all the way to Fort Worth, just to see the pair of you backed up against a wall and gunned down."

"It hasn't happened yet," Mark said, "but for the sake of your slimy hide, you better hope it does."

Elkins laughed. "Oh, I do hope it does. You gents have had a hell of a natural increase on what used to be your spreads, and I'm anxious to get my rope on the rest of them new mavericks."

Mark and Bill sat on their bunks, grinding their teeth in silence.

Waco, Texas. June 30, 1866.

The distance to Fort Worth was about seventy-five miles. Lieutenant Henry and his three companions picked up their prisoners and departed at exactly eight o'clock. Resting the horses, the journey could easily be made in a day. There was no talk. The soldiers were grim, so Mark and Bill kept their silence. Reaching Fort Worth, they were admitted, taken into the guardhouse, and their shackles removed.

"Well, pardner," said Mark when they were alone, "we wrestled the devil and lost big time. What'll we do now, wait for 'em to load their guns?"

"Oh, there'll be some kind of a trial," Bill said. "*Then* they load their guns."

But nothing was said about a trial, and after three days, both men had begun to wonder what exactly would be their fate.

Fort Worth, Texas. July 5, 1866.

Two soldiers came for them, and they were taken to the office of the post commander, Captain Ferguson. When Ferguson answered the knock on his door, the corporals saluted.

"At ease, corporals," said the officer. "You'll remain outside. Rogers, you and Harder will come in and be seated, he said, closing the door. "I am Captain Ferguson."

"I wish I could say I'm pleased to meet you, sir," said Bill, "but not under these kind of circumstances."

"Same feelings here," Mark said.

"I have spoken to your former commanding officer," said Ferguson, "and the two of you had distinguished careers with the Confederacy. Now you're both facing a murder charge. Why?"

"Because we come back to our proved up land and found it had been taken for taxes while we wasn't here," Bill said angrily. "That wasn't fair."

"I agree," said Ferguson, "but violating the law didn't help your cause. As you have no doubt heard, the murder of President Lincoln by a Southern sympathizer has official Washington furious. Northern congressmen have retribution on their minds."

"So they get back at us by stealing our land," Mark said bitterly. "We wasn't near the president. All we wanted was to forget about war and come back to Texas."

Captain Ferguson sighed. "The president wanted us *all* to forget about war, to allow the scars to heal. Now, God knows if they ever will."

"Everything you've said is true, sir," said Bill, "but it's of no help to us. What will become of Mark and me?"

"I *could* have you court-martialed for murder," Ferguson said. "Conviction calls for a mandatory death sentence."

"You speak as though there's some other choice," said Mark.

"Maybe there is," Ferguson said. "For some time, I've had a mission in mind that only a truly desperate man might consider. The two of you certainly qualify."

"If it's anything less than the firing squad," said Bill, "I'd be interested in hearin' it."

"It may be every bit as dangerous as the firing squad," Ferguson replied. "Have either of you ever heard of Wolf Estrello and his whiskey runners?"

Mark and Bill shook their heads, and Captain Ferguson continued.

"Rotgut whiskey is being brought by steamboat to Fort Smith," said Ferguson, "and wagoned from there to Estrello's stronghold in Indian Territory. This poison is being sold to the Kiowas and the Comanches. During the war, when we lacked the manpower to strike back, Estrello built a formidable empire, creating a haven for deserters from both sides of the conflict. Now we're ready to infiltrate Estrello's outfit and finish him once and for all."

"That's interesting," said Bill, "but it means nothing to us."

"Suppose there's a way the two of you can help destroy these whiskey runners, and in so doing, regain your freedom, your confiscated property, and full amnesty? Would it still mean nothing to you?"

"Great God almighty, what I wouldn't give for such a chance," Mark said.

"Amen," said Bill reverently.

"Then listen to me," Captain Ferguson said. "I want the two of you to work your way into Estrello's confidence. He's getting the whiskey from an illegal distillery somewhere near St. Louis, and then steamboating the loaded wagons along the Mississippi and the Arkansas to Fort Smith. Your mission will be twofold. I want you to escort the wagons by boat from St. Louis, and then become teamsters from Fort Smith to the Estrello hideout. Am I getting through to you?"

"Yes, sir," said Bill. "You want us on the inside of Estrello's whiskey-runnin' outfit. You're wantin' it rode into the ground. Just how many men are we up against?"

"Perhaps as many as fifty," Ferguson replied, "but we're prepared to grant amnesty to all who are willing to desert. Except for Estrello himself, of course. We want him dead."

"I'm beginning to understand what you have in mind," said Mark. "You aim for us to free all these varmints that's willing to give up whiskey running, and kill the others."

"Putting it bluntly, yes," Captain Ferguson said. "It was the president's dream to heal the nation, to forgive those deserving of it, and to eliminate the hard-core criminals who are beyond redemption. I believe you two can be rehabilitated, while helping to make the president's dream a reality. Needless to say, you are sworn to silence, and until such a time as you've successfully completed your mission, you'll be outlawed, with prices on your heads."

"What kind of prices?" Bill asked.

"Ten thousand dollars on the heads of each of you," said Captain Ferguson. "That's the same bounty on the heads of all the Estrello gang. I might add that those who aren't interested in amnesty and must be eliminated are subject to having their bounties paid to you, if you earn them. That's in addition to amnesty for yourselves and the return of your spreads near Waco, free and clear of all taxes."

"We're not concerned with bounty," said Bill. "We only want our spreads back and the freedom to live there."

"Nevertheless, there'll be some bounty," Captain Ferguson said. "Some of Estrello's bunch is hardened criminals. When it comes to a showdown, they'll shoot or be shot. Any questions?"

"Yes, sir," said Mark. "At which end of this 'Whiskey River' showdown do we buy in? At the start of it, where the wagons are loaded on the steamboats in St. Louis, or where the teamstering begins at Forth Smith?"

"If you value your lives," Ferguson said, "you'll find the Estrello stronghold in Indian Territory and hire on as teamsters if you can. Estrello will have you shot dead if you seem to know too much. I presume the two of you *are* qualified teamsters."

"Don't insult us, Captain," said Bill Harder. "We're Texan to the bone. We can saddle and ride anything with hooves and hair and hostle anything up to a six-horse or mule hitch, includin' a stagecoach."

"No insult intended," Ferguson said. "I just wanted to be sure I'm not sending you to your deaths. Are you prepared to break out tonight?"

"The sooner the better," said Mark. "How will we be armed?"

"Colts, seventeen-shot Winchesters, and a hundred and forty-four rounds for each of them," Captain Ferguson said.

"No Bowies, then," said Bill.

"No," Captain Ferguson said. "Remember, you're breaking out. You can't appear too well armed, or Estrello will get wise to you. Obviously, you'll be taking military mounts, and there'll be nothing in the saddlebags but military issue and some jerked beef. You'll have to make contact with Estrello and gain his confidence."

"Captain," said Bill, "you're a gambling man. You've just given us a chance to ride out of here for parts unknown, not knowing if our word is worth a damn or if our intentions are any better. How do you know we won't just ride out and keep going?"

"Let's just say I've become a good judge of men," Captain Ferguson said. "All my military commands have been in Texas, and I've never yet had a Texan betray my trust. Even if it cost him dearly. I've never asked or expected more than a handshake."

Without a word, Bill Harder and Mark Rogers got to their feet, and each man extended his right hand across Captain Ferguson's desk. Ferguson shook their hands, a slight smile on his rugged face.

"One thing more," said Captain Ferguson. "When you ride out, each of you will have a wanted dodger in your saddlebag. There'll be an artist-drawn likeness of you, with a price on your heads of ten thousand dollars each. The charge will be murder. If things go sour, it could well be the death of you, but there's no help for it. You'll need it to sell Estrello that you're on the dodge."

"One more question," said Mark. "How are we to convince any of Estrello's outfit that the offer of amnesty is for real if they run for it?"

"With these," Ferguson said, presenting each of them with a paper-thin oilskin packet. "In this is a copy of my agreement with you men, along with amnesty to as many of the Estrello men as you can convince. Hide these beneath the insoles of your boots, and don't remove them until you absolutely must. If Estrello even suspects, you're both dead."

"Bueno," said Mark. "We're ready when you are."

"After midnight, during the sentry change," Captain Ferguson said. "Your horses will be hidden in the darkness just south of the front gate, rifles in the saddleboots, with your Colts and ammunition in the saddlebags. We must make this look like an authentic break, so I'll have to sound the alarm. You'll have five minutes start. Head for Indian Territory. You'll get there well before daylight, and you won't be tracked after you've crossed the Red. Good luck, and *vaya con Dios.*"

"Thank you, sir," said Mark and Bill in a single voice.

They were fed especially well in the guardhouse, then took advantage of the remaining few hours to sleep. Shortly after midnight the door to their cell clicked open. They saw nobody, even as they crept across the compound to the front gate. It stood open just far enough for them to slip through. The saddled horses were waiting, and the two fugitives only took the time to remove their gun rigs from the saddlebags and belt them on. Then came the sound of an ominous bugle call, awakening the camp to a possible escape.

"That's us," said Bill. "Let's ride."

They swung into their saddles and circled wide of the post, galloping their horses along a deadly trail that might well be their last.

Chapter 1

There were eight whiskey-laden wagons. A dozen salty out-riders rode shotgun. Wolf Estrello, leader of the smugglers and lead rider, reined up.

"Whoa up," Estrello shouted. "Time to rest the mules."

The mounted men and the teamsters got down to stretch their legs. Jake Miles, oldest of the teamsters, had been on the outs with Wolf Estrello for weeks. Estrello wasted no time in threatening Jake with what the old man most feared.

"Jake," said Estrello, "I've waited long enough. When we reach camp, I'm takin' them two girls of yours to wife."

"Both of 'em?" an outrider asked.

"Both of them," said Estrello. "You think I ain't man enough?"

The expected trouble came from the expected quarter. Jake Miles was squeezing the trigger of his Colt when Wolf Estrello—heller with a pistol—drew and shot him twice. Jake, dying, stumbled back against the mules, and the animals reared in panic.

"Somebody steady them damn mules," Estrello bawled.

Carl Long and Lee Sullivan caught the bridles of the leaders, and all the men gathered around, looking at the bloody body of Jake Miles. While nobody spoke, the silence became all the more accusing.

"Damn it," said Estrello, "every man of you seen him draw. I shot in self-defense."

"It didn't come as no surprise," said Todd Keithley, a tall young man wearing an old used-up black Stetson and two guns. "You been houndin' the old man about them two gals for nigh a month now."

"My right, and none of your damn business, unless you'd like to take up the fight where old Jake left off," snarled Estrello.

Keithley's right hand was near the butt of his Colt, while the weapon on his left hip was turned butt forward, for a cross-hand draw. He eyed Estrello without fear, and it was the outlaw chieftain who backed down.

"This ain't the time or place for a fight," Estrello growled. "Let's move out. I'll take the lead wagon."

"Nobody's goin' anywhere until we've buried Jake proper," said Keithley.

Some of the men looked at Wolf Estrello with thinly veiled hate in their eyes, for there wasn't a man among them that Jake Miles hadn't befriended in some way. They were just a heartbeat away from open rebellion, and Wolf Estrello knew it.

"Then git a couple of shovels from the wagons and bury him," Estrello said. "The mules can use the extra rest."

Estrello had given in with poor grace, and they all knew it. He was leader of the band for two reasons. First, he would slit his own mother's throat if necessary, and second, he had been a major in the Union Army, stationed near St. Louis. He knew where and how to buy the illegal whiskey, and who to pay off. Nobody liked or trusted Estrello, and that had made him all the more bitter and hard to tolerate. He

had been caught bottom-dealing, and none of the outfit
would play poker if he sat in. The man stayed alive because
of his chain-lightning speed with a Colt and his willingness
to use it. Lee Sullivan had joined Todd Keithley in digging
a grave for Jake Miles. The unpleasant chore finished, they
dropped their shovels into one of the wagons. Wolf Estrello
sat on the box of the lead wagon and without a word swatted
the mules with the reins. The wagons lurched into motion,
five days from their camp south of the Washita River.

Indian Territory. Washita River. July 14, 1866.

Amanda and Betsy Miles had been born within minutes
of one another and were near a year past twenty-three. The
blue of their eyes was dazzling, their hair corn silk yellow,
and the only difference between them an obscure birthmark
no man had ever seen. They had spent the better part of two
days debating their precarious situation in the outlaw camp.

"Five years since Ma died, and five years among outlaws," said Amanda.

"But we're alive," Betsy replied, "and we owe old Jake
for that. We knew consumption was taking Ma from us, and
Jake saved us. He took us in and gave us his name. I think
now we'll have to trust him when he says he'll free us from
this hellhole."

"I do trust him," said Amanda. "It's the rest of the bunch
I'm afraid of. Any one of them could shoot Jake in the back,
and where would that leave us?"

"On the road to hell, I suppose," Betsy replied. "Estrello
will use both of us, without old Jake standing in his way."

"Oh, please stop talking that way," said Amanda. "You're

speaking of Jake as though he's already dead, and we're at Estrello's mercy."

"Perhaps he is," Betsy said. "Remember those terrible moods that Ma always had, just before somebody died? Well, I've been having them, too. The third one last night. If it's not you or me, then it's Jake. There's nobody else."

"Dear God," said Amanda, "what are we going to do? If we wait to talk to Jake, the whole gang will be here."

"I think that's why we have to take two horses and make a run for it tonight," Betsy replied. "I've heard one of the men say we're not more than fifteen miles north of the Red. After that, we'll be in Texas."

Indian Territory. North of the Red. July 14, 1866.

"I think we've dawdled around too long at this end of the Territory," Mark Rogers said, as they sipped their breakfast coffee.

"I don't," said Bill Harder. "Like Captain Ferguson said, they kind of got to discover us. Give 'em the idea we're here looking for them, and we're dead meat. Maybe tonight we can ride a little more to the east. Long as they've been doing this, there's bound to be some ruts from wagon wheels that'll put us on their trail."

"By the time Ferguson made his deal, I was ready to kiss his feet," said Mark. "Now I'm not all that sure he's done us any favors. This bunch, when we find 'em, is gonna be about as loyal as a pack of coyotes, and they'll all have their eyes on us."

"Well, hell," Bill said, "if we hire on as teamsters, all we got to do is drive a four- or six-horse hitch. You and me can do that with our eyes shut, can't we?"

"I reckon," said Mark, "but something about all this bothers me. Reminds me of a time I drawed a full house and should have raked in about a thousand bucks. But the bastard on the other side of the table had a straight diamond flush."

Bill laughed. "I seem to recall it bein' closer to fifty bucks. Ever'time you think back on it, there's more money on the table. I think you're gettin' a case of the whim-whams. Hell, all we got to do is keep ourselves alive until we can bust up this gang of smugglers. How could that get any more complicated?"

But that was before the intrepid Texans encountered the naked Amanda and Betsy Miles in their desperate bid for freedom.

Outlaw camp on the Washita. July 17, 1866.

Wolf Estrello had left eight men in camp, and they had ignored the two women. By the time Amanda and Betsy Miles had convinced themselves their only hope lay in taking two horses and riding for their lives, the event they most dreaded happened. They heard the distant rattle of approaching wagons.

"God help us," said Amanda. "We waited too long. Tonight there'll be thirty men here in camp."

But the situation immediately worsened, because when the lead wagon appeared, Wolf Estrello was at the reins. That position had always belonged to Jake Miles.

"Something's happened to Jake," Amanda said fearfully.

One by one, the wagons drew up. The teamsters began unharnessing the weary teams, and as Amanda and Betsy fearfully approached Wolf Estrello, the outlaw made it a point to ignore them. It was Amanda who asked the dread question.

"Where's our Pa? Where's Jake?"

"Dead and buried," said Estrello unfeelingly. "The old fool got gun-happy, and I had to shoot him. Now you two pieces of baggage had better be nice to me, or the trail could get damned rocky."

But things got complicated quickly in a manner Wolf Estrello hadn't expected. Amanda and Betsy, of a single mind, threw themselves at the surprised outlaw, cursing and crying. They tore at Estrello's hair, smashed their small fists into his cruel face, and in her fury, Amanda was able to plant a well-placed boot in his groin. Estrello's outfit looked on with some admiration, and nobody became alarmed until the two women had Estrello facedown, stomping him. It was Carl Long and Lee Sullivan who finally dragged the women away. When Estrello finally sat up, his face was a bloody mess. His swollen eyes came to rest on Todd Keithley, who was openly grinning.

"By God, it took the lot of you long enough to drag them off me," Estrello snarled.

"It never crossed our minds you needed help," said Keithley. "How many times have you said you could handle both of 'em?"

"I won't be forgettin' you, smart mouth," Estrello said. "Long, you and Sullivan take them hellions to my tent. I'll take care of them after I've cleaned myself up."

"You want we should tie 'em hand and foot?" Lee Sullivan asked.

"No," said Estrello, "they've been coddled too long. If they try anything foolish, put a slug through any part of their carcass that appeals to you."

Some of the men laughed, while others eyed Estrello coldly. His was an outfit divided, and he was of a mind to use these stubborn females to establish his undisputed leadership. When he reached the tent that was his quarters, Amanda and Betsy sat on the ground. The two outlaws guarding them had their Colts drawn.

"Do we go or stay?" Carl Long asked nervously.

"You don't do a damn thing, either way, until I say so," Estrello snarled, "and I ain't give you no orders. You women get to your feet and strip."

"You murdering son-of-a-bitch," said Amanda with a hiss, "go ahead and shoot me. It's the only way you'll ever see me without my clothes."

"That goes for me as well," Betsy said.

Both girls clasped their hands to still their trembling, but the fire in their eyes was unmistakable.

"Spirited, ain't you?" said Wolf Estrello. "I like that, be it in a horse or a woman. Now I aim to ask you one more time to get on your feet and strip."

"Why don't you strip us yourself, big man?" Amanda said. "I have a place in mind to plant my other boot."

Defiantly, both women had gotten to their feet, their backs to the rear of the tent. The outlaw said no more, and when Amanda taunted him, he moved like a lightning bolt. His heavy fist struck the girl below the left ear, and she fell back against the canvas, sliding to the ground.

"Damn you," said Betsy, leaping toward Estrello.

But Carl Long slammed the muzzle of his Colt against her head, and Betsy joined her sister on the ground.

"Now the two of you get the hell out of here," Estrello ordered.

They went, carefully closing the tent flap behind them. Estrello wasted no time, lest the women regain consciousness before his lowdown intentions had been accomplished.

He first drew off Amanda's and Betsy's boots. Their only other garments were men's shirts and Levi's. He stripped Amanda first, and then Betsy, catching his breath at their unspoiled beauty. He laughed as the girls came to their senses, frantically trying to cover vital parts of their bodies with their hands.

"Look, you bastard," said Amanda. "That's all you'll ever have a chance to do."

"There'll be no supper for either of you," Estrello said, "and breakfast depends on how nice you are to me the rest of the night. I'll see you again after supper."

"Bring all your gunmen with you," Betsy taunted. "You'll need them."

For all their bravado, the two women stared at each other in terrified silence. They had only their boots and Wolf Estrello's promise to return. Of his evil intentions, they had not the slightest doubt.

"It'll be dark in a few minutes," said Amanda. "Then we can crawl out from under the back of this tent."

"Stark naked and without horses," Betsy said. "They can just wait for daylight and then track us down like starved coyotes."

"When it's dark enough, perhaps we can get to the horses," said Amanda.

"No saddles," Betsy said. "Settin' your naked behind on a horse's backbone will be like straddling a corral fence without your britches."

"I'd prefer *that* to having Wolf Estrello straddle *me,*" said Amanda, "if you know what I mean."

"I know very well what you mean," Betsy said, "and I'm not disagreeing with you. I'll stand anything a horse can do to my behind, as long as that pig Estrello keeps his dirty hands off me."

Amanda and Betsy pulled on their boots, waiting for darkness. They could hear the rattle of pots and pans as the outlaws prepared supper.

"I'm hungry," said Amanda.

"So am I," Betsy said, "and they'll be counting on that. Our only hope is reaching and crossing the Red before daylight. Surely, someone in Texas will help us."

"Us being naked won't help our cause," said Amanda.

"No," Betsy agreed, "but we must get beyond the dirty hands of Wolf Estrello. I'll be willing to gamble on anybody else. And I do mean *anybody*."

Darkness came, and the supper fire outside created weird dancing shadows on the side of the old canvas tent in which Amanda and Betsy waited. The sounds of supper became less and less. Time was short.

"If we can slip under the back of the tent, it'll be between us and the horses," Amanda said.

"Estrello, bastard that he is, may have a double guard posted," said Betsy. "Suppose we're discovered before we can mount horses?"

"Head for the shadows along the Washita," Amanda said. "The important thing is, they must not catch us. Estrello has plans for us tonight. It's time to go."

They worked a tent peg loose, allowing them to crawl under the canvas. Briars and a variety of thorns tore at their exposed flesh, until finally they were free, crawling on their hands and knees. They could see some of the outlaws beyond the tent. Slowly, they crept toward the grazing horses and mules. Estrello insisted on riding a half-wild black stallion, and the black raised his head and perked his ears, listening. Amanda and Betsy took just a single step. Spooked, the black reared, nickering long and loud. He sidestepped, and the rest of the animals followed his lead.

"They're after the horses," Estrello bawled. "Shoot to kill."

All hope gone, Amanda and Betsy ran for the shadows along the Washita. Lead sang like bees, and a slug burned a furrow along the inside of Amanda's left thigh. Lead ripped across Betsy's chest from left to right, and she fell.

"How bad?" Amanda demanded, dropping to her knees beside Betsy.

"It took some hide off my chest where I can't afford to lose any," said Betsy.

The two fugitives got to their feet, and the shooting had all but died away.

"Save your shells," shouted Wolf Estrello. "I want some of you watching those horses and mules for the rest of the night."

"There goes our only hope," Amanda said. "If we escape, it'll have to be afoot. We'll have until dawn to reach the Red and cross into Texas."

"We don't know they won't cross the Red and come into Texas after us," said Betsy. "We humiliated Estrello, and he'd planned on using us to make up for that tonight. Now he's hotter than seven kinds of hell."

"I wish we could follow the river," Amanda said. "It'll be awful easy for us to get lost and turned around, traveling in a circle."

"We must travel south, toward the Red," said Betsy. "We'll be sure the North Star is always behind us. Come on."

Indian Territory. July 17, 1866.

"Maybe you was right, pullin' away from the Washita," Mark Rogers said. "If we was told the truth at Fort Worth, that bunch of outlaws is holed up somewhere along the river a few miles north of the Red. We can make a better case for ourselves, ridin' north, which is the quickest way out of Texas."

"For that matter, the Washita flows into the Red," said Bill, "but it's too far south. If that bunch of renegades is holed up in Indian Territory, they won't be camped on or near the Red. I figure we can follow the Red south, until just before it crooks into Arkansas. From there, we'll follow the Washita north. At least, it won't look like we come straight from Fort Worth."

Still avoiding the Washita River, Mark and Bill found a spring hidden away in a mass of trees and boulders. Their supper fire wouldn't be visible for more than a few feet away, and the trees would dissipate the smoke. They unsaddled their horses. Bill started a fire, while Mark hacked off some bacon. Suddenly, Bill dropped to the ground belly-down, pulling his Colt. Unsure as to what had startled Bill, Mark had drawn his own weapon.

"You're covered," Bill said. "If you have weapons, throw them out ahead of you and come out with your hands up."

"We don't have any weapons," said a frightened voice. "It's my sister and me, and we don't have a stitch of clothes between us. We're hungry."

"Come on, then," Bill said.

The two of them came forth, so weary and hungry it seemed their nakedness no longer bothered them. One of them had a lead burn across her chest, while the other had bled from a wound inside her left thigh. Briars and thorns had raked them unmercifully, and they were a bloody mess. But Mark Rogers and Bill Harder were temporarily speechless. The two girls seemed identical in the pale starlight. Mark recovered first.

"The two of you need some doctoring. We have some clean bandages and a couple of tins of salve, if you . . . uh . . ."

"We trust you," said Amanda. "While you're doing that, we'll tell you what's happened to us. I'm Amanda Miles, and this is Betsy, my sister. We ran away from a bunch of outlaws, after the leader of the gang stripped us."

"It's not nearly as simple as it sounds," Betsy said. "Perhaps we'd better start at the first, when old Jake took us to the camp."

Bill had spread a blanket. The girls lay down, allowing their boots to be removed. Betsy began talking as Bill Harder began to cleanse her wounds. Finally, Amanda took up the story as Mark doctored her as well as he could.

"So you spent five years in an outlaw camp with a man who wasn't your father," said Bill. "He should have gotten you out of there."

"It wasn't that easy," Amanda said heatedly. "Jake had a price on his head, like most of the others. He protected us as long as he could."

"Until this Wolf Estrello killed him," said Mark.

"Yes," Amanda said. "Estrello wants Betsy and me for . . . for . . ."

"I reckon we have a pretty good idea what he wants you for," said Bill, "and neither of you would have him if he was solid gold."

"I'd rather be dead than have his hands on me," Betsy said.

"So would I," said Amanda with a shudder. "Will you help us escape?"

"I wish we could," Bill said, "but we killed a pair of Yankee tax collectors, and we got a price on our heads. That's why we're settin' here in the Territory."

"Oh, God," cried Amanda, "they'll be coming for us at first light."

"Suppose we stand up to them and don't let them take you?" Mark asked.

"It would be ever so brave of you," said Amanda, "but there are thirty armed men. An order from Wolf Estrello, and they'd shoot you dead."

"There must be an answer to this," Bill Harder said. "If old Jake stood up for you and kept Estrello at bay, why can't Mark and me do the same?"

"Jake was able to do it because Wolf Estrello thought Jake was our father, and we can't make that claim of either of you," said Betsy.

"Maybe Bill and me have an even stronger hold on you," Mark said. "Suppose the two of you were committed to us back before we went to war? You reckon this Estrello's got the sand to try and steal two women who were promised to us more than five years ago in Texas?"

"I . . . I don't know," said Amanda. "The outfit's divided. Some of the men don't get along hardly at all with Estrello."

"You're not sure every man would back Estrello in a showdown over the two of you, then," Bill said.

"Most of the outfit's loyal to Estrello only because of the money," said Amanda. "With no money involved, he can't count on more than half his men. Perhaps not that many."

"Just one thing wrong with that," Betsy said. "We have no right to ask either of you to risk your lives to save us. You can't do it."

"Oh, but we can," said Mark. "When we left to join General Lee, Bill, these two little shirt-tail gals was just seventeen. You remember 'em promising themselves to us, once the war was over? There was Betsy and you, Amanda and me."

"I remember it like it was yesterday," Bill said. "Come daylight, we'll straighten out this damn bunch of outlaws. But we got to have your help, girls. Can you convince this bunch of bastards that you been spoken for, that you're hog-wild crazy about Mark and me?"

"Save us," said Betsy, "and I'll go anywhere with you, doing anything you ask of me."

"She's speaking for me, too," Amanda said.

"Then we have some heavy talkin' to do," said Bill. "We got to know as much as the two of you can tell us about your lives in Texas, before you were brought here. Betsy, do you object to being my promised bride when we face that bunch tomorrow?"

"Not in the slightest," Betsy said. "Just don't be shocked at how far I'm willing to go when I have to."

"Amanda," said Mark, "it's you and me. Can we convince the varmints you've been promised to me for five years?"

"I'm willing to become a wife to you even if we never stand before a preacher," said Amanda. "I'll die before Wolf Estrello takes me."

"Damn it, the two of you deserve better than being tied down to a pair of outlaws," Mark said. "We have prices on our heads, too, and you're just swapping one bad deal for another. Even if we had extra horses, we couldn't take you away from here."

"We know that," said Betsy, "but you're willing to risk your lives to save us. It may be more difficult than you expect. If this is to work out like we're planning, the two of you will have to join Estrello's gang. He's a devil with a pistol, just looking for a chance to kill. I'm afraid for you—for all of us."

"In anything like a fair fight, Mark and me can face Estrello down," Bill said, "but we must avoid any gun trouble if we can. We need time to divide the outfit, to win the favor of some of the men who might be willing to turn on Estrello. If it's our guns against the whole bunch, then the odds go to hell."

"We need to know as much about this Estrello as we can," said Bill. "Like how far can we push the situation shy of a gunfight?"

"Estrello has the pride of a dozen men," Betsy said. "That's why some of the men hate him. He's pistol-whipped them for no reason. He vowed to take both me and Amanda to bed last night, and that's why we ran away. He's a cruel beast who will beat a horse until he breaks its spirit."

"That's why he left us our boots," Amanda added. "He *wanted* us to run away, knowing we didn't have a chance without clothes or horses. Now he'll feel all the more justified in punishing us."

"That's the answer, then," said Mark. "He's busy gettin' a mad on tonight, justifying what he aims to do tomorrow, after he's run the two of you down. We'll turn that around and use it against him, forcing the bastard to pull a gun if he has the nerve."

"Oh, dear God, no," Amanda said. "He *has* the nerve. Nobody will draw against him. We heard one of the men say he shot Jake twice, although Jake drew first."

"Now don't you worry," said Mark. "Bill and me have an edge. There's one thing that every bull-of-the-woods gunman is afraid of, and that's comin' face-to-face with a better man, a faster gun. This lowdown son-of-a-bitch is about to meet two of them, all in the same day."

"You're risking your lives for us," Betsy said. "I feel so . . . so guilty."

"Don't," said Bill. "Remember, we're on the dodge ourselves. We got enough jerked beef and bacon for a week. If we stay in Indian Territory, we'll have to throw in with Estrello. The only way we can do that is to purely scare hell out of him."

"I'm so afraid for you both," Amanda said. "A fight over us will hurt your chances."

"Wrong," said Mark. "Many a man who's an outlaw and killer will still respect a good woman. Just bear in mind that after four long years of war, Bill and me come lookin' for the two of you, expecting you to live up to your promises. Not to say that Estrello won't try to kill us somewhere along the trail, but we can shame him before his outfit, once he comes looking for you."

"We know you don't have much food," Amanda said, "but could we have something to eat? We weren't allowed any supper."

"We still got a pretty good chunk of bacon," said Bill. "We'll broil you some of that and make a fresh pot of coffee."

After eating, Amanda and Betsy went to the spring, where they filled their tin cups with fresh water.

"My God," Mark said softly, "did you ever see two more beautiful girls? I'd fight my way through fire and brimstone and wrestle the devil for a smile from either of them."

"By the time we bust up this Estrello gang—if we can stay alive—we'll each have a woman beside us that'll rattle the eyeballs of every man in Texas. But we ain't takin' 'em without going before a preacher, are we?"

"Not if we can avoid it," said Mark, "but this Estrello may be just cruel enough to see that the girls live up to their promises to us, with or without a preacher."

"We're a mite shy of blankets," Bill said when Amanda and Betsy returned from the spring. "Betsy, you take my blankets, and Amanda, you'll take Mark's. We won't have you lying naked on the ground."

"The wind is cold," said Amanda, "but it's not fair, us taking your blankets. Perhaps we can share them."

"Yeah," Bill said. "The two of you sharing Mark's, with Mark and me sharin' mine."

Mark almost choked, while the girls burst into laughter.

"Mark will sleep next to me," said Amanda, "while Bill sleeps next to Betsy."

"Yeah," said Bill, "and you got nothin' to be afraid of. We only take off our hats."

Chapter 2

Outlaw camp on the Washita. July 18, 1866.

Wolf Estrello decided against further humiliating Amanda and Betsy Miles. He was just vain enough that he didn't want any man in the outfit seeing them naked, so he folded their clothing and placed it in his saddlebag. For appearances' sake, he would take some of his outfit with him, carefully choosing those who wouldn't question whatever he did.

"Jules Hiram. Hugh Odell, and Bert Hamby, you'll ride with me," Estrello said.

"Four of you against two scared, naked girls is a mite one-sided," said Todd Keithley. "I'll just ride along and see that the girls aren't mistreated and their clothing's returned."

"You'll go nowhere against my orders," Estrello shouted. "I'll have you bound and horsewhipped for insubordination. Now two of you saddle two extra horses."

"Then you'd better include me in whatever you have in mind," said Ed Stackler. "Jake Miles was my friend. I should have gut-shot you last night, before you stripped those two girls and drove them out of camp. I'll be riding with you this morning, like it or not."

Wolf Estrello found himself in trouble. As Todd Keithley backed away from the group, Ed Stackler stood beside him.

Behind the two of them came Carl Long, Lee Sullivan, Nick Ursino, and Vernon Clemans. Every man carried two guns. Some of the other men looked doubtfully at Estrello, perhaps of half a mind to join the opposition. It had soured them, seeing old Jake Miles baited into a gunfight he couldn't win and being shot down.

"Then I'll take four men," Wolf Estrello said. "Keithley, you and Stackler can go, and I'll take Hiram and Odell. Does that strike everybody as fair?"

"As far as it goes," said Stackler. "You've made your brag, but you won't be taking either of those girls against her will."

"I'm with you on that," Keithley said.

There was immediate agreement from the others. While these men were outlaws, there was a streak of decency within them all that forbade this disgraceful thing Wolf Estrello had in mind.

Without a word, Keithley and Stackler saddled their own mounts and then a pair for Amanda and Betsy. They rode out behind Estrello, Hiram, and Odell. The trail wasn't difficult to follow, for the girls had kept close to the riverbank, and their boot tracks were plain. There were bits of dried blood on leaves on the ground and on tree trunks.

Hiram laughed. "Looks like they got cut up some, or nicked by some lead."

But his laughter withered quickly away when the cold eyes of Keithley and Stackler met his.

"Rein up," Estrello ordered. "I smell smoke."

"Them two wouldn't have no way to start a fire," said Odell.

"Who says it's their fire?" Estrello said. "It could be the law. We'll leave the horses here and go on afoot. We got the wind in our favor."

But in the camp a quarter of a mile distant, Mark Rogers and Bill Harder waited, not depending on the wind. Each man stood next to his grazing horse, and when the animals raised their heads and perked their ears, their riders quickly caught their muzzles before they could nicker. Amanda and Betsy had covered themselves with the blankets.

Estrello led the way, followed by the other four. None of them expected what they encountered.

"That's far enough," Bill Harder said. "You're covered. Who are you, and why are you invading our camp?"

"I'm Wolf Estrello, and I'm here to claim a pair of runaway females that's been in my camp for near five years. Turn them over to us and save yourselves some trouble."

"They've told us about their experiences in your outfit, including the shooting of Jake Miles, their pa. But that won't make any difference to you."

Suddenly from beyond the spring, Mark Rogers stepped out, and it was he who spoke.

"I'm Mark Rogers, and my *amigo* is Bill Harder. Amanda and Betsy Miles are twenty-three years old. Five years ago, before Bill and me joined the Confederacy, Amanda and Betsy were promised to us. They would wait until the war was done. Now Bill and me are callin' in those claims, with or without your approval."

"Wolf," said Olson excitedly, "these *hombres* got prices on their heads. I saw the wanted dodgers while we was in St. Louis. Hell, they're worth twenty thousand dollars, dead or alive."

Wolf Estrello laughed. "So you're no better than we are. What do you aim to do, here in Indian Territory, with two females on your hands?"

"We thought we might do the same thing you're doing," Bill Harder said coolly. "After all, you don't have a government franchise to sell rotgut whiskey to the Comanches and Kiowa, do you? Mark and me can handle anything up to a six-horse or -mule hitch."

"Compete with me?" Estrello roared. "I have thirty men. By God, both of you will be dead by this time tomorrow."

"Wolf," said Stackler, speaking for the first time, "you have maybe fifteen men who will likely pull a gun for you. The others will turn on you, if only to revenge old Jake's death. Wouldn't you say so, Keithley?"

"I would," Keithley replied, "and Wolf, I think it's time Amanda and Betsy had their clothes returned. I saw you put them in your saddlebags."

"I'll see that they get them," said Estrello angrily. "Where are they hiding?"

"Don't you come near us, Wolf Estrello," Amanda shouted. "We're living up to our promise of five years ago. Let Mark or Bill bring our clothes to us."

There was no help for it, and removing the rolled-up garments from his saddlebag, he silently passed them to Bill. But Estrello wasn't the kind to take water, and as Bill turned away, Estrello went for his revolver. Mark made no move until he was sure of Estrello's intentions. Drawing left-handed, he put a slug through Estrello's gun hand, and the outlaw dropped the weapon as if it were hot. In an instant, Bill had drawn his own Colt, holstering it when he saw it wasn't needed. Keithley and Stackler were watching Hiram and Odell as though they might take a hand if the other two outlaws bought in.

"Here are your clothes," said Bill when he reached Amanda and Betsy. "I don't think they can see you from here, but maybe I'd better hold a blanket in front of you."

"Please do," said Betsy. "Who fired the shot?"

"Mark," Bill replied. "Estrello's just learned he's not the fastest gun around anymore."

"That will help you," Amanda said, "but would you and Mark go up against Estrello's bunch? It's awful dangerous. It wouldn't be just him after you. The federals will be, too."

"That was a bluff, threatening to start an outfit of our own," said Bill. "Fortunately, two of the men Estrello brought with him dealt us a royal flush. We now know that with a little prodding, half of Estrello's outfit can be hazed off in another direction. I think, after he's thought about it, he'll want Mark and me to join him, if only in the hope of gunning us down."

"Oh, God," said Betsy, "he'll be looking for ways to kill you. Every time you ride out, we'll remember what happened to Jake."

"Don't speak a word to Estrello, unless it's to answer a question we've already agreed on," Bill said. "If he feels threatened enough to take us into his outfit, there's going to be a condition. There's room enough on a wagon seat for two, and wherever Estrello sends us, you'll be going, too. Dangerous, maybe, but no more so than leaving you in camp with some of his outlaws. Estrello could always send away all who might turn against him, leaving you at the mercy of the others. Can either of you fire a rifle or revolver?"

"Yes," said Amanda. "We learned in Texas by the time we were twelve, thanks to the regular visits of the Comanches."

They had been taking their time, for Bill wanted to reassure them of the need to join Estrello's gang. When they were dressed, except for their boots, Bill folded the blankets, and they were ready to face Estrello. They found him gritting his teeth, a bloody bandanna wrapped about his injured hand.

"I reckon," said Estrello when he finally spoke, "you'll

need horses and saddles for these troublesome little wenches. I'm figurin' two hundred and fifty dollars per horse and saddle."

"Then you'd better do some more figurin'," Stackler said. "These are the horses and saddles they rode when Jake first brought them to the territory. Right, Keithley?"

"Right," said Keithley, "and there's Jake's two Henry rifles and his Colt. All that should go to Amanda and Betsy."

"I shall make up my own mind what I intend to do," Estrello snarled, "and I'll listen to no more speculation at my expense. Before I make any decisions, I want the rest of the outfit to know what those possible decisions are."

"Then let's mount up and ride," said Mark. "You and your men lead out, and the rest of us will follow."

It was clearly an insult, and the outlaws took it exactly as Mark had intended. While Hiram, Odell, and Estrello were furious, there was just a hint of a smile on the faces of Stackler and Keithley. Estrello's men watched in silence as the riders approached the camp. They had heard the shot Mark had fired, and their attention was immediately drawn to Wolf Estrello's bandaged hand. Amanda, Betsy, and the two strange riders were careful to remain behind the outlaws. Estrello wasted no time. Dismounting, he turned to the men who had gathered and began speaking. Some outlaws grinned when they learned Amanda and Betsy had been claimed by Mark Rogers and Bill Harder.

"That ain't so hard to figure out," said Alfonso Suggs. "Let 'em take the women and ride out. I wasn't ever in favor of Jake bringin' 'em here."

"Me neither," said Burrel Hedgepith, the black man.

"They refuse to ride out," Wolf Estrello said. "They're threatening to build an outfit of their own and horn in on us."

"Like hell," shouted one of the outlaws. He reached for

his revolver, only to find himself covered by Colts in the hands of Mark and Bill. Without a word, he let his weapon slide back into the holster. It was enough to convince the rest of the gang, for Estrello already nursed an injured hand, and none of the outlaws had ever seen him beaten to the draw.

"These *hombres* is Rogers and Harder," said Estrello. "I'm thinking it won't be a bad idea if they was part of our bunch. We all end up fighin' among ourselves, and none of us makes any money."

"We ain't makin' none now," Skull Worsham said. "Not after your fifty-percent cut."

"I'm willing to lower my share to forty percent," Estrello said. "It would be worth it to get some new teamsters. We're already two men shy."

"They're bluffin'," said Waddy Jackman. "Ain't no way they can raise an outfit here in the Territory, and they got no mules or wagons."

"When the need arises," Mark said, "we'll have riders. As for our wagons and teams, we're figurin' on using some of yours."

There was surprise on the face of every man in the outfit, and several were violently angry, but nobody made a move toward his gun. Not a man of them wanted to challenge these gun-handy strangers, and they began to understand the predicament Estrello faced. But knowing Estrello, they believed he was taking in Rogers and Harder only to dispose of them at some convenient opportunity.

"All right," said Estrello, "it's time for a vote. Anybody object to us takin' in Harder and Rogers as teamsters?"

Nobody said anything, although some were obviously tempted.

"That's settled," Estrello said. "Harder, has you and Rogers got anything to say?"

"Matter of fact, we have," said Mark. "Wherever we go, Amanda rides the wagon box with me, while Betsy rides with Bill. As all of you now know, they've been promised to us, and we aim to see that nothing happens to them."

"Take 'em with you, and welcome," Wolf Estrello said, "but the first damn troublesome mischief they bring down on the outfit, all of you will answer to me."

The outlaws didn't have a common fire for preparation of food. Instead, they worked in teams of two or three, hunkering down to eat alone when their food was done.

"There'll be food in the wagon Jake drove," said Amanda. "All those supplies belong to me and Betsy."

"Bill and me will keep watch," Mark said. "The two of you search the wagon for grub, and while you're looking, keep an eye out for those weapons that belonged to Jake. I'd bet my saddle some of these coyotes have already claimed them."

Most of the wagon was filled with barreled whiskey, and there was room for little else.

"Jake's Colt's here," Betsy said, "but there's no sign of the rifles or ammunition."

"Come on," said Mark. "We'll need those Henry rifles and whatever ammunition there is. If Estrello didn't take them, he'll know who did."

With Amanda and Betsy accompanying them, Mark and Bill paused half a dozen yards from where Estrello stood watching them.

"Jake had a pair of Henry rifles," Bill said. "We want them, along with any available ammunition."

"Whoever took them Henrys and ammunition, fetch 'em," said Estrello.

Sheepishly, Phelps Brice and Chad Graves stepped forward.

"We took 'em," Graves said. "Jake was gone, and —"

"Shut up," Estrello growled, "and get them."

The Henry repeaters were brought, along with four tins of ammunition. Bill passed one of the weapons to Betsy, while Mark gave the second one to Amanda.

"Now, ain't that something?" said Dutch McCarty, grinning. "Couldn't neither one of 'em hit the inside of a barn with the doors shut."

The roar of a Henry seemed unusually loud in the stillness. Dutch McCarty's hat took a wild leap off his head, and Amanda stood ready to fire again if need be. But there was no need. Some of the outlaws laughed, while Estrello seemed not to believe his eyes. These damn women could and would shoot a man, if provoked. Mark nodded to Amanda, and she and Betsy retreated to what had been Jake's wagon.

"Estrello," Bill said, "if you aim for us to haul wagonloads of booze somewhere, then it's time for us to know where and when."

"It goes no farther than right here," said Estrello. "You take the wagons off the boats at Fort Smith, and bring them here. Our . . . ah . . . clients come here for the product. The day after tomorrow, you'll take the empty wagons to Fort Smith, where you'll wait for their return by steamboat."

Snider Irvin laughed. "Folks is startin' to call the old Arkansas 'Whiskey River.' "

Mark and Bill spent the rest of the day near the wagon Jake had driven, cleaning their weapons and watching the outlaws. When suppertime was near, Amanda and Betsy prepared the meal.

"Estrello hasn't told us much of anything," said Amanda while they ate. "He could be setting us up for an ambush at Fort Smith."

"He could be," Mark said, "and we'll have to be ready. It's a risk, but there's no other way. Keithley and Stackler aren't too fond of Estrello. Somehow, we must find a time and place to talk to them, without the rest of the gang knowing."

"Who were the teamsters from Fort Smith when Jake was killed?" Bill asked.

"Besides Jake," said Betsy, "there was Jules Hiram, Hugh Odell, Bert Hamby, Alfonso Suggs, Snider Irvin, Elgin Kendrick, and Burrel Hedgepith."

"Eight wagons," Bill said. "Always eight? Never more or less?"

"Always eight," said Betsy, "and a dozen outriders. None of the outriders are allowed on the wagon boxes. It's as though Estrello doesn't trust them."

"Estrello aims to send the wagons back to Fort Smith the day after tomorrow," Mark said. "What will he do with all this barreled rotgut loaded on these wagons?"

"Oh, you haven't seen the worst of it," said Amanda. "Tomorrow the Comanches and Kiowa come to trade for whiskey. They'll trade stolen horses, pelts, gold, silver, and anything Estrello will accept."

"How many Indians?" Bill asked.

"Five hundred or more," said Betsy. "Sometimes they'll tap a few barrels of the stuff and get crazy drunk right here."

"That's a hell of a lot of Indians," Mark said, "when there's maybe forty-eight barrels of whiskey. Somebody will lose out"

"No," said Amanda. "Estrello's thought of that. He's set his prices high enough that no single Indian can afford a large amount of the whiskey. They're forced to combine whatever they have to trade and then share as much whiskey as Estrello will sell them. There's a few of the Indians— Comanches, I think—who manage to trade for four or five barrels of whiskey. They load each barrel on a travois behind a horse and haul it back to their camp. Jake always said they would resell or trade the whiskey for ten times what it was worth."

"Tarnation," Bill said, "with thirty-six gallons of pure alcohol per barrel, these Indians could stay crazy drunk for God knows how long. If we're leaving the day after tomorrow for Fort Smith, what happens if all this whiskey hasn't been sold?"

"It will be," said Betsy. "When it gets down to the last few barrels, there'll be fighting over what's left. One Indian tried to trade his squaw for a barrel of the stuff."

"Makes me wonder why Estrello don't add some more wagons and haul in more of the stuff," Mark said.

"Jake said Estrello's too smart for that," said Amanda. "By limiting the whiskey, he's able to demand a higher price. If he brought in too much, the bidding wouldn't be nearly as fierce."

"With so many men in camp, where do the two of you usually sleep?" Bill asked.

"Under Jake's wagon, when it's here," said Betsy. "When it's not, we try to hide out in the brush."

"Then take your place under the wagon tonight," Bill said. "We'll be close by."

But to the surprise of Mark and Bill, Estrello had plans for them.

"Them Indians knows the whiskey's here," Estrello said. "On the first watch, I want Rogers, Harder, and all you men." He pointed at eleven others. "The rest of us will take the second watch at midnight."

Hiram, Odell, Hamby, Suggs, and Irvin knelt behind one of the wagons, rolling smokes.

"It's us against them," said Ursino. "No good reason to

have so many men on the first watch. Them five coyotes hunkered behind the wagon is there to keep an eye on us."

"I suspect you're probably right," Clemans said. "Estrello's been watching us almighty close ever since he shot Jake. He's expecting some kind of revenge."

"He's damn well going to get it," said Long, "unless he gets me first."

"One thing you ain't considering," Sullivan said. "There's as much a price on our heads as there is on Estrello's. If we cash in Estrello, we lose contact with that bunch at the illegal distillery. Then there'll be no more whiskey, and we'll have every damn Indian in the Territory after our scalps."

"I'm about ready to saddle up and ride," said Stackler, "price on my head or not."

"I'm of the same mind," Keithley said, "but the time's not right. I think we're all on trial, along with Rogers and Harder."

"I think you're right," said Mark. "When you and Stackler sided with Bill and me, Estrello got suspicious. Now he aims to keep an eagle eye on us. It would be almighty easy for some of us to be shot off the wagon box in the middle of the night, without any proof as to who done the shooting."

Outlaw camp on the Washita. July 19, 1866.

The night passed uneventfully. It was barely dawn when the Indians began arriving. With an eye for business, Wolf Estrello had tapped a keg of the brew and allowed each of the Indians a single tin cupful. It being summertime, many of the Indians wore only a loincloth and moccasins. From beneath Jake's wagon, Amanda and Betsy were watching as the trading began.

"It seems downright indecent, the two of you watching these half-naked Indians get drunk," said Mark. "A loincloth don't cover much."

"It won't cover anything at all after they've had enough whiskey," Betsy said. "The loincloth comes off. We've been watching this for five years, and we're not shocked anymore."

More and more Indians arrived. Many of them led horses and mules for trading, whose brands attested to their having been stolen. One Indian arrived leading three heavily laden horses. Each animal was loaded with prime pelts, and a shouting argument ensued as the Indian and Estrello got into a trading mood. Slowly, Estrello began to give in to the Indian demands, and the Indian grinned delightedly. He was about to best the white man in a trade. He demanded and received three full barrels of whiskey for his three horse loads of pelts.

"My God," said Bill, "he's swapped two thousand dollars worth of pelts for three barrels of rotgut that ain't worth fifty dollars a barrel."

"They do that all the time," Amanda said. "The only things they won't swap are their weapons. Lots of them own repeating rifles."

"All these horses and mules they're trading are branded," said Bill. "How does Estrello dispose of them?"

"Somewhere near St. Louis," Betsy said. "He has an out-of-the-way corral somewhere along the river. When the wagons go after more whiskey, the livestock the Indians have traded are taken along."

"Have you and Betsy ever been allowed to go to St. Louis?" Mark asked.

"No," said Amanda, "but Jake was. He told us the little that we know. He didn't like leaving Betsy and me here with outlaws while he was away. That's why Estrello killed him."

The Indian who had traded for three barrels of whiskey had tapped a keg and was selling the lethal brew in lesser amounts to other Indians who didn't have much to trade. As it turned out, Betsy and Amanda told the truth. As the whiskey took hold, the Indians lost whatever inhibitions they might have had. Many a loincloth was discarded, leaving a band of naked drunken Indians cavorting like mad.

"They've got enough whiskey to stay drunk for a week," said Bill. "What happens if they're still here tomorrow, and there's another whiskey run?"

"Estrello will leave enough men here to keep them in line," Betsy said. "Their whiskey will be gone before the wagons return with another load. They know better than to cause Estrello any trouble. There wouldn't be any more whiskey."

"Well," said Keithley, seating himself with his back to a wagon wheel, "you've just had a firsthand look at why Indians hate the white man. When that stuff wears off, they'll all be wishing they were dead, and some of them may be."

"When are we going to find out what plans Estrello has for us tomorrow?" Bill asked.

"You'll know sometime tonight," said Keithley. "He'll take a dozen outriders with him, and they'll be watching you every minute. Estrello doesn't trust anybody."

"From the sound of things," Mark said, "I don't see how Estrello holds this outfit together. Even if he takes only forty percent of the money, that can't leave much for the rest of us."

"After Estrello's share, the rest of us generally get five or six hundred dollars," said Keithley. "He's got the only game in town, so you can't make any demands. Nobody who's ever complained about the low pay is around anymore. They're all dead."

"We'll keep that in mind," Bill said, "but just because we

have prices on our heads, it don't mean we work for nothing. Not for Estrello, or nobody else."

Keithley laughed softly. "Like I told Stackler, there's more to you two gents than meets the eye. Some of the rest of us are ready to bust out of this whiskey smuggling, and when you're ready to make your play, we'll side with you."

"Don't let what you see fool you," Mark said. "We've each got a price of ten grand on our heads, and if all we can make is five or six hundred dollars a haul, it'll be better than nothing. Outside the Territory, and the law would have us behind bars in a week."

The conversation trailed off, for someone was coming. It was Estrello, and he spoke abruptly.

"Keithley, you'll have the lead wagon tomorrow. Following you will be Long, Sullivan, Clemans, Ursino, and Stackler. Rogers and Harder, the two of you will drive the last two wagons. There will be no lagging behind. My outriders will see to that."

"Will we be driving the wagons into town for loading?" Bill asked.

"You will not," said Estrello. "All of you will remain in a prescribed area until every wagon has been loaded and returned. You will then load the wagons on steamboats, to be transported to Fort Smith. From Fort Smith, we will return here. Rogers and Harder, I'll be watching the two of you until you've proven yourselves. Don't do anything foolish." With that, he was gone.

"Damn him," said Keithley softly, "he suspects something."

"Let him," Bill said. "Mark and me aim to do exactly what we're told."

Stackler arrived quietly and hunkered down by the wagon. "Harder, you and Rogers are on trial. Estrello's outriders will be watching you like hawks, and they'll shoot you on suspicion."

Indian Territory. July 20, 1866.

The wagons had been lined up in the order Wolf Estrello demanded. In the last wagon—the one that had belonged to old Jake—Mark sat on the wagon box, Amanda by his side. Just ahead of them, in next to the last wagon, sat Bill and Betsy. With the popping of a whip, the lead wagon lurched into motion, and the other wagons followed. Two of Estrello's outriders made it a point to stay directly behind the last two wagons.

"They're watching us," Amanda said nervously.

"Let them," said Mark. "We'll give them no cause for doubt."

The empty caravan moved on toward Fort Smith. There it would board steamboats for St. Louis, delivering another cargo of rotgut poison to Indian Territory.

Chapter 3

Bound for St. Louis. July 22, 1866.

Estrello knew his way well in the darkness. Their only stops were to rest the horses and the mules. Mark and Amanda talked, speaking softly.

"What's this?" Mark asked as he kicked the inside of the wagon box. "Sounds like metal of some kind. Maybe boilerplate."

"It is metal," said Amanda. "If there was an attack, Jake could belly-down in the wagon box and shoot back with little chance of being hit. I hope Estrello allows you to keep this wagon. It could save your life."

"Since this wagon did belong to Jake, we'll insist on keeping it," Mark said. "If it comes to a shoot-out, there's room for Bill and Betsy in here with us."

"Estrello and his bunch have been attacked before while returning with the whiskey," said Amanda. "One of the outriders was killed and a teamster wounded."

"Were they attacked by the law or another gang of outlaws?" Mark asked.

"Jake said they were renegade Indians," said Amanda, "led by a Kiowa known as Many Horses. There might be as many as two gangs after us. The danger will be greatest after we leave the steamboats near Fort Smith, with the whiskey."

"I'll have to get word to Bill and Betsy when we stop to rest the teams," Mark said. "If there's an attack, and there's time, they can get in here with us."

When it was again time to rest the teams, Mark slipped to the rear of the wagon and managed to get Bill's attention.

"Maybe that's why Estrello was willing to take us on," said Bill. "Maybe it's about time for old Many Horses to launch another attack."

"If it comes, and there's time," Mark said, "you and Betsy join us in Jake's wagon. He had the sideboards lined with some kind of metal. Amanda says if we're attacked, it likely won't happen until we've unloaded the whiskey at Fort Smith."

Mark slipped back into the wagon, put his arm about Amanda, and drew her close. The girl didn't resist, and Mark's heart leaped. The lie he had told about Amanda belonging to him for five years was taking on more truthful proportions all the time, and he could see her dressed in gingham as she tended his little shack on the Brazos.

Bill was having similar thoughts, and he quietly put his into words. "If Mark and me can get you and Amanda out of here alive," Bill said, "where will you go? What do you aim to do?"

"I promised to go with you five years ago," said Betsy. "If you'll have me, I'll go with you as soon as we're free of Estrello and his bunch."

"Then when we're free of this damned smuggling, you'll have a home, Betsy." His hand was on her shoulder and she moved closer to him.

The wagons rolled on, and just as dawn was breaking, Estrello ordered a halt. It was time for breakfast and a few hours' rest. Horses and mules were unharnessed, and fires were started along a creek. There was evidence of old fires where teams and men had rested before, but no sign of recent tracks. Nobody spoke. They all set about broiling their bacon over small, smokeless fires. After the outfit had eaten and rested for several hours, they harnessed the teams and moved on.

It was far into the night when Estrello's band reached the makeshift dock on the Arkansas, near Fort Smith. Quietly, Estrello made the rounds of all the teamsters. "There's been a change in plans," he said. "We'll all be goin' on to the loadin' dock in St. Louis." He said no more.

There was a whisper of sound as a horse drew up next to old Jake's wagon. "We're bein' followed," Ursino said. "Estrello didn't expect them until we returned from St. Louis and the whiskey was loaded into the wagons. Be ready."

But there was no immediate disturbance. The wagons, along with the livestock Estrello had taken in trade, reached the secluded dock two hours before dawn. The four steamboats were already there, chuffing, without running lights.

"Betsy, you and Amanda stay in the wagon," Mark cautioned. "Bill and me will be on the ground under the wagon. If we're attacked, don't return any fire."

The attack began suddenly, lead screaming off the iron wagon tires. But the attackers had been expected, and the return fire was fierce. Bill and Mark, firing from beneath the wagon, accounted for four of the invaders. The attack ended as suddenly as it had begun. The surviving attackers galloped away, leaving their dead behind.

"What in tarnation was that about?" Bill wondered. "No whiskey on the wagons."

"They aimed to kill or wound some of us," said Bert Hamby. "Anybody been hit?"

"Ezra Shadley stopped one with his right arm," said Walsh Tilden, "and Gid Patton took one in his right leg. We'll see to them after we reach the creek ahead."

When they reached the creek, only Long, Sullivan, Clemans, Keithley, Ursino, and Stackler were there. Mark and Bill led two of the runaway horses they had managed to catch.

"By God," said Tilden, "Rogers and Harder done some powerful shootin'. There was four dead *hombres* behind their wagons."

"Keithley," said Estrello when he arrived, "you got a medicine chest. Patch up those who are wounded. The bastards stampeded most of our extra horses and mules, and that's money out of your pockets. Sullivan, take some men and tie these teams to trees and see that nobody goes near them. The rest of us will remain afoot until dawn. If anybody refuses to answer a challenge, cut him down."

"Damn it," Bill hissed, "the showdown's comin' too soon. We don't even have the whiskey, and some good men may die unless we're able to back their play."

"I know," said Mark, "but this is not exactly the showdown we were expecting. Those sneaking varmints seemed willing to kill us for the wagons and the teams."

"You could be right," Bill said. "If they wanted Estrello out of business in a hurry, killing his men and stealing his wagons and teams would just about do it."

"At first light," said Estrello, "we'll take their trail and ride them down."

While none of his men had died, Estrello had lost many horses and mules intended for trade. A chill wind blew out of the west, and distant fingers of lightning warned them a storm was in the making. Some of the men hunkered down under blankets, their Winchesters ready.

"Let's eat," said Estrello at first light. "Then we got some killing to do."

But the attackers had expected pursuit, and instead of running, had set up an ambush. As soon as Estrello's outriders and teams were within range, the bushwhackers cut loose.

"Gun the bastards down," Estrello shouted.

Amid blazing gunfire, Mark, Bill, and the rest of the teamsters fought to control the frightened teams. Lead struck the metal wagon parts, singing off with a deadly whine. Estrello's group fought their way toward the wagons, for it seemed the rival band of outlaws was determined to kill the teamsters. Estrello was furious, and his Winchester roared. The fire from Estrello's outfit was deadly, blazing through the trees, and those begging to surrender were shown no mercy. No prisoners were taken. Pounding feet indicated some of the outlaws running for their lives, their horses having been killed or mortally wounded.

"Save your ammunition, men," Estrello shouted.

"Let's follow the bastards and kill the others," Drew Wilder shouted.

"Damn it, no," said Estrello. "We got to round up them stampeded horses and mules. There's a storm coming."

A westerly wind brought gray sheets of rain sweeping down upon them. Lightning far to the west was much closer, lighting the leaden skies with golden brilliance.

"We'd never find them now, even if we had the ammunition and the time," said Ursino.

"Put away your guns," Estrello shouted, "and try to find yourselves a horse or mule to ride. We got to catch as many of those stampeded horses and mules as we can."

"It's rainin' so hard you can't see your hand in front of

your face," Snider Irvin said. "Let's scrap this damn run and go after the gold Jake had. You women know where he hid it before he was caught. The gold's still there, and some of us will trail you to hell to find it.

"We'll never tell any of you anything," Betsy replied. "But we'll tell the law you're hauling and selling illegal whiskey to the Indians, and searching for that stolen gold you blamed on Jake four years ago."

Estrello laughed. "Nobody can prove we had anything to do with that stolen gold. Old Jake's dead, and that leaves just the two of you, and you won't be talkin' if you're dead."

"You lying, thieving varmints," Betsy shouted. "The jury acquitted us. They never once believed we knew where the gold was hidden, and the law won't believe it now."

"Insurance companies don't take a beatin' like that, without makin' it almighty hot for somebody," said Estrello. "Sooner or later, we'll find that gold, and then leak word out to the law and the newspapers that the two of you went back and got it."

"My God," Bill whispered, unbelieving. "Is all this true?"

"Mostly," said Betsy, refusing to look at him. "We almost had Jake talked into nothing more dishonest than freighting in illegal whiskey. He was Estrello's second-in-command then, and he wasn't even with the bunch the day they stole the gold. Trying to save Jake, Amanda and me took the gold, managing to hide it before a sheriff's posse caught us."

"So you fought the law and won," Mark said, "and now nobody else knows where the stolen gold is. Just what the hell did you aim to do with so much money?"

"Our ma was consumptive," said Amanda, "and we wanted money for her. But she didn't last that long, and all we could think about was giving back the stolen gold. We had some terrible fights with Jake, because he didn't know where we'd hidden it."

"If I had to bet," Bill said, "I'd bet a horse and saddle the metal Jake used to line the bed of his wagon is the missing gold."

"No," said Amanda. "Betsy and me wouldn't lie to you."

"Not after all you've done for us," Betsy said. "The sheriff's posse caught up to Jake in the wagon, and he hadn't had the time to hide the gold."

"But you and Amanda did," said Mark. "What do you aim to do with it?"

"Return it to the express office from which it was taken," Betsy said.

"You can still be prosecuted," said Bill. "I believe that's grand larceny, and there's a seven-year statute of limitations."

"But we never spent a dollar of that gold," Amanda protested. "We've waited for most of five years for a chance to return that stolen gold. We only wanted to spare old Jake a prison sentence. They still sentenced him to a year."

"You should have used the gold to bargain with the court," said Bill. "Jake's not here to testify that except for concealing the gold, neither of you had anything to do with it. It could now become your word against that of Estrello and his outlaws."

"He's right," Mark said. "I don't figure the opinions of Bill and me will be worth a damn, with a pair of ten-thousand-dollar rewards on our heads."

"Oh, damn it, how did we get caught up in this mess, just trying to help Jake," Betsy cried. "He didn't do that much wrong."

"He took a pile of money that wasn't his," said Mark, "and that generally creates one hell of a misunderstanding."

"Oh, God, how can we return the stolen gold without going to jail?" Betsy cried.

"I don't know," said Bill. "Somehow you'll have to win the confidence of the law, and the best way to do that is to invite Estrello to put up or shut up. You can always tell the court that you did what you had to, trying to save Jake."

After a few moments of silence, Betsy shouted angrily, "Go ahead and call the law, Estrello. I'll gladly go there if your dirty carcass is locked in the next cell. You can't hurt Jake anymore, and we can testify we saved the gold."

"Betsy," said Bill, "you don't know the gold's still there. If it isn't, then all you've done is drag yourselves into a five-year-old robbery."

"Damn Estrello," Betsy said. "I'm willing to risk it."

Estrello only laughed as Betsy and Amanda forced themselves to remain silent. The rain became more intense.

"It looks like a Mexican standoff," said Mark. "This is the kind of rain that works its way in from the High Plains and hangs on for a week."

"The least of our worries," Bill said. "This bunch we just chased off may attack us at any time. They left a pile of dead bodies behind, and they don't strike me as the forgiving kind. Our camp's divided, and that will hurt us."

"Yeah," said Keithley, "and next time some of those dead bodies may be ours. As far as we're concerned, there are twenty-five men who might decide to split with Estrello. Should there be a split, those *hombres* could finish us with a single volley of lead."

"In Estrello's outfit," Bill asked, "who's second and third in command?"

"Drew Wilder's next, after Estrello," said Keithley. "After him comes the Spaniard. Alonzo Bideno."

"One's no better than the other, then," Bill said.

"No," said Keithley. "The two of you were allowed to keep your weapons after all that fancy shootin' you done back yonder at the creek. If this bunch has a falling-out, anything can happen. If Estrello decides to rule with an iron hand, he's a dead man. There's thirty-five men in the outfit, and I can't see more than ten of us throwing in with Estrello."

"I was hoping we might create a quarrel within the outfit and divide them," Bill said.

"That's been tried," said Keithley. "Estrello killed two of his own men."

"I need a way to get outside, to find out how closely they're watching us," Bill said. "Will you help me, Betsy? If we're caught, we'll have to convince this bunch we got some fooling around on our minds. I won't be able to do it without your help."

"I'll do what I can," said Betsy.

"Good," Bill said. "Those on watch are behind us, and I've loosened our wagon canvas on the left front side. If they're watching close enough to catch you, don't resist. Tell them you have to go to the bushes."

The rain had slackened, but the sky was still cloudy, and the dark dress Betsy wore was an advantage. But her foot slipped off a front wheel hub and she came down in the mud on her knees.

"Don't you take even one extra breath, woman," said a cold voice. "You get back into that wagon, and do it now."

"But I have business outside," Betsy protested.

"You just think you do," said the gunman. "Now get back in that wagon."

There was a roar, and a slug from a Colt struck an iron wagon tire just inches from Betsy's hand. Without a word, she got to her feet and climbed back into the wagon.

"Damn them," said Bill.

"It's cloudy and I couldn't see much," Betsy said, "but there's at least three of them."

"From here on," said Mark, "I think we'd better play some parts. There's enough of these varmints to split the outfit and fight among themselves. If it rains long enough and hard enough, mud will bog down these wagons hub-deep. That may light the fuse to some short tempers. We still have those stampeded horses and mules to find, if we can."

Bill laughed. "I was just thinking the same thing. Listen to the sound of music on the wagon canvas. It's raining again."

Thunder boomed three times in a row, shaking the earth. Horses and mules went wild.

"Damn it," Estrello shouted above the thunder, "you men get out there and hold them teams. I'm chargin' every one of you for anything that happens to your teams or wagons."

Men slipped, slid, and cursed. Lightning struck somewhere close, and one of the mules stampeded, dragging a teamster belly-down behind him.

"Well, that tells us something," Keithley said. "Estrello didn't call on anybody but his trusted men to calm the horses and mules."

"I think Estrello has some kind of deadline for picking up that rotgut in St. Louis," said Mark, "and he can't afford to lose any of the teams. Let one of us bust a wheel or an axle in the dark, and Estrello may be in big trouble."

"That's correct," Keithley said, "but there's bigger trouble than that. None of these men are satisfied with Estrello taking the lion's share from whiskey sales. We're building up to a split and a fight within this outfit, and with no more guns than he can muster, Estrello will be on the short end of it."

"I expect you're right," said Bill. "The only reason we're still armed is that we're still mostly unknown, except for the shooting Estrello's seen us do. He needs our guns, and at some point he'll try to force us to commit ourselves to him."

"Yeah," Mark agreed, "and we'd better be damned convincing. When this thing comes to a showdown, every man will want a share from the whiskey and gold there on the spot. From here, how far is it to where the gold's buried?"

"Perhaps twenty-five miles," said Betsy.

"It's workin' out against us," Keithley said. "Somehow we must finish this run to St. Louis and nail Estrello with some hard evidence. These killers have to be convinced it's better to go for the gold after they've wagoned in the whiskey."

"That might buy us some time," said Mark, "but what good will it do?"

"Maybe none," Keithley said, "maybe plenty. Believe it or not, I was once a Ranger, and every day I could avoid gettin' shot was another day I had to live."

"Including Betsy and Amanda, there's ten of us," said Mark. "That means odds against us are almighty long. I know this is dangerous talk, but one of us is goin' to have to raise some opposition, some reason for delaying a showdown."

"That makes sense," Keithley said, "but how?"

"If we're looking at this thing right," said Bill, "even with ten of us throwing in with Estrello, we're still hopelessly outgunned. We'll have to stand behind the bastard at least until we can free ourselves from this snake pit."

"If I ain't gettin' too nosey for my own good," Keithley said, "are you expecting help from somewhere?"

"To be truthful, I'd have to say no," said Bill. "I'm just lookin' at the odds, at all the possible hands we can play. God knows, we don't have many."

"Keithley," Mark said, "if there's any hope of us bustin' out of this outfit without a life sentence at Huntsville or our backs to the wall before a firing squad, will you throw in with us?"

"To the bitter damn end, whatever it may be," said Keithley. "I'd rather die on my feet than live on my knees."

"There's Long, Sullivan, Clemans, Ursino, Stackler, you, Betsy and Amanda, and Bill and me. Is there anybody else?" Mark asked.

"None that I'd count on," said Keithley. "The men you named are capable of settling down and going straight, given a chance. The others are outlaws by choice."

"You've spoken to the six we can count on, then," Bill Harder said.

"Yes," said Keithley said. "Once after Estrello gunned down a teamster who opposed him, and again after he killed Jake. If there's any hope, we'll stand with our backs to the wall and make them pay dearly for every one of us."

"I can tell you only this much," Mark said. "We have a fighting chance to come out of this alive and redeem ourselves in the eyes of the law. Whatever happens, we must not allow our weapons to be taken from us. We must convince Estrello that the ten of us are with him, and it won't be easy. The odds will still be impossibly long."

"If we're aimin' to make a move," said Keithley, "then you'll know about when and where. Is this somethin' me and the others are allowed to know?"

"Frankly, we're not sure," Bill said. "There's planning to be done. What's your opinion on the gold Amanda and Betsy have hidden? Five years is quite a spell. I believe the gold's still there, but how can we be sure? If we lead Estrello's bunch that way, and the gold's gone, we're in big trouble."

"Estrello believes the gold's still there," said Keithley. "In fact, he believes there's as much as a hundred thousand. The only thing that's kept him reined in is that he's had so few men he could count on. Wilder and Bideno got as many of the bunch together as they could, demanding that the gold be recovered and divided. Estrello's trying to buy some time. The only thing that's kept him in command is that he's had to agree to a division of the gold, once we return from St. Louis with a final load of whiskey."

"That's the truth," Betsy said.

"The only thing that makes this stolen gold hard to swallow," said Bill, "is that there's so many outlaws, and none of them have any idea where the gold is."

"Amanda and me can find it," Betsy said.

"Damn it," said Mark, "this is getting deeper and deeper. Betsy, I'm not doubtin' your word or Amanda's, but what's kept these outlaws at bay for nearly five years? Why is it nobody's brought the water to a boil over this hidden gold?"

"Estrello's had old Jake to thank for that," Betsy said. "When this outfit came together for the first time, Jake was second in command to Estrello himself. Back then, most of the men were loyal to Estrello and Jake, and the two of them wanted to freight in the illegal whiskey to the Indians. Their thinking was that the gold was safe enough, and that it could be recovered after the whiskey smuggling became too great a risk."

"There's no reason for us not to believe that Betsy and Amanda know where the gold is," said Keithley, "but something's botherin' me. When you gents showed up at Estrello's camp, he had killed Jake and had driven both girls naked into the woods. That don't make a hell of a lot of sense, with only them knowin' where the gold is."

"Not until you consider Estrello and the way he thinks,"

Betsy said. "He ran Amanda and me out of camp, naked, be-lieving we'd come crawling back on his terms. But when he found us, we had Mark and Bill with us. Now he has less reason than ever for expecting Amanda and me to tell him where the gold is."

"Perhaps there's one thing we're overlooking," Amanda said. "Only Betsy and me can find the gold, and as long as we're unwilling, Estrello's in trouble. Suppose that changed? Suppose we agreed to lead Estrello to the gold, in exchange for our freedom?"

"As a last resort, it might work," said Keithley, "but it would take some almighty powerful acting to pull it off."

"I don't favor that," Bill said. "Suppose it falls through? The girls end up there under Estrello's blankets, and the rest of us end up dead."

"But it may be the only real hope we have," said Betsy. "Can't you imagine what this bunch would do if they sud-denly had a hundred thousand dollars in gold to divide among themselves? They'd murder us all to silence us."

"She has a point there," Keithley said. "That could hold everything together until we're back from St. Louis, but what happens when we can't stall any longer, and it's time to divvy up the gold? I'm not a very trusting *hombre,* and I'm the kind who would expect a double-cross. Especially with us hopelessly out-gunned."

"I can't deny that," said Mark, "and somehow we have to split this outfit. The gold—or even the promise of it—might do that, but the subject must be brought up without it in-volving Amanda and Betsy. Is there anybody in this outfit who can likely stir up trouble over this gold, without creat-ing suspicion?"

"Clemans and Ursino," Keithley said. "They was part of

the original gang, and they fell out with Estrello when he allowed Jake and the girls to take the gold. I'd say it wouldn't take much to get Vernon and Nick up to a fighting pitch, since Jake's gone and only Amanda and Betsy know where the gold is."

"That settles it," Bill said. "We'll have to figure some way to get this bunch in a fight over this gold. Any ideas?"

"Clemans, Ursino, and Stackler are old-timers with this bunch. Soon as they saw the way the stick floated, they started tryin' to work their way in with Estrello. But Estrello felt like Jake had betrayed him, and he ain't trusted nobody since. Those three old-timers have long been in favor of bustin' up this outfit," Keithley said.

Mark sighed. "That gets us back to having to trust somebody. Can you find out just how far we can go with Stackler, Ursino, Clemans, Sullivan, and Long?"

"I think so," Keithley said, "but it's a touchy situation. We have to stir up enough hell to send 'em all after the gold, without them goin' before we're ready."

"Then we'll have to let these other men in on the scheme to give up the gold, so we can count on them when we come up against Estrello," said Bill. "Do you reckon we can depend on Clemans or Ursino to raise some hell when we're ready for it?"

"Either or both," Keithley said. "They ain't liked Estrello since he took over the outfit, after they had that first fallin'-out over the gold."

"It gets complicated," said Mark. "What we must do is return that stolen gold and see that this whiskey smuggling along the Arkansas is stopped. For those who are willing to join us, the reward is freedom from prosecution, among other things. Those who are unwilling and insist on fighting must be gunned down to the last man."

"The two of you talk like federal men," Keithley said. "Can you tell me for sure who's siding you?"

"The state of Texas and the federal government," said Bill. "When the time comes, we have the necessary proof. But before we do anything else, we must organize as many men as we can, who will stand their ground when there's a showdown with Estrello."

"Yes," Keithley said, "and they've got to hold off until we've completed this whiskey run from St. Louis. Let me talk to Nick, Vernon, and Ed. I think they're about ready to give up on the whiskey smuggling anyway. They got so much of a price on their heads, they might just hang it all up if the amnesty deal is good enough."

"It'll be good enough," said Mark, "but we must convince everybody involved that the run to St. Louis must come first. Any amnesty deal is a two-edged sword. Those accepting amnesty will have their crimes forgiven, while those who refuse will die with their guns in their hands."

"Now I can see which way we're headed," Keithley said. "We must separate the sheep from the goats. By the time we haul this load of whiskey from St. Louis, we should have two different camps: one ready to keep smuggling, and the other willing to give it up in return for freedom from prosecution."

"That's what is all boils down to," said Mark. "Somehow this whiskey problem must be resolved, and the only way we can do it is divide and conquer. Even then, the odds will be unbelievably long."

Chapter 4

Contrary to what Wolf Estrello had hoped, a new cloud mass moved in from the west, and instead of the rain ceasing, it took a new start.

"Damn it," said Estrello, "we can get these empty wagons to the landing at Fort Smith aboard the boats bound for St. Louis. By the time the boats return from St. Louis with the wagons and whiskey, the ground should be dry."

Wilder laughed. "Estrello, you sweat and worry like an old woman."

Some of the other outlaws laughed, reason enough for Estrello to wonder how many of them would side with him in an open rebellion. Estrello chose to ignore the remark, and gave an order. "I want these teams hitched and the wagons ready to go at daylight. I want you riders strung out the length of the caravan, and don't concern yourselves with only what's ahead. An attack could come from any quarter."

Todd Keithley hurriedly harnessed his teams. His wagon was close enough to Ed Stackler's to allow Keithley a chance for some fast talking.

Stackler took only a minute to make up his mind. "I'd shuck it all, Keithley, for a chance to ride back to Texas and start over. Just to be able to lie down at night without a pistol in my hand."

"There's not much I can tell you," said Keithley, "except the State of Texas and the federal government aims to offer amnesty. Those choosing not to accept will be hunted down to the last man."

"I can understand that," Stackler said. "How long before the showdown?"

"Sometime on the last leg of the run with the whiskey," said Keithley. "Probably after we take the loaded wagons off the boats beyond Fort Smith. I need your help in getting to Ursino, Clemans, Long, and Sullivan. Can you do it without Estrello or his bunch deciding something's wrong?"

"If I can't do it today, I will tonight," Stackler said. "Where do the new men stand?"

"With us," said Keithley, "and that's all I can tell you."

The wagons were ready to go at dawn, and despite the soggy ground and the continued rain, Estrello shouted for them to move out. Mark and Amanda were on the box of the wagon that had belonged to Jake Miles, Bill and Betsy had the wagon directly behind. The remaining wagons were strung out to the rear. They hadn't progressed a hundred yards when trouble struck. One of Mark's lead mules stepped into a leaf-filled stump hole, and as a result of the shock and pain, the animal reared, trying to escape the harness. One of the outriders—Drew Wilder—drew his rifle from the boot and swinging it hard as he could, struck the spooked mule in the head. Stunned, the unfortunate animal sagged to its knees. That was as long as it took Mark Rogers to launch himself from the wagon box. He swept Wilder out of the saddle, and when the two got to their feet, Wilder had his hand on the butt of his Colt. When Mark hit him, he lay on the muddy ground and began cursing Mark.

"Nobody manhandles Drew Wilder and lives to talk about it," he snarled.

"Nobody mistreats an animal when I'm around," said Mark. "Next time—if there is one—I'll kill you."

"What the hell's holding things up?" Estrello shouted, reining up.

"One of the mules stepped into a deep hole and got spooked," Clemans said. "Wilder slugged the varmint with the muzzle of his rifle. Rogers came off the wagon box like a cougar, after Wilder. It ended just like you likely saw it."

"I did see most of it," said Estrello. "Wilder, you're not a teamster. If you ever lay a hand on one of these animals again, you'll answer to me."

"When I choose to talk to you," Wilder snarled, "you'd better have a cocked pistol in your hand."

The Spaniard—Alonzo Bideno—stood tense, his hand near the butt of his Colt, for he and Wilder were friends. Only when he saw Mark watching him did he let it go. Some of the other men had turned hard eyes on Wilder. Mark ignored him, however, and was examining the injured mule.

"How badly is he hurt?" Estrello asked.

"He's not going to be working for a few days," said Mark, "and you can see where he was hit by Wilder's rifle."

"Damn you, Wilder," Estrello said. "We don't have another mule to replace him."

"Well, use a horse," snarled Wilder.

"You do not mix horses and mules," Estrello said in disgust. "Rogers, this is part of your team. What do you suggest?"

"Mules and horses don't pull the same," said Mark, "but they can work together when they're harnessed right. Bring me two horses that ain't easy spooked."

The two horses were brought. Mark left the first two mules in harness. Ahead of them, he harnessed the two horses.

Finally—ahead of the horses—he harness two more mules. The remaining two mules—including the injured one—he tied to lead ropes behind the wagon.

"Hell, that ain't never gonna work," Tull McLean said.

"It wouldn't for you," said Mark, "but it will for me."

Outlaws they were, but they had respect for a man's ability to handle his horse. Mark took the time to speak to the skittish horses, ruffling their ears. Amanda still sat on the wagon box, and Mark climbed up beside her. After several false starts, the two horses settled into their harness, and the wagon was again moving.

Not until after supper did Keithley have another chance to talk to Bill and Mark. "All the men in question are with us," Keithley said. "You got Wilder a mite upset with you, though. He's trying to turn the others against us."

"*Bueno,*" said Mark. "That gives him a reason for hating me, without involving the stolen gold or the illegal whiskey. That was a damn fool thing to do, hurting a mule when you don't have one to replace it, but it worked to our advantage. Wilder didn't make himself any friends, and he may have hurt his standing with Estrello."

"I'm on the second watch tonight, with Nick, Vernon, and Ed," said Keithley. "I aim to answer any questions they may have. At some point, one of you will need to talk to Long and Sullivan. There's so few of us, we must nail down what we have."

Fort Smith. July 25, 1866.

Despite a night and most of a day of rain, the empty wagons were no trouble. The outfit made camp one day away from their rendezvous point beyond Fort Smith. Wilder made no secret of his dislike for Mark Rogers, but nobody seemed to take him seriously. At night, his wagon empty, a teamster generally slept in or under it. Since Betsy was with Bill, and Mark with Amanda, they chose to tie the canvas puckers at front and back and spend their nights in the wagons. It afforded some privacy, while providing endless material for crude jokes among the other men. Amanda and Mark sat within their wagon, while behind them, Betsy and Bill occupied the second wagon.

"While I appreciate the wagon," Amanda said, "I can't imagine why Estrello's allowing us to use it. He never allowed Jake or anybody else to sleep in the wagons, even when there was room."

"I can," said Mark. "Estrello's being forced to change some of his habits. Bill and me have created some trouble for him because we ruined his plans for you and Betsy, and he's not sure where we're going to stand when the showdown comes."

"Lord, I wish this was all over and we could just ride back to Texas," Amanda said.

"So do I," said Mark, "but the worst is yet to come. Rough as it may be, we have to give thanks to the Almighty. There's a small chance that some of us will be able to redeem ourselves. Sooner or later, a man ridin' the owlhoot trail will forget for just a little while who and where he is. Just long enough for somebody to pull a gun maybe half a second quicker."

Amanda shuddered and moved closer to him. She tried changing the subject. "If I tell you something about me, will you promise not to laugh?"

"Things being the way they are, I think I can safely promise that," said Mark.

"Ever since you and Bill rescued Betsy and me," Amanda said, "I find myself believing the story you told Estrello—that Betsy and me were promised to you and Bill five years ago, that you've come to hold us to that promise."

"We have," Mark said.

It was pitch dark within the wagon. She couldn't see his face, and there wasn't a hint of humor in his voice that might have branded the whole thing a joke.

"You . . . have?" Amanda asked.

"Of course we have," said Mark. "We've told you that. I think there's a destiny laid out by the Almighty for every man choosing to try and follow the straight and narrow. I believe our destiny—mine and Bill's—includes you and Betsy. Is that good enough for you?"

She crept closer and responded with a kiss.

"That answers a lot of questions," Mark said. "I just wish you and Betsy had somethin' to wear under your shirts. Way it is now, when you . . . ah . . . jiggle about, it could send a man's mind gallopin' down the wrong trail."

She laughed. "Would one of those minds belong to you, and another to Bill Harder?"

"Damn," he said, "I always take everything one step too far."

In the second wagon, conversation lagged. Betsy and Bill had discussed their situation and their chances of survival until they were just plain weary.

"God," said Betsy. "I'm so tired of this wagon, I could get out and start walking."

"I'm of about the same mood," Bill Harder said. "I feel like somebody took a single tree and just beat hell out of my back and shoulders. There's some fool people around who

thinks all a teamster has to do is set on his behind and signal
the teams when to stop and go."

"What else *does* a teamster do?" she asked, apparently
deadly serious.

"This," said Bill. Hanging her belly-down over the wagon
seat, he proceeded to wallop her behind. When he turned
her loose, she sat up with a giggle.

"Damn you, Bill Harder, before I stand before a preacher
with you, I aim to have me some canvas underpants, some
pantaloons, a girdle—"

"All that stuff's against the law in Texas," said Bill. "If a
man has to fight his way over a desert populated with grizzly bears and rattlesnakes, the trip had damned well better
be worth it. I think that was in Sam Houston's platform
when he ran for governor."

She laughed. "Am I worth a desert full of grizzly bears
and rattlesnakes?"

"One or the other," said Bill. "Not both."

"Amanda and Mark are sitting in that wagon in the dark,"
Betsy said. "What do you think they're doing?"

"How the hell should I know?" Bill demanded. "Why
don't you ask Amanda?"

"You don't have to get miffed," said Betsy. "It just seems
like . . . with us planning to go before the preacher . . . that
we . . ,"

"Ought to be doing considerably more than settin' here
holdin' hands," Bill finished.

"All right," she snapped, "but if the time ever comes,
you'll have some idea as to where to start, won't you?"

He couldn't see her face, but he seized her shoulders and
drew her so close their noses were touching. When he spoke,
it was barely above a whisper.

"I reckon you're entitled to your opinion, but in the part

of Texas I call home, a man don't sample a woman's favors until a preacher's read from the book. Not unless he's in a whorehouse and paying. *Comprende*?"

"Yes," she said angrily, drawing away from him. "I'll be twenty-four years old in October, and I'm . . . I'm . . ."

"Unused and unspoiled," said Bill. "You can last a few more days. One way or another, we'll be free of this outfit."

"Being dead is a kind of freedom," she said sarcastically.

"That's gospel," said Bill, "but whatever happens, you and Amanda won't be any worse off than if Mark and me hadn't come to rescue you. Would you rather wait a little longer for me, or share a bed with Estrello and Amanda?"

"That's the trouble with damn Texas men," she said, somewhere between a laugh and a sob. "They have answers to everything, and they're always right."

The following day they circled wide, avoiding Fort Smith. Half a dozen miles east of town, they unharnessed the teams. Sundown was an hour away.

"The four boats will be here sometime tonight," Keithley said when he had a chance to talk to Mark.

"It ought to be interesting," said Mark. "Have you come up with any reason why he's taking the entire outfit to St. Louis this time?"

"No," Keithley said. "He's never done this before. It's almost like he's building up to a big showdown of some kind. A fight that could get some of us killed."

After supper Estrello sought out his first and second in command, Drew Wilder and the Spaniard, Alonzo Bideno. Wilder, still barely on speaking terms with Estrello, said not a word. When Estrello spoke, he tried to seem as jovial as possible.

"*Amigos,* I suppose you are wondering why this journey is different from the others."

"I personally don't give a damn," said Wilder. "This is my last run. Then you can take this first in command thing and stuff it where the sun don't shine."

"Ah," Estrello said, his voice cold, "a grudge is the hardest load with which a man can burden himself. What are your feelings, Alonzo?"

"That we are pushing our luck, *señor,*" said Bideno. "They tell us our price be going up this time. Our shares are already small. Now they threaten to become smaller, with as much or more opportunity for an *hombre* to die with his *pistola* in his hand."

"Suppose I told you this is the last run, and that it will cost us nothing?" Estrello asked. "The war's over, and there's talk in Congress of sending the military to clean up Indian Territory. If and when that happens, I don't aim to be here."

"So you aim to take them wagonloads of whiskey without paying," said Wilder. "That's why you brought every man of us. We're gonna have to shoot our way out of a damn double cross, with all that whiskey to slow us down."

"You're forgetting something," Estrello said. "The whiskey will be brought to the usual landing south of St. Louis, and we have more than thirty men."

"Last time, we had to pay before they'd allow us to go aboard," said Wilder. "You got any ideas it'll be better this time?"

"As a matter of fact, I have," Estrello said. "I will cheerfully pay them whatever they ask. Whatever it takes to get possession of the whiskey, because we'll be reclaiming all that we've paid them."

Wilder laughed. It was the lowdown kind of double cross he appreciated.

"We must get some men aboard each of the boats, then," said Bideno.

"We'll have men aboard as usual," Estrello said. "At least enough to silence each of the four-man crew aboard the vessel."

"Those aboard must die, then," said Bideno. "Who will man the boats?"

"Use your head," Estrello said. "Nobody dies until the wagons leave the boats at the Fort Smith landing. Until then, every ship's crew will be under the gun."

"That might work," Wilder said grudgingly. "There ain't a man among us sharp enough to pilot one of them boats from St. Louis to Fort Smith."

"When the boats reach the landing here at Fort Smith, sixteen men must die," Bideno said. "That part I do not like, *señor*."

"What the hell would you have us do, Bideno?" Wilder shouted. "Maybe we can just take the whiskey and send them all back to St. Louis, so they can get the law after us that much sooner."

"That's enough, Wilder," said Estrello angrily. "I understand Bideno's objection. In our business, it is necessary to kill a man occasionally, but what we're considering now is premeditated murder. A massacre. Unfortunately, there is no other way."

"When we have done the killing and taken the whiskey, let us anchor the boats somewhere," Bideno said. "It is better than setting them adrift, as derelicts."

"You're right about that," said Estrello. "The first steamer up the Arkansas bound for Fort Smith will report the killings. We'd better be long gone by then."

"Since you aim to take the whiskey without paying,"

Wilder said, "that means extra money in our pockets. How much are we talkin' about?"

"I'm not sure," said Estrello cautiously.

"When you *are* sure," Wilder said, "tell me. Then I'll decide if a shootin' showdown's worth it."

"Like hell," said Estrello. "You're either in or you're out, Wilder. There'll be no last-minute decisions. If you're with me, I want a commitment now. If you're not, then I want you to saddle up and ride. You're not welcome here."

"By God, you're a caution," Wilder said. "You've just told me you aim to murder the steamboat captains and firemen, and you're offerin' *me* the chance to just ride out? I think I'll stick around and collect my share of the money."

Estrello laughed. "A wise move, Wilder. You've already done enough killing to face the rope ten times over. I'm sure the law would like to get its hand on you."

"I'm sure that some back-shootin' son-of-a-bitch would turn me in," Wilder said, "if he can do it without risking his own hide."

"*Señor* Estrello, you must tell the others," said Bideno. "When?"

"Tonight," Estrello said. "You think I trust you and Wilder to keep your mouths shut until some better time?"

Bideno laughed. "Ah, *señor,* is it not a joy to be among *amigos* who are predictable?"

The fire had burned down to a bed of coals when Estrello called a meeting. He spoke for only a few minutes before it all erupted into a storm of shouting and cursing. Estrello drew his Colt, and two blasts from it silenced them.

"Now I'll answer any legitimate question," said Estrello, "except for the money, I think we'll just have to wait and see how it works out. All of you know what has to be done. I think we'll cut the cards. Those with low numbers will become our executioners."

"My God," Betsy whispered fearfully, "suppose you or Mark draws a low card?"

"We'll face that if and when it happens," said Mark, "but I can promise you that we'll not take part in these planned murders."

Estrello had produced a new deck of cards and proceeded to shuffle. Each man took a card on the draw. Estrello then began calling names, and each man responded with the card he had drawn. Men drawing the eight lowest cards were Irvin, Jabez, Shadley, Worsham, Jackman, DeWitt, Graves, and McLean. There would be other outlaws aboard, but these eight were the executioners.

"That's how it stands then," Estrello said. "Any one of you that ain't got the sand for this piece of gun work, let me hear from you now."

Nobody spoke, and Estrello nodded in satisfaction. It had gone smoother than he had expected.

Mark and Bill returned to their wagons.

"I'm glad neither of you drew a low card," said Amanda.

"There was some deck-stackin' goin' on," Bill said. "Nobody drew low cards except the men who are solid behind Estrello. I get the feeling that there's some of us old Wolf just don't trust."

"I've had that same feeling for a while, myself," said Mark, "and I don't think you've taken it quite far enough. We've just heard Estrello choose eight killers to eliminate the steamboat crews. What's to stop him from choosing another bunch to rid himself of some of the rest of us he's not especially fond of?"

"I don't like to think about that," Bill said, "but it's a possibility we'll have to face. If there are fewer men to claim the money, each share increases. Keithley's with us on the second watch. Let's see how he feels."

By the start of the second watch, Keithley had already spoken to Long, Sullivan, Clemans, Ursino, and Stackler. They all seemed to share the same doubts, concerning the expected showdown.

"I think we'll be safe enough, until Estrello has eliminated the steamboat crews and has taken the whiskey," said Keithley. "I expect him to make his move after we reach the landing near here, just east of Fort Smith, on the return journey."

"Why can't Estrello be satisfied with just taking the whiskey?" Betsy asked. "Why does he have to murder the steamboat crews?"

"To silence them" said Keithley. "A man on foot could reach Fort Smith within maybe two hours, and they'll have the telegraph there. Estrello's afraid of that."

"I don't know how we can prevent this mass murder Estrello has in mind," Bill said, "but I'll feel like less of a human being if we don't try."

"But there's not enough of you," said Betsy. "They'll just turn their guns on those of you who try to stop them."

"She's dead right about that," Keithley said. "We need help."

"There's the telegraph in Fort Smith," said Amanda.

"We'd never make it," Keithley said. "The moment one of us is missed, Estrello will be ready to send killers after him. Besides, unless you have some ideas, there's nobody we can reach by telegraph who might get here in time to help us."

"No," said Bill, "and the big question is, can we get help from *anywhere* in time to stop Estrello's conspiracy?"

"We still have to take the steamboats to St. Louis, load

the whiskey, and return to this landing near Fort Smith," Mark said. "That'll take some time. Todd, is there some way I can get pencil and paper for a message?"

"Ed Stackler has a notebook," said Keithley. "How soon do you need it?"

"Right now," Mark said, "and I'll need some light. Who's got a lantern?"

"I have," said Keithley, "but you'll have to be careful. Some of these *hombres* on the second watch are Estrello men to the bone."

"Let me go with you, Mark," Amanda said. "If anybody gets curious about the light, I can tell them I'm sick and that Todd sent me to his wagon for some medicine."

"They'll never believe that," said Mark, "but we'll have to try. Getting caught with the message I'm about to send will be the death of Bill and me."

"Go ahead," Keithley said. "You know where my wagon is. Circle around, comin' in from the north side. Don't light the lantern until you have to. I'll have Stackler get to you with pencil and paper. Good luck."

Mark and Amanda reached Keithley's wagon without being discovered, and within a few minutes, Stackler was there. Silently, he passed the stub of a pencil and two sheets of paper to Mark. He then vanished into the shadows. The lantern was at the very rear of the wagon box. First Mark helped Amanda into the wagon, and following her, drew the rear pucker, and tied it as securely as he could. He then tightened and tied the front pucker. Then he lit the lantern, keeping it on the floor of the wagon box, well beneath the overhead canvas. Kneeling near the lantern, the paper against the rough boards of the wagon box, he began to write. It took but a few minutes for the lantern to draw attention.

"All right, damn it," Wilder said, "Who's usin' that lantern, and why? That you, Keithley?"

"It's me—Amanda," came the reply. "I'm sick and Keithley has a medicine chest. I'm looking for some laudanum."

"Then find it, and put out that lantern," Wilder growled.

"Bless you, Amanda," said Mark softly.

Mark wrote rapidly, of necessity keeping the handwriting small, so that he might get as much into the message as possible. When he was finished, he quickly blew out the lantern.

"I want you to go on back to the wagon," Mark whispered. "I still have to get this on its way, if I can."

"But how—?"

"Later," said Mark. "Now get going."

Mark waited in the shadow of Keithley's wagon until he believed Amanda had returned to their own wagon. He then walked down near the river, where the horses and mules were grazing. Suddenly, there was the snick of a Colt being cocked, followed by the rough voice of Snider Irvin.

"Stand where you are and identify yourself. What'n hell are you doin' among the stock in the middle of the night?"

"Mark Rogers," said Mark, "and I have as much business here as you. I'm part of the second watch."

"Then mind what you do after dark," Irvin growled. "Cat-footin' up on a man when he can't see you is a damn good way of gettin' your hide ventilated."

"Thanks," said Mark. "I'll try to remember that."

Mark walked on toward the river, seeking the roan horse he had ridden to the outlaw camp from Fort Worth. The difficult portion of his task still lay ahead. When at last he could see the roan, he quickly found his saddle. From the boot he removed the Winchester. In one of the saddlebags he placed the written plea for help. Very slowly, he led the horse so that it might appear the animal was grazing, should anybody notice. Holding his breath, expecting a challenge at any time, he went on. He led the saddled horse for more than a mile westward. There he tied the reins securely to the saddle horn and slapped the roan on the flank. The horse trotted a few yards and looked back, clearly undecided as to what was expected. Again Mark swatted the roan on the flank, and this time the animal neither paused nor turned back.

"Old son," said Mark softly, "I hope you still think of Captain Ferguson's post as home. If you show up in the morning here in Estrello's camp, I've ridden my last trail."

Chapter 5

Keithley and Bill stood in the shadow of one of the wagons. Quickly, Mark explained the desperate move he had just made.

When he had finished, Bill spoke. "It ain't often I disagree with you, *amigo,* but I'm goin' to this time. I just wish you'd taken the time to talk about this. We're at least three hundred miles from Fort Worth. A drifting, riderless horse could take a month getting there."

"One other thing you should have considered," Keithley said. "Give a horse two weeks on a particular range, and he considers it home. The critter might return to our old camp on the Washita."

"I reckon I'll have to agree with both of you, as much as I hate to," said Mark. "Come daylight, if that saddled roan is grazing along the river, I'll have to come up with answers to some mighty hard questions."

"Oh, God," Betsy said, "the horse might follow us then."

"Yes," said Mark, "and I should have considered that. It was just a desperate move to try to get a message to Fort Worth."

"That's the second time the two of you have mentioned Fort Worth," Keithley said. "Is that your federal contact?"

"Yes," said Mark. "You might as well know, and you can tell the others who are with us. The post commander is Captain Ferguson. We don't know if there'll be any lawmen who can get here in time to help us. We may all have to run for our lives, and I want all of you, should you have the chance, to be prepared to telegraph Ferguson at Fort Worth. Mention Bill and me, and I promise you that will get Ferguson's attention."

Keithley laughed softly. "I knew there was more to you *hombres* than a pair of outlaws on the run. Now that I can tell the others, it'll pull us all closer together."

"See that they know tonight," said Bill. "If that saddled roan's here at daylight, Mark may be needin' us all."

"The boats still must go to St. Louis, pick up the whiskey, and then return to Fort Smith," Bill said. "How long does that take?"

"Figure eleven days," said Keithley. "Whenever they're loaded, the steamboats won't leave St. Louis until after dark. Dangerous as hell, travelin' the Mississippi without running lights, but they're doin' it."

"Seems to me that's doin' it the hard way, taking the Arkansas to Memphis and then the Mississippi from there," Mark said. "The stuff could have been freighted overland from St. Louis without involving steamboats."

"Sure it could," said Keithley, "but how do you cross that much territory with loaded wagons on a regular basis without raising some hard questions? The steamboats are Wolf Estrello's idea, and I'll have to give the murderous bastard credit. It's worked for almost two years. Steamboats have become so common, nobody stops to think that some of them are involved in illegal activities."

"This outfit doing the freighting is as guilty as Estrello and his bunch," Bill said.

"They are, and they know it," said Keithley. "That's why this arrangement with Wolf Estrello has worked so well. If anybody talks, there's evidence enough on both sides to hang the whole damn bunch from the same limb."

"What bothers me is the possibility that we may have to risk our necks trying to save theirs," Bill said. "From what Estrello's said, he won't waste any time, once his need of the steamboats is past. Whatever we aim to do, we'll have to do it before those steamboats dock near Fort Smith with the whiskey. Once the wagons are off the boats, they can be well into Indian Territory in an hour or two."

Indian Territory. July 26, 1866.

Some eighty-five miles west of Fort Smith, a Kiowa, returning from an unsuccessful hunt, had stopped to rest his horse. He would lead the animal to water at the great lake.*

The Kiowa stared at the distant expanse of water, and at first believed his eyes were deceiving him. A roan horse, wearing a white man's saddle, grazed along the lake shore. First, the Kiowa led his thirsty horse to drink. Then he turned his attention to the roan. The reins had been knotted about the saddle horn, suggesting that the horse, for some unknown reason, had been set free.

As the Kiowa went closer, the roan nickered, perking up its ears. The Kiowa spoke to the horse until he was close enough. He then took his knife and slashed the double rigging, and removed the saddle he neither needed or wanted. Gratefully, the roan lay down and rolled in the grass. The Kiowa laughed, waiting for the horse to get to its feet. When it did, the Kiowa had a long rawhide lead for use as a bridle. It was then that he saw the brand on the roan's left hip.

* Sardis Lake, near present-day town of Clayton, Oklahoma.

While the Kiowa didn't know what "U.S." meant, he had seen it on many *soldado* horses, and that made his good fortune all the sweeter. He had taken a blue coat's horse without endangering himself. Leading the roan, he rode west, deeper into Indian Territory.

Fort Smith. July 27, 1866.

During the night, the four steamboats arrived. They were stern-wheelers, allowing them easy access to the prepared dock. The firemen fed just enough wood into the fireboxes to keep up steam. Dawn came, and Mark stood looking at the horses and mules. His roan wasn't among them, and he sighed with relief.

"You've just done yourself out of a horse and saddle," Bill said.

"I reckon I'm a mite selfish," said Mark, "but I like to think my hide's worth more than a horse and saddle."

"Now we go to St. Louis for the whiskey," Betsy said. "Maybe one of us can escape to a telegraph office and ask for help."

"The boats will be loaded a considerable distance south of St. Louis," said Keithley. "I doubt any one of us would make it to St. Louis alive."

"Mark," Amanda asked, "where's your Winchester?"

"In the wagon," said Mark. "If everything just goes to hell and we have to run for it, I'll have to take me a horse and saddle from one of these owlhoots."

"We'd better split up," Keithley said. "Wilder keeps lookin' over here. If I don't do anything else, I'd like to ventilate his ugly carcass before I split the blanket with this bunch."

Two wagons and their teams were to be taken aboard each of the four steamboats. To make them harder to track, no names appeared on the boats; but everyone in the gang was familiar with the *Aztec, Goose, Midnight,* and *Star.* Then came the horses belonging to Estrello's outriders, and the many horses and mules Estrello had taken in trade for whiskey. Counting himself, Estrello had thirty-four men. When it came time for them to board the steamboats, Estrello had a list of names.

"On the fourth boat, the *Star,*" said Estrello, "I want Long, Sullivan, Clemans, Keithley, Ursino, Stackler, Rogers, Harder, and their women. Irvin and Suggs will see there is no problems aboard that particular boat. On the *Midnight,* boat three, I want Hiram, Odell, Hamby, Kendrick, Hedgepith, Shadley, Patton, and Tilden. Shadley, you and Tilden are in charge. On the *Goose,* boat two, I want Worsham, Bideno, Jackman, Cordier, Haddock, DeWitt, Graves, and Wilder. Wilder, you and Bideno are in charge. On the *Aztec* with me, I want Brice, McCarty, Schorp, McLean, Renato, and Jabez. I'll be in charge. Graves, you will be my second in command."

"Of all the rotten luck," said Betsy. "We get Suggs and Irvin in charge of our fourth boat."

"Luck had nothing to do with it," Mark said. "Estrello's not about to take any chances with us. He planned it this way. We have Irvin and Suggs in charge, but we can take them if we have to. I'm surprised we're not in the first steamboat, where old Wolf can keep a close watch on us."

"He has an ego nine feet tall and a yard wide," said Carl Long, who had just joined them. "Even if we salted down Suggs and Irvin and took possession of the *Star,* we would still be stuck behind the others, with no place to go except farther west."

"That's not a bad idea, taking control of the fourth steamboat," Lee Sullivan said. "Is it part of our plan?"

"I don't think we actually *have* a plan," said Stackler. "Mark, you and Bill brought us together. What do you think?"

"I think taking over a steamboat will be the quickest way to get all of us killed," Bill said, "unless I change my mind. Have another look at the upper deck of the first steamboat, where they've removed the canvas covering."

"By the Eternal," Nick Ursino said, "it's a Gatling gun. That thing could wipe out an entire tribe of Indians in just a few seconds."

"Is this the kind of thing Estrello's done before?" Mark asked.

"Not in all the time I've been with him," said Stackler. "He's always taken maybe three or four men from each steamboat. The rest of us just waited here for them to return."

"He always took varmints like Wilder and Irvin," Clemans added. "He's partial to those who will kill without question."

"We still don't have a plan," said Ursino.

"We'll have to plan as we go," Mark said. "We don't know what's likely to happen before we reach St. Louis, load the whiskey, and return here. As for taking over a steamboat, let's give it some thought. The Aztec has the Gatling gun on the forward deck, and it'll take some time to turn that boat around. But if there's no other way, we can cut down Suggs and Irvin, ground the steamboat, and ride for our lives."

"I don't like the sound of that," said Bill. "Estrello will still have enough men so they can track us down, riding in relays. I believe Estrello would leave the steamboats loaded with whiskey and come after us."

Keithley sighed. "I'm inclined to agree with Bill. We'd

better give serious thought to this situation. It's unlikely
that we'll have any advantage during the loading in St. Louis.
There should be a four-man crew aboard each steamboat.
Generally, there's a captain and three fireman, but they're
not short-horns. Every man of them is armed with a Winchester and knows how to use it."

"Rogers and Harder, drive your wagons aboard the *Star,*"
Estrello shouted. "Take them where you are told, unhitch
the teams, and chock the wagon wheels."

The steamboat crew had brought heavy oak ramps for the
loading and unloading of the wagons. It required four men,
including the steamboat's captain, to get the ramp in place.
When it was ready, Mark guided his team up the ramp, taking the wagon to a position one of the crew had pointed out.
There he unharnessed the mules, and again following one
of the crew, led the animals to a lower deck. By the time he
returned to chock the wheels of the wagon, Bill's wagon
was aboard, and he was unharnessing the teams.

"Be damn sure you chock them wheels right," said one of
the crewmen.

"I ain't never chocked no wheels before," Mark said with
all the sarcasm he was able to muster, "but I'll do my best."

Irvin had arrived just in time to hear the exchange.

"Rogers," said Irvin, "I'm in charge, and there'll be no
smart-mouthing. Do as you are told, or you'll answer to me."

"If I had a gun, I could kill him myself," Betsy said softly.

"Not so loud," said Bill. "Like it or not, we're stuck with
him and Suggs until we decide what we have to do."

"I'm wondering if these steamboats weren't built for
smuggling," Mark said. "Except for the ramp to each deck,
the rest of the rim has maybe a three-foot-high wall that
looks like steel or iron. A few men with that kind of cover
and plenty of ammunition could hold off a small army."

"It's something to keep in mind," said Stackler. "Some of us don't have that much ammunition. Estrello's kept us out of towns, and we've been limited to the shells he's been allowing us."

"Then we'll just have to make good use of what we have," Mark said.

There was some delay when some of the horses and mules to be sold shied at the boat ramp. Instead of going aboard boat three, the animals whirled and ran back the way they had come. Shadley and Hiram were run down in the unexpected stampede. They lay there in the mud, cursing, while others in the outfit thought it hilariously funny.

"Damn it," Estrello bawled, "you outriders go after those animals. And be sure you get them all."

But it was no easy task, for the horses belonging to the outriders had been unsaddled and were on a lower deck. Considerable time had passed before the pursuers were able to leave the steamboat, and by then, the escaped horses and mules had disappeared into the brush and undergrowth along the north bank of the Arkansas.

Keithley laughed softly. "That's the first time that's ever happened."

"Wolf Estrello's greed is the cause of that," said Sullivan. "He's taking twice as many mules and horses as he's ever taken before."

"Every one of them's wearin' a brand of some kind," Bill said. "Horse stealing can get a man hung quicker than anything else. How does he get around that?"

"Another of his crooked contacts in St. Louis," said Ursino. "By the time Estrello gets this stolen stock off the boat, he'll have what passes for a bill of sale on every one of the critters."

Slowly, the disgruntled outriders rounded up the stampeded horses and mules, driving them onto the steamboat two or three at a time. They were still missing a pair of mules when Estrello gave it up.

"Let the others go," he shouted.

The outriders were only too glad to do exactly that. When they again got aboard the steamboat, they had been bloodied by briars and thorns, and their tempers were on a short rein. They led their horses to a lower deck, again unsaddling them. A stranger with dark hair to his collar and a three-day beard stood on deck, watching the last of the runaway horses and mules being led aboard. When he spoke, it was loud enough for all to hear.

"I am Captain Jenks, and I am in full command of this vessel. My word is final, and I suggest all of you keep that in mind. None of you is allowed in my quarters, in the pilothouse, or the boiler room."

But there was immediate conflict. Their hands near the butts of their revolvers, Irvin and Suggs faced the arrogant captain. "I'm Irvin, and this is Suggs. We are in charge of everybody on this boat until it has traveled to St. Louis and returns here. That's by order of *Señor* Estrello."

"I am the captain," Jenks said, "and any man disobeying my rules will be shot. That specifically includes both of you."

Jenks had a Colt belted around his middle and looked perfectly capable of using it. His hard eyes bored into Irvin and Suggs, and the surly pair allowed common sense to overcome their pride. They backed off, and Captain Jenks eyed the rest of the men as though daring somebody to take up the argument where Irvin and Suggs had left off. None of the other men had anything to say, but there was a half smile on Stackler's rugged face, and a definite twinkle in the eyes of his companions.

"Damn it," Suggs complained to nobody in particular, "we'll be settin' here all night while they load the other three boats."

"Mister," said Captain Jenks, who had overheard, "feel free to take your horse and ride on ahead if that suits you. Otherwise, shut the hell up and stay out of the way."

When the fourth steamboat was loaded and the loading ramps raised, the men assigned to the third boat, the *Midnight,* wrestled the ramps into place. The two wagons were then taken aboard, followed by the outriders' horses. Last came some horses and mules Estrello would sell or trade in St. Louis. The loading of the first and second boats went smoothly, and not quite an hour before sundown, the four steamboats were ready to depart. Black smoke poured from their twin stacks, as firemen added wood and stoked the fires beneath the boilers.

"I'm hungry," Amanda said. "What about food?"

"Mostly cold biscuit and jerked beef," said Lee Sullivan. "That's all this outfit provides, unless Estrello pays extra, which he won't. There is a barrel of fresh water, though."

The stern-wheelers rolled on, leaving a backwash of muddy water behind them. Before dark, Captain Jenks spoke to Long and Sullivan.

"You men come with me. There's food to be brought to the upper deck."

Sullivan's prediction of jerked beef and cold biscuits proved correct, but there was enough of both to satisfy their hunger.

"This is goin' to be one hell of a long ride," said Bill, "without decent grub."

Mark laughed. "I recall you sayin' once that a Texan could survive for a year on good old jerked beef."

"He can," Bill grumbled, "but that don't mean he has to like it."

Darkness fell, and there was only faint starlight to illuminate the muddy Arkansas. Bill, Betsy, Mark, and Amanda stood beside the rail, their eyes on the big paddle wheel.

"Something like this could be fun," said Betsy, "if things were different."

"Things *will* be different when we ride back to Texas," Mark said. "Maybe we'll spend a couple of weeks in Austin, eating and sleeping."

"I admire your optimism," said Bill.

"So do I," Amanda said. "As much as I want to believe we'll live through this, there's doubt that's tearing me apart. It seems like nothing ever works out for Betsy and me. We lost Ma to consumption, and old Jake took us in, seen we were fed, and had something to wear. Of course, we were with these outlaws, but Jake protected us. After Jake was killed, it would have been the end of us, if the two of you hadn't been there. Now it looks like we may all meet the same grisly end together."

Taking off his hat, Mark touched Amanda's cheek with his own. The girl was weeping silent tears for what might have been. He said nothing, for there was nothing he could say that would change their precarious circumstances. Bill and Betsy were silent, and it seemed Bill might be comforting the girl as best he could. After a prolonged silence, it was Betsy who spoke.

"I have to go to the bushes. What am I going to do?"

"There has to be some private place on this steamboat," Bill said. "Captain Jenks can't fault us for asking about that. Come on."

They found Captain Jenks on the main deck, eating jerked beef and a biscuit. He was civil enough when Mark asked him the all-important question.

"The facilities—the head—is on the deck just below this one," said Jenks. "You will be permitted down there."

"I'm afraid to go alone," Betsy said. "Bill, will you come with me?"

"Come on," said Bill. "We're not even sure what we're looking for. I'll go and see that nobody bothers you."

"Perhaps I'd better go along, too," Amanda said. "It's that, or go later."

"Let's go, then," said Mark. "It bothers me, with all these men on board."

"I'm not afraid of any of them, except Suggs and Irvin," Betsy said. "Of course, we don't know the firemen."

"I don't look for any trouble from the firemen," Mark said. "Bill and me will stay near enough to hear you if anything goes wrong."

There was only an iron-runged ladder leading down to the next deck, and at the foot of the ladder was a lighted lantern. Bill took it, and they began looking for what Jenks had called "the head." They found it at the far end of the deck, and it was in no way enclosed. A kind of bench had been constructed out of rough lumber, with a convenient hole at each end. Beneath them they could hear the rushing of the river.

Bill laughed. "Why this ain't nothin' but an old cow-country outhouse."

"Not quite," said Mark. "There's no walls, no door, and no privacy."

"Well, hell," Bill said, "a good lightning bug could turn out more light than this old lantern. We'll just blow it out until you're finished."

"No," said Betsy, "leave it lighted. It's so awful dark down here."

"Something touched the back of my neck," Amanda cried. "It was cold and wet."

Mark laughed. "You've been nuzzled by one of the mules. Some of the extra mules and horses are down here."

"Laugh, damn it," said Amanda. "It scared me half to death."

"The two of you had better get over there and use that contraption," Bill said, "before the rest of the horses and mules get interested and come to see what you're doing."

"At least they could have built some walls around the thing," Betsy complained.

"It's dark now," said Amanda. "In daylight, we'll be sitting right there for anybody to see us."

"I don't believe there's a man on this steamboat that won't respect your privacy," said Mark, "unless it's Irvin and Suggs. Bill and me can handle them."

"One or both of you could be killed," Betsy said. "Our privacy's not worth that."

When they were ready to return to the upper deck, they hung the lantern back where they had found it and climbed the iron-runged ladder. Amanda and Betsy went first, Bill and Mark following. There in the dim starlight stood Irvin, a scowl on his ugly face.

"The captain said there wasn't gonna be no roamin' around on this steamboat," Irvin said. "Where the hell you been?"

"The ladies had to visit the facilities on the lower deck," said Bill, trying to contain his temper. "We asked the captain, and he gave his permission."

Somehow they made it through that first long night. Shortly after daylight, the four boats stopped at a crude landing, where the firemen loaded additional wood to continue the journey. On the *Star* the comrades watched the activity, pondering their situation.

"The way all this is stacking up," said Long, "we'll have to make our move on the return trip from St. Louis."

"You may be right," Mark said. "When Bill and me were first lured into comin' after Estrello's outfit, not too much was said about the bunch in St. Louis that Estrello's dealing with. Now that we're neck-deep in the situation, it looks like these steamboat crews and their owners may be as troublesome as Estrello's bunch."

"I think we'd better spend our time thinkin' of some way to save our own hides," said Clemans. "These steamboat crews don't trust *any* of Estrello's outfit, including us. There are eight of us against Estrello's twenty-six men. Add the gun-totin' captains and their crews to that, and we'll have more than forty men against us in a showdown."

"I've been considering that," Stackler said. "I think, before these steamboats return to Fort Smith, some of us will be forced to jump ship. Mark, while I appreciate the agreement you and Bill had with the military at Fort Worth, there's no way eight of us can go up against forty gunmen and come out of it alive."

"Don't forget Betsy and me," said Amanda. "We have rifles, and we can shoot."

"Bless both of you," Mark said, "but the odds are still too high."

"I hate to mention this," Keithley said, "since we have problems enough, but why didn't Estrello assign two or three of us to each steamboat? I think he *wants* us to plan some kind of rebellion. All of us have opposed him in one way or another, and when he's ready to dispose of those steamboat crews, he aims for us to die along with them."

"I'm considering that, too," said Stackler, "and it's looking more and more like it's what Estrello's planning to do.
Let's face it. There are wanted dodgers on us all, except for
Betsy and Amanda. Suppose all of us and all the steamboat
crews die in a shootout? It will leave behind enough evidence and dead men to convince the law there's been a
falling-out among thieves and killers."

"But there won't be any of the whiskey," Ursino said.
"Estrello wins the pot."

"We can't let him do it," Betsy cried.

"There's a way out," said Bill. "There's always a way
out. We just have to find it."

The second day there was unexpected trouble on the *Star,*
the fourth steamboat.

"Mark," Amanda said. "I need to go down to the lower
deck. Do you suppose it will be safe in daylight? I hate taking down my Levi's among this many men, even if they're
all mostly our friends."

"I'll go with you," said Mark. "I'll wait near the ladder
and head off any of the men who might not know you're
there."

The way seemed clear, for there was nobody in sight on
the lower deck. Near the improvised "outhouse" were some
horses and mules, and they looked curiously at Amanda.
She had been there only a few seconds when from the corner of her eye she caught some movement among the mules.

Suggs stepped out into the open, an evil grin on his scarred
face. "Well now, girlie," said Suggs, "I've always wanted a
better look at you. Leave them britches down around your
boot tops and stand up."

Amanda sat there in horrified silence, and from behind
Suggs, Mark spoke.

"Suggs, you low-down skunk, you don't know how much I'd like to kill you where you stand. Get the hell out of here while you still can."

Suggs laughed. "I got as much right down here as she has. I'm waitin' my turn."

It was too much. Mark took a step forward, and his right fist cracked against Suggs's chin. The outlaw was flung back among the horses and mules and, frightened, they started a commotion. Suggs, attempting to use some of the animals for cover, went for his gun.

But Mark had been expecting that. He rolled under one of the mules, seizing Suggs by his legs and slamming him to the floor. Suggs's Colt roared, further disturbing the captive livestock. Seizing the front of Suggs's shirt in his left hand, Mark hauled him to his feet and hit him again. He went down and didn't get up. But there was more trouble. Captain Jenks stood in the narrow corridor, a cocked Colt in his hand.

"Mister, tell me what happened here, and it had better be good."

Mark quickly explained, as Amanda—with white face and shaking hands—stood beside him. Suggs finally sat up, rubbing his jaw. Stackler, Keithley, Clemans, and Ursino stood in the narrow corridor behind Captain Jenks, but he ignored them. He spoke to Suggs.

"The ladies have priority down here, and the right to privacy. If I ever again catch you involved in such a shameful affair on my steamboat, I'll kill you."

Suggs got to his knees and finally his feet, staggering a little. He laughed, and then he spoke to Captain Jenks. "I aim to see that Wolf Estrello knows about this, big man. Next time, you may not have the gun."

"Be sure you tell Estrello," Captain Jenks said, "and if

there is a next time, it may be you lacking a gun. One of you men find his pistol and turn it in to me. Maybe he'll get it back, and maybe he won't."

Irvin had come down the ladder to see what had caused the disturbance, and he was just in time to hear Captain Jenks demand Suggs's Colt. Irvin said nothing, climbing up the iron-runged ladder to the upper deck.

Chapter 6

The rest of the day, Irvin and Suggs kept to themselves.

"From now on," Mark said, "they'll be looking for some excuse to come down on us."

"Let them," said Bill. "If there's trouble between them and Captain Jenks, my money's on the captain."

Near sundown, the steamboats again drew up alongside a crude landing, where the firemen began loading more wood for fuel. Irvin and Suggs made their way down the ramp to the riverbank. From there they walked to the first boat, the *Aztec*. On deck, Estrello saw them coming and went to meet them before they boarded the craft. If there was trouble, he had no desire for the rest of the outlaws to become aware of it.

"What the hell are you two doin' here?" Estrello demanded. "Trouble aboard?"

"You might say that," said the surly Suggs. "Your snooty captain threatened to kill me, and he took my Colt."

"All for no reason, I suppose," Estrello said.

"Aw, hell," said Irvin, "he run into one of them females on the second deck."

"You invaded her privacy, then," Estrello said.

"Yeah," said Suggs. "You could say that. So what? That

bastard ain't talkin' down to me like I'm nobody. He's captain of a steamboat, not God."

"Whatever *you* think of him makes no difference," Estrello said angrily. "He *is* captain of the steamboat, and if either of you create any more disturbance aboard that boat, you won't have to concern yourselves with the captain. I'll come after you myself. Now get the hell aboard and stay there."

Irvin and Suggs said nothing, but started back toward the *Star*.

Stackler laughed, for he and his comrades had seen the confrontation.

"I'd of give five hundred dollars to have heard what Estrello told them," said Keithley.

"They didn't much like it," Mark said. "Look at their faces. They're killing mad. Maybe we can use that to our advantage."

Fort Smith. July 29, 1866.

The Barton gang, who had attacked Wolf Estrello's outfit, had suffered a great loss, for eleven of their number—one of whom was Frank Barton himself—had been killed. Near the landing where Estrello's wagons had boarded the steamboats, what remained of the Barton gang sat in silence, drinking coffee, including Liz, Barton's redheaded, short-tempered wife, with whom he had constantly fought.

"Damn it," said Green Perryman, "we might as well call it quits. There ain't enough of us for a gang."

"We're not giving up," snapped Liz Barton. "Attacking Estrello, trying to kill his men, was a foolish move. It was Frank's idea, and he paid for it."

"And took ten men with him," Will Macklin said. "I've enjoyed all the Barton luck I can stand."

"Don't be so quick to run," said Liz in a more soothing tone. "We'll add some more riders, and when Estrello returns with the whiskey, we'll be ready."

"Ready for what?" Hez DeShea asked. "Some more buryings?"

"Don't get sarcastic with me," snarled Liz. "Frank Barton was a fool. I did everything except shoot him, trying to prevent that attack on Estrello, but the rest of you went along like sheep. Where the hell were you when it counted?"

"I reckon you got us there." said French Loe. "We thought Frank knowed what he was doing. Hell, we had the edge."

"Eleven men died," Liz said. "You call *that* an edge?"

She was right, and it silenced them. The looks on their faces suggested they might just saddle up and ride away. Liz tried again, more tactful this time.

"From now on, we'll make no moves until everybody agrees," said Liz. "I won't ask or expect anything foolish of you, like Frank did."

"You?" Tobe Havre said. "Why, you're just a . . . a . . . ."

"A woman," Liz said, "but I can out-draw and out-shoot any one of you. I was there in the midst of a stupid attack that cost us eleven men, doing my part."

"Then I reckon it's safe for me to say I disagreed with some of Frank's ideas," Sterns said. "He had a mad on for Wolf Estrello, and what would it have gained us if we'd killed a few of his men? The damn territory's full of outlaws."

"That's what I asked him, after he made the decision to strike," said Liz. "From now on, we don't concern ourselves with anything that doesn't pay. Now who's going to throw in with me?"

"I like the way you talk," Sterns said. "I'll stay a while."

"Count me in," said DeShea.

"I like the idea of us all agreein'." Loe said. "I'll ride with you."

"That goes for me, too," said Lefty Paschal.

Whit Sumner, Will Macklin, Tobe Harve, and Green Perryman voted to stay.

"That's more like it," Liz said. "Now we have to come up with a solid plan to take the whiskey from Estrello's outfit without a face-to-face gunfight."

"We have maybe eight or nine days," said Sumner, "if this trip takes them as long as the others. How many more men are you wantin'?"

"Since we're going up against Estrello's bunch," Liz said, "we could use twenty more. I am open to suggestions. Do any of you know where we might find these men in the time that we have?"

"If you don't have any objection to working with Indians, I can get you two hundred," said Loe. "We could pay them in whiskey."

"I don't like the sound of that," Sumner said. "It's got double-cross wrote all over it. Them Indians—Comanche and Kiowa—trade with Estrello. They know what them wagonloads of whiskey's worth when they reach the Territory."

"I don't want nothin' to do with renegade Indians," said Macklin. "I purely don't trust the varmints. Maybe they'd help us slaughter Estrello's bunch, but after they're done with that, what's to keep 'em from turning on us?"

"French," Liz Barton said, "we're obliged for the suggestion, but we can't depend on a bunch of renegade Indians. Like Will said, even if they joined us and we took that load of whiskey from Estrello, the renegades might turn on us. We'll have to come up with something better."

"Nothin' to do, then, but ride back into the Territory and ask around," Harve said, "but who's going?"

"I suppose that's up to me," said Liz.

"Nobody—especially a woman—rides into Indian Territory alone," Loe said. "You'd better take us all with you."

"No," said Liz. "Too many riders, and they have the look of a posse. Lefty, you ride with me, and the rest of you wait here. We don't have much time."

Lefty Paschal saddled a horse for Liz and one for himself. They mounted and started out eastward, toward Indian Territory.

"Well," said Lefty, "now that old Frank's cashed in his chips, you and me don't have to slip around, do we?"

"Frank being gone doesn't have a damn thing to do with whether or not I see you," Liz said angrily. "You have the same problem as all men. A few rolls in the hay, and you think you own me."

"Well, hell," said Lefty, "if my claim on you ain't no stronger than that, maybe I'll just ride back and join the rest of the boys. Then you can go huntin' grizzly bears with a switch if it suits your fancy."

"Damn you." Liz said, "I chose you to go with me, and you're going. Whether or not you share my blankets is my decision, not yours. Now let's ride."

Lefty Paschal said no more. He realized, although they had slipped around behind her dead husband's back, that he really didn't *know* Liz Barton. Her Colt revolver was tied low on her right hip, and he knew for a fact she could pull iron and shoot like hell wouldn't have it. For the first time, Paschal saw her as more dangerous than Frank had ever been. Nothing more was said until they eventually stopped to rest the horses.

"If it ain't asking too much, do you have a plan for taking

those four steamboats when they return with the whiskey?"
Lefty asked.

"I do," said Liz, her green eyes on him, "and you'll learn
what it is when I decide to tell the others."

North on the Mississippi. July 31, 1866.

The four steamboats swept past Little Rock in the middle
of the night, and not until the third day did they reach the
Mississippi, at a point south of Memphis, Tennessee.

"If anybody calls their hand," said Stackler, "it'll be on
the Mississippi."

"We didn't see another boat on the Arkansas, all the way
from Fort Smith," Ursino said. "Seems like there ought to
be more traffic, at least to Little Rock."

"Too dangerous," said Stackler. "The last few months have
been almighty dry, and in the best of times, rivers have shallow water in some places. I imagine these captains of the
Estrello steamboats know where these treacherous waters
along the Arkansas are."

"I've heard a good captain can 'grasshopper' a steamboat
across a sandbar," Clemans said. "These gents are not very
sociable, but they know their jobs."

"I sort of like Captain Jenks, after he told off Irvin and
Suggs," Betsy said. "Whatever else he may be, he's a
gentleman."

"I hope he *still* is when we return with all that whiskey,"
Long said.

"I wonder if we can't talk some sense to Captain Jenks
before we return to Fort Smith with the whiskey," said Bill.
"Suppose he knew—as we know—that the steamboat cap-

tains and their crews are supposed to die when the need for them is past?"

"It would be our word against Estrello's," Mark said, "and these steamboat people are not making any money off us. Of course, we can't dismiss the idea entirely, because we have no idea what's likely to happen before we return to Fort Smith."

"All right," growled Irvin as he arrived in their midst, "what's going on here, a tea social?"

"We were taking a vote," said Clemans. "We're trying to decide whether we'd prefer to see you hung, or backed up against a wall and shot."

"We compromised," Ursino said. "We decided we'd prefer to see you hung, but while you're kicking air, we'll shoot your carcass full of holes."

"Where's Suggs?" Stackler asked. "Did the captain have to kill him?"

"He's with his own kind," said Betsy. "On the lower deck with the mules."

"There ain't a damn one of you got anything to be funnin' about," Irvin said. "There'll come a time to shut your mouths, and I'm looking forward to it." With all the arrogance at his command, he walked away.

"There it is," said Mark. "He as much as told us Estrello aims for us to die."

"Oh, Lord," Amanda said, "that means he intends to kill the rest of you, and then force Betsy and me to lead him to the gold. I'll drown myself in the river before I'll do it."

"I'll join you," said Betsy.

When darkness fell, Bill, Betsy, Mark, and Amanda took refuge in the wagon that had belonged to Jake Miles.

"I swear I'm going to stop drinking water until this is

over," Amanda said. "I hate going to that lower deck after dark."

"So do I," said Betsy. "I keep looking for Suggs to show up."

"Bill and me can go with you," Mark said.

"I have a better idea," said Betsy. "We'll stay on this deck, and get over there near the edge. When it dries, nobody will be the wiser."

"Be sure there's nobody around," Mark cautioned.

But they had barely reached the point near the edge of the upper deck when there was a shout. Irvin and Suggs came charging out of the shadows. Mark and Bill scrambled out of the wagon, but the damage had been done. With a shriek, Betsy and Amanda went over the side into the dark, muddy water below. Mark drew his Colt and fired three times. It was an accepted signal of danger on the frontier. One of the men on the third boat, the *Midnight*, fired three answering shots, and in the distance there were more shots as someone on the *Goose* relayed the distress signal. Making their way toward shore, the steamboats were grounded shy of it, for there was a lengthy sandbar. Men from the first three boats were wading in mud and water, and as Mark and Bill left the *Star*, they encountered Wolf Estrello.

"What the hell . . ." Estrello bellowed.

"Betsy and Amanda are in the river," Mark shouted.

Captain Jenks arrived with a lantern and was told what had happened.

"We'd better begin walking the banks," said Jenks. "Can they swim?"

"We don't know," Bill said.

"I want to know who's responsible for this," said Estrello, "and I want to know now."

"I heard the shots," Captain Jenks said, "But I saw nothing."

"I fired the first three shots," said Mark. "Betsy and Amanda were near the edge of the upper deck. Irvin and Suggs ran out of the darkness, startling them. That's when they went over the side."

"Damn them," Estrello said. "They've cost us the gold."

"Damn the gold," Mark shouted. "Let's look for Amanda and Betsy."

"Some of you get aboard boat four," said Captain Jenks, "and I'll take you across. We will have to search both riverbanks."

All the men scrambled back aboard boat four. Captain Jenks guided the craft as near the opposite bank as he could, and the men aboard descended again into mud and water. Estrello was stomping the deck of boat four, bawling for Irvin and Suggs.

In the dark waters of the Mississippi, Amanda and Betsy fought the backwash from the steamboat's huge paddle wheel. When the vessel was far enough away and the water calmed, they swam for the nearest riverbank. They crawled out on their hands and knees, bellied down, and coughed up river water.

"Damn," said Betsy, "are we in a mess. Estrello probably won't even look for us."

"The hell he won't," Amanda panted. "We know where the gold is. There's somebody with a lantern across the river. The question is, should we allow ourselves to be found? This might be the answer to our prayers, where Bill and Mark are concerned. Suppose we could reach a telegraph office and send a message to Fort Worth?"

"It might be worth a try," said Betsy, "if we can send it

collect. We don't have a cent between us. But it'll scare the hell out of Bill and Mark. They'll think we drowned."

"I hate that, but we're trying to help them," Amanda said. "Along a river like this, I can't believe there won't be a lesser town somewhere between here and St. Louis. Let's go upstream, the way the boats were going."

They started walking, resting when exhaustion made it necessary. Soon the sounds of the search and the shouts of men were behind them. They could hear only the sound of the river and could see nothing in the darkness. There was no moon, and the twinkling stars seemed dim and far away. When they were able to walk no farther, they sprawled in the grass beneath a tree and fell into exhausted sleep.

Mark and Bill walked the riverbank at least two miles downstream without seeing or hearing anything. Clemans and Ursino were with them.

"We might as well turn back," Bill said. "If they're alive, they won't be this far downstream."

"And we don't even know if they could swim or not," said Ursino.

"No," Bill said, "and if they could, we may not find them. They're the kind who would use this as an opportunity to send that message to Fort Smith if they can."

"I think you're right," said Mark, "and if they're alive, they'll be somewhere upstream, the way the steamboats were headed. What's bothering me is how long Estrello will look for them before saying the hell with it and going on to St. Louis."

But Estrello wasn't about to give up so easily. He found Irvin and Suggs hiding in Bill Harder's wagon on the *Star*.

"Come out of there, you troublemaking sons-of-bitches," Estrello shouted.

"We didn't do nothin'," Suggs whined. "We saw some-body on deck and come up here to see who it was. It was all an accident."

"You damned bunglers," snarled Estrello. "If we don't find them, we've lost the gold, and I'll personally hang the two of you upside-down over a slow fire. Now get the hell off this boat and join the search."

In their haste to escape Estrello's fury, Irvin and Suggs leaped over the side into neck deep water and mud. Quietly cursing Estrello, they stumbled up the riverbank not too far from where Betsy and Amanda had reached safety. Cap-tain Jenks returned to the steamboat, to find Estrello pacing the deck.

"It's going to be impossible to find them in the dark," the captain said. "Shall we just go on?"

"Hell, no," said Estrello. "We're going to stay right here until first light and look some more, until we find them or their bodies."

"It's going to cost you," Captain Jenks said.

"You'll get everything that's coming to you," said Es-trello ominously.

Finally, exhausted from the search and having seen no sign of Betsy and Amanda, the men returned to the steamboats.

"We can't find them in the dark, Captain," Bill said. "What's going to be done?"

"Estrello has ordered us to lay over here until daylight," said Captain Jenks. "He will find the ladies or their bodies before we continue."

Mark and Bill climbed into Jake's wagon, where they slept not a wink. They were wet, muddy, and exhausted, but none of that mattered. Amanda and Betsy were gone.

When the gray of approaching dawn crept over the eastern

sky, they went in search of the captain. "Captain Jenks," Mark said, "if we had horses, we could do this much quicker."

"Then put one of the ramps in place and take your horses," said Jenks.

"Nick," Bill shouted, "will you and Vernon help us get this ramp in place?"

"Sure," said Nick. "If you're taking your horses, we'll take ours. Mark, you don't have a horse or saddle."

"I will," Mark said. "Suggs and Irvin have saddles and horses. I'll borrow one, and I'll dare either of the skulking coyotes to say a word."

Seeing the ramp in place, all the men from the *Star*—except Irvin and Suggs—took their horses for the search. It was Ursino who found a boot print where Amanda and Betsy had emerged from the river.

"They're walking upstream," Nick shouted.

"I wonder if we're doing them any favors, tracking them down," said Bill, as he and Mark galloped to join Nick.

"There's not much else we can do," Mark said. "There may not be a telegraph office any closer than St. Louis. We can't leave them stranded on their own, without food."

But as it turned out, Bill and Mark had no choice. As though he feared just such a possibility, Estrello had ordered men from boats two and three to unload their horses and join in the pursuit. Amanda and Betsy heard the horses coming and turned to look. Bill and Mark leaped from their saddles while the horses were still moving. Wearily, Betsy and Amanda stumbled to them, tears streaking the mud on their faces. Some of the men from boats two and three reined up.

"You're wasting time here," Wilder said. "Get them on horses and back to the steamboats."

"This is none of your damn business, Wilder." said Mark.

"I'm makin' it my business," Wilder said.

Wilder seized Mark's shirt by the collar from behind. Mark tore loose, and with a long night of bottled-up fury and frustration behind it, smashed his fist into Wilder's jaw. He went down and didn't get up.

"If Estrello don't kill you for this, you lead a charmed life," said Stackler.

"I'm sorry we dragged you and Bill into this, Mark," Betsy said.

"I'm not," said Bill. "If Estrello wants to blame somebody, let him go after Irvin and Suggs. They started all this."

Wilder sat up, a thin stream of blood trickling from the corners of his mouth. He looked at Mark and spoke in a venomous tone. "You don't do that to me and live to talk about it, bucko. One day you and me will meet where we're not bound by Estrello's ten commandments. Then we'll see just who's the better man."

"I'm looking forward to that day, Wilder," said Mark. "Until then, I'll be careful not to turn my back on you."

Mark and Bill lifted Amanda and Betsy to their horses and mounted behind them. They soon arrived at the waiting steamboats, and with the ramp still in place, the riders trotted their horses aboard. When Amanda and Betsy were helped down by Mark and Bill, Captain Jenks actually smiled.

"You men get those horses below deck and unsaddled," said Estrello. "We've lost too much time as it is."

"Not until we settle something with you," Mark said. "We're damn tired of Irvin and Suggs dogging us. The next one of them that steps out of the dark without warning will get a dose of lead poisoning."

"I've taken care of that," Estrello said shortly.

Not wishing to remain alone on deck, Amanda and Betsy

went with Mark and Bill to the lower deck, waiting while they unsaddled the horses.

"In a way, I'm glad you found Betsy and me," said Amanda, "and in another way, I wish you hadn't. We might have had a chance to send that message for you."

"That's what we planned to do, after we thought about it," Betsy added.

"I'm glad we found you, whatever the consequences," said Mark. "We'd have lost our minds, not knowing if you were alive or dead."

"What do you suppose Estrello's done with Irvin and Suggs?" Betsy asked.

"They're on the boat somewhere," said Bill, "but I don't think they'll be bothering you or Amanda."

"I'm surprised Estrello didn't shoot them both," Mark said. "I think he's keeping himself a mental list, and when he starts killing folks, the troublemakers within his own outfit will be the first to go."

"If I had the chance to shoot just one of these coyotes," said Bill, "I think I'd rid us of Wilder. He's as much or more a danger than Estrello himself."

By the time they reached the upper deck, the steamboats were moving again. Clemans and Ursino stood by the rail, watching the backwash from the big paddle wheel.

"Lord, how I envy you, Mark," Ursino said. "That's the first time anybody's ever laid a hand on Wilder. Of course, you'll have to kill him."

"I reckon," said Mark. "I don't take any pleasure in that, but he looks and acts like one of the varmints that won't have it any other way."

"I think most of Estrello's outfit's of the same mind," Clemans said, "and that won't make it any easier on us."

"That's likely the worst part of this kind of life," said

Ursino. "Live by the gun long enough, and you know you're goin' to die by it. You become fatalistic, refusing to settle for anything less than a shoot-out."

"Let's go sit in the wagon," Betsy suggested. "I feel like we're being watched."

"We are," said Mark. "Irvin and Suggs have been told to back off, but that won't stop them from watching us every minute."

They climbed into Jake's old wagon. It seemed they had a little privacy.

On the lower deck Irvin and Suggs sulked, suffering from the stinging rebuke they had received from Wolf Estrello. "Just what the hell kind of magic has this Harder and Rogers got, anyhow?" Suggs wondered. "I never seen any man so much as *threaten* Drew Wilder, but Rogers laid him out cold."

"You wasn't there," Irvin said. "How would you know?"

"No," said Suggs, "but Walsh Tilden was, and he couldn't believe it."

"We've made some mistakes in our time, *amigo,* but this ranks among the worst," said Irvin. "I think by the time Estrello collects for this last batch of rotgut whiskey and gets his hands on that gold, you and me will be very, very expendable."

"Hell, it won't be just you and me," Suggs said. "Estrello's a greedy bastard that don't like nobody. I think we need to get some of the boys together that he's stomped on, and before he can get us, we cut his string."

"After he's sold the whiskey and found the gold, we double-cross him," said Irvin. "I'm not opposed to it on religious grounds, but we got the same damn trouble with some of these other varmints. Suppose we join some of these other *hombres* in double-crossing Estrello, and them that we've joined double-cross *us*? I wouldn't trust Wilder as far as I can flap my arms and fly, and I'd put at least half the others in the same pile."

"Ah, hell, I don't know exactly what to do," said Irvin. "I've never had a true friend in my life, nobody I could count on not to let me down."

"Have I ever let you down?" Suggs asked.

"It was you bully-raggin' them damn females that got me in trouble with Estrello and Captain Jenks," said Irvin.

Suggs laughed. "That ain't exactly like shootin' you in the back. Hell, how do I know *you* wouldn't double-cross *me,* if the pot was big enough?"

"You don't," Irvin said. "You got my word, just like I got yours."

Chapter 7

St. Louis. August 1, 1866.

Fifteen miles south of the St. Louis town limits, a huge warehouse covering many acres had all its entrances secured except the one that led to the offices near the front. In a large leather-upholstered chair sat Taylor Laird. Standing before the desk was Burt Wills, Laird's second-in-command, who engineered most of Laird's shady deals.

"Now just where the hell is Estrello and his bunch?" Laird wondered. "They should be here by now."

"Maybe they had a fallin'-out," said Wills. "When they get here, the new whiskey's in the kegs and waiting. It's near the dock, under heavy guard."

Laird laughed. "I like that term, 'new whiskey.' You reckon anybody will notice that we watered the stuff down?"

"I don't see how," Wills said. "It's been strong enough to melt a horseshoe. It'll just take more of it for a man to get owl-eyed drunk."

"I haven't spoken of this before," said Laird, "and I suppose it's time that I did. After this, Captain Jenks, his crewmen, and his steamboats will no longer freight our whiskey to the landing at Fort Smith."

"I reckon they got a reason," Wills said.

"They *think* they have," said Laird. "They think we've about run our course, that the law could come after us any time."

"Well, they're right about that, I reckon," Wills said, "but they'll never make this kind of money freighting livestock, produce, and fertilizer from St. Louis to New Orleans, and from New Orleans back to St. Louis. There's no chance of them staying on?"

"Oh, there's a chance," said Laird, "but they want more money."

"Which you don't intend to pay," Wills said.

"No," said Laird, "I don't."

"But you're going to charge Estrello *more* for this whiskey than he's ever paid. Will he stand still for that?" Wills wondered.

"He has little choice," said Laird. "This swill we're selling him is bootleg. If he bought the legitimate stuff, with taxes, it wouldn't be worth his while. I intend to tell him the cost of steamboat freighting just went up, and that we're adding the difference to what he's been paying."

Wills laughed. "He'll go through the roof. You want me and some of the boys to ride down to the dock and wait for 'em? Estrello will have a load of horses and mules, and if we don't drive 'em back, his outfit will."

"I don't want anybody but Estrello near this place," said Laird. "Take nine men with you, and see that the Estrello outfit stays there at the landing until it's time for them to board the steamboats and depart. Any horses or mules taken in trade, you can bring with you when you return."

"All the other details involved in the sale, you'll handle here, then," Wills said.

"Yes," said Laird. "He'll have authorization from me. After he's shown it to you, see that him and his outfit goes aboard those steamboats and they get the hell out of here."

"What about the money owed to Captain Jenks and his crews?" Wills asked.

"You'll be taking it with you," said Laird. "I told Jenks the last time we negotiated I wouldn't pay another dollar. I'd as soon not have him here."

"What about the horses and mules Estrello will want to trade toward the whiskey?"

"Credit him with fifty dollars for every horse and mule he has to trade," Laird said, "but only if he has something that can pass as a bill of sale. And whatever you do, don't bring the animals here. They'll have brands all over them. Drive them directly to Bundy's place and dispose of them quickly."

"Fifty dollars per horse or mule?"

"If you can get it," said Laird. "I had a hell of a fight with Bundy. He's wantin' to cut us back to twenty-five."

"Do you aim to take the cut if he won't go any better?"

"Only if there's no other way," said Laird. "If there's anything we *don't* need, it's being stuck with branded stock and a handful of questionable bills of sale. Begin by asking for fifty a head. Bundy won't agree to that, so use your own judgment."

"I'll round up the boys and we'll get started," Wills said. "They're bound to get there this evening or sometime tonight."

Indian Territory. August 1, 1866.

It was near dark when Liz Barton and Lefty Paschal reined up their horses. The wind was out of the west and brought the distinctive odor of wood smoke.

"We might as well ride on in," Lefty said. "We're down-wind, and they've heard us by now."

It was a sensible assumption, and Liz didn't argue. When they were close enough to see the fire, there was nobody in sight. Then a cold voice issued a challenge.

"Who are you, and what do you want?"

"I'm Liz Baron, and this is Lefty Paschal. We were hoping for some supper."

"This ain't no damn cafe," the voice said, "but we'll share what we got. Dismount, and keepin' your hands where we can see 'em, come on to the fire."

Liz and Lefty obeyed the command. Within the surrounding darkness, a dozen men had been concealed. Now they stepped out into the light, their hands near the butts of their revolvers. Black Bill Warnell was the leader of the bunch, and it had been he who had challenged the newcomers. He leaned his Winchester against a pine tree and turned to face Liz and Lefty. Liz Barton found herself intimidated, but there was no help for it, and she spoke as confidently as she could. Quickly, she explained what she had in mind, and some of the outlaws laughed. Black Bill spoke.

"You Bartons don't learn from your mistakes, do you? Old Frank got himself and ten other gents salted down, and now you're lookin' for some damn fools to replace them. No, ma'am, thank you."

"Now that Frank's gone," one of the outlaws asked, "who's *segundo* of the outfit?"

"I am," said Liz. "What of it?"

The outlaws laughed, and there was nothing Liz Barton could do, except stand there, her face flaming red. Finally, striving to control her temper, she spoke.

"I can out-shoot and out-ride any one of you. What I'm

proposing to do is take those wagonloads of whiskey from Wolf Estrello and his outfit, but I need riders."

"I reckon there's folks in hell needin' spring water," said Black Bill. "We know about the whiskey Estrello's been haulin' in, but we also know he's got maybe forty men. Besides old Frank, how many of your boys cashed in?"

"Too many," Liz said, at a loss for words. "So you're scared of Estrello's bunch?"

"Hell, we're scared of *anybody's* bunch, ma'am," said Black Bill, "when they can ride through an ambush and salt down as many men as you lost. How many of Estrello's bunch did your outfit gun down?"

"I . . . I'm not sure," Liz said.

"None," said Black Bill. "Two of 'em were slightly wounded. Now I got one more thing to ask you. Why in thunder did Frank attack Estrello's bunch on their way to *get* the whiskey? The damn wagons was empty."

"Frank hated Estrello and wanted to kill as many of the outfit as he could," Liz said. "I didn't favor it. We don't intend to get involved in *anything* from now on if there's no money in it."

"Well, you got *that* part of it headed in the right direction," said Black Bill. "Trouble is, if you go after Estrello's bunch and those wagonloads of whiskey, you'll be joining old Frank in hell, or wherever he turns up."

"Let's go, Lefty," Liz said.

"You're welcome to stay and eat," said Black Bill. "We got a bottle of whiskey, and we can drink to old Frank's memory."

"Damn them," Liz gritted.

"That fool attack that got Frank killed is gonna hurt us," said Lefty. "If this bunch has heard of it, the others will have, too."

South of St. Louis, on the Mississippi. August 1, 1866.

When the steamboats again stopped to take on wood, Estrello made his way from the *Aztec* to the *Star*. He said nothing to Captain Jenks, but sought out Amanda and Betsy. He ignored Bill and Mark when he spoke.

"Ladies, we'll reach St. Louis sometime tonight, and we'll be returning to Fort Smith as soon as possible. Putting it bluntly, the two of you know where the gold is, and one way or another, you're going to lead me to it. I prefer not to get nasty, but I can and I will if you force my hand. Are you going to cooperate?"

Amanda and Betsy looked helplessly at Bill and Mark.

"If you do them any harm, Estrello, you'll do it over our dead bodies," Mark said.

Estrello's laugh was an ugly sound. "That can be arranged."

"If we lead you to the gold," Betsy pleaded, "will you let those of us go in peace, who are tired of this kind of life?"

"Why shouldn't I?" asked Estrello. "Neither of you can implicate me. It'll be your word against mine. Now I want some general idea as to where we'll be going."

"No," Amanda said. "We'll tell you when we return to the Washita."

"You'll tell me now," said Estrello ominously.

Irvin and Suggs, sensing trouble, leaned against the pilothouse within gun range. Their thumbs were hooked in their belts near the butts of their Colts. Estrello was in the position of having them in a crossfire if he chose.

"Go ahead and tell him the general area, Amanda," Mark said. "Nothing specific."

"It's within twenty-five miles of the Washita," Amanda said, "and that's all you'll be told until we return there."

"Very well," said Estrello, "I shall count on that. I trust

neither of you will forget the penalty for lying to me, or attempting to double-cross me."

"There'll be a considerable penalty if *you* pull any tricks on *us*," Bill warned.

"I said the ladies are free to go, once I know where the gold is," said Estrello. "I'm not including anybody else in the deal."

"You lie," Betsy shouted. "Amanda wasn't asking for freedom for just the two of us, and you know it."

Estrello laughed. "So you have friends who wish to forsake me and ride with you. I'll assure you I have a reasonably good idea as to who they are, and when the time comes, I will deal directly with them."

He said no more, but made his way down the ramp, past the sweating men who were bringing wood aboard the steamboat. Amanda and Betsy stood there, clenching their fists and gritting their teeth. Irvin and Suggs grinned, aggravating Amanda and Betsy all the more.

"Come on," Mark said, "and let's get away from here, I don't like the smell."

They walked to the far end of the deck. The six men they had come to think of as their friends were all there, and they looked grim.

"Bad news, I reckon," said Ed Stackler.

"The worst," Mark replied. "He's agreed to free Amanda and Betsy if they'll lead him to the gold. That gives us a pretty good idea what he has in mind for the rest of us."

"I'm not taking him anywhere," said Betsy. "Once he has his hands on the gold, he'll kill Amanda and me. I just know it."

"I think so, too," Amanda said, "but when the whiskey's unloaded at Fort Smith, we'll still be nearly three hundred miles from our old camp on the Washita. We'll have a little more time to perhaps think of some way out."

"The more I think about it," said Nick Ursino, "the more certain I am that we'll have to shoot our way out."

"I think you're right," Vernon Clemans said, "but there's so many of these varmints I'd like to ventilate, I won't know where to start."

"We've got to do better than that," said Ed. "In a stand-up fight with all these gun-throwers, we don't have a prayer."

"Ed's right," Mark said. "We'd be gunned down before any of us even got off a shot at Estrello, and when you're fighting for your life, you don't sell out cheap. We're in need of a plan, a possible means of escape."

"Then, damn it, let's come up with one," said Bill. "Do they always time their return to Fort Smith after dark, unloading the whiskey before dawn?"

"They always have before," Todd Keithley said, "and I can't think of any reason why they won't do it the same way, this time."

"I don't believe Estrello will come after any of us until we're well away from the river and Fort Smith," said Carl Long. "Sound carries at night, and it's not more than six or seven miles to Fort Smith, cross-country."

"That's a good argument for making our move *before* the whiskey's been unloaded from the wagons," Lee Sullivan said.

"We could make our move at the wood stop between Little Rock and Fort Smith," said Vernon, "but I expect the price would be more than we want to pay."

"You know it would," Mark said. "Before those ramps are let down to bring the wood aboard, Estrello has two men on deck, armed with Winchesters. He can have two dozen more after us within minutes. Our only chance is to get the hell off this steamboat and out of gun range before they realize we've made our break."

"That brings us back to a possibility we've already rejected," Ed said. "If we take them by surprise, we'll have to run this steamboat aground. In the dark, without any running lights, the bunch on the other three steamboats won't notice if we slow down and fall a little behind."

"We rejected it before," said Bill, "and now it's one of the few possibilities any of us have of getting out of this alive. I think we'd better consider it again. The big rocks in the road will be Captain Jenks and his firemen. Are we prepared to kill them all?"

"All we need of the captain is to have him run this steamboat aground," Mark said, "and if he's not smart enough to figure out what Estrello has in mind for him, I believe he'll become a lot more agreeable with a cocked pistol at his head. The same goes for his firemen."

"That's gospel," said Vernon. "Even if we were that murderous, we can't afford having those on the other steamboats hear the shots."

"There are the horses," Betsy said. "What about them?"

"We'll have to decide if they're worth the risk," said Todd. "I doubt Estrello would send his bunch after us afoot, and while they're saddling up, that would gain us a little time."

"We could saddle our horses ahead of time," Amanda said, "and have them ready."

"Much as I hate bein' afoot. I'd have to say no to that," said Todd. "We can't afford to wait until we reach the dock when all four steamboats come together. Should we take over this steamboat, we'll have to ground it at some unlikely place. There won't be time or opportunity to set up the ramp for the horses. We'll have to go over the side and run for it."

"It's starting to sound more and more like our only hope," Nick said. "A lot depends on the time of night we make a run for it. We'll have to reach Fort Smith before dawn, and we may still have a fight on our hands. There's bound to be a lawman, but he won't be of any help to us against all that bunch ridin' with Estrello."

"Maybe there are soldiers garrisoned at Fort Smith," Ed said.

"Maybe," Mark said, "but up against Estrello's gang, they might be as outnumbered as we are. Anyway, I doubt we could get any help from them in a hurry. At best, they might telegraph Captain Ferguson at Fort Worth before lifting a hand."

"So we're going to run for it on foot," said Betsy, "and even if we reach the town, we can't depend on anybody to help us. Even if we escape in the dark, Estrello may just wait until dawn and begin the search all over again."

"He damned well might," Bill agreed. "They can unload the wagons and the whiskey while they wait for daylight."

"There's no perfect way of doing this," said Mark. "I believe we can successfully get off this steamboat and into the woods, but from there on, we'll be taking our chances. It will depend almost entirely on what Estrello decides to do."

"He'll come looking for Betsy and me," Amanda said. "He's promised to find and share that gold with his outfit, and if he fails, they'll turn on him."

"I think she's right," said Nick. "When Amanda and Betsy were lost in the river, Estrello just went crazy. Not because he cared a damn for either of them, but because they know where the gold is hidden. Estrello will have them looking for us in the dark."

"We do have a bit of an edge," Vernon said. "A man on a horse is easier to see than a man on foot. Maybe we can even the odds some."

"Each time you fire in the dark," said Ed, "your muzzle flash makes a good target. We'll have to do more hiding than shooting. Let's let Estrello's bunch spend the night looking for us while we make our way to Fort Smith. We don't know what we'll be facing there, but we'll be among other people, and Estrello will hate that."

"*Bueno,*" Mark said. "One of us may still reach the telegraph office."

"But if there are no fighting men to help us at Fort Smith," Carl Long said, "there'll be no time for the post commander at Fort Worth to send help. They're too far away, and we have too little time."

"Amanda," said Mark, "you told Estrello that gold is within twenty-five miles of the Washita. Is it?"

"No," Amanda said. "Betsy and me told him that so he'll have to return to the old camp on the Washita. With loaded wagons, that's almost a week from Fort Smith, and we thought it might allow us a little more time to come up with a plan of our own."

"Excellent," said Ed, "but suppose the worst happens? Suppose we're unable to free ourselves, and you have to go on to the Washita with Estrello? He may shoot both of you for lying to him."

"Whoa," Mark said. "This talk about returning to the Washita just gave me an idea. If just one of us can reach the telegraph in Fort Worth, we can have a company of soldiers waiting for Estrello when he gets there."

"That can be done," said Bill. "Men on horseback can easily ride from Fort Worth to the Washita, well ahead of

Estrello's loaded wagons. Captain Ferguson can have enough men there to wipe out Estrello's bunch."

"Once we break loose—granted that we do—" Ed Stackler said, "there are two things we must do. We must avoid being captured or shot, and we must get that telegram on its way to Fort Worth."

"Risky from start to finish," said Lee Sullivan, "but it's something definite that has a chance to succeed."

At least it was a plan, and their sagging spirits were lifted a little.

St. Louis. August 2, 1866.

Burt Wills had nine men waiting at the landing when the four steamboats arrived. The sun was still two hours high, about enough time for Wills and his men to conceal the mules and horses Estrello had brought for trade. He didn't like Estrello, and it left a bad taste in his mouth when he remembered what Taylor Laird had told him. He would have to negotiate with Estrello over the value of the livestock, giving the outlaw credit for what he owed for the whiskey. The ramps had been put in place, and even then men were leading the extra horses and mules off the steamboats. Estrello looked around, apparently for Taylor Laird, finally fixing his eyes on Burt Wills. He approached Wills with a question that was blunt.

"Where's Laird?"

"You're riding upriver to see him this time," said Wills.

"Oh?" Estrello said. "Why?"

"Prices are goin' up," said Wills, "but not on branded mules and horses. We're lowering that to twenty-five."

"Like hell you are," Estrello shouted. "So he wants to see me, does he?"

Wills watched as Estrello flung a saddle on the first horse he came to. He spoke to one of his men and was brought a mule on a lead rope with packsaddle. Estrello shouted to one of his men who had remained on the upper deck of the first steamboat. The man disappeared, and a few minutes later, left the steamboat. He carried a heavy burlap sack, which he secured with rawhide thongs to the packsaddle. That, Wills knew, would be the gold with which Estrello would pay for the whiskey. Wills joined his nine men, gathering the horses and mules Estrello had brought for trade.

"Fifteen mules and seventeen horses," Wills shouted after a count.

Estrello said nothing. Leading the pack mule, he reined up where only Drew Wilder could hear what he had to say.

"I want all that whiskey in the wagons and on those steamboats before dark," Estrello said. "I'm going after our money, and then we're movin' out."

"There he goes," said Mark, "and there goes our chance to learn where he's getting the whiskey."

"Captain Ferguson didn't tell us we have to go that far," Bill said. "He wants us to help bust up the gang. We'll be damn fortunate if we can do that and come out alive."

"So Estrello goes alone to settle for the whiskey," said Mark. "Has he always done it that way?"

"Every time I've been with him," Ed said. "The varmint sellin' that slop would sell to anybody who can pay, and Estrello's always taken care to see that none of us has any idea as to who supplies him the rotgut."

"I've been with him from the first," said Vernon, "and the rest of us are left here to load the whiskey on the steamboats, while Estrello goes somewhere to pay for the stuff."

Estrello was barely out of sight, when Wilder began giving orders.

"All you teamsters bring the wagons off the boats, and be quick about it."

"Notice the Estrello men with Winchesters," said Todd. "Ten to one they've been ordered to shoot us if we so much as look like we intend to run for it."

With Winchesters were Wilder, Suggs, Irvin, DeWitt, Bideno, and Jabez.

"Come on, Bill," Mark said. "We might as well harness the teams and get the wagons down here."

Once the wagons were off the steamboats. Wilder took charge of getting all the barrels loaded. They were heavy and difficult to handle, and it required three men to lift one into a wagon. Once there, it had to be slid forward to make room for others that would follow. The men from the *Star*—except for Irvin and Suggs—had to load the two wagons that Bill and Mark had driven from the steamboat. The men armed with Winchesters did nothing, except to curse the weary laborers who paused to wipe the sweat from their eyes. Amanda and Betsy watched as the outlaws with Winchesters shouted at the men who were moving the heavy barrels. When Mark's wagon had been loaded, the six comrades from steamboat four started loading Bill's wagon.

"My God," Bill groaned, "my back will never be the same."

"Well, don't be in too damn big a hurry," said Ed. "If we finish first, we'll be told to help the others. Wilder would like that."

Finally the back-breaking ordeal was over, and the wagons were driven to the steamboat from which they had been taken for loading.

*   *   *

Wolf Estrello reached the huge headquarters of Taylor
Laird and was elated to find only one horse standing in the
shade of an oak. Of late, Laird had seen to it that most of his
men were occupied elsewhere when he was expecting Estrello. Conducting all of their business after dark, Laird
made sure that few of his men ever saw Estrello, or knew the
purpose of his visits. Estrello tied his horse and the pack mule
to a hitching rail. Taking the heavy sack from the pack
mule, he made his way toward the entrance. Suddenly, the
door opened.

"You took long enough. You should have been here last
night," Laird said.

"No business of yours," said Estrello, "long as you get
your money."

"The damn whiskey was at the dock yesterday," Laird said,
"and I had to pay extra, hiring men to stand watch over it."

"Well," said Estrello, "are we goin' inside, or do you aim
to stand out here and bitch my time away?"

"Come on in, damn it," Laird growled. "I want to settle
this thing, so you and your outfit can go. Last time you were
here, the captain on a commercial steamer coming from St.
Louis reported your four steamboats without running lights."

Estrello laughed. "Your concern is touching, Laird."

"Concern, hell," Laird snorted. "I don't personally give a
damn if you and every man in your outfit is caught and
strung up. I just don't want any incident involving you and
your scruffy bunch to suck me in."

Laird took a seat in the big leather chair behind his desk.
He didn't invite Estrello to sit, and the outlaw stood there
waiting.

Finally, Laird spoke. "Like I told you last time, the brew's
gone up twenty-five dollars a barrel. I trust you have come
prepared to pay the increase?"

"I have," said Estrello. "There's twenty horses and twenty-two mules."

Laird laughed, for Estrello always gave him false figures. But from now on, it wouldn't matter, at the lower prices.

"Twenty-five dollars a head," said Laird. "No more."

"I'll accept that," Estrello said, suddenly agreeable. His hard eyes were on the big safe behind Laird's desk. It stood partially open.

"Empty the sack on the desk," said Laird. "I trust you won't be insulted if I count it."

Laird's greedy eyes were on the gold, and he failed to see Estrello's right hand drop to the butt of his Colt. Estrello fired three times, and the lifeless body of Taylor Laird struck the wall and slid down to the floor.

Chapter 8

Taylor Laird's body was sprawled before the big safe, his big leather-upholstered chair lying partially on him. Estrello dragged the chair away, and then, seizing Laird by the feet, he dragged the body out of his way. He then knelt before the big iron safe, swinging the door open. He caught his breath when he beheld the contents. There were bundles of currency, each bundle neatly tied with string, and the safe was packed full. In his excitement, Estrello dragged most of it out on the floor, finding that apparently all the bills were of hundred-dollar denominations. This was no time to count it, but Estrello had an eye for such things, and he figured there was thousands of dollars—perhaps hundreds of thousands— within the safe. His heart raced like a galloping horse as he pondered his next move. Possibilities boggled his mind, and he could see himself somewhere in Mexico or South America, living like a king.

But Estrello couldn't afford the luxury of dreaming. He must have another sack for all the currency, and he began looking for one. In one office after another he dragged out desk drawers and rummaged through closets. Eventually, he found a suitable burlap bag, and its contents were heavy. Estrello upended the bag, dumping everything on the floor. There was a massive amount of old gun parts, including cylinders, triggers, frames, and walnut grips. Estrello took the now empty bag and hurried back to Laird's office. Quickly, he looked out the window, but all he saw was Laird's horse and his own horse and mule. Kneeling before the safe, he began stuffing bundles of currency into the sack. There was barely room for it all, and seizing a ball of heavy twine from Laird's desk, Estrello had a difficult time tying the neck of the sack. He then returned the gold he had brought to the other sack, and found he was unable to carry the gold and the currency at the same time. He took the sack of gold to the pack horse, and hurriedly lashed the heavy bag to one side of the packsaddle. He then returned for the currency and thonged the bag to the other side of the packsaddle.

Leading the pack mule, he started downriver, reining up when his excitement subsided and common sense took control. He had no idea how many men Laird employed, or how soon they might discover his body. Ten of them had taken the horses and mules to some location downriver and might soon be returning to Laird's place of business. In fact, he might meet them, and the loaded pack mule might quickly arouse their suspicions, for this was the first time he had ever left Laird's with anything but the horse he rode. He quickly rode more than a mile east of the river before again riding south. He knew he must reach the steamboats before encountering anybody.

Burt Wills felt uneasy without fully understanding why. Estrello hadn't seemed all that put out over the impending increase in the cost of the whiskey or a reduction in the price Laird had been paying him for horses and mules. Why?

"Pick up that gait, boys," Wills shouted. "There may be trouble at Laird's."

The riders swatted the horses and mules with their lariats. Nobody questioned Wills's demand for haste, for he had long been Laird's second-in-command. Reaching the hidden corral where livestock of questionable ownership was kept, they drove the horses and mules inside the corral. Toomey and Grant, two of Laird's men assigned to keep watch, leaned against the six-rail fence, watching. It soon became apparent that the new arrivals didn't intend to dismount.

"Hey," Toomey shouted, "ain't you unsociable varmints gonna stop and jaw a while?"

"Not now," said Wills. "We don't have the time."

Wills and his riders kicked their horses into a slow gallop, and when they came within sight of the huge structure Laird owned, Wills knew something was wrong. There was no lamplight from any of the windows, and even in the starlight, he could see the lone horse where Laird always picketed his mount.

"Trouble," Wills said, reining up. "We'll go in on foot."

Reaching the entrance, they found the door open. On the wall inside hung a lantern. Wills lighted it, holding it in his left hand, well away from his body. In his right hand was his Colt, cocked and ready. Wills said nothing, but his nine companions did not follow him. Someone had to go in, and Wills took the risk. At first the office seemed empty, but when Wills reached the big desk, he could see Laird's dead face in the dim light from the lantern. With shaking hands, he lighted the lamp on Laird's desk. That was the signal for the rest of the riders to enter, and they did so, freezing as they viewed the remains of their late employer.

"That son-of-a-bitch Estrello," said Wills.

"He cleaned out the safe, too," one of the riders observed. "What'n thunder we gonna do now? There wasn't nobody but him."

"Wrong," Wills said. "There's me, and there's the money

Estrello took. I want each of you to find as many of our bunch
as you can. Have them waiting near the landing where Estrello's four steamboats were. We're goin' after the bastards."

"How?" a rider asked. "We can't run down them steamboats."

"We can if we have a steamboat of our own," said Wills.
"Laird has a private steamboat and a crew to pilot it. All of
you be waiting where I told you, and I'll have the boat there
within two hours."

"You can take Laird's private steamboat?" one of the riders asked.

"Hell, yes," Wills snapped. "Now all of you mount up
and ride. I especially want men who have Sharps .50 buffalo guns. There's going to be a running fight."

Estrello was thankful for the darkness, for his men had
seen to it that everybody went back aboard the boats. Carrying the sack of gold, he went aboard the first steamboat.
He had a key to a personal locker he was allowed to use, and
dropping the sack of gold inside, he locked the steel door
and went back for the bag of currency. Wilder stood on
deck, apparently wondering what Estrello was doing, but he
said nothing.

"Why the hell are you standin' there?" Estrello demanded.
"Get back aboard the *Goose,* where you were assigned. We're
pullin' out in a few minutes."

When Estrello returned with the sack of currency. Wilder
was no longer there. Captain Savage, in charge of steamboat one, met Estrello as he came aboard.

"Are we ready to depart?" Savage asked.

"Yes," said Estrello, "but with one change. I want this
steamboat to exchange positions with the *Star,* with the *Star*
taking the lead. We'll bring up the rear on this one."

"Changing positions in the dark without running lights requires a great deal of difficulty," Captain Savage said. "We don't turn around in the dark. Is this necessary?"

"It is," said Estrello. "I have reason to believe we may be pursued by a pack of thieves, and we may need the Gatling gun to defend ourselves."

"I think not," Captain Savage said coldly. "We have not been paid to defend you and your men against a running attack with your enemies."

"Maybe this will change your mind," said Estrello. In an instant, his Colt was in his hand, taking the startled captain by surprise.

"You fool," Captain Savage said, "you can't keep me under the gun all the way to Fort Smith."

"I can't," said Estrello, "but I have enough men so that one of us can. Now you get into the pilothouse and turn this thing around."

"The other captains must be told of the change," Captain Savage said.

"I'll see that they're told," said Estrello. "Now you do as you're told."

Some of the men from the lower deck had heard the conversation. Tull McLean and Dutch McCarty had climbed the ladder and stood on the upper deck, looking at Estrello in surprise.

"Don't stand there like damn fools," Estrello shouted. "I want you to escort this gent to the pilothouse and keep him covered. He's going to turn this steamboat around so that it brings up the rear back to Fort Smith."

"Why?" McLean asked.

"By God, because I said so," snapped Estrello.

"He's being pursued," said Captain Savage, "and intends

to use the Gatling gun. I'd say he's gotten himself and the rest of you in big trouble."

"Is that true?" McCarty asked.

"I had trouble over the price of the whiskey," Estrello lied. "There was some shooting, and there may be gunmen after us."

"How in hell do you chase a steamboat?" McLean asked in disbelief.

Captain Savage laughed. "In another steamboat."

"Give me fifteen minutes," Estrello told Tull and McLean. "The other captains have to be told about the change in formation."

Convinced, McCarty and McLean drew their Colts, covering Captain Savage. Estrello hurried to his locker to dispose of the sack of currency, and from the shadows stepped Wilder. His Colt was steady in his hand as he said, "I saw you bring the gold aboard. The gold you took to pay for the whiskey. Now I'm wonderin' what you got in that *other* sack. Open it."

Estrello had no choice. He untied the neck of the burlap bag, and Wilder's eyes went wide at the sight of the currency. He laughed. "No wonder you're expectin' somebody to come after you. That, and what you didn't pay for the whiskey is quite a pile. When do you aim to divvy it up?"

"Certainly not now," Estrello snarled. "I must talk to the other captains and get these steamboats moving. We may not have much time."

"Then put that sack in there with the other one," said Wilder, "and don't be gettin' no ideas. Some of us will be watchin' you every damn minute."

Estrello put the sack of currency in the locker, closed the door, and locked it. He then turned away and ran toward the ramp, cursing his rotten luck. Wilder had his circle of friends, and before the night was over, they would all know of his treasure. Gangplanks to the second, third, and fourth steamboats had been raised, preventing Estrello from going aboard. He shouted, seeking to attract the attention of someone on the upper deck of boat two.

"Yeah," said Skull Worsham, "what is it?"

"Get Captain Lytle for me," Estrello shouted. "I need to talk to him."

Captain Lytle took his time, saying nothing until Estrello had told him of the change in the order of the steamboats.

"You've spoken to Captain Savage, I presume," said Captain Lytle. "What did he say?"

"He's agreed to the change," Estrello said. "Now get ready to move out."

As quickly as he could summon them, Estrello spoke to Captain Stock, captain of the *Midnight,* and Captain Jenks, captain of the *Star*. Estrello hurried back to the *Aztec* and found Captain Savage had done nothing toward reversing position. McCarty and McLean still faced him with drawn Colts.

"Well?" Estrello growled.

"He's captain of the damn steamboat," said McCarty. "What you expect us to do, shoot him?"

"Yeah," McLean said, "without him, how do we get this thing back to Fork Smith?"

"Savage," said Estrello, "if we're attacked, you can die just as quick as any of us. I've talked to Lytle, Stock, and Jenks, and when you turn this steamboat around, they'll lead out."

The first three captains had already begun the tedious job of reversing their boats, and having little choice, Captain Savage entered the pilothouse. The rest of the men aboard Captain Savage's craft were aware a change was taking

place and had gathered on the upper deck. Their attention
was drawn to the pilothouse, where McCarty and McLean
stood before it with drawn Colts.

"What'n hell's goin' on?" Ike Jabez wanted to know.

"I shot an *hombre* over the price of whiskey," said Estrello desperately, "and some of the gang may be coming after us. We're moving this steamboat into fourth position so
we can use the Gatling gun if we have to."

At that point, Wilder stepped out of the shadows. "He
ain't told you all of it. He brought back the gold he took to
pay for the whiskey, and besides that, a sackful of bills.
Thousands and thousands there, I reckon. Now we just need
Estrello's word that he aims to divide all that money and
gold, fair and square, once we're back in the Territory."

"That's exactly what I'm planning to do," Estrello said.
"The bastard I had to shoot over the whiskey had a safe full
of money. What was I supposed to do, just leave it?"

"Hell, no," said Wilder. "You can't hang but once. We ain't
against what you done. We just want to be damn sure you
ain't forgot who your friends are when it's time to divide the
loot. Now you just mind your business, and don't get no funny
ideas about a double cross."

Captain Jenks's steamboat, the *Star,* had turned around
and had now become the leader.

"What in tarnation's he doin' that for?" Bill wondered.

"Who knows?" said Mark. "It's hard to see by starlight,
but it looks like the other three steamboats are turning around.
Ours will be first in line."

"This will hurt our chances of jumping ship just before
we reach Fort Smith," Vernon said. "If we run this steamboat aground, with the other three behind us, they'll know
what we aim to do before we can escape."

"That's a chance we'll have to take," said Nick.

"Something must have happened, causing this change," Amanda said.

"I think you're right," said Mark, "and it may mean big trouble for Estrello."

"It may mean big trouble for us all," Ed said. "At least one of those Gatling guns has a cylinder it takes ten shells to fully load. In practice it's been evaluated and is supposed to fire four hundred times a minute. Enough hits could sink us."

"That, or explode the boilers," said Nick. "In either case, we're finished."

"Well, it hasn't happened yet," Bill said, "and if this bunch from St. Louis comes after us, we'll still have three steamboats between us and them."

"We'll need them," said Lee, "but until they get closer, our Winchesters won't be of any use."

"You're right," Todd said. "We'll just have to pray that Estrello has men who can operate the gun, and enough ammunition to feed it. Five volleys, if it's the big Gatling, and there's two thousand shells."

Burt Wills eventually found ten additional men to join in the chase. It took longer than he had expected, because he finally had to tell them of the robbery and murder of Taylor Laird. Some of them were difficult to convince.

"Look," said Wills, "I know this business backward and forward, as well as sideways and upside-down. I can operate it as well as Laird did, but we can't do it broke. We *need* the cash and the gold that Estrello took, and we need to teach that varmint a lesson. Now, who's got the sand to go after them?"

The ten men stepped forward, and, mounting his horse, Wills led out. As expected, the four loaded steamboats were

gone. In their place was the black-and-gold stern-wheeler
that had belonged to Laird. It was an impressive sight, reas-
suring them that Wills could do exactly what he planned to
do. Didn't he have control of Laird's steamboat, a fancy
craft that few of them had ever seen, and that some didn't
know existed?

The steamboat already had up steam, smoke boiling from
its twin stacks. The nine men Wills had sent on ahead waited
on the upper deck, and he noted with approval they all had a
Sharps .50 buffalo gun, as did the ten men he had brought
with him. Wills hurried to the pilothouse, where Captain Tyndall waited. Tyndall had not been told the purpose of this
expedition, and without beating around the bush, Wills told
him the truth.

"If we don't catch up to this bunch of thieves and killers,"
Wills concluded, "then we'll be broke and out of business."

"I don't know if we can catch them or not," said Tyndall,
"since they have a considerable head start. Suppose we *are*
able to catch up to them? What do you intend to do?"

"There are twenty of us armed with Sharps .50 buffalo
guns," Wills said. "We can stay out of Winchester range and
give them hell. These big guns can cut their pilothouses
down to the bare deck. I aim to take up where Laird left off,
and I'll begin by making an example of these varmints that
done the killing and robbery."

"You're the boss, then," said Tyndall. "Let's get started."

Within minutes, the black-and-gold steamboat was on its
way south, traveling at top speed. Grimly, twenty men lined
its upper deck, shading their eyes, hoping to see the quarry
somewhere ahead.

Not quite a hundred miles south of St. Louis, the four
steamboats bearing the Estrello outfit were forced to stop

and take on wood. Men from the fourth steamboat—now Estrello's—quickly went ashore, supposedly to stretch their legs. One of these men was Drew Wilder.

"Where the hell you been, Wilder?" Gabe Haddock asked. "You was supposed to be on the *Goose,* and I ain't seen you since before we left, last night."

"I been on the *Aztec,* talking turkey with our *amigo,* Estrello," said Wilder. "Get the others over here from the second, third, and fourth boats. This is something you all need to hear."

Except for McCarty and McLean, the men gathered to hear what Wilder had to say. Before he finished, there were shouts of anger. Elgin Kendrick said what all of them were thinking. "Damn it, now there won't be any more whiskey, no more easy money."

"There may not be any money at all if they have a steamboat and catch up to us," said Wilder. "Estrello cleaned out the safe, and there must be hundreds of thousands, besides the gold we saved by not payin' for the whiskey. I saw the money and the gold Estrello put in his locker. We'll all have to watch Estrello if we aim to keep him honest. If there's no other way, shoot the varmint. We can manage without him if we have to."

Bert Hamby laughed. "Keepin' Wolf Estrello honest is like teachin' a rattler to behave like a salamander."

"From here on to Fort Smith," Wilder said. "I'll be on the *Aztec,* watching Estrello. He'd kill us all for that pile of money and gold he brought back."

"Not if we kill him first," said Burrell Hedgepith.

"Only if there's no other way," Wilder said. "He *did* what he should have done, bringin' back the gold and the stolen money. So he gets a chance to share it with the rest of us. But at the first sign of a double cross, he's fair game."

Shouts of approval erupted as the men again boarded the steamboats.

"I need to talk to the other captains," said Captain Savage, aboard the *Aztec*.

"You ain't talkin' to nobody," McCarty said. "Far as they know, they're follerin' your orders, and it's gonna stay that way."

St. Louis. August 4, 1866.

At the military outpost in St. Louis, Sergeant Ember knocked on the post commander's door and was bid enter. He saluted, had it returned, and then presented Captain Hailey with a lengthy telegram. Quickly, Hailey read the telegram.

"By the Eternal," said Captain Hailey, slamming his fist down on the desk, "we've been right about Taylor Laird and this whiskey running, but there was never any conclusive evidence. Now it's startin' to add up. I want you to detail men to search *all* Laird's warehouses, destroying any illegal whiskey."

"Yes, sir," said Sergeant Ember, "but what about the killers? Two days ago, those four steamboats were seen headin' south, without running lights. Don't you reckon those whiskey runners have a load of the stuff aboard?"

"I'm sure they do," Captain Hailey said, "but with a two-day start, there's no way we can catch up to them from here. They're on their way to Indian Territory."

"You could telegraph Fort Smith," said Sergeant Ember.

"Good idea," Captain Hailey said, "except it's a small post with a handful of troops, and most of the lawmen in the area are deputies, out somewhere in the Territory with their tumbleweed wagons."*

"Maybe there's a better way, sir," said Sergeant Ember. "Remember, a month or so ago when you got a letter from Captain Ferguson at Fort Worth? He had sent two men to try to join Estrello's outfit."

"Sergeant, that's classified, and you're not supposed to know," Captain Hailey said. "Consider yourself reprimanded."

"Yes, sir," said Sergeant Embler. "What I was about to say is that if Estrello and his outfit are bound for Indian Territory with loaded wagons, Captain Ferguson could send a company of soldiers to head them off. Soldiers from Fort Worth could be there in not more than three days."

"Soldier," Captain Hailey said, "that's good thinking. Of course, it'll be up to Captain Ferguson as to whether or not he wants to send soldiers in the hope of destroying the Estrello gang. We don't know for *sure* they're involved. It could be a wild-goose chase."

"Yes, sir," said Sergeant Ember, "but suppose it's not. Suppose there's a genuine chance to put the Estrello gang out of business permanently. Whatever Captain Ferguson decides to do with the information, doesn't he still need to know?"

"I suppose you're right," Captain Hailey said. "I can telegraph him as much as we know, and let him decide how far he wants to take it. Give me a few minutes, and you can take the message to the telegrapher."

"If it pans out, sir, you could receive a promotion for this," said Sergeant Ember.

"Soldier," Captain Hailey said, "with the ranks frozen,

---

* In Fort Smith the law was represented primarily by Judge Parker, the "hanging judge." Tumbleweed wagons were driven by lawmen into Indian Territory, seeking outlaws.

neither of us will live long enough for promotion. Now get this telegram on the wire as soon as I finish it."

Aboard Captain Savage's steamboat, the *Aztec,* he was constantly under guard. Not having been allowed to speak to captains of the other steamboats, he felt reasonably sure that none of them had been told about possible pursuit and use of the Gatling gun on the deck of the *Aztec.* The armed outlaws kept an around-the-clock watch on Savage, and he realized he wouldn't have a chance to warn his companions on the other steamboats before they reached the landing at Fort Smith. Savage, Lytle, Stock, and Jenks were useful to the outlaws only until they reached Fort Smith. After that, the steamboats would not be needed. What was going to happen to the steamboat captains and their crews? Captain Savage shuddered at the possibilities.

Aboard what was now the first steamboat in line, the *Star,* Amanda had just gone to the lower deck, and, not wishing to reveal her presence at the makeshift outhouse, she felt her way, leaving the lantern hanging by the hatch that led to the upper deck. At first she thought she had been followed, un- til one of the men laughed. They didn't know she was there! Quickly, Amanda got as far away as she could, where the dim rays of the lantern wouldn't reach. There she hunched, trembling, and what she heard set her heart to pounding with excitement. Mark had come with her, and she had no idea how he had managed to conceal himself. Irvin and Suggs were discussing a murder and robbery involving Wolf Estrello!

"I got to give the varmint credit," said Irvin. "He could have just gunned down old man Laird and took the gold that was to be paid for the whiskey, but he robbed the damn safe.

Besides the gold, Wilder says there may be thousands of dollars in greenbacks. A big sack full of it."

"Wilder's got the right idea," Suggs said. "If Estrello had got all that aboard without any of us knowin' it, he'd double-cross the hell out of us. We still may have to kill the greedy son-of-a-bitch when we get back to the Territory."

The duo headed back down the narrow corridor that led to the overhead hatch to the upper deck. Amanda stayed where she was until Mark spoke.

"Go ahead and use that thing, and let's get out of here before that pair of varmints start wonderin' where we are."

"I think I just had it scared out of me," Amanda said. "Let's go back and tell the others."

They reached the upper deck without seeing Irvin or Suggs. As had become their custom, they joined their companions who shared their predicament. Quietly and quickly, Mark and Amanda repeated what they had heard.

"Thank God," Betsy cried, "that's the split we were hoping for."

"Yeah," said Bill, "but it may not work out to our advantage. With so much at stake, the whole damn gang may line up against Estrello. He's just one man, and we're still outgunned."

"A lot depends on what they decide to do about the stolen gold," Ed said. "If they decide to forget the gold and go with what they have, then Amanda and Betsy are in big trouble."

"I think Estrello will insist on going after that hidden gold," said Nick. "It's likely all that'll keep him alive."

"It's all that will save Amanda and me," Betsy said, "but I don't believe they'll forget the gold. Not after they've fought over it for five years, and they believe Amanda and me know where it is."

"You mean you *don't* know?" Bill asked.

"I didn't say that," Betsy snapped. "Who knows if we can find it again? Because of it, Amanda and me have survived five years in this damn outlaw camp."

Mark was looking at Amanda, and her eyes failed to meet his. He tilted her chin, and at the corners of her eyes was the beginning of tears.

"I don't know if we can find it again," said Amanda. "I just don't know."

Chapter 9

Indian Territory. August 4, 1866.

Liz Barton and what remained of the Barton gang soon found that word of their ignominious defeat and the death of Frank Barton had spread throughout Indian Territory. Nobody wanted to join the Barton gang—whatever the possibilities—and some laughed openly when they learned Liz Barton had taken over leadership.

"Now what?" Lefty Paschal wanted to know.

"I'm not sure," said Liz. "One thing for certain, we won't be taking the whiskey away from Estrello's outfit."

They rode back to their camp alongside a creek and found the rest of the riders were trying to beat the August heat by dunking themselves in the stream.

"Get out of there," Liz ordered. "There's something you need to know."

"I reckon we already know," said Whit Sumner. "You and Lefty come back alone. That tells me nobody wants any part of the Barton bunch."

Without another word, they crawled out of the creek. They pulled on their trousers, buttoned their shirts, and stomped their feet into their boots. Buckling on their gun belts, then putting on their hats, they headed toward their picketed horses.

"No," Liz cried, aware of what they were about to do. "We can make it. We just need more time."

"Time just run out," said Hez DeShea.

They saddled their horses, mounted, and rode away toward Indian Territory.

"Now what, boss?" Lefty Paschal asked.

"Before I do anything else," said Liz, "I'm going in that water and wash myself."

"Am I permitted to join you?" Lefty asked. "I'd hate to shock your modesty."

"Do whatever you please," said Liz. "I'm not your keeper."

Southbound on the Mississippi. August 5, 1866.

Fully aware of the riches Wolf Estrello had brought to them, the outlaws let it appear that Estrello still had control of the gang. Only Captain Savage knew otherwise, and he had not been allowed to speak to the other captains. Attempting to demonstrate his authority and strength, Estrello again entered the pilothouse.

"What's wrong with these damn boats?" Estrello demanded. "Is this top speed?"

"It is," said Captain Savage shortly.

"Then why ain't we makin' as good a time as we did goin' upriver?"

"Because the boats are fully loaded now," Captain Savage said. "Get out of here and leave me alone."

Wilder no longer thought of himself as "second-in-command," and when Estrello left the pilothouse, Wilder came up to him and said, "He ain't speeded up none."

"Captain Savage says they're at full speed. Anyhow, we're in fourth place now. Orders must come from Captain Savage. Damn it, we can't go any faster than the other boats. Are you prepared to tell the other captains why you want more speed?"

"No," Wilder admitted, "I reckon you're right. We got to keep this thing a secret from the rest of the captains until we get to the landing near Forth Smith."

"Renato, Jabez, and Schorp," Estrello shouted.

"What are you wantin' them for?" Wilder asked suspiciously.

"To take care of something we should have thought of before," said Estrello.

He said nothing more until the trio arrived, and Estrello spoke to them. "Go to the lower deck where the horses are, and move them all to the other end of the steamboat. Stretch a rope from one side of the boat to the other, to keep them there."

"Why?" Franklin Schorp asked.

"To keep them out of the line of fire if there's shooting," said Estrello. "You want to reach the landing at Fort Smith and find your horse has been killed by a stray slug?"

The three men looked at Wilder, who said irritably, "Go ahead and do what he says. It makes sense. We don't know what kind of weapons Laird's bunch may have aboard that steamboat."

"Now," said Wilder, when the three had gone, "you have so much confidence in that Gatling gun, don't you reckon it's time to find out if there's any ammunition for it, and where you can find it?"

"I suppose," Estrello said, hating the smug look on Wilder's face.

"Then get with it," said Wilder. "I'm sure Captain Savage would like to see you."

When Estrello entered the pilothouse, Captain Savage ignored him.

"Damn it," said Estrello, "I'm talking to you. Where's the belts of ammunition for the Gatling gun?"

"I have no idea," Captain Savage said. "The gun was mounted there by order, over my protest, and if any ammunition was brought aboard, I don't know where it is."

"You lie," said Estrello, drawing his Colt.

"Put the gun away," Captain Savage said calmly, "unless you have a man who can pilot this steamboat."

Wilder still had a guard posted outside the pilothouse, and through the glassed-in portion, McLean watched with interest, as Estrello drew his Colt. Just as quickly, Estrello replaced the weapon and stomped out of the pilothouse. Frustrated beyond words, the next person Estrello encountered was Wilder. He said nothing, and it was Wilder who spoke.

"Well, where's the ammunition for the gun?"

"Savage claims he don't know if there is any, or where it is," said Estrello. "You want me to go back in there and shoot the bastard?"

"I want *you* to find the ammunition for that damn Gatling gun, wherever it is," Wilder said. "It was you brought all this down on us."

Estrello considered asking for help from some of the men, but thought better of it. All of them, while excited over the wealth with which he had returned, seemed to blame *him* for the expected pursuit. Estrello found nothing on the first deck and went on to the next deck, where the horses were. He went in among the animals, and one of the horses reared, nickering.

"Settle down, damn you," Estrello growled.

It was at that end of the deck, in among the horses, that

Estrello finally found what he was seeking. A dirt-encrusted brass ring had been sunk into the wooden deck, and with a mighty heave, Estrello raised the trapdoor. There he counted a dozen wooden boxes, only one of which had been opened. From the open box he took a full belt of ammunition. Saul Renato and Phelps Brice claimed to know how to fire the Gatling gun. Now was the time to find out. Estrello was in no mood for Wilder again, but the outlaw was watching for him.

"Well," said Wilder, "I see you found it. How much is there?"

"A dozen cases, six hundred rounds each," Estrello growled.

"Just in case you get gunned down, you'd better tell me where it is," said Wilder.

"Go to hell," Estrello said. "Look for it like I did."

Estrello found Brice and Renato, and they followed him to the upper deck, where the Gatling gun had been mounted.

"How much shells?" Renato asked.

"According to the boxes, 7,200 rounds," said Estrello. "I'll show you where the rest of it is, but first I want to watch you get this gun ready. We're likely to need it any time."

Brice turned the gun's crank, finding that it moved easily. Renato fed in the belt of brass cartridges, lining up the first ones in firing position.

"She ready to shoot," Renato said.

"This one has six chambers instead of ten," said Estrello. "How fast does it shoot?"*

"Depends on how fast you can crank the cylinder," said Brice. "We're damn lucky this one's mounted on the deck. Them with wheels jump around some, and it ain't easy findin' the range."

*The Gatling gun was invented in 1861, and reportedly could fire 400 times a minute.

"Need more shells," Renato said. "This be two, maybe three volleys."

"Come on," said Estrello. "The rest of 'em are on the lower deck."

On the *Star,* Clemans and Nick Ursino stood by the rail facing the huge paddle wheel. It was difficult to see anything except the three steamboats following them.

"That amnesty we've been talkin' about seems to be gettin' farther and farther away," Nick said. "Not only are we in the midst of a bunch of varmints who would kill us for any reason or no reason at all, we're being pursued by a boatload of *hombres* with revenge on their minds."

"Let us not forget the revelation that Amanda and Betsy may or may not be able to find that hidden gold," said Vernon. "I'm startin' to wonder if there *is* any gold."

"Oh, there's gold, all right," Nick said. "I think old Jake Miles feared for his life, and he allowed Amanda and Betsy to take the gold and hide it. I believe it was Jake's way of keeping them alive after he was gone."

"Now they're not sure they can find the gold again," said Vernon. "If they can't, they won't be of any use to Estrello and these outlaws. You know what that means."

The negative conversation came to an end when Mark, Bill, Amanda, and Betsy joined the duo at the rail.

"If they're coming," Mark said, "I'm surprised they haven't caught up to us."

"Maybe they're waiting for dark," said Nick. "Vernon and me was just wondering what had become of them."

"Don't be so anxious," Bill said. "This could be more dangerous than anything else we have to face. There's so much metal on these steamboats, a ricochet could take a man's head off."

"You're right about that," said Mark. "If they do catch up to us, Amanda, I want you and Betsy on the lower deck."

"Let's talk some more about that missing gold," Nick said.

"There's nothing more to be said," Bill replied, irritated. "It's been five years, and with wind, rain, and snow the land can change."

"I don't want any of you sparing my feelings," Betsy said. "We all have to pay for our mistakes. Amanda and me made a big one."

"Not necessarily," said Nick. "After Jake had tried to be a father to both of you, how could you refuse to help him? I don't fault either of you for that."

"We'll just play out the hand," Todd Keithley said. "It's all we can do."

Brice and Renato brought up half a dozen cases of ammunition for the Gatling gun. At sundown, McCarty shouted a warning.

"Another steam boat comin', follwerin' us."

"We don't know for sure it's them," Wilder said.

"Brice, Renato, get the Gatling ready," said Estrello.

Drawn by the excited commotion, Mark, Bill, and their companions hurried down the upper deck. By then the black-and-gold steamboat was within range of Estrello's *Aztec*. The first shot from a Sharps .50 shattered the glass in the captain's cabin. The shooting became more intense, lead screaming off the metal parts of the steamboat.

"Amanda, Betsy, come on," Mark said. "Lower deck, and stay on the side farthest from that approaching steamboat."

Amanda and Betsy went without complaint. Some of Estrello's men were firing their Winchesters without effect. The range was still too great.

"They're using Sharps .50s," Wilder shouted. "Damn it, fire that Gatling gun before they cut us to ribbons."

"They ain't close enough," Brice snarled.

But the shooting from the pursuing steamboat continued. Jabez took a slug in his chest and was dead when he struck the deck. Leaving Amanda and Betsy on the lower deck, Bill and Mark ran for the upper deck. Their Winchesters were in the wagons, and a hail of lead plowed into the wooden main deck of the steamboat as they ran toward their wagons. Clemans, Keithley, Ursino, and Stackler were bellied down on deck, firing their Winchesters, seemingly without effect. McCarty hunkered down behind the damaged pilothouse, watching Captain Savage. Dodging lead, Estrello reached the pilot's cabin. He drew his Colt, and when Captain Savage turned to face him, Estrello spoke.

"They're running just out of range of the Gatling gun and our Winchesters," Estrello said. "It'd dark enough so they can't see us all that well. Slow this thing down some, so they can get closer."

"No," Captain Savage shouted.

Estrello seized the front of Savage's shirt in his left hand, while the Colt in his right had its muzzle directly under the captain's nose.

"Listen, damn it," Estrello shouted, "they're gonna sink us if we don't stop them. You slow this steamboat down, or by the Eternal, I'll shoot you and take my chances."

Estrello let go of Captain Savage, and the captain turned back to the controls. Slowly, the steamboat lost speed, and Estrello yelled at the two men prepared to fire the Gatling.

"Fire! They're close enough. Fire the Gatling!"

Aboard the pursuing steamboat, the men were jubilant. While their fire was raking the deck of the steamboat ahead, their quarry was still out of Winchester range, unable to effectively return the fire. Wills made a run for the pilothouse and Captain Tyndall. Lead shrieked all around him as the buffalo guns cut loose a covering volley.

"Tyndall," said Wills, "stay within range of our buffalo guns, but not within range of their Winchesters."

"They've slowed down some," Tyndall said. "I'll try to match their speed."

But the sun was down, dusk fast approaching, and visibility wasn't good. With a crash like rolling thunder, the Gatling gun sent a fusillade of lead at the pursuing steamboat. Two of Wills's men were killed, and two more seriously wounded.

"Tyndall," Wills shouted, "fall back! Fall back!"

Tyndall had slowed some, but they were still within range of the Gatling gun. Another blast from the big gun wounded two more men. Finally, they were out of range.

"Gatling gun," said one of Wills's men. "We ain't no match for that."

"Its range is considerably more than that of a Winchester," Wills said. "We'll stay well out of reach of their guns and cut down on them with ours. They can't see us all that well in the dark."

"Hell," said one of the outlaws, "that same dark won't let us see them. We're shootin' blind now."

"Then hold off on the gunfire," Wills said. "There'll be a moon later, and if we still haven't stopped them, we'll be right on their heels come daylight. Some of you take the men who are wounded down to the second deck, where we can use a lantern to see to their wounds."

"They've stopped shooting," said Estrello. "We hurt them some. Anybody hit besides Jabez?"

"No," Irvin said. "They're going to the second deck, below us."

"They're holdin' off, likely until moonrise," said Wilder. "Maybe even until first light."

"Captain Savage has got somethin' to say," McCarty announced.

"Stay where you are, Wolf," said Wilder. "I'll handle it."

Hating Wilder, Estrello said nothing, for some of the other outlaws were watching.

"Within the hour," Captain Savage told Wilder, "we'll be forced to make a wood stop. How do you intend to accomplish that, without us being blown to bits?"

"We'll load the wood before moonrise, when they can't see well enough to shoot."

Burt Wills was in what remained of the pilothouse, and Captain Tyndall had some bad news.

"We're low on wood," Tyndall said, "and those other boats will be up against the same problem. Trouble is, they can load before moonrise when we're blind, and then hold us at bay until all the fuel we have is gone."

"We're not gonna let that happen," said Wills. "We'll wait for moonrise if we have to, but as soon as we can see well enough, we'll deal them some more lead poison. Two of our men are dead and four wounded. We'll have to end this fight before they can do us any more damage."

"I'm afraid there's more at stake here than just ending the fight," Captain Tyndall said. "Were you ever aboard a steamboat when the boilers exploded?"

"No," said Wills.

"Well, I was," Tyndall said, "and that particular time, nobody was shooting at us. I've tried to tell Laird he needed some iron sheathing on this steamboat, but he wouldn't listen. Now you'd better listen. That last volley from the Gatling sent three slugs into the boiler room. They didn't hit anything vital . . . this time."

"I understand," said Wills. "We're going to try to put them out of business before the Gatling gun can be used again."

Aboard the *Aztec* steamboat, Wolf Estrello stomped into Captain Savage's pilothouse.

"Why the hell have you slowed down so much?" Estrello shouted. "You've practically stopped."

"Like I told Wilder, we must have fuel, or we're not going much farther," said Captain Savage. "I'm waiting for the first three steamboats to get into position. Then I'll take my position behind the *Midnight*."

"Damn it," Estrello groaned, "they'll catch up to us."

"Wilder says we can load our wood before moonrise," said Captain Savage. "He thinks if they can't see us, they can't shoot at us."

"Oh, damn Wilder," Estrello said. "That Gatling's an overgrown scattergun. Fire it in the general direction of anything, and it spits out a stream of lead two yards wide. We got to get them before they get us."

"Tell it to Wilder," said Captain Savage. "He's giving the orders."

Estrello's beefy face turned crimson with fury, and, covertly watching, Captain Savage wore a half smile.

"Wilder," Estrello said, "if we make this next wood stop, that damn bunch is gonna get close enough to cut down on us again."

"Estrello," said Wilder, with barely concealed fury, "if

we *don't* stop for fuel, they'll have us dead in the water. We're making the stop for wood whether you like it or not."

When the first three steamboats were in position to take on wood, Captain Savage took his place behind the third craft. Wilder had men ready to lower the ramps, and the crew immediately began loading wood from the dock. Far up the river, well out of range, they could see the shadowy hulk of the pursuing steamboat. The Mississippi being so wide at that point, the black-and-gold steamboat was keeping to the farthest bank.

"He's working his way even with us," Estrello shouted. "That'll put them in range of all our steamboats."

"And them within range of our Gatling gun," said Wilder. "Let 'em come a mite closer. Then swivel that gun around and fire at 'em. This thing you're shootin' ain't a Winchester. It lays down a wide swath of lead, and even in the dark, it can be deadly."

But the pursuing steamboat stopped just out of range.

"The damn nerve of them," Estrello shouted, "they're waiting for us to move on, so's they can take on wood. Let's just set here until their wood runs out, and see how far they can go."

"Set here till moonrise," said Wilder, "and they're in position to broadside all four of our steamboats. By God, can't you see that's what they got in mind?"

Aware of the possible danger, all the steamboat crews were hurriedly loading wood. In the next hour the moon would rise. Brice and Renato still crouched beside the Gatling gun, and it already held a belt of cartridges.

"Hell, we're within range," said Brice. "Let's blast 'em out of the water."

"No," Wilder said. "We'd only get one shot. When we move on, they'll have to take on wood. That'll put us well ahead of them. We'll wait and go after them when their boat's on the open river."

Wilder had no sooner spoken when there was the roar of gunfire from the other steamboat. McCarty lay on the deck unconscious, bleeding from a deep gash above his left ear. Irvin and Suggs crumpled to the deck of the *Star* as all the boats came within range, docked as they were. It was too much.

"Fire," Wilder shouted.

But Brice and Renato hadn't waited for the order, and the clattering roar of the Gatling gun drowned out everything else.

"Hold your fire!" bellowed Burt Wills. "We're too close. Back it up."

Captain Tyndall backed the steamboat up beyond range, and there was no more firing. But the Estrello outfit had three more wounded men. McLean was down, lead in his right leg, but he still clung to his Winchester. McCarty had a graze to his head and a wound in the shoulder. And Brice had been hit twice, once in the shoulder and once in the leg. Estrello's steamboat had only four men who hadn't been hit, except for Captain Savage and his crew. In the confusion, Captain Savage slipped off the steamboat, and for the first time since the race with death had begun, the captains had a chance to talk. Savage spoke rapidly, for even then, Wilder was headed for them, his Winchester ready.

"Break it up," Wilder snapped. "Back to your steamboats."

The captains obeyed, but the damage had been done. For the first time, the men piloting the first three steamboats knew why Estrello had reversed the order of the first and fourth steamboats. They also knew if the heavy gunfire in any way damaged the steamboat with the Gatling gun, the first three steamboats would have no defense except Winchesters.

"Damn it, that was a waste of ammunition," said Estrello. "Whose side are you on, Wilder?"

"Shut your mouth, Wolf," Wilder said. "I ain't gonna set here like a frog with a pair of busted legs, taking their fire without returning it. You don't know it was ammunition wasted."

"You damn fool," said Estrello. "You're gonna get us all killed. Where's Brice, one of the two men assigned to the Gatling gun?"

"Flat on his back on the deck, with two wounds," Renato said.

"Mr. Wilder," said Estrello, his voice dripping with sarcasm, "if you don't mind, I'll help Renato man the Gatling gun."

"Go ahead," Wilder said. "Get up there and get shot, so I don't have to do it later."

Aboard the *Star,* the latest volley from the pursuing steamboat had wounded three more men. Vernon Clemans, Todd Keithley, and Nick Ursino had been stuck by the flying lead. Nick was out cold from a slug that had burned its way across his skull. Todd and Vernon had both been struck in their upper thighs. Bill and Mark were seeing to the wounded men, using the medicine chest from Keithley's wagon. Amanda and Betsy had remained on the lower deck.

"Mark," said Keithley, "why don't you tell Carl, Lee, and Ed to hold off with their Winchesters? They'll end up wounded or dead, and we don't owe Estrello's bunch anything. Another volley or two, and Estrello won't have an outfit. Let him fight his own war."

"Todd's right," said Mark. "I'll get to them before there's any more shooting. The fewer fighting men this outfit has, the better our chances of breaking away."

* * *

"They're movin' out," Captain Tyndall shouted.

Slowly, the four dark hulks crept from the crude loading dock into the main stem of the Mississippi.

"No shooting," said Wills. "We'll catch up to them after we've replenished our fuel."

Feverishly, the crew began loading firewood, and before they had completed their task, the moon had risen. The steamboat took to the river again at full speed, and within less than an hour were again within sight of their quarry.

"Here come the bastards again," Wilder shouted.

The gold portion of the steamboat's hull shone brightly in the moonlight. After having so many wounded, Estrello's outfit had given up returning fire with Winchesters and were depending on the Gatling gun.

"Slow this thing down some," Wilder demanded, and Captain Savage did so.

"Whatever you plan to do," said Captain Savage, "you'd better do it quick. The pilothouse and my controls can't stand another hit like the last one."

"Just a little closer," Wilder said, "and we'll let the Gatling talk again."

But their pursuers, with the long-range Sharps .50s, cut loose again. A slug caught Estrello in the shoulder and laid him out on the deck. Wilder leaped to the dais on which the Gatling gun was mounted, and helping Renato feed a new belt of shells into the weapon, soon had it ready to fire. The steamboat had imperceptibly slowed, catching the captain of the pursuing steamboat by surprise.

"They're within range, damn it," Estrello shouted. "Fire!"

Wilder kept cranking out fire from the Gatling gun until

the belt of shells was gone, but it no longer mattered. There was a massive explosion, as steam, smoke, and fire engulfed the black-and-gold steamboat. A deadly ricochet had hit one of the boilers, and three of the four had exploded.

Chapter 10

The black-and-gold steamboat broke in half, and the remains sank quickly. But a half a mile downstream, a commercial steamboat, The *New Orleans,* paused on its way to St. Louis. Captain Virgil Troy had observed most of the spectacle through a spyglass the steamboat's pilot, Hankins, had handed him.

"What do you make of that?" Hankins asked.

"A running fight," said Troy. "One of the four steamboats has a Gatling gun, and that seems to have made a difference."

"We can get around the wreck and go on," Hankins said.

"We can, but we're not," said Troy. "If we play by the rules, we'll have to take aboard any survivors. Under the circumstances, the authorities must be told. Those four steamboats without markings could be involved in hauling the illegal moonshine we've been hearing about."

"Maybe that was the law after them, that got sunk," Hankins said.

"I doubt it," said Troy.

Keeping as near the farthest bank as possible, the four steamboats were soon past the commercial craft. Hankins piloted the big steamboat as near the bank as he safely could, near where the explosion had occurred. He beheld six bloody, dripping-wet men standing there, watching the steamboat as it came toward them. Wills, Tyndall, and four of the gang had survived the blast.

"You men are welcome aboard," Captain Troy shouted. "We'll take you to St. Louis."

"To St. Louis and the law," said Captain Tyndall. "They must have seen the fight before we sank."

"Well, damn it, we can't just stand here in the middle of nowhere," Wills said. "Better that we get back to St. Louis and see if there's anything left of Taylor Laird's empire."

"I hope somebody's found and buried the varmint if we're goin' back there," said one of the men. "Otherwise, he'll be ripe enough to puke a buzzard."

"Damn shame we didn't take time to bury him," Wills said. "Not for his sake, but for ours. He might not have been missed for a while."

The *New Orleans* had gotten as close to the bank as it could. Wills and what was left of his men waded into deep water and with ropes thrown to them, made their way to the big steamboat's deck. No questions were asked of them, and the survivors had nothing to say regarding their predicament.

"Something uncommonly strange about all this," Hankins said as he and Captain Troy watched the six survivors come aboard.

"That's exactly why I intend to report it," said Captain Troy. "The law in St. Louis is too far afield for it to matter, but the military should be interested. We've been hearing of steamboats traveling to St. Louis and loading illegal whiskey. I think what we've just seen were four such steamboats."

"I still think the law might have been aboard the boat that sank," Hankins said.

"We'll find out when we reach St. Louis," said Captain Troy. From the inside pocket of his blue-and-white jacket he took a .31 caliber Colt revolver. After checking the loads, he returned the weapon to his pocket.

St. Louis. August 7, 1866.

Lieutenant Banyon knocked on the post commander's door and was bid enter. He did so, saluting Captain Hailey.

"At ease," said Hailey, returning the salute. "Take a seat."

The lieutenant handed Captain Hailey a sheaf of papers.

"That's a complete report on what we learned about Taylor Laird, sir," Banyon said.

"I'll read it at my leisure," said Captain Hailey. "Give me a brief report."

"There were six of us," Lieutenant Banyon said. "We found Taylor Laird dead, shot three times. The safe was standing open and virtually empty, so the motive could have been robbery. We checked out every bank in town, and Laird had no accounts in St. Louis of any kind. Apparently, he kept all of his money in the safe. Except for the offices near the front of the building, it was full of whiskey, thirty-six-gallon drums. I sent a detail of men there to dispose of it."

"Good, Lieutenant, good," said Captain Hailey. "Were you able to find other properties owned or controlled by Taylor Laird?"

"Three more locations," Lieutenant Banyon said, "and more whiskey. They'll be taken care of before the end of the week. We can't do much about what happens in the territory, but we may have busted up this end of the whiskey smuggling."

"More so than you realize," said Captain Hailey. "Just a while ago, I learned six men were taken into custody after the sinking of a steamboat somewhere far to the south. A commercial steamboat, the *New Orleans,* was near enough for the captain to see the tag end of an on-the-river fight in progress between the steamboat that sank and four others. The four had no identifying marks, and I suspect they're involved in the transporting of illegal whiskey."

"Then there are witnesses?"

"Yes," said Captain Hailey. "The captain and his pilot were close enough to see it all through their spyglasses. From their report, one of the four boats that escaped was equipped with a Gatling gun. Hankins, the pilot, said the boilers exploded on the ship that sank."

"That's it, then," Lieutenant Banyon said.

"Not quite, Lieutenant," said Captain Hailey softly after the lieutenant had gone. Again Hailey reread the telegram he had received in response to his own, from Captain Ferguson at the Fort Worth outpost. It was painfully brief and worded so that if intercepted, it wouldn't make sense. It read:

"The long shots are the ones that pay. Mucho gracias."

It was simply signed "Ferguson," without a hint of what the captain intended to do, if anything.

On the Mississippi. August 9, 1866.

Estrello's boats had ten wounded men, including Estrello himself. Only Jabez had been killed. Ed Stackler had taken the medicine kit from the wagon and was doctoring the wounds of Vernon Clemans, Todd Keithley, and Nick Ursino. Nick's was the least serious, it being just a painful burn across his skull. Vernon's and Todd's were more serious, being in the thigh, and blood was draining into their boots. Amanda and Betsy were back on the upper deck, going from one man to another, attempting to help. On the *Aztec,* Renato was working over McCarty, for McCarty had been wounded in the shoulder, as well as the head. The other five wounded men had been hit in arms or legs, and the bleeding had been minimal. Bill, Mark, Amanda, and Betsy brought blankets from the wagons, seeing to the comfort of their wounded companions. Suddenly, there was a strange look in Bill's eyes, and he collapsed on the deck, facedown.

"Bill!" Betsy cried.

"Help me get his shirt off," said Mark. "He might have been hit."

Removing his shirt, they found that had indeed been the case. While there hadn't been much blood, a jagged piece of lead had whipped through Bill's shirt just above the waist, leaving an ugly, jagged hole.

"I've just used the last of the disinfectant," Ed said. "We'll have to tap one of those barrels of moonshine."

On the *Aztec,* Renato turned to Wilder. "We're out of disinfectant. Should we use the whiskey?"

"Hell, no," Estrello shouted, having overheard. "Leave that whiskey alone."

Despite their situation, Wilder laughed. "Maybe this is God's way of gettin' back at you, Wolf," Wilder said. "You'll have to drink some of your own poison."

Meanwhile, on the *Star,* they stretched Bill out on a blanket next to Vernon, Todd, and Nick. Stackler returned with a wooden bucket full of whiskey.

Mark poured some of the whiskey into Bill's wound, and he sat up with a gasp.

"Don't get up," Betsy begged. "You've been hit."

"I feel like I've also been set afire." said Bill. "What'n hell was *that*?"

"Some rotgut whiskey from one of those barrels in my wagon," Mark said, "and it can get worse. Come down with a fever, and you'll actually have to drink some of the stuff."

"God forbid," said Bill, closing his eyes.

Amanda and Betsy made the rounds of the wounded outlaws on the *Star*. They brought a progress report.

"I saw Irvin and Suggs get it," said Todd, "and that was almost worth takin' a slug myself."

"I wish I'd seen Wilder plugged but, you can't drown a man that's born to be hanged," Vernon said.

"Give him some of that whiskey," said Bill. "He's out of his head."

"Thanks," Vernon said. "I'll do something nice for you sometime."

"I hate to bring this up," said Carl, "but in another day or two, we'll be back at the Fort Smith landing. How do we free ourselves from these outlaws with four of you hurt?"

"Simple enough," said Todd. "Those of us who aren't able to make a break for it will have to stay. Carl, you, Lee, Mark, Amanda, and Betsy will have a chance if we stick to our plan."

"Damn the plan," Betsy said. "I'm not leaving Bill behind."

"Then all any of us have done to save you and Amanda will be lost," said Bill. "Some of these outlaws will take you, having their way with you. Then, if you can show them to that hidden gold, they'll kill you."

"Much as I hate to admit it," said Mark, "he's right."

"If Betsy stays, I stay," Amanda said. "She's my twin sister, and we've been through too much together."

"If Amanda stays, then so do I," said Mark. "That leaves only Carl, Lee, and Ed."

"I'm not running out on the rest of you," Ed replied. "I'd feel like a Judas."

"Then it's up to Carl and Lee," Bill said. "We still need that telegram sent to Captain Ferguson at Fort Worth. Fort Smith is our last chance. Then it's Indian Territory."

"You think me and Carl won't feel like we've let the rest of you down?" Lee Sullivan asked. "Maybe Estrello will wait for his wounded men to heal before taking the wagons on into the Territory. That will allow our wounded time to heal."

"I hate to say it," Carl said, "but unless some of us take them by surprise, making our break at Fort Smith, you all know we're not likely to get another chance."

"Then let me make the break," said Ed Stackler. "One man might have a better chance than two. Soon as we're near the landing, I'll go over the side and into the water. There's a chance they won't miss me."

"There's also a chance they'll cut you to ribbons with Winchesters or Sharps .50s," Carl said. "If Lee and I run for it, one of us might make it."

"Damn it," said Stackler, "let's cut the cards. The low card goes."

"Where do we get a deck of cards?" Carl wondered.

"In Jake's wagon, under the seat," said Betsy. "They were Jake's, and they're wrapped in oilskin."

"Shame on you, Betsy," Amanda said. "You're sending one of these men out to die."

But it was the only fair thing to do, and Stackler went and brought the cards. It was he who shuffled them. Mark drew the first card, Carl the second, and Lee the third. Ed then drew the fourth card.

"Face-up time," Ed said.

Carl dropped his card, the king of clubs. When Lee dropped his, it was the ace of diamonds. Almost reluctantly, Mark dropped his card, and it was the queen of hearts. Ed dropped his card, the four of spades.

"Damn it, Ed," said Lee, "you stacked that deck."

Ed laughed. "I did not. I always beat you gents at poker because you're not that good at it. It's settled. I'm going to make a run for it, jumping ship before any of these steamboats has a chance to dock. If I make it to Fort Smith alive, maybe I can get a telegram off to Captain Ferguson in Fort Worth in time to free the rest of you."

"It's a long-shot chance," said Mark. "How far are we from Estrello's old camp on the Washita?"

"About two hundred and fifty miles," Carl said.

"With loaded wagons, even if there's no trouble, that's twelve to fifteen days," said Ed. "Ferguson and a company of soldiers could *walk* from Fort Worth in that amount of time. Depending on how serious Captain Ferguson takes that telegram, it's our only way out."

"Ferguson won't let us down," Bill said. "According to my count, it's been thirty-six days since we left Fort Worth. I think Captain Ferguson will be looking for something that will tell him we're alive and successful, or that we've failed and are dead."

"That's my impression of Captain Ferguson, too," said Mark. "That's why it's important that we complete this mission. Captain Ferguson trusted us when all we had to look forward to was a rope or the firing squad."

"The wounded will give me a slight edge when it's time to make a break," Ed said. "They may not be so quick to grab their Colts, and those arm and shoulder wounds will limit their use of Winchesters."

Estrello's outfit on the *Aztec* was a surly lot, as those who hadn't been wounded were forced to tend to their comrades who had been less fortunate.

"Hell, I ain't no doctor," said Franklin Schorp.

"Me, neither," Renato said.

"You got no choice," said Wilder, "same as I don't. Do the best you can, so the wounds don't get infected. Somebody tap another one of those kegs and bring me some more whiskey."

"You'll have to get it yourself," Schorp said. "The rest of us got our hands full."

Finally, all of the wounded Estrello gang, including Estrello, had their wounds taken care of, and the upper deck of the steamboat looked like a battlefield. Captain Savage was no longer being watched, for the few men who hadn't been wounded were exhausted from the August heat and tending their wounded comrades. When the sun sank below the western horizon and twilight approached, there was a cooling wind out of the west.

"Here's where we leave the Mississippi for the Arkansas," said Carl, watching from the deck of the *Star*. "There'll be one more wood stop before we get to the Fort Smith landing."

"I might be able to escape during the wood stop," Ed said, "but it's a long way back to Little Rock, and even farther to Fort Smith, without a horse."

"I hate it, you having to go afoot," said Mark. "I feel like that's the responsibility of Bill or me, since we made the agreement with Captain Ferguson."

"I don't see it that way," Ed said. "The deal for amnesty includes me, and I don't expect something for nothing."

"I don't think any of us will be getting it for nothing," said Lee, "and I don't fault anybody for that. I joined Estrello's outfit because I had a price on my head and nowhere to run."

"Same as the rest of us," Carl said. "Somehow, it didn't seem all that bad, right at the first. We were selling whiskey, and the Indians were buying. I couldn't see it coming to this, some of you lying wounded on a steamboat, while we choose one man to risk his neck trying to break loose to bring help."

"Don't worry about me," said Ed. "I've done more than my share of fool things, with a lot less to be gained."

A hundred and thirty miles east of Fort Smith, the steamboats again stopped to take on fuel. Wilder, Schorp, and Renato stood watch with Winchesters to be certain that nobody left the Star except the crew for the loading of wood. Men left steamboats two, three, and four stretching their legs.

"What about us?" shouted Stackler.

Wilder looked at him like he was sizing up a deer.

"We're gonna' have us a little change."

"What?!" cried Amanda and Betsy in unison.

"We need to even up the men on the boats," Wilder said, grinning.

Mark stepped up. "If you're talking about me and Bill, here, the women are stayin' with us."

Silence fell across the boat as Wilder rubbed his jaw where Mark had hit him earlier. Every heart held still as both men stared at each other, their hands slowly sliding towards their weapons.

Bill groaned. It wasn't loud, but it was enough to break the spell.

"All of you get on over to the Aztec," growled Wilder.

"And the women?" Demanded Mark.

"I said 'all of you,' didn't I? And the wounded, too. We want to keep all the casualties in one place."

"All those they're suspicious of, is more like it," muttered Sullivan.

"Oh Lord," said Betsy, "I thought that was gonna be it."

Stackler helped to lift Bill. "Guess we're all in the same boat now."

With enough wood to see them the rest of the way to the Fort Smith landing, the four steamboats again moved out. But they were unable to travel at top speed because of the occasional sandbars around which they had to maneuver. In places, the river was shallow, and care had to be taken to keep the steamboats in deep water.

"Time for some whiskey," said Mark. "Bill's running a fever. Vernon and Todd won't be far behind."

"I reckon I got off easy, just gettin' my skull creased," Nick said. "I don't envy the others, having to drink that God-awful whiskey."

Within the hour, Vernon and Todd were running fevers, and they had to be given large doses of the terrible whiskey. The night wore on, and at dawn there was only jerked beef for those able to eat. Bill, Vernon, and Todd were sick from the whiskey, although it had served its purpose and eliminated the high fever. The other outlaws on the *Aztec* had fared no better. McLean and McCarty threw up on deck, while the others moaned in fitful, restless sleep.

"What we gonna do when we get to Fort Smith?" Renato asked Wilder. "Men are sick, and there is no room for them in the wagons."

"I ain't decided yet," said Wilder. "Maybe we'll get into the Territory a ways and just lay over there until the wounded are healed enough to ride."

Irvin was awake. "You aim to go lookin' for that stolen gold old Jake had?"

"Damn right I do," Wilder said. "Them women know where it is."

"Whiskey running is shot to hell," said Schorp. "What

will we do, once we sell this whiskey and find the missing gold?"

"I'm taking my share of the loot and going where the law can't touch me," Wilder said. "Maybe Mexico."

"Only three men on this boat to concern us," said Lee Sullivan. "Ed, when you make your break, we can gun down Wilder, Schorp, and Renato."

"No," Stackler said. "Kill them, and the rest of Estrello's outfit will kill you. There's no point in me going for help if the rest of you are dead before it gets here."

"We'll be reaching the landing at Fort Smith late tonight," Sullivan said, "but not before moonrise. We can still pull a gun on the good captain and have him run this steamboat aground somewhere shy of the landing."

"No," said Stackler. "We'll have to scrap that part of our original plan. Forcing a stop shy of the landing will alert everybody on the other three steamboats that we're up to something, and the moonlight will make me a good target in the water."

As the day wore on, the rest of the wounded outlaws on the *Aztec* slept off their fevers and awoke.

"Wilder," said Suggs, "we was supposed to gun down the captains and their crews at the Fort Smith landing. Are we still aimin' to?"

"Not on this steamboat," Wilder replied. "There's just three of us that ain't been hurt and are trustworthy, and we can't spare anybody to go after the captain. Those on the other boats can do as they please, but this steamboat needs its crewmen."

"There's Long, Sullivan, Stackler, and Rogers, besides the two women," said Irvin, "and they're all still armed."

"They joined us in the fight against the Taylor Laird gang," Wilder said. "We'll reward them by letting them live until we find that gold them women buried."

"We're near two weeks' away from the Washita," said Suggs. "What if we just split the money and the gold we got, and them wantin' to hunt Jake's gold can do it, while the rest of us just go our way?"

"You're crazy as hell," Irvin shouted. "After all we been through, I aim to get my share when this rotgut whiskey's sold, and I can't do that if we split up now."

"Nobody's leaving," said Estrello, who had awakened, "and as for that hidden gold, we leave it be until the whiskey's been sold."

"Wolf's right about sticking together," Wilder said. "We may need the guns of every man of us. Suppose them hundreds of whiskey-drinking Indians was to decide to just *take* the whiskey, instead of buyin' it?"

For a change, Estrello and Wilder had agreed on something, and the rest of the outlaws nodded their approval. Vivid in their minds were tales of white men who had gone into Indian Territory without protection and were never seen again.

The August sun bore down with a vengeance, and not a breeze stirred. The wounded men, some without shirts and others without trousers, sweated. The bad whiskey had done its job, for nobody had any fever.

"Wolf," said Brice, "you think this is the end of whiskey running into Indian Territory?"

"As far as I'm concerned it is," Estrello said. "You saw the *New Orleans* take on the survivors from Laird's steamboat, and there are witnesses to the sinking. All it'll take is for just one man to talk. Taylor Laird built an empire, but without him it's as dead as he is."

"It was you that gunned him down," said Wilder. "Maybe you should have given it a little more thought. It'll be hell finding bootleg whiskey now."

"I gave it some thought," Estrello said. "Laird had just raised the price on whiskey, and I couldn't see us taking all the risk while he took none, at a higher price. I had no idea there was money in the safe until Laird was dead. What *else* do you do with a gent you don't need anymore, except get rid of him? If I'd left him alive, he'd have followed us all to hell and come in after us."

"I can't argue with that," said Wilder, "but there's somethin' you'd better keep in mind where these whiskey-drinking Indians are concerned. One word to any of them about this bein' the last of the whiskey, and they won't need us anymore. There'll be enough of them to just *take* this load of whiskey, along with our scalps."

"Hell's fire," Estrello shouted, "how big a fool do you think I am?"

"I'm not sure," said Wilder with an evil grin. "You continue to amaze me."

"This whiskey didn't cost us nothin'," Renato said. "We sellin' it to the Indians at the old price, or will we ask for more money?"

"Keepin' in mind what Wilder just said about our scalps," said Estrello, "I think we'll have to sell to them at the old price."

"Hell, I don't," Irvin said. "This is our last haul, and I'm for milkin' it dry. I'm for *doubling* the price."

There was an uproar as the outlaws agreed or disagreed.

"By God," Suggs shouted, "let's vote on it."

"We're not votin' on it because we ain't raisin' the price," said Estrello.

All eyes turned to Wilder, and his response surprised them. "Wolf and me have had our differences, but this time, we fully agree. I reckon some of you don't value your scalps all that much. Let a bunch of likkered-up Indians get a mad on, and we're all dead men."

There was some grumbling among several of the outlaws who didn't like the decision to sell the whiskey at the old price, but they soon became silent, for Estrello and Wilder were both looking at them in a way that made them uneasy.

Now on board the *Aztec,* Bill, Betsy, Mark, Amanda and their companions waited uneasily as the outlaws argued over raising the price of whiskey.

"The greedy varmints," said Vernon. "That rotgut didn't cost them a cent, and some of them want to double the price to the Indians."

"Thank God Estrello and Wilder ain't as stupid as some of the others," Carl said. "There's a chance we'll be stuck with this bunch until they unload this whiskey, and those Indians won't draw any lines between us and the rest of Estrello's outfit."

The day wore on, and as they approached the final landing near Fort Smith, the stars had been sprinkled over the purple of the sky. It would be dark soon.

"I'm gettin' a break," said Ed. "No moon yet."

"There soon will be," Mark said, "if they decide to go after you."

"Oh, they'll go after him," said Betsy. "Even though this may be his last whiskey run, Wolf Estrello don't like to lose. He's the cause of all this trouble."

"Let's don't forget Wilder," Bill said. "He's done his share."

The outlaws seemed to have forsaken their vow to gun down the steamboat captains and their crews, for the first three steamboats were guided in close to the crude landing. The *Aztec* eased in behind them.

"Get those ramps down," Estrello shouted.

"That's my cue," said Ed quietly. "Wish me luck."

Amanda and Betsy kissed him quickly, and Ed shook the hands of the rest of his friends. He then went to the side of the deck opposite where the unloading ramps had to be let down. His companions watched him disappear over the side and into the darkness. But other eyes had witnessed Stackler's escape.

"Wolf," an outlaw shouted, "somebody went over the side."

"He won't get far afoot," said Estrello. "Wilder, take half a dozen men from boats one, two, and three, and go after him."

"Hell, I ain't stompin' around in the brush and thickets afoot," Wilder said. "I aim to take my horse."

"Then *take* your horse and have the others take theirs," said Estrello, "but don't come back without the varmint who ran out."

It was Renato who took the time to see who was missing. "It was Stackler that went over the side."

"When you run him down," said Estrello, "don't be gentle. Let's make him an example to the rest of them."

Chapter 11

Fort Smith landing. August 11, 1866.

Stackler swam upstream far enough that he judged the outlaws couldn't see him in the dark waters of the Arkansas. Reaching a shallows, he waded out on the Fort Smith side of the river. His teeth chattered, for his sodden clothing made the evening wind seem cold. The moon had risen and appeared to be balanced in the tops of the trees, adding its light to that of millions of glittering stars. After climbing out of the river, Stackler rested just long enough to catch his breath. He then set out for Fort Smith, somewhere to the north.

Aboard the *Aztec,* Stackler's friends watched in anger and dismay as Wilder and six other outlaws unloaded horses and saddles for use in the search for Stackler.

"It's so unfair," Betsy cried. "He won't have a chance, being afoot."

"They're off to a slow start, taking time to saddle their horses," said Bill, "and it'll be darker in the woods, where the moonlight can't get through."

"The trouble is," Mark said, "they'll know he's bound for Fort Smith. There's nowhere else to go from here."

The others said nothing. They fully expected the outlaws to ride Stackler down and doubted they'd see their friend alive. The outlaws finally got their horses saddled and clattered down the ramp.

"Now," Estrello shouted, "eight of you that ain't been hurt, harness the teams and get them wagons off the boats."

Long, Sullivan, and Rogers started for their wagons.

"Hold it," said Estrello. "That order don't include Stackler's friends. The rest of you stay where you are. Take your Colts and Winchesters and lay 'em on the deck, and when you've done that, walk away from them."

"I was afraid of that," Carl said. "Now we're depending entirely on Ed."

They were covered by three of the outlaws, including Estrello, their Colts steady in their hands. The men—even the wounded—had no choice. All their weapons were piled on the steamboat's deck. Leaving two men to cover the captives, Estrello began carrying the weapons down the ramp and off the steamboat.

"I can't see what he'd doing with our guns," said Carl.

"We can't see any of the wagons from here," Lee said. "Maybe he'll leave them in one of the wagons."

But Estrello had thought of a better hiding place. Beneath each wagon's bed there was a stretched, firmly attached cowhide, useful for hauling dry wood for cook fires. Estrello piled the weapons into the "possum belly" of the very wagon that had been Ed Stackler's.

"Without our guns, I feel like we're a step closer to the grave," said Betsy.

"We still have Jake's Colt," Amanda said. "Estrello forgot about that."

"Where *is* Jake's Colt?" Mark asked.

"Beneath my shirt, tucked under my waistband," said Amanda. "Do you want it?"

"No," Mark said. "It's safer where it is. We're likely to need it."

Briars ripped and tore at Stackler, for he couldn't see them in the dark. Beneath the trees, the ground was mottled with splashes of light, where the moonlight had managed to get through the foliage of the many trees. Behind him, Stackler could hear the voices of the outlaws who were looking for him.

"Damn it," Wilder shouted, "spread out. We'll never find him riding single file."

Stackler began using the little light there was to the best advantage, looking for a place that he might hide. If they passed him in the dark, they might conclude he'd made it on to Fort Smith and abandon the search. But in his heart, he knew better. As vindictive a man as Wolf Estrello was, he wouldn't settle for anything less than death for one he felt had betrayed him. Suddenly, a horse nickered, sounding much closer. Stackler got to his feet and hurried on. His boots had begun to dry, and he could feel the stiffening leather starting to blister his feet. He must find a thicket so dense his pursuers wouldn't consider the possibility he was hiding there. When he found such a thicket, he plunged as far into it as he could, and lying belly-down in fallen leaves, faced back the way he had come.

Wilder was the first to cross a small clearing where the moonlight identified him. After Wilder's command, the outlaws who accompanied him had spread out in a skirmish line, each man fifty yards from the next. To Stackler's relief, Wilder rode on past the concealing thicket. Eventually, they would be forced to abandon the search if they thought Stackler had reached Fort Smith. But Ed Stackler's luck had run out. Somewhere, perhaps from the town itself, came the

baying of a dog. As the baying seemed to grow louder, it
was apparent the animal was nearing Stackler's thicket.
Stackler heard leaves rattling as the dog approached. It didn't
bark again until it was but a few feet away.

"Dog," said Stackler desperately, "stop that. I'm your
amigo, your friend."

But the troublesome dog believed otherwise, for he continued barking. The significance of it wasn't lost on the outlaws searching for Stackler.

"That dog's got somethin' or somebody treed," Wilder
said. "Maybe the gent we got to find. We must have passed
him in the dark. Let's ride back."

With the barking dog to guide them, the outlaws soon
found the dense thicket where Stackler had hoped he'd be
safe. They surrounded the thicket.

"Stackler," Wilder shouted, "we know you're in there.
Are you comin' out, or do we have to get you our way?"

"Have a go at it your way," said Stackler.

The dog had stopped barking, and Stackler could hear the
outlaws mumbling.

"Let's just riddle that thicket with lead," DeWitt said.
"Estrello didn't say nothin' about him bein' alive when we
drag his carcass back."

"No shooting until I give the order," said Wilder. "We got
a use for him and the rest, at least until we get to the Washita."

Stackler heard the tag end of the conversation. He decided it was for his benefit, to throw him off guard. He remained where he was, then suddenly heard the slight rattle
of the dry leaves that littered the ground. At first he thought
the dog had returned, but there was a lengthy pause between
the rattling of leaves. One of them was trying to get to him,
taking one cautious step at a time.

"Come on, damn you," Stackler gritted under his breath.

In a small patch of moonlight Stackler caught a glimpse of his pursuer. Drawing one of his Colts, he fired. He then rolled as far as he could from his original position. There was no answering fire.

"Damn you, Jackman," snarled Wilder. "Why didn't you fire at the muzzle flash when you had the chance?"

"Because I was hit in my gun arm," Jackman shouted. "I'm comin' out."

There was the rustle of leaves, but Stackler didn't fire again. He believed he'd need all his ammunition and that in fact, he might not have enough.

At the river all eight wagonloads of whiskey had been removed from the steamboats, and the captains were ready, when the last wagon rumbled off onto the solid ground, to back away. Farther downstream the river would be wide enough for them to turn the steamboats around. Their immediate goal was to get as far from the Estrello gang as possible.

"I hear a dog barkin' his head off," said Odell. "Could be barkin' at Stackler."

"More than likely, he's barking at Wilder and the others who are looking *for* Stackler," Estrello said.

Just as suddenly the dog ceased barking, and after a prolonged silence, there was the distant sound of a shot.

"What the hell?" said Estrello.

"Maybe Stackler shot the dog," Renato said.

Back at the thicket where Stackler was hiding, there was talk among the outlaws as one of them tied a bandanna around Jackman's wounded arm.

"Wilder," said Tilden, "there's plenty of dead leaves and grass. Why don't we just set the brush afire?"

"Because Fort Smith's within hollerin' distance of here,"

Wilder said. "You want the whole damn town down on us? A nice big fire would bring somebody on the run."

"So will a lot of gunfire," said Haddock. "Whatever law there is in Fort Smith will be almighty interested in what's goin' on."

"So what'n hell are we gonna do about Stackler?" Tilden demanded. "You aim for us to surround this thicket until he gets hungry?"

"I'm damn tired of some varmint questioning everything I do," said Wilder. "Take hold of this and go any way that suits you. Just be sure you tell Estrello that it was your idea and not mine."

"I've already been shot," said Jackman, "and we ain't so much as laid eyes on the varmint that done it. I'm for ridin' back and tellin' Wolf we're up against something we can't handle."

"I've never shot an *hombre* in the back in my life, Jackman," Wilder said, "but if you ride back to tell Estrello *anything* such as that, you're a dead man."

Wilder had raised his voice in anger, and suddenly there were two shots from within the thicket. One of them struck Wilder's left arm just above the elbow, while the second tore a gash along his left side, under his arm. Lightning quick, Wilder drew his Colt and emptied it into the thicket. But Stackler had changed positions, and the lead wasn't even close.

"Well," said Haddock, "if somebody in Fort Smith didn't hear that—"

"Haddock, just shut the hell up!" Wilder said.

Jackman laughed. "It didn't bother you when the bastard shot *me*, Wilder, but now *you* got a taste of his lead, how do you like it?"

Wilder said nothing. He had removed his shirt, and even

in the moonlight the outlaws could see blood dripping from a terrible gash along his left side. The lead had gone on through the flesh of his left arm, and it also bled profusely.

"Wilder," said Tilden, "you'd better ride back to camp and have that tended to. You're losing an almighty lot of blood."

"I'll ride back when we take Stackler with us," Wilder snarled. "If I want advice from you or anybody else, I'll ask for it."

He wrapped his shirt about the bloody wound in his side, tying the sleeves in front to hold it in place. The wound in his upper left arm he ignored. He then reloaded his Colt and spoke to Stackler.

"There's enough of us to take you, Stackler. It's just a matter of time, and I don't care if you go back dead or alive, but by God, you're goin'. Now you can come out of there and make it easy on yourself, or you can force us to get mean. What's it gonna be?"

But Stackler was no longer in the thicket. While much attention had been devoted to the wounded Wilder, Stackler had quietly slipped out the other side of the thicket while it was momentarily unwatched.

"Damn what Fort Smith thinks," said Wilder. "All of you get your Winchesters. We're goin' to fill that thicket with lead. Fan your shots out in a half circle, firing low and then high. We won't give the varmint anywhere to hide."

The seven outlaws fired their Winchesters—seventeen shots per weapon—until they were empty. When the thundering roar died away, there wasn't a sound.

"We got him, by God," said Wilder.

"You can't be sure of that without goin' in there," Tilden said.

"Hell," snarled Wilder, "you think I don't know that? But

it's not just me. All of us are going in. He can't gun down all of us in the dark."

"I wouldn't be too sure of that," Shadley said. "He's fired three times just at the sound of our voices, and two of us have been hit."

Wilder seemed not to have heard. "Fan out," he said. "We're all goin' in there at a different place. If he's alive and fires, pour the lead to the left and right of the muzzle flash. He'll change positions."

Fearing Wilder's wrath, the unwilling outlaws entered the thicket, growing bolder when they they weren't greeted with lead as they had half expected. They emerged on the other side of the thicket, having found nothing. Wilder was cursing bitterly.

"Well," said Patton, "we lost him, but we've told all of Fort Smith we're here."

"We ain't lost him," Wilder snarled. "We can still catch him before he gets to town. Mount up and let's ride."

Stackler hadn't expected to hit anything with his two shots. They had been intended to give pause to the outlaws, while Stackler tried to slip away. The ploy had worked better than Stackler expected, and he had escaped the thicket well before the outlaws had cut down with their Winchesters. Stackler stopped to catch his wind and to listen. He drew his Colt, for there was the rustling of leaves somewhere behind him. Finally, he laughed, for in the moonlight a tan-and-white hound stood there looking at him.

"Pardner," said Stackler, "under different circumstances, I'd enjoy your company, but you've already give me away once. Wherever you belong, be on your way. Vamoose."

But the dog didn't move until Stackler did, and the animal continued trotting along behind him.

"Damn it, dog," Stackler said, "you'll be the death of me."

The seven riders in pursuit found it tough going, for there were briars that had crept up trees, leaving thorny branches sweeping down from low-hanging limbs. Wilder, having used his shirt to bind the wound in his side, had his back and shoulders raked repeatedly. Finally, a thorn-ridden branch swept off his hat.

The massive amount of lead poured into the thicket had been heard by Estrello and the rest of his outfit, back near the river.

"Damn them," Estrello roared. "How much lead does it take to cut down one man?"

The ominous significance of the shooting had not been lost on Stackler's friends, either.

"Dear God," cried Betsy, "they must have him trapped somewhere."

"Maybe not," Todd said. "This bunch is likely shooting at their shadows. I'd say the first three shots we heard might have been fired by Ed. But it had to be Wilder and his bunch that cut loose with what we just heard."

"Ed knew there would be nothing any of us could do to help him," said Mark. "If anybody can make it, I believe Ed can. If we had all made a run for it, some of us wouldn't have made it. Anybody who was caught probably wouldn't have lived until help arrived."

"That means they won't be bringing Ed back alive, then," Amanda said.

"Best not to expect it," said Bill. "Wilder's not a compassionate man."

"I'm wishing we had all been able to run for it together, before they took our guns," Vernon said. "They're goin' to make an example of Ed for the benefit of the rest of us."

"I'm expecting Estrello to keep us alive until we get these

wagons back to the Washita, at least," said Bill. "When you think about it, there's not a professional teamster in all that Estrello outfit. They aim for us to handle those wagons just as we have right up to now. That'll keep us alive a few more days."

"That won't help Ed," said Nick. "Ed, Vernon, and me have been pards since before the war."

"I don't know how or when it will happen," Nick said, "but the bastards that kill Ed Stackler are goin' to die. As long as I'm alive they're livin' on borrowed time."

"Some of us haven't known Ed as long as you gents have," said Mark, "but we feel the same way about him."

Stackler fought his way through brush, unable to see. Clouds had swept in from the west, hiding the moon and stars. The tan-and-white hound was at his heels, and Stackler made no further effort to rid himself of the dog. Shards of rocks thrust up out of the soil, and Stackler stumbled over them. He couldn't see the stone ledge with a drop-off of a dozen feet, and he went over the edge, headfirst. He slammed into the hard ground on his shoulders and the back of his head, and there he remained, unconscious, until Wilder and the other riders found him.

"Get up, Stackler," said Wilder.

Stackler had already been disarmed, and there was nothing he could do except obey. He stood up, leaning against the stone drop-off to steady himself. One of the outlaws bound his hands behind him, and he was forced to walk to where the horses had been left. But the outlaws had no intention of allowing him to ride. Wilder shoved Stackler, who, because of his bound hands, couldn't regain his balance. Wilder had a lariat, and when Stackler fell, Wilder looped one end of the lariat around Stackler's ankles. The outlaws mounted their horses, Wilder's mount dragging Stackler across the rocky soil, through brush and all manner of brambles. Stackler vowed not to cry out or plead with them. He closed his eyes to protect them, gritting his teeth against the constant pain of being dragged. It seemed they would never reach the river and the Estrello camp, but finally they did. The moon had broken through the clouds in time for Estrello's outlaws to see their comrades coming, dragging the unfortunate Stackler.

"Damn them," said Mark, "They've got him. They've got Ed!"

Amanda and Betsy were weeping, while Bill swore under his breath.

"He may still be alive," Vernon said. "Otherwise, why bring him back?"

The first thing Estrello did was give Wilder hell for all the unnecessary shooting.

"If he's alive, cut him loose," Estrello said.

"He's alive," said Wilder, "but damn it, he shot two of us before we—"

"You got his guns?" Estrello asked.

"Yeah," said Wilder. "You think I'm a damn fool?"

"Turn him loose," Estrello said.

"Why should I?" Wilder asked. "He done his best to kill us."

"Good for him," said Estrello. "He's a better man than any of you."

Stackler lay facedown. Estrello whipped out his knife, slashing the bonds on Stackler's wrists. He then cut the lariat loose from Stackler's ankles.

"Damn you," Wilder shouted, "you've ruint my lariat."

"After all that unnecessary gunfire," said Estrello, "I ought to slit your damn throat. Get up, Stackler, if you can."

Stackler was game, but he got only as far as his hands and knees.

"Carl, Lee," Mark said. "Let's go get Ed."

Wilder saw them coming and drew his Colt. "Nobody sent you any invites," he said. "The bastard stays where he is until he can get up on his own."

"Wilder," said Estrello, "put the gun away."

"Estrello," Mark said. "Ed's hurt. We want to do for him what we can."

"Take him, then," said Estrello.

"No," Wilder said, cocking the Colt.

But Wilder's hard eyes were on Carl, Lee, and Mark. Calmly, Estrello drew his Colt and slammed the muzzle of it against Wilder's head, just above the ear. Wilder went down, his Colt blasting lead into the dirt at his feet. Without a word, Estrello took the Colt from Wilder's hand, shoving it under his own waistband. Stackler was again trying to get to his feet, and again he failed. Carl and Lee each took one of Stackler's arms, while Mark took his feet, and they managed to get him back to their own little camp near Stackler's wagon.

"I'll get some whiskey from the wagon," said Carl.

Carl took the wooden bucket and tapped one of the kegs in Stackler's wagon. The outlaws said nothing. Betsy and Amanda had hurriedly brought blankets. Stackler had been placed on his back, and unconscious, he still groaned in pain. He face was gashed in many places, and his chest was a mass of blood to his waist, for all the buttons had been torn from the front of his shirt.

"He may have some hurts we can't see," Betsy said. "Take off his Levi's."

Stackler had livid bruises all over his lower back, thighs, and legs.

"Much as I hate to suggest it," said Nick, "I think we'd better give him enough of that whiskey to knock him out for a while."

"He hasn't been shot, at least," Amanda said.

"He might be in better shape if he had been," said Vernon. "Tomorrow, he'll be in real misery, and whether he has fever or not, the whiskey's a good idea. Let him sleep through as much of the pain as he can."

With Carl and Lee holding Stackler in an upright position, Mark forced a large quantity of the whiskey into the wounded man. Ed groaned, and with the shock of the whiskey, just for a few seconds, he opened his eyes.

"Sorry, pardner," said Lee. "You've been bad hurt, and the whiskey will help."

Stackler tried to speak, but the words trailed off, and he closed his eyes. Then from the woods behind them there came a slight noise.

"Damn it," Mark said, "and we're unarmed."

Finally, from the brush emerged a tan-and-white hound. The animal sat down, fixing his eyes on the wounded Stackler.

"Maybe that's the dog we heard barking," said Amanda.

"I wouldn't be surprised," Vernon said, "and it may have been him that attracted Wilder to Ed's hiding place."

The dog made no move. Stackler's companions began doctoring his many wounds as best they could.

St. Louis. August 15, 1866.

Dan Rowden, St. Louis county sheriff, knocked on the door of the post commander's office and was given permission to enter. Rowden got right to the point. "I've heard you and your men have taken into custody some of the outlaws smuggling whiskey into Indian Territory, Captain."

"Indirectly, Sheriff," said Captain Hailey. "Through a streak of good luck and some solid thinking on the part of the crew of the *New Orleans,* we seemed to have gotten our hands on some of the scum from these parts who were producing the whiskey. Have any of them decided to talk?"

"They're all singing like birds," Sheriff Rowden said, "hoping to escape federal prosecution. That was Taylor Laird's steamboat, and one of the six survivors—Burt Wills— had access to the boat. He was Laird's second-in-command, and as soon as he discovered Laird was dead, he got nineteen men together, and they set off in Laird's steamboat, with .50 caliber Sharps buffalo guns. Of course, you know the rest. They came up against a Gatling gun, and it was too much for them. That's all we've been able to get out of them."

"The four steamboats hauling the whiskey didn't belong to Taylor Laird, then," said Captain Hailey.

"We could find no evidence of it," Sheriff Rowden said, "and Burt Wills claims Laird made arrangements for the steamboats. He believes the steamboats Laird contracted for came from New Orleans. We've checked out all local sources."

"I suppose that's possible," said Captain Hailey. "During the war, when the government had its hands full, there's been all manner of smuggling into and out of New Orleans. As I understand it, there's a crime syndicate—a ring of criminals—in or around New Orleans, where a man with money can buy anything he wants, including murder."

"And Taylor Laird had money," said Sheriff Rowden. "My God, did he *ever* have it. From what Wills and his friends have told us, the outlaws who killed Laird not only took the gold they should have paid Laird for the whiskey, they cleaned out the safe as well. If Wills and his bunch hadn't taken Laird's steamboat and had just quietly buried Laird, they might have taken over this entire bootleg whiskey operation without anybody being the wiser."

"You can prosecute the six captives you have, then," said Captain Hailey.

"We can, and we will," Sheriff Rowden said. "I just want to ask a favor of you."

"Go ahead," said Captain Hailey.

"Indian Territory is considerably out of my jurisdiction," Rowden said, "and I'd be interested in knowing if, and when, you capture that bunch of outlaws who escaped with those four steamboats loaded with whiskey. That's a lot of rotgut, and all it can do is further fan the flames of hatred that already exist."

"I fully agree," said Captain Hailey. "There's a chance that we're about to bust up this particular band of Indian Territory outlaws. If and when it happens, I'll let you know."

Fort Smith. August 15, 1866.

Ed Stackler, dosed with whiskey, slept for most of three days. During that time, Wilder and Estrello avoided one another, except for exchanging occasional hostile looks. On the fourth day, Ed sat up. The tan-and-white hound was still there, and it was the first thing Ed saw when he opened his eyes.

"Somebody reach me a gun," he said. "That's the varmint that gave me away as I was hidin' from Wilder and his bunch."

"None of us have our guns," Todd said. "After you made a run for it, all our weapons were taken by Estrello."

"Damn," said Ed bitterly, "all I managed to do was get us in deeper. Now what in thunder can we do?"

"We haven't been able to come up with anything," Mark said. "Betsy managed to hide Jake's Colt, and there's five shells in it, but that's all we have going for us."

"Estrello and the others who were wounded on the steamboats are healed enough to ride," said Todd, "but I see Jackman and Wilder picked up wounds of their own tonight. Good shootin' in the dark, *amigo*."

"Not good enough," Ed said. "Good enough would have been to bore the varmints dead-center."

Conversation died, for Estrello was headed their way. For a moment he looked at Ed and then he spoke. "Tomorrow we leave for the Washita. I hope that meets with everybody's approval. Stackler, are you in shape to handle your teams?"

"I am," said Stackler, his hard eyes meeting those of the outlaw leader.

"*Bueno,*" Estrello said. "I'll count on you."

Chapter 12

Fort Smith. August 16, 1866.

During the night, the storm that had been threatening for several days broke, and by first light there was a virtual sea of mud.

"We ain't goin' nowhere in this," Estrello said. "We'll try again tomorrow."

But the rain continued all day and for the most part of the night.

"The rain will help us," Carl said. "Those of you who have been wounded will get a little more time to heal."

"I don't think I've ever seen so much rain in August," said Lee. "We may be stuck here for another week."

"That means the showdown will be delayed a few more days," Bill said. "Something may change in our favor by then."

"I wish I could believe that," said Betsy.

"Oh, let's look on the bright side," Nick said. "Ed got himself a dog."

"Ah, go to hell," Ed said.

But the tan-and-white animal had remained with them and, as added assurance that he wouldn't be driven away, had made friends with Amanda and Betsy.

Estrello waited two days after the rain had ended, then gave the order to move out. But the terrain was still hazardous and muddy. In the afternoon, Lee's wagon broke a rear axle, and the caravan traveled no farther that day. The following day, the left rear wheel of Ed's wagon slid into a leaf-filled, invisible hole, splintering the wheel.

"Damn it," Estrello raged. "We've had two major breakdowns in two days. You damn teamsters better start watchin' for holes and drop-offs."

"It's impossible to see through a pile of drifted leaves," said Ed. "Why don't you cut Wilder a brush broom and let him walk ahead of the wagons, brushing all those dead leaves out of the way?"

Estrello ignored the comment, but the others didn't. Some of the outlaws laughed, and Wilder was furious. He eyed Stackler as though measuring him for a coffin, and Stackler grinned at him. After two days on the trail, they hadn't traveled more than twenty miles, and on the third day, they found Indian sign in abundance.

"Unshod horses," Vernon said. "Must have been near a hundred."

"Wilder," said Estrello, "follow them a ways and see if they went on, or doubled back. It looks like they rode north, and I doubt they were headed for Fort Smith."

Wilder said nothing, doing as he was told. In two hours, he caught up to the wagons. "The varmints rode to the Arkansas and set up camp not far from where the steamboats docked," he said. "No squaws. Looks like a war party."

"How many of 'em?" Estrello asked.

"Could be a hundred, maybe more," said Wilder. "I couldn't get any closer."

"We know they're not here to attack Fort Smith," Estrello said, "so that leaves us."

Ed and his companions had heard the exchange, and Ed spoke. "This is the time to demand that Estrello return our weapons. If nobody else feels up to walking into the lion's den, then I will. We must defend ourselves."

"I'll do it," said Mark. "You've done more than your share."

Mark stalked down to the outlaws' main camp with a show of confidence he didn't feel. The outlaws saw him coming, and nobody said anything. Mark spoke to Estrello, ignoring all the others. "Estrello, we heard what Wilder told you about that party of Indians. I'm here to tell you we want our weapons back. If you're attacked, don't you think ten more guns might make a difference?"

"We'll take our chances," Wilder shouted. "You ain't gettin' 'em back. Not after Stackler shot me and Jackman."

Mark laughed. "Wilder, if somebody was out to kill you, wouldn't you shoot back?"

Some of the other outlaws laughed, for it was a telling point. Wilder's face went red.

Before he could respond, Estrello spoke. "We'll likely need all the guns we can get. Go ahead and take them. They're in the 'possum belly' under Stackler's wagon."

"No, by God," Wilder roared. "Arm that bunch, and before we're done, we'll end up on the business end of their guns."

"Wilder," said Estrello in a dangerously low voice, "you just looked in on what you claim was a hundred or more Indians. I'm concerned with us keeping our scalps, not your personal likes and dislikes."

"Hell, it wasn't you that Stackler shot," Wilder snarled. "He shot Jackman and me."

"Damn good shootin' in the dark," said Hedgepith.

Most of the other outlaws laughed, making Wilder all the

more angry. Spitefully, he shouted so that all could hear him. "How many of you think old Wolf's took leave of his senses, givin' back the guns to Stackler and that bunch?"

Suggs, Irvin, and Jackman sided with Wilder.

Estrello ignored them, and Mark headed for the wagon. Clemans, Keithley, Stackler, and Ursino joined him.

"It's times like this," Nick said, "when Estrello seems almost human."

"Don't get too soft on him," said Mark. "Before this is over, you may be face-to-face with him, his Colt spittin' lead."

As night approached, Estrello had something to say, and it was met with some mixed emotions. "Until this Indian threat is over, we're going to stand guard over the wagons. Half the outfit until midnight, the rest of it until dawn. The first watch begins at dusk." He pointed to Wilder, Mark, Bill, and ten others. "You're on the first watch until midnight. The rest of us will take over the second watch. Keep your eyes open, your guns loaded, and your mouths shut. There won't be a moon until late."

"I hate it, all of you being on the same watch with Wilder," said Betsy. "He could shoot one of you and blame it on the darkness."

"I think he's made it a little obvious he doesn't like any of us," Nick said. "It's to our advantage. If he starts taking shots are us, Estrello will know why."

"With Bill and Mark and the rest of us, and five of them on the first watch, there'll be enough of us to watch one another's back," Vernon said.

"There's a chance the Indians won't show up after dark," said Carl. "Some of the tribes are superstitious about fighting at night. With our luck the whole bunch is likely Comanches. They'll kill at midnight as readily as they will in the middle of the day."

Darkness crept in, bringing with it a few stars. Carl and Lee worked as a team, Vernon and Todd as a second, Nick and Ed as a third, while Mark and Bill made up a fourth. Of Estrello's men, there was Hiram, Odell, Hamby, Suggs, Wilder, and Irvin. The wagons had been half circled, with the circular side to the north to provide some protection for the defenders should the expected attack come from that direction. The teamsters stood watch over the first five wagons, while the six Estrello men took the last three. The moon had yet to rise, and the darkness seemed all the more intense when drifting clouds covered the faraway stars.

But there was no sign of the Indians during the first watch. Estrello and the rest of the outfit took over at midnight, while the first watch rolled into their blankets. Nothing seemed amiss until first light. Irvin and Suggs had taken it upon themselves to watch Nick's wagon, which was the last in line.

"I aim to take a look at my wagon," said Nick. "I wouldn't put it past Suggs and Irvin to tap one of the kegs and drink some of the stuff."

By the time Nick reached the wagon, he could smell raw whiskey. He loosened the rear canvas pucker, and all the barrels still had sealed lids. Finally, he looked under the wagon and saw the dribble of whiskey. The rest of the outfit was having breakfast when Nick got Estrello's attention.

"They got to us last night," Nick said. "You'd better have a look."

Estrello slammed down his tin cup and without a word headed for Nick's wagon. Nick hunkered down, pointing to the thin stream of escaping whiskey.

"Barrel may have sprung a leak," said Estrello.

"I doubt it," Nick said. "See those wood shavings on the ground? One of 'em managed to cut through the wagon box, and then through the bottom of one of the kegs."

"Hell's fire," shouted Estrello, "that would have taken him half the night. I want to know when this happened and who was responsible for watching this wagon."

"The moon rose late," Nick said, "and from the puddle beneath the wagon, I'd say the Indians did this before midnight."

Estrello said nothing, making his way back to the rest of the outlaws. His eyes roamed over them all, and finally he spoke. "Who had watch over that last wagon over yonder, during the first watch?"

"Irvin and me," said Suggs. "Why?"

"Because while you two were standing there jawing, an Indian got under the wagon and cut a hole all the way into a whiskey barrel. God knows how much whiskey he took, and the rest is being wasted on the ground."

"Ah, hell," Irvin said, "I don't believe that. I'll see for myself."

"So will I," said Suggs.

Estrello said nothing. The proof was undeniable, and when the two returned, he would give them hell, making of them an example for the other outlaws.

"Damn it," said Suggs, "it was black as the inside of a stovepipe last night. Couldn't see nothin'. Besides, how do you know it didn't happen on the second watch?"

"Too much whiskey's been wasted," Estrello said. "With that and what the Indian took, the barrel must be near empty. I want the two of you to get in the wagon, get to that leaking barrel, and set it out here. We'll plug the hole and save any whiskey that's left."

"Get us some help," said Irvin. "That's a hell of a lot of work for two men."

"Two men stood by and let it happen," Estrello said. "Now get started."

In silent fury the two outlaws began their task while Estrello watched. They had to remove four full barrels before they reached the leaking barrel.

"Move it down here upside-down," said Estrello.

When that had been done, Estrello cut off a piece of a dead pine limb as big as his thumb. With his knife he fashioned a wooden stopper that he drove into the hole where the barrel had been leaking. Using the butt of his Colt, he drove the stopper in as tightly as he could. From the wagon box he then took a small crowbar and pried the lid off the whiskey keg. They could see the bottom of the keg, for there wasn't more than a gallon or two of the murky liquid remaining.

"Nail something over that hole in the bed of the wagon," Estrello ordered, "and then reload the four barrels you took out. Bring that near empty one with you. I want all the others to see what happens when a man on watch is doin' something else."

Aware that their ordeal wasn't over, the furious duo began wrestling the heavy kegs of whiskey back into the wagon. Finished, they leaned on the wagon's tailgate, trying to catch their wind.

"He still can't be sure that happened on our watch," Suggs said.

"Ah, hell," said Irvin, "he's right. There's too much whiskey gone through that little hole. It had to drip for most of the night, and we don't know how much the Indian got."

Seizing the nearly empty keg, they took it with them. Some of the outlaws who didn't particularly like either man were grinning. Estrello looked grim.

"I want every man of you to look in there," Estrello ordered. "Stackler, that includes you and your bunch."

Estrello removed the keg's lid, waiting for them all to file past the keg for a look. Ed and his companions waited until the rest of the men had finished.

"Stackler," said Wilder, "how could that damn dog of yours allow an Indian to sneak in that close? Where was the varmint when he could have been useful?"

"Likely tryin' to catch himself somethin' to eat," Ed said. "So what? It was Suggs and Irvin who had guns and were supposed to be watching that wagon."

"He's dead right," said Estrello. "Tonight, Tilden and Worsham will move to the first watch, while Suggs and Irvin go to the second with me. Let down your guard for just one minute, and I'll be watching. If this happens again, whoever's responsible can saddle up and ride out. That is, if I don't kill him first."

None of the outlaws were smiling, for the ultimatum had been directed at them all. Not until Bill, Mark, and their companions returned to their camp did any of them speak.

"The Indian couldn't have taken much whiskey," said Betsy. "The rest just leaked out."

"That the Indian took any whiskey at all is bad news," Mark said. "Now they know what these wagons are loaded with, and they won't be satisfied sneaking around in the dark, stealing a little at a time."

Mark's prophecy came to pass before the end of the day. The wagons had moved on, covering maybe twelve miles, and the wary outfit stopped for the night an hour before sundown.

"Here come the Indians!" one of the outlaws suddenly shouted.

The outlaws seized their Winchesters. Mark, Bill, and

their companions made no hostile moves, for the Indians were headed for the main camp, where Estrello waited.

"That looks like some of the same Indians Estrello's been selling to," said Amanda. "The big Indian with the crooked nose is Broken Nose. He's always managed to get a keg of whiskey for his own use. We may not get to the Washita. Estrello may have to sell to them right here."

"I don't see any packhorses of pelts and no horses or mules to trade," Bill said. "It's possible they aim to just take the whiskey without paying."

"My God," said Vernon, "there's enough of them to kill us all ten times over. If they decide to fight, are we siding Estrello and his bunch?"

"We'll have no choice," Ed said. "They've seen us on the wagon boxes, and as far as they're concerned, we're part of the Estrello gang."

The horde of Indians separated. Twenty or more of them paused within a few yards of Mark, Bill, and their companions. The larger body rode on, coming face-to-face with Estrello and the rest of the gang. Estrello said nothing, waiting. Broken Nose spoke.

"Want whiskey."

"The whiskey's for sale when we reach the Washita," said Estrello.

"Want whiskey now," Broken Nose said.

"Sell whiskey for pelts, horses, and mules on Washita," said Estrello.

"No pelt, no horse, no mule," Broken Nose said. "Want whiskey now."

Broken Nose wore a single feather in his hair, and suddenly, when a Colt roared, the feather disappeared. Quick as a cat, Estrello moved, smashing his fist into Wilder's snarling face. Wilder went down, dropping the Colt. Broken

Nose and his companions had not moved. The Indian spoke again, this time more demanding.

"Want Whiskey. You give."

"No," said Estrello. "We sell whiskey at the Washita."

Broken Nose wheeled his horse and rode toward the west, his companions following.

"Now what?" Hiram wondered.

"We get ready for a fight," said Estrello. "Some of those Indians are the same ones who have been buying from us on the Washita. What the hell's happened to them?"

"They're actin' like they know that this is the last of the whiskey," Schorp said.

Wilder sat up, rubbing his jaw.

"You hotheaded son-of-a-bitch, I should shoot you," Estrello said. "Next time, I will."

"We'll have to fight anyway," said Wilder, "unless you aim to give 'em the whiskey."

"We may have to fight," Estrello said, "but only a damn fool hurries it up."

"For a minute, there, I thought all of us were dead," said Todd.

"We would have been, but for one thing," Nick said. "Indians want an edge, to strike when they're least expected. They didn't like the odds."

"Nick's right," said Ed. "They're more likely to jump us on the trail at first light, or near sundown, when we're give out."

"Do we just wait on them to come after us?" Betsy asked.

"If I had any choice, I wouldn't," said Vernon.

"Neither would I," Mark said. "They left a trail we can follow in the dark. Our only hope is to get them before they get us."

"Kill them all?" asked Amanda.

"No," Mark said. "An attack against such numbers would be foolish. The Comanches once trapped a few Texans, including me. We didn't have a chance, but during the night, we found that Comanche camp and scattered their horses to hell and gone. While the whole lot of them was afoot, looking for their horses, we saddled up and got the hell out of there."

"It makes sense to me," said Ed, "but do you aim to suggest it to Estrello? The less trouble we have, and the sooner we reach the Washita, the sooner this bunch will cut our string."

"We may have to," Mark said, "to save our own hides. Trouble is, if we stampede the horses, leaving that many Indians afoot, can we make it to the Washita before they find their mounts and come after us?"

"I have my doubts," said Lee. "We've been on the trail three days, and I doubt we've covered more than ten miles a day. If we take their horses, we'll really give this bunch somethin' to fight about, once they catch up to us."

"It's a risk we'll have to take," Mark said. "We can't save ourselves without saving the rest of these varmints. I'll talk to Estrello."

They watched Mark approach the band of outlaws.

"Estrello," said Mark, "I need to talk to you in private."

An uproar of shouting and cursing erupted among the outlaws, but Estrello ignored them. He nodded in agreement, following Mark toward the wagons. Quickly, Mark told the outlaw leader of his plan to leave the Indians afoot.

"I like that," Estrello said. "If it comes to a fight, we're finished. Have you done this before?"

"Once, in Texas," said Mark. "The trick is to run their horses far enough for us to be well out of their reach before they find their mounts. There's just one big problem. They'll know you're going to the Washita, and we can't run their horses far enough to avoid having them get there ahead of us. Of these particular Indians, how many of them have been buying from you?"

"A few," said Estrello cautiously.

"We're going to have to trail them, find where they're camped, and then stampede their horses," Mark said, "and we'll have to do it tonight."

"By God, you're mighty concerned with my well-being," said Estrello.

"I'm concerned about me, my woman, and my friends," Mark said. "I'll help you to save them. If we're forced into a fight with that many Indians, some of us will die."

"I reckon that makes sense," said Estrello. "How many men?"

"As many as you'll send, as well as me and my friends," Mark said.

"I'm leaving some of my men with the wagons," said Estrello, "and just so you don't get any ideas beyond chasing Indians, your women will stay here, too."

"Then get your outfit saddled and let's ride," Mark said.

Estrello left nine of his men with the wagons.

"Amanda," said Mark, "you and Betsy stay near the wagons, and keep your guns close. Stay away from those men Estrello is leaving here."

"Do be careful," Betsy cried.

Estrello led out, and there was no difficulty following the trail the Indians had left. The moon had risen early, and the purple sky was a profusion of silver stars. Directly behind Estrello's group rode Carl, Lee, Vernon, Todd, Nick, and Ed, led by Bill and Mark. Nobody spoke. There was only the steady thump of horses' hooves. Finally, when they stopped to rest the animals, Estrello dropped back to talk to Mark.

"Rogers, you say you've done this before. From here on, take the lead. You'd better not be leadin' us into a fight we can't win."

They were riding westward into Indian Territory, the night wind in their faces, and at the smell of wood smoke, Mark reined up, raising his hand. The rest of the riders reined up behind him, dismounting when he did.

"We'll have to go on foot the rest of the way," Mark said, "but first we must know how their camp is laid out and where the horses are. I'll take one man with me."

"Then I'll go," said Estrello.

"I'd prefer Clemans or Ursino," Mark said.

"Damn it, *I said I'm going*," said Estrello.

"Suit yourself," Mark said.

They crept along on foot until the smell of wood smoke grew stronger. Slowly, they made their way through a heavy stand of trees to the crest of a ridge. Below them, in a canyon and along a stream, was the Indian camp.

"By God," grunted Estrello, "it's a box canyon, with the horses at the boxed end, and all them damn Indians fencin' 'em in. We can't stampede them horses unless we're behind them."

"Then we'll have to get behind them," said Mark. "We're going to look at the boxed end of this canyon and find a way down. Then we can stampede their horses right through the camp."

Estrello said nothing as they followed the ridge, carefully keeping below the skyline. A stream flowed out of solid rock at the boxed end of the canyon, and even in the dim light from the moon and stars, it appeared there was no possible way to take horses down the slope.

"That damn canyon wall is solid rock and near straight up," said Estrello. "They ain't no way you can get a horse down that."

"I don't aim to take horses down there," Mark said. "I aim to take seven men with me, and we're going in afoot. After we've stampeded the horses, I want you and the rest of the men mounted, near the open end of this canyon. When those Indian horses pour out, I want all of you behind them, yelling and shooting like hell wouldn't have it. I want those horses run a good fifty miles from here. *Comprehende?*"

"Yeah," said Estrello, "but my men ain't likely to take to the idea of goin' afoot among that many Indians."

"I've decided who's going with me," Mark said. "Long, Sullivan, Clemans, Keithley, Ursino, Stackler, and Harder. I want the rest of you near the open end of that canyon. The success of this whole thing depends on how far all of you are able to stampede those horses, once we start 'em running."

"I can't figure you out, Rogers," said Estrello. "You and your friends are goin' into an Indian camp afoot, leavin' me and my boys mounted."

"That's it." Mark said. "I want you and your men down there at the lower end of that canyon, and I don't want so much as a whisper out of any of you. If anybody lights a smoke, and the Indians don't kill him, I will."

"Where you goin' now?" Estrello asked.

"Back after my *amigos*. By the time we return, the moon should have set, which will suit our purpose," said Mark.

"I'll take the rest of my men down canyon to wait for the stampede," Estrello said, "but don't get any ideas about a double cross."

"That's the trouble with being a lyin', cheatin', murderin' varmint," said Mark with as much venom as he was capable of. "You can't trust anybody else to keep his word."

"There's something damned strange about you and your bunch taking all the risk, just to save us and my wagonloads of whiskey," Estrello said. "My boys ain't gonna like this."

"Then, by God, send your boys into that box canyon to stampede those horses. I'll be glad to just back off and let you handle it any way you damn please," said Mark.

"No," Estrello said. "Do it like you got it planned. I'll take the other nine *hombres* to the lower end of the canyon to wait for you and your bunch to stampede the horses."

They reached the picketed horses and Estrello quickly explained the plan.

"Rogers, Harder, and their few friends ain't been nothin' but trouble, ever since we left the Washita," said Suggs, "and now you're puttin' everything in their hands. Damn it, I don't like it."

"The trouble with you and a few of the others, Suggs, is that you let your likes and dislikes get in the way of common sense. Somebody's *got* to get down that canyon wall and stampede those Indian horses. I'm ready to back off and let you and your stubborn *amigos* handle this the best way you can," Mark said angrily.

"Suggs," said Estrello, "he's speakin' the truth. If that whole damn bunch of Indians is able to come after us, we're dead men. So is Rogers and his *compadres*. Now unless you and seven others want to do what Rogers and his *amigos* aim to do, then just shut the hell up. I want all of you at the lower end of this canyon when we return with the other men. Hide your horses well away from the canyon mouth, and keep them there until we get back to you."

"No noise, no smoking, and no talking," Mark said.

"Pay attention to him," said Estrello. "Spoil this, any one of you, and I'll personally peel your hide off, a strip at a time."

Mark mounted up, riding back the way they had come. Estrello and the nine men who had come with him mounted their horses and began a roundabout ride toward the open end of the canyon.

Chapter 13

Mark rode back to where his companions still waited with their horses. Quickly, he told them of his plan.

"It's as good a plan as we're likely to come up with," Ed said. "That is, if Estrello and his bunch can keep the stampede going."

"They'd damn well better," said Mark, "or we'll be trapped in that canyon with a passel of screaming Indians after our scalps."

"Tell me Estrello and his bunch didn't take our horses with them," Bill said.

"They didn't," said Mark. "Our horses are where we left them before Estrello and me went looking for the Indian camp."

"We can't take the horses down the canyon wall, and if we could, they couldn't climb out again," Carl said. "How do *we* get out of that canyon? With that many Indians, some of them may grab a horse, even as they're stampeded."

"We'll take our horses well beyond the mouth of the canyon, where they'll be well out of the way of the stampede. We'll picket them there. When we're down the canyon wall, we'll each take an Indian pony and begin the stampede. After the horses are free of the canyon, we'll ride back and get our own horses, leaving Estrello and his bunch to keep the stampede going."

"What about the Indian ponies we'll be riding?" Lee asked. "We can't just turn them loose. The Indians could use them to help gather the others."

"We'll take the Indian ponies back to camp with us," said Mark. "Any more questions before we head for the canyon?"

There were none. Mark led out, his companions following. They left their horses not far from where Estrello and his men waited. From there, it was a mile or more back to the boxed end of the canyon, and they had to walk.

"I don't mind facin' a hundred or so kill-crazy Indians," Ed said, "but walkin' in these boots could be the death of me."

They reached the boxed end of the canyon, Mark taking the lead, each man bringing the lariat from his saddle. Mark held up his hand, and his companions halted. He would make the ascent first. Finding a large pinnacle of stone that he judged strong enough, Mark secured one end of his lariat to it. Carl, Lee, Vernon, and Todd passed him their lariats. He judged them more than long enough to reach the canyon floor below. The fires within the Indian camp had burned down to coals, and the occasional wind stirred a spark or two. Mark hitched up his gun belt, pulled his hat a bit lower, and started down. His feet against the rocky canyon wall, hanging on to the extended lariats, he "walked" down. Bill followed, and within minutes all eight men were on the floor of the canyon. Water fell from a head-high crevice in the wall, helping to conceal any sound. Some of the horses had ceased grazing, and the eight men waited for the animals to settle down. When they did, Mark quickly got his arm around the neck of a bay. He held the animal steady until his companions had captured mounts. At his signal, each

of them mounted, bareback, drew their Colts, and began firing over the heads of the remaining horses. The herd broke
into a fast gallop, the eight riders right behind them. Some
of the sleeping Indians barely escaped the thundering hooves,
while some of them were able to catch a horse on the run.
Mark shot two mounted Indians off their horses. His companions followed his lead, and finally the horses had run
through the Indian camp, and there were no more mounted
Indians. By the time some of the Indians got their rifles,
the range was too great and the sky was dark with gathering clouds. Some Indians fired arrows or threw lances, all
of which fell short. When the herd of Indian horses was
out of the canyon, nine more riders swept in behind them.
Mark and his companions cut out of the canyon and back
along the rim, far enough from the edge that the Indians
couldn't see or hear them. Estrello and his men kept up
the firing until Mark and his companions could hear it no
longer.

"They've given up the chase, or they're too far away for
us to hear the shooting," said Ed.

But all the Indians, seeing the futility of it, hadn't taken
part in the chase. Suddenly, out of the dark, a brawny arm
was around Mark's throat, and he could see his companions
engaged in similar struggles. The Indians had discovered
the rope! Mark's adversary tried to throw him over the canyon rim, but Mark tore himself free and threw the Indian
over, instead. Slowly, the eight men got the best of their opponents, several of whom were thrown over the canyon rim.
The others were simply knocked senseless with the muzzle
of a Colt. There was no shooting. Quickly, Mark hauled up
the knotted lariats, and mounting their bare back Indian
ponies, the eight men returned to their own horses. Each

leading a captured horse on a lead rope, they set out for the wagons.

"Was anybody hurt?" Amanda and Betsy cried, running to meet them.

"Some Indians, as far as we know," said Mark. "Estrello and some of his bunch are stampeding the horses. If they got hurt, it's their own fault."

It didn't take long to stir the interest of the outlaws Estrello had left behind.

"Where's the rest of our outfit?" Wilder demanded.

"They're busy," Mark said.

He told them nothing more. The riders hobbled the captured Indian horses, leaving them to graze.

Estrello and the rest of his outfit didn't return for another two hours. Estrello made it a point to speak to Mark. "By God, Rogers, it worked. We run them horses until our own was give out. I got to give you credit."

"Before you get too excited," said Mark, "you'd better assign a heavy watch. It may be too far for those Indians to find their own horses tonight, but their camp's not that far from ours. They could sneak in and rustle our stock, including the mules."

"It ain't but six hours until dawn," Estrello said. "Wilder, choose a dozen men and take the first three hours. I'll pick some men to join me for the second watch."

To Mark's surprise, he and none of his companions were chosen for either watch.

"Old Wolf seems to be softening up some," Amanda said. "This is one of the few times he hasn't put all of you on watch."

"I think this is for the sake of his outfit," said Vernon. "He doesn't want his bunch to get the idea he's all that dependent on us. We've already cleared out the Indians with very little help from him. Once we stampeded that herd, a bunch of schoolgirls could have kept it running."

"Don't say that loud enough for Estrello or any of his outfit to hear it," Nick said. "Let them think they might find us useful again."

"Not against those Indians," said Mark. "They're not fools. That trick won't work for us again. When they finally catch up their horses, you can bet they'll have sentries watching over the herd every night."

During what remained of the night, Amanda and Betsy slept beside Mark and Bill. Not far away, a lonely cry drifted across the stillness.

"That's the first coyote I've heard in a long time," Amanda said, sitting up.

"That's no coyote," said Mark. "Listen when it comes again. Listen for the echo."

The cry came again, trailing off mournfully.

"Yes, I heard the echo," Amanda said. "What does it mean?"

"It means you've just heard an Indian making like a coyote," Mark said. "A coyote's cry won't echo, but the human voice will."

"Lord," Betsy said, "does that mean they're ready to come after us? Could they have found their horses so soon?"

"I doubt they'll find their horses for several days," said Bill, "but we can't be sure. I just hope the *hombres* Estrello's got on watch keep their eyes and ears open. It's like Mark told Estrello. It wouldn't be a bit unusual for the Indians to sneak into our own camp, taking enough horses and mules to round up their own mounts."

Indian Territory. August 20, 1866.

But the remainder of the night was quiet, and Estrello had the outfit harnessing the teams, following a hurried breakfast.

"Those Indians know where we're bound," said Vernon. "That leaves us wide open for an ambush."

"Again we're at Estrello's mercy," Mark said. "We'll be strung out in the wagons and can be picked off one at a time. Somebody should be scouting ahead, looking for Indian sign every day. If they're able to take us by surprise, we'll be wiped out."

"It's terrible," said Amanda. "To save ourselves from Indians, we also have to save all these thieves and killers."

"There'll come a time when there's nothing any of us can do," Ed said. "These Indians know we're bound for the Washita, and there have been as many as four or five hundred there to buy whiskey. All they have to do is join forces with the hundred or so who are after us now, and we're all dead."

"Maybe the others won't try to take the whiskey without paying," said Betsy.

"I'm afraid they'll all be of the same mind," Todd said. "This bunch after us now just got a little impatient. I don't doubt they've had an eye on us since the whiskey was unloaded from the steamboats."

When the teams were harnessed, the caravan moved out, heading west.

"I had hoped Estrello would be smarter than this," said Bill.

"He hasn't had that much Indian trouble," Betsy said. "He's counted on the whiskey to keep him on good terms with the renegades, and up to now, it has."

"He can't depend on that anymore," said Bill. "With this

bunch of Indians ready to kill us and take the whiskey, why wouldn't the rest of them be of the same mind?"

"I'm afraid they will be," Betsy said, "and if the rest of them are waiting for us at the Washita, I fear what's going to happen."

Amanda had taken her usual place beside Mark on the wagon box, and it was a while before either of them spoke.

"I hate for you to do anything more to help this bunch of outlaws," Amanda said, "but do you suppose, for our sake, you should tell Estrello he needs a man scouting ahead for Indian sign?"

Mark sighed. "I reckon I'll have to. Trouble is, Estrello will send some coyote such as Wilder, who may or may not be capable of reading sign."

Eventually, when they stopped to rest the teams, Mark approached Estrello.

"You ought to have a scout riding ahead, looking for Indian sign," said Mark.

"Yeah?" Estrello said. "You really think that bunch will have caught their horses by now? Hell, we chased 'em a good fifty miles."

"That's just one group of Indians," said Mark. "You have no idea where the others are, or what they might do. I can promise you one thing: Word of what we did last night will spread, and whiskey or not, our scalps won't be safe anywhere in the Territory."

"Maybe you're right," Estrello conceded. "Tomorrow I'll send a rider ahead with an eye for Indian sign."

But tomorrow would be too late. Shortly after midnight the Indians struck. Not for the purpose of killing, but to stampede the horses and mules. The first warning they had was a spine-chilling war whoop, echoed many times by other warriors. Horses nickered in terror, mules brayed, and at least half the animals stampeded to the west. Suddenly, all was quiet, as the thunder of hooves died away.

"Anybody hurt?" Estrello shouted.

There was no answer, except a bitter laugh from Wilder. "Hell, we're more than hurt. They just give us a dose of our own medicine. We likely don't have enough mules left to draw even one or two wagons. Now they can come back whenever they damn please and finish us."

"Estrello," Mark said, "you didn't stampede those horses far enough. They all likely started drifting back toward that Indian camp. We gained only one day."

"Damn it, we run them horses a good fifty miles," said Estrello. "Your plan just didn't work, that's all."

"Then I'll let you decide how you aim to gather those horses and mules," Mark said. "Vernon and Nick are taking a count to see how many we've lost."

Vernon and Nick had grim news. "They stampeded all the mules except five," said Vernon. "Our horses—including those eight we brought back from the Indian camp—were picketed and didn't run. Most of the rest of them—loose and grazing—are gone. There's only ten of those horses."

"Wouldn't make no difference if we had a hundred horses," Irvin said. "We'll never find our horses and mules in the dark, and come first light, the Indians will round 'em up."

"Not if we round 'em up first," said Estrello. "Every one of you who still has a horse, saddle up. There's a moon, and before moonset, we'll gather as many of our animals as we can."

"That's a damn fool idea, Estrello," Wilder said.

"Maybe," said Estrello through gritted teeth, "but unless you can come up with something better, we'll go with it."

Bill, Mark, and their teamster companions saddled up,

Mark taking one of the eight horses they had ridden from the Indian camp the night before.

"There's eighteen horses left," Estrello said. "Saddle up as I call your names." He mentioned seventeen names. "You'll be riding with me. The rest of you will remain here with the wagons."

"Do be careful," Betsy warned. "They may be expecting you."

Mark, Bill, and their companions allowed Estrello and his men to take the lead. They then rode out—eighteen strong—toward the west, the direction in which the stampede had gone.

"Just like the varmints to stampede 'em into Indian Territory," Suggs growled. "It'll be hard as hell to see anything in the shadows of the trees."

Warily, they rode on, and not more than three miles distant, they heard shuffling in the dead leaves and brush. They reined up, waiting. In a patch of moonlight two mules appeared.

"Hiram, Odell," said Estrello, "catch and hobble them. Then we'll go looking for the rest of them."

That proved more difficult than they had hoped. They rode almost five miles before finding several of the horses and another mule.

"We'll never get them all before first light," Shadley said.

"Yeah," said Wilder, "and in daylight, we'll likely get ambushed by them Indians."

"Rogers," Estrello said, "do you have any ideas?"

"Why would you want another of my ideas?" Mark asked. "You didn't halfway live up to the last one."

"Try me again," said Estrello. "We have to have those mules and horses."

"You'll find them at the Indian camp," Mark said. "The

five animals we've found were lost along the way. The Indians took the rest of them, so we couldn't round them up."

"They'll all be expecting us to come after our horses and mules," said Bill, "so there'll be a heavy guard. Waiting for the first light will cost us our scalps."

"You're sayin' we should go after 'em tonight at the Indian camp?" Estrello asked.

"I am," said Mark.

"So am I," Bill said.

"I see the sense of it," said Estrello, "but they won't fall for that stampede a second time."

"Nobody said anything about another stampede," Mark said. "This time, we'll have to attack the camp itself, shooting to kill. If the horses and mules scatter, then so be it, but we have to end this Indian threat before we go looking for our livestock."

"There's twenty-six of us," said Estrello. "You'd have us attack a hundred or more Indians?"

"Hell's fire," Suggs growled, "we'll be out-numbered more'n five to one."

"If we set here until they jump on us," said Clemans, "they'll *still* outnumber us. We got to do as Mark suggests, and move first, if we're to have a chance."

"Wolf," Wilder said, "why don't you just step aside and let Rogers run the show entirely? He's got all the answers."

"Wilder," said Mark, "I don't claim to have all the answers, but I have some of them. Bill and me fought Comanches in Texas since we were twelve years old. All you've done is look down your damn nose and criticize. Unless you have something worth bein' heard, back off and shut up."

"I'll second that," Hiram said. "Rogers told it straight when we stampeded them Indian horses. We just didn't run 'em far enough."

"I judged it was plenty far enough," said Estrello angrily.

"You judged wrong," Mark said, "or these Indians giving us hell would still be afoot, looking for their horses."

"Rogers was right about the stampede, like it or not," said Estrello. "Why not give him his head and see what he can do this time? Remember, if you don't like his plan, then before you disagree, you'd best have a better one."

"Yeah, let Rogers do it," Irvin said. "I want to watch him round up the horses and mules in the dark."

"You'll have a long wait, Irvin," said Mark. "We'll gather our stock in the daylight. Tonight we must find that Indian camp and eliminate as much of that threat as we can. It's a favorite Indian trick to stampede the horses and then pick us off one or two at a time while we're rounding 'em up."

"Then let's go looking for that damn Indian camp," Estrello said. "It ain't that long till first light."

"With most of us gone, it'd be a good time for them to come back for the whiskey," said Patton.

"No, they won't," Stackler said. "The next move is ours. They're expecting us to try to avoid a fight because of their greater numbers. Then when we begin looking for our stock, they'll ambush us two or three at a time, just like Mark said. When there's no way out of a fight, choose your own ground and your own time."

The twenty-six of them rode west, the way the stock had stampeded. This time, Mark took the lead, the others following. After riding some ten miles, they stopped to rest their horses.

"Mark's dead right, so far," said Ursino. "We've seen no horses or mules, reason enough to believe they've either scattered them all over creation, or driven them on to their camp. The three or four animals we found just managed to break away while they were being driven."

"One thing in our favor," Hiram said. "We're ridin' into the wind, and there's less chance of us stumbling into them before we know they're there."

"It's too late at night for a fire," said Bill, "so there won't be any smoke to guide us this time."

The first warning they had was the distant braying of a mule. Mark reined up, speaking barely above a whisper.

"We'll leave the horses here, and some of us will go ahead on foot. We'll need a look at their camp. Bill, you come with me. The rest of you wait with the horses. Be watchful—they may have scouts circling the camp."

Mark and Bill crept carefully on. Suddenly, a pair of shadows came at them, the light of twinkling stars reflecting off the knives in the upraised hands of the enemy. As they had learned long ago in Texas, Bill and Mark each seized the wrist of the hand wielding the knife and fought for possession of it. Slowly but surely, the Texans forced their opponents to release the weapons, which they then used to silence their foes.

"By the Eternal," said Bill, "I hope we're not close enough for the rest of them to have heard us. Better wait a minute."

They waited, holding their breath, but there was no sign the scuffle had been heard. Cautiously, they moved on, pausing when they heard a horse nicker. The camp was close, their danger great, but they had to know what kind of situation they were facing. Again one of the horses nickered, and Bill paused, his hand on Mark's arm.

"There's some of 'em in with the horses and mules," Bill whispered. "That's our horses and mules, and the Indians are spooking them."

"Let's get a little closer," said Mark softly. "We need to know where their camp is in relation to the horses and mules. They'll stampede when we attack, and we want them to run back toward the wagons if possible."

It was a bold move, for if the horses and mules ran west—deeper into the Territory—they would be all the more difficult to gather. Some of them might never be seen again. Suddenly, a horse nickered only a few feet away, and there were soothing voices as Indians tried to calm the animals. Of a single mind, Bill and Mark turned and went back the way they had come. They dared not go any closer. Reaching the place where they had left the two dead Indians, they froze. The bodies were gone! Before they could make a move, they were surrounded by seven Indians, all armed with lances and three of them with Winchesters. Bill and Mark were forced around the grazing horses and mules, on into the Indian camp. Surprisingly, although there was no fire, the camp seemed alive with activity, a virtual certainty the Indians planned an attack at dawn. Bill and Mark had their weapons taken, their wrists and ankles bound with rawhide, and were then shoved facedown.

"The only question is, will they kill us before or after they attack the wagons," Bill said.

"Before, unless a miracle takes place," said Mark. "I don't expect one out of Estrello or any of his bunch, but we have six *amigos* out there who'll help us if there's any way."

"Damn it," Estrello hissed, "they've been gone plenty long enough to have been back. Some of us had best go looking for 'em."

"No," said Keithley. "They may have been captured, and if they have, the Indians will set a trap for the rest of us. Let's get back to the horses and decide what to do."

When they reached the picketed horses, it was Clemans

who spoke. "I think the horses and mules are on this side of the Indian camp, under a considerable guard. That means Bill and Mark have likely been captured, and there's a good chance they won't live past first light unless we make our move before then."

"Hell, they're dead men any way we go at it," Wilder said. "They'll use them to suck in the rest of us. While we're settin' here on our hunkers, Harder and Rogers may already be dead, and this bunch of Indians may attack the wagons at first light. We ain't doin' no good here."

"All of you who feel that way, mount up and ride," said Ed. "Me, I aim to do what I can to save them."

"So do I," Nick said. "They'd do it for us."

Quickly, Todd, Vernon, Lee, and Carl made similar vows.

"Way I see it," said Estrello, "if Harder and Rogers are alive or dead, these Indians are still plannin' to attack the wagons, probably at dawn. If we aim to do anything on our own, we'd best be decidin' what and when."

"From the sound of horses and mules," Carl said, "the livestock is between us and the Indian camp. When we attack, that'll stampede the horses and mules again. Unless we want to drive them deeper into Indian Territory, we'll have to circle around and attack from the west."

"Then let's ride," said Estrello. "Couple of you bring the horses belongin' to Harder and Rogers."

The twenty-four men rode several miles wide of the Indian camp, approaching it from the west. They dismounted, listening. They were now downwind from the Indian camp, and the slightest noise could easily be heard.

"Some of us still have to get close enough to learn if Bill and Mark are alive," said Nick. "If they are, we can't just ride in shooting."

"Even if they're alive," Wilder said, "there won't be a hell of a lot we can do for 'em."

"Maybe not," Nick said, "but I aim to try."

"I'm going with you," said Vernon. "The rest of you wait here. Give us half an hour."

"That's all," Estrello said. "If they aim to hit the wagons at first light, we can't spend any more time here."

Leaving their horses, Nick and Vernon crept through the brush. The first light of the approaching dawn had already grayed the eastern sky. From a thicket Nick and Vernon were finally able to see part of the Indian camp, and what they saw made their blood run cold. Bill and Mark were tied to a pine tree, back-to-back, and even as Nick and Vernon watched, Indians were piling brush around the base of the tree.

"Let's go," said Vernon. "We don't have much time."

Estrello and his men waited expectantly.

"Bill and Mark are alive, about to be burned at the stake," Vernon said.

"What do you aim to do about it?" Estrello asked.

"Vernon and me aim to cut 'em loose," said Nick. "All of you have your Winchesters. Go in shooting and make every shot count. Once you're through the Indian camp, drive the horses and mules ahead of you. We'll lead our horses as far as we can."

The men set out for the Indian camp, working their way slowly through a concealing thicket. When they could see the camp, a fire had been started, and from it a pair of Indians were preparing torches for the captives tied to the tree.

"Mount up," Nick said. "Shoot fast and straight."

"Don't give up, pards," said Ed, "Texas is comin' after you."

With piercing Rebel yells, they galloped their horses toward the Indian camp, firing as they rode. Nick and Vernon had knives in their hands as they leaped from their saddles.

Chapter 14

Aware that they were about to lose their captives, the Indians directed most of their fire toward Nick and Vernon, allowing their companions to unleash a withering fire with their Winchesters. Nick went down, an Indian arrow through his left thigh, and on hands and knees, he reached Bill. He slashed the bonds that secured Bill, who helped him to his feet. Unwounded, Vernon cut Mark free, and Mark paused.

"Our Colts!" Mark shouted.

Their gun belts had been placed on a blanket, and despite the danger, Mark seized them before leaping up behind Vernon's saddle. Bill had helped Nick up first, then swung up ahead of him. Estrello's bunch had unleashed a devastating fire, and the Indians could no longer concentrate on the escaping captives. Hedgepith was flung from his horse, an Indian lance driven through his middle. Kendrick was struck twice in the back by arrows, and then took a Winchester slug through the chest. The mules and horses, spooked by all hell having busted loose, were off and running, taking with them most of the horses belonging to the Indians, as well. Soon the desperate riders were out of range, and had to

slow their horses. But the stampeded animals had calmed
down and some were attempting to graze.

"Get those horses and mules running again," Mark shouted.

Finally, after half a dozen miles, Mark reined up, waiting
till the others caught up to him before he spoke. "Those of
you who are wounded, go on back to camp and have your
wounds tended. The rest of us are going to make it damned
hard for this bunch of Indians to round up their mounts this
time."

Besides Nick, two of Estrello's gang had been wounded.
Tilden had been struck a glancing blow by a lance, and the
entire left side of his shirt was bloody. Wilder had been shot
in the right shoulder. Nick had to be helped to mount one of
the saddleless horses. He then followed the two wounded
Estrello men back toward camp. Having kept the horses moving for what Mark judged was twenty miles, he reined up.

"This ain't far enough," Estrello said.

"We're not done with them," said Mark. "We're going to
cut out our own horses and mules, and you can drive them
back to camp. Bill and me are going to take these Indian
horses far enough to keep this bunch afoot for a week."

"By God, see that you do," Estrello said. "I lost two good
men, thanks to you and Harder gettin' yourselves caught."

"You'd have lost a lot more than that if you'd waited for
them to attack us," Ed said.

Most of the men were quiet, having looked death in the
face and survived. Quickly, the riders separated their own
stock from the Indian horses. Bill and Mark recovered their
own mounts, and Nick's saddled horse was among those
being driven back to camp. When only the Indian horses remained, Bill and Mark continued driving them to the north-
east, toward Fort Smith.

"You know, there ain't more than fifty horses here," Bill

said. "Is that all the Indians there was in that camp, or did we miss some of the horses?"

"I think this was an entirely different bunch of Indians," said Mark. "A smaller band. I believe we might have unfairly criticized Estrello for not having run the horses far enough. We've overlooked the fact that we're back in Indian Territory, and that all Indians don't ride together. The bunch whose horses were scattered night before last are likely still out looking for them."

"You're right about that," Bill said. "That means we still have two hundred miles from here to the Washita, and if we live long enough to get there, we'll still have to face all of Estrello's four or five hundred Indians come to buy whiskey."

"Unless it's Broken Nose and his bunch," said Mark. "If they still got it in their heads to just take the whiskey, it'll all be over for us."

"If I had anything to say about it, I'd just let them have the damn whiskey in return for 'em leaving us alone," Bill said. "Estrello's on the prod because he lost two men coming to our rescue, yet he'll risk everybody's lives to save those loads of rotgut whiskey."

Bill and Mark continued driving the stampeded Indian horses until the sun was well past noon high.

"I'd say we've brought them sixty miles," said Mark.

"At least that far," Bill agreed. "There's a possibility we're overlooking. We must have killed at least a dozen of them, and that's enough to convince an Indian he's having a bad medicine day. They may just go after their horses and leave us be."

"That would be great," said Mark. "It's gonna be hell if we have to fight Indians all the way to the Washita, and then come face-to-face with Broken Nose and four or five hundred of his bunch."

Judging that the Indian ponies had been driven far enough, Bill and Mark rode west to their camp. The wounded had been seen to. Nick had a bandage on his thigh. Wilder had his shoulder bandaged, while Tilden had a bandage around his middle.

"I reckon you run them ponies far enough this time," said Estrello.

"We figured sixty miles," Mark said, "but there was one thing that didn't look right to us. There were only about fifty of those Indian ponies, and I don't think we lost more than three or four—if that many—in the stampede."

"Hell's fire," Estrello fairly shouted, "you're sayin' this ain't the same bunch of Indians whose horses we stampeded the night before last. I never had this kind of trouble in the Territory before."

"You've got it now," said Mark. "We may have to fight every damn horde of Indians between here and the Washita, and when we get there, face up to Broken Nose and four or five hundred of his bunch. It's something to look forward to."

"We move out tomorrow at first light," Estrello said.

"Then you don't aim to allow the wounded time to heal," said Mark.

"They can heal as they ride," Estrello said coldly.

Mark said no more, but went to talk to Nick. Vernon was with him.

"Sorry about your leg, Nick," said Mark. "I just want to thank you both for coming after us. It was about to get downright hot where we were."

"It was no more than you'd have done for me or Vernon," Nick said. "Estrello told us we're moving out tomorrow. I reckon he didn't want us gettin' the idea we might be able to heal first."

"He's a cold-hearted bastard by anybody's standards,"

said Bill. "At least you'll be on the wagon box with your sore leg. Tilden and Wilder will be in the saddle."

Amanda and Betsy were excited when Bill and Mark rode in, but they waited until the duo had spoken to Nick and Vernon. From there, Bill and Mark hurried on to meet Betsy and Amanda.

"We're so glad you're back," Amanda cried. "Estrello said two men were killed, and when we didn't see either of you, we thought . . ."

"Not quite," said Mark. "We drove about fifty Indian horses a good sixty miles before turning 'em loose."

"I thought there was a hundred or more Indians," said Betsy. "Why so few horses?"

"Likely because this was a different bunch of Indians," Bill said. "A smaller bunch."

"Dear God," said Amanda. "Broken Nose and his bunch are just part of the problem."

"I'm afraid so," Mark said. "Bill and me were just considering the possibility that we'll be fighting different bands of Indians all the way to the Washita, and that when we get there, we'll have to face Broken Nose and four or five hundred of his followers."

"Lord, what are we going to do when we finally reach the Washita?" Betsy asked.

"I wish I knew," said Mark.

Fort Smith. August 25, 1866.

After Frank and most of the Barton gang had been wiped out and the remainder of the gang had deserted her, Liz Barton headed for the nearest town. She was hungry, with only a Colt and the clothes on her back, a result, she thought bitterly, of having shared Frank Barton's name and his bed for half a dozen years. She stopped at a stream and did what she could to freshen herself, aware from her reflection in the water that she was still a beautiful woman. Her years in the bawdy houses, saloons, and dance halls hadn't changed that. She needed a man gullible enough to fall for her charms, and strong enough to take all that she wanted from life. Reaching Fort Smith, Liz reined up before the Territorial Saloon. Until the man she sought came along, she must feed herself.

Buckshot Orr, owner and bartender, saw Liz come in. It was still early afternoon and the place was deserted.

"I'm looking for work," said Liz.

"What kind of work?" Orr asked.

"Saloon work," said Liz. "I can mix drinks, dance, sing, or anything else you require."

Orr laughed. "I can appreciate that kind of talent. Who *are* you?"

"Just call me Liz. I can start any time. I'm hungry and need a place to sleep."

"You can start tonight," said Orr. "Your pay will depend on your performance. There's a room for you at the head of the stairs, and there's plenty of grub in the kitchen. Help yourself."

It was all Liz Barton had hoped for, and more. She dined on ham and eggs in the kitchen, and then made her way upstairs to the room Orr had assigned her. There was more than just the single room. In fact, the entire upper floor looked suspiciously like the cribs in a whorehouse. Removing her gun belt, hat, boots, and clothing, she stretched out on the bed. She had begun to doze when Buckshot Orr opened the door. Liz didn't scream, flinch, or even speak. She lay there calmly, her eyes meeting those of Buckshot.

Orr laughed. "I just wanted to see if you got what it takes, Liz."

"Are you satisfied?"

"Yeah," said Orr. "For the time being. I might have other plans for you. You're more than just another saloon woman."

Liz laughed. "Just so we understand each other, my talents don't include sleeping with the owner of the saloon."

"You could do, and have done, worse, Liz Barton," Orr said. "I knew Frank. He was a damn fool who was long on ambition and short of temper. He finally got what was coming to him. I've always thought you could have done better."

"So you knew Frank," said Liz. "I don't remember you."

"You wouldn't," Orr said. "I busted up with Frank before he got his hooks into you. Frank had an eye for the women, and he caught me in . . . shall we say, a bad position . . . with a little gal who wasn't nearly as talented as you."

"If you knew Frank, you know the rest."

"The outlaw bit?" said Orr. "Frank Barton didn't have the makings of an outlaw. He wasn't smart enough. Had some good men, though."

"I know," Liz said, a bit more friendly, "I tried keeping them together, but they didn't like the idea of following a woman. I've been wondering where they went."

"They're with Sim Bowdre. He's been a mite shorthanded. Now he's got twenty-two men. He's in here regular."

"No price on his head?" Liz asked.

"None that I know of," said Orr. "He's too smart for that. He likes town living, warm beds, and warm women."

"Sounds like my kind of man," Liz said.

"Don't count on it," said Orr. "He didn't like Frank either.

You got anything to wear besides the shirt and britches you just got out of?"

"No," Liz said. "Frank thought they were good enough for lying out in the Territory."

"Well, they ain't good enough for here," said Orr. "When you get up, go to the mercantile. Get you some decent shoes and a dress or two. Charge 'em to me."

"Thanks," Liz said.

Orr closed the door, and Liz smiled to herself. So Sim Bowdre had twenty-two men, including what was left of the Barton gang. There might be enough gunmen to take those wagonloads of whiskey from Wolf Estrello . . .

Indian Territory. August 25, 1866.

When the wagons were ready to roll, Estrello sent Hiram to scout ahead for possible Indian sign.

"It took him long enough to see the need for that," said Amanda as she took her place beside Mark on the wagon box.

"I'm not sure it'll do much good," Mark said. "Those Indians haven't come off too well with us. I don't expect they'll be leaving any unnecessary sign. Still, we can't afford not to be as careful as we can."

"I always thought Indians attacked moving wagon trains," said Amanda. "None of these have, so far."

"Tribes are most likely to do that," Mark said. "These within the Territory are mostly renegades, and they're not very predictable. The average Indian likes a good fight, while most of what we encountered seems to prefer stampeding our stock and picking us off one or two at a time."

"But that hasn't worked for them," said Amanda. "Do you suppose they've given up?"

"No," Mark said. "They know what these wagons are hauling, and they're not about to give up on them. God knows what they'll do next. We'll just have to be ready for anything they throw at us."

Estrello was in a foul mood because of the numerous delays. "Let's get these damn wagons moving," he shouted, "and you teamsters watch where you're going. We got no time for breakdowns."

"He has his nerve," said Betsy. "Breakdowns have been the least of our troubles, and if it hadn't been for you, Mark, and the other teamsters, this whole bunch would have been scalped by now."

Bill laughed. "I think what we've been through so far will be nothing compared to what we'll face when we reach the Washita. If there are three or four hundred Indians there, and they decide to take these wagons, there won't be a damn thing any of us can do except die."

"What about those Indians whose horses you ran off last night? Can they catch up to us after they find their horses?"

"Yes," Bill said. "Trouble is, they may not be the problem. I don't think there were more than fifty in the bunch. That means there may be lesser groups of them somewhere along the way. But the main trial is yet to come—when we reach the Washita."

Hiram returned after a little more than an hour, reporting no Indian sign.

"Bueno," said Estrello. "There's nothin' standin' in our way."

But the left rear wheel of Ed's wagon chunked into an unseen hole, splintering the wagon wheel. Estrello galloped back, reining up before Stackler's wagon.

"By God, didn't you hear me when I said no more breakdowns?"

"Estrello," Ed said, "a man can't avoid what he can't see. Some of these holes and drop-offs are full of dead leaves, and you ought to have sense enough to know it. If you want somebody to replace me at the reins, then say so. I'm fed up with your hell-raising every time there's trouble with a wagon."

Bill was off his wagon box and was already coming to help Mark and Ed replace the damaged wheel. Estrello turned away, seething in silence.

The repair cost them the better part of an hour, and the wagons rumbled on toward whatever destiny awaited them at the Washita.

Sim Bowdre was speaking to his band of outlaws, but it was mostly for the benefit of what was left of the old Barton gang.

"I don't want any of you in town if there's a price on your head."

"Damn," said Hugh Sterns, "that eliminates all of us who was with Barton."

"So be it," Bowdre said. "If you get yourself locked in the *calabozo,* don't holler for me, 'cause I won't know you. Them of you as rides in, do it one or two at a time."

Bowdre was the first to ride in, for it was still early afternoon and the saloons would not be crowded. Bowdre went directly to the Territorial Saloon, for Buckshot Orr had once been a member of Bowdre's band of outlaws. Orr was quick to pass along to the outlaws any useful information and was amply rewarded. The saloon was empty, except for Liz and Orr. Bowdre was a big man, six feet five without his hat, and seeing Liz, he doffed his hat and bowed. Liz repaid him with a smile.

"About time Buckshot added some class to this place," Bowdre said.

"Yeah," said Orr. "Now if I could just populate it with a better class of *hombres* . . ."

Bowdre wasted no time making his way to the table where Liz sat. He hooked a chair with his boot and sat down.

"Mind if I set, ma'am?"

"Don't 'ma'am' me, damn it," Liz said. "You know who I am."

Bowdre laughed. "I just took over what was left of Frank's old outfit."

"They all have prices on their heads," said Liz.

"That's why you won't see 'em in town," Bowdre said. "I forbid it. I was right sorry to hear about old Frank. We hated one another's guts and the treacherous varmint got himself shot before I had a chance at him. I reckon you're free now, ain't you?"

"Not free," Liz snapped, "but reasonable."

As other patrons entered the saloon, Liz was drawn away from Bowdre, but she felt his eyes on her. Bowdre eventually left, not returning until near closing time. He wasted no time speaking to Liz.

"When Buckshot closes, can we talk?"

"I suppose," said Liz. "Where?"

"Here," Bowdre said.

Orr locked the door to the saloon and blew out all the lamps except one, which was turned low.

"I'll be in the kitchen, Sim, when you want out," said Orr.

They sat down at a table, and Bowdre wasted no time. "Your boys—the rest of Frank's gang—want to go after that shipment Wolf Estrello has brought into the Territory. What can you tell me about it?"

"Why should I tell you anything?"

"Because it'll take somebody like me to take it off his hands. All old Frank got out of it was a piece of lead," said Bowdre.

"I can't tell you anything you don't already know," Liz said.

"Oh, but you can," said Bowdre. "Now that old Frank's out of the picture, what are my chances?"

"That depends on what's in it for me," Liz replied.

"A hotel room in town, good grub, decent clothes, and money," said Bowdre.

He dropped five double eagles on the table before her.

Liz laughed. "Is that all?"

"Damn it, woman," said Bowdre, "with me payin' the hotel and buyin' everything else, a hundred dollars will last you a week, won't it?"

"I suppose," Liz said.

"I got a room at the hotel. We'll go there. Buckshot, come unlock the door."

After Orr had let them out, Liz turned back and spoke to him. "Sorry, Buckshot, I got a better deal."

For the time and place, the hotel was fancy. There was a dining room with solid oak tables and chairs. There was plush carpet, even in the hall. Bowdre's room was on the second floor. When they entered the room and Bowdre turned around, Liz had skinned out of the dress, and she had worn nothing else.

"Well?" said Liz.

"Well, I think it's bedtime," Bowdre said.

Indian Territory. August 26, 1866.

The Indian attack came as a total surprise. It came from the rear, and the only warning any of them had was gunfire from the three outriders trailing the last wagon. Teams were reined up, and teamsters grabbed their Winchesters. The rest of the outriders had dismounted and had let loose with a hail of lead, forcing the attackers to turn and ride for their lives. By some miracle, none of the teamsters had been hit.

"Anybody that's wounded," Estrello shouted, "come to the first wagon."

Hiram, Odell, and Hamby showed up. All had arrow wounds. Hamby was wounded in the side, but the barb had gone on through. Hiram and Odell each had an arrow in the thigh.

"Hell, we can't take the time for any doctorin' here," said Wilder. "That bunch may hit us again."

"We'll see to our wounded before goin' any farther," Estrello said. "Keithley, bring the medicine chest from your wagon. One of you see how many of the varmints we accounted for."

Vernon and Nick had already gone to take a body count.

"Vernon and me counted seventeen of 'em," said Nick.

"That's enough to bring the others back for revenge," Wilder said.

"Not necessarily," said Ed. "There weren't more than fifty of them, and that being the case, we cut down a third of them. That's bad medicine for Indians."

"Ed's right," said Todd. "They won't try another direct attack. At least, this bunch won't. They'll come at us in camp, where we all don't have our Winchesters in hand and expecting them."

Ed cleaned and bandaged the wound in Hamby's side, while Estrello himself drove out the arrows in the thighs of Hiram and Odell.

"Them of you that's wounded have to make it on to the next camp," Estrello said. "Then you can take enough whiskey to sleep off the pain and fever."

The wounded were hurting before Estrello judged it was time to end the drive for the day. The three wounded men were dosed with whiskey and were stretched out on some of their blankets.

"My God," said Betsy, "suppose two hundred of them came after us like that?"

"We'd get some of them," Bill said, "but some of them would get us. We'll just have to hope that if Broken Nose aims to take this whiskey, he'll wait until we get it to the Washita River. If he's got two hundred renegades, or even a hundred, we've had it."

"Tonight," said Estrello, "the first and second watches will be cut in half. One half of each watch will watch camp, while the second half circles our horses and mules. We're not taking a chance on that bunch coming back. If they do, we'll be ready."

Estrello himself got up far in the night, and finding his three wounded men feverish, dosed them with more whiskey. By morning, they were much improved, except for massive hangovers. The trio was unable to ride, and despite Estrello's impatience, the caravan was forced to sacrifice another day.

"Damn it," said Estrello, "this is the perfect time for that bunch to come after us."

But despite their increased watchfulness, they were not disturbed during the night, and by the next morning, the wounded men were able to ride. The wagons again took the trail, the outriders keeping a careful watch in front and behind.

Fort Smith. August 26, 1866.

Liz Barton found her alliance with Sim Bowdre entirely to her liking. She knew that sometimes he would be in town twice a week, and sometimes not at all. He was by no means critical and would never demand to know what she did while he was away. Her room was in the nicest hotel in town, and nobody questioned her presence when Bowdre wasn't there. The second night he spent with her, he had some questions.

"Liz, I keep hearing about eight wagonloads of whiskey bound for the Washita. I hear that Estrello has done this before, avoiding trouble with the Indians because they want the whiskey. What can you tell me about that?"

"Not much," said Liz. "I know they're on their way to the Washita now. Frank's idea at first was to waylay them on the return trip and take the whiskey. Then he changed his mind, and before the wagons reached Fort Smith, he attacked them."

"Empty wagons?" said Bowdre. "What in hell for?"

"He hated Wolf Estrello," Liz said, "and hoped to cripple him. But Estrello's bunch turned it around, crippling us. We lost eleven men, including Frank."

"How many men does Estrello have?"

"I don't know exactly," said Liz. "Frank said more than thirty. We had nineteen."

"I have twenty-two including what's left of Frank's bunch. They're clamorin' to go after that whiskey."

"Be careful if you do," Liz said. "Besides the teamsters, there were more than twenty outriders, every one with a Winchester."

"I'm obliged for what you've told me," Bowdre said. "If we can pull this off, there'll be something nice in it for you."

Liz laughed. "You're my kind of man, Bowdre. You do something nice for me, and I'll go on doing nice things for you."

Indian Territory. August 27, 1866.

"I've made up my mind," Sim Bowdre told his band of outlaws. We're going to take all that whiskey off Wolf Estrello's hands and sell it ourselves. We'll ride at first light. Does anybody object to that plan?"

"No," they shouted in a single voice.

"I got a question," said Will Macklin, once a Frank Barton rider. "Are we goin' in, all of us shootin' and raisin' hell, or do you have a plan that won't get us all shot dead?"

"Before anybody pulls a gun, I'll have a plan," said Bowdre.

Chapter 15

Indian Territory. August 27, 1866.

Wolf Estrello pushed the men and animals to the limit. They were still a hundred and fifty miles from the Washita.

"You're pushing too hard, Wolf," said Wilder. "The men can take it, but look at the horses and mules. They're gaunt, and these twelve-hour days is gettin' to 'em."

"Mind your own damn business, Wilder," Estrello said. "I'm still bossin' this outfit."

But Wilder's warning proved almost prophetic. Two mules came up lame and had to be replaced with horses. Worse, the eight Indian mounts they had captured were not broken to harness, and Estrello gave up on them. Instead, he used the saddle horses belonging to Carl and Lee.

"Somebody's going to pay," Lee said, "if I find whip marks or any other signs of mistreatment."

"Count me in on that," said Carl. "When I threw in with this outfit, there wasn't nothin' said about my horse pulling a wagon with a bunch of damn lop-eared mules."

"Then keep your eyes well ahead of your teams, lookin' for trouble spots," Estrello said. "Some of these damn delays can be avoided."

"A man can't see beyond the lead team of a six-mule

hitch," Todd said. "He's just got to take his chances. I'm gettin' a mite tired of the teamsters gettin' the blame when a mule stumbles or a wheel breaks. You've got a heavier load on these wagons than ever before. I think it's time you considered that."

"The loads ain't too heavy," said Estrello. "Just teamsters who are too careless, or just don't give a damn."

"I don't like the sound of that," Vernon said. "If you think that poorly of us, you might just decide not to pay us at the end of this run."

"Once we reach the Washita and settle with the Indians, you'll get everything that's comin' to you," said Estrello.

"I'm obliged for the warning," Todd said.

"Yeah," said Vernon, "we're obliged."

Fort Smith. August 28, 1866.

Liz was already awake when Sim Bowdre sat up in bed and rolled and lighted a cigarette.

"You distracted me some last night," Bowdre said, "and I didn't get around to telling you I've decided to go after Estrello's wagons. I figure them renegade Indians will buy from me as quick as they will from Estrello. Such a haul will take us plumb out of the outlaw business, I figure."

"Watch your step," said Liz, "or you may get put out of the outlaw business in a way you're not counting on. Some of those men with Estrello are carrying two Colts, with the extra loaded cylinder in their pockets. They shot Frank's outfit all to hell, without one of them taking the time to reload."*

---

* Two fully loaded Colts with an extra loaded cylinder was first attributed to the Texas Rangers. The extra cylinder could quickly be changed for a full one, allowing a man with twin Colts to fire eighteen times without reloading.

"Hell, I wasn't born yesterday," Bowdre said. "I don't aim to ride headlong into them. We'll get far enough ahead to set up an ambush."

"He's got outriders who do nothing except watch for trouble," said Liz. "They're all armed with Winchesters, which they used until they were close enough for their Colts. And then they started cuttin' us down."

Bowdre laughed. "How many did you shoot?"

"Not a damn one," Liz admitted. "When they gunned down Frank, I got the hell away from there. So did the others who lived to talk about it."

"Well, they're ready to have another go at it, and so are my bunch," said Bowdre. "I'll be gone for a few days. Wish us luck."

"I will," said Liz. "You'll need it."

After a leisurely breakfast with Liz, Bowdre rode back to his camp on the outskirts of Indian Territory, not far from Fort Smith. His bunch was hunkered around a small fire, drinking coffee from tin cups. Bowdre dismounted, took a tin cup, and poured himself some coffee before he spoke.

"Tomorrow we ride to relieve Wolf Estrello of that load of whiskey. I'm told he's got more than thirty men. Some of them carry two Colts. Probably an extra loaded cylinder, too."

"Hell, I thought they *all* had two Colts and an extra cylinder," said French Loe, one of the survivors of the attack that had taken Frank Barton's life. "The lead was comin' so thick and fast, we couldn't get close enough without bein' shot to doll rags."

"That's what you get, ridin' headlong into 'em," Bowdre said. "We'll have to get well ahead of them and set up a foolproof ambush."

"You think Estrello ain't sending a scout ahead, looking for Indian sign?" Whit Sumner asked.

"He is, unless he's a damn fool," said Bowdre. "It'll be our business to lay an ambush without leaving any horse tracks if we have to walk five miles."

"Then leave me out of it," Weaver Upton said. "I ain't walkin' no five miles."

"You ain't sharin' in the loot, either," said Bowdre. "Damn it, do what you're told, or saddle up and ride."

"Aw, I was just joshin'," Upton said, trying to cover his mistake with a grin.

"Now," said Bowdre, "who can drive a six-mule hitch?"

"I can," Hugh Sterns said.

"So can I," said Hez DeShea.

"Me, too," Whit Sumner said.

"I can do it," said Kirk Epps.

"Same here," Tasby Winters said.

"Same goes for me," said Wilson Soules.

"It goes for me, too," Cordell Kazman said.

"I can," said Blake McSween.

"So can I," Burly Grimes said.

"*Bueno,*" said Bowdre, "that's nine, and I only need eight. Now who wants to ride out today, get well ahead Estrello's outfit, and set up an ambush?"

"I'd like to go," said Lefty Paschal. "I owe that bunch a dose of what they give us."

"Not that I don't trust your judgment, Lefty," Bowdre said, "but I'm sending Upton with you. He's part Comanche. Set the ambush far enough ahead to allow us to get there well before the wagons."

"How do we know which way they'll be goin', except somewhere in Indian Territory?" Cordell Kazman wondered.

"They've done this before," said Bowdre, "so there'll be

wagon ruts. Anybody got any reason to believe they won't follow the same route this time?"

Nobody spoke. It was all laid out carefully, and the outlaws nodded in satisfaction. But things got complicated when Paschal quietly took a horse after dark and rode into Fort Smith. He headed for the Territorial Saloon and wasn't all that surprised when he found Liz Barton there, working as a house dealer. He winked at her, but she didn't so much as nod in his direction. Paschal got bold and approached the table.

"Liz," said Paschal, "I want to talk to you in between games."

"I never saw you in my life, and I have nothing to say to you," Liz said.

"Well, I say different," said Paschal. "We had more than a few rolls in the hay. You ain't forgot that, have you?"

Buckshot Orr—carrying his sawed-off namesake—saw trouble coming and headed for Paschal, who made no move toward his Colt.

"You'd better make yourself scarce, pilgrim," said Orr. "That's Sim Bowdre's woman."

"I don't see Bowdre's name on her nowhere," Paschal said. "Anyway, all I want is just to talk to her. Is there any harm in that?"

"I reckon not," said Orr. "But get on the bad side of Bowdre, and it's your funeral."

When the poker game ended and the players left the table, Paschal drew back a chair and took a seat.

"What the hell do *you* want?" Liz asked in a deadly low tone.

"Maybe I want my woman back," said Paschal.

"I've never been your woman, and I'm not now," Liz replied.

Paschal laughed. "We had us some good times behind old Frank's back. Ain't no reason we can't have some more."

"You're a damn fool, Lefty Paschal. I know you're part of Bowdre's gang, but here you are, looking for a roll in the hay with me. I'll do one thing for you. If you get out of here and promise not to come back, I won't tell Bowdre you were here."

"I ain't afraid of Bowdre," Paschal said.

"That's good," said Liz. "Here he is now."

Lefty looked toward the door and his blood ran cold. Sim Bowdre had followed him to town and stood there with his thumbs hooked in his gun belt, near the butt of his Colt. Sensing trouble, Orr brought out his sawed off twelve-gauge.

"I want no trouble in here, gents. If there's blood to be spilled, spill it in the street."

"I'll meet you in the street, Paschal," said Bowdre, "unless you're yellow."

Paschal got to his feet and started toward the door. Liz Barton remained at the table, saying nothing. Bowdre had walked about twenty yards down the dirt street. There was no moon, only the light from distant glittering stars and the lamplight that bled through the saloon windows. Bowdre still stood with his thumbs hooked in his gun belt, just above the butt of his Colt.

"I don't see the need for this," said Paschal. "Liz has been everybody's woman. She was mine while Frank Barton was still alive, and she'll be somebody else's woman when she's tired of you."

"Maybe," Bowdre said, "but she's mine now. Pull iron when you're ready."

There was no help for it. Paschal drew faster than he ever had in his life, but before his finger could tighten on the trigger, he saw flame burst from the muzzle of Bowdre's Colt.

Paschal stumbled backward and sat down in the dusty street. Finally, he lay down flat on his back and didn't move again. Doors of other saloons burst open as men rushed out to see what had happened. Several men had drawn their guns, covering Bowdre.

"Somebody get the sheriff," a man shouted.

Sheriff Glen Taggart had held the office for many years, and with most of the outlaws holed up in Indian Territory, there had rarely been any trouble in town.

"Anybody witness this shootin'?" Taggart asked.

"I did," said Orr. "It started in my place, over a woman. I made 'em come out to the street. The dead man went for his gun before the other made a move."

"What's your name, stranger?" Sheriff Taggart asked, turning to face Bowdre.

"Simmons Bowdre. This varmint come in and challenged my right to a woman that had no interest in him. I invited him out, and he wasn't fast enough. You need anything else from me, Sheriff?"

"I suppose not," said Sheriff Taggart, "but stick around town for a while. This *hombre* may have a price on his head. If he has, you're entitled to the reward."

"I'm not anxious to claim blood money," Bowdre said, "but I'll be in the Territorial Saloon for a while."

Lefty Paschal's body was carried away, and Sim Bowdre went back into the saloon. It had suddenly all the patrons it could handle, as men discussed the shooting. Some of them were sneaking looks at Liz, who sat alone at the poker table. Bowdre boldly walked over, dragged out a chair, and sat down beside Liz. Those who had been watching her quickly turned their attention elsewhere.

"An interesting situation," said Bowdre. "Was he before Frank or after Frank?"

"During Frank," Liz said.

"That ain't sayin' a hell of a lot for your loyalty," said Bowdre.

"I didn't promise loyalty," Liz said. "At least, not to you. Besides, I was done with Lefty before I met you. He was here trying to rekindle the fire. I told him to get lost. He was about to do that when you showed up."

"You're my woman, damn it," said Bowdre, "and if any more of your old fires flame up, I'll put them out just like I did this one. Let's go back to the hotel for a while."

Liz got up and started for the door with Bowdre.

"Liz," Orr shouted. "I need you to deal. We got a full house."

"Liz will be back in an hour," said Bowdre. "Until then, deal 'em yourself."

"Damn it," Liz said, "you didn't have to tell the whole town where we're going and what we'll be doing."

Bowdre laughed. "Them that knows me will know what I'm doin', and after this, I don't reckon there'll be any varmints tryin' to move in on you."

When it was time for Liz to return to the saloon, Bowdre went with her. They found Sheriff Taggart there.

"Bowdre," said Taggart, "that *hombre* had a three-thousand-dollar price on his head. I'll put in for the money, and you can pick it up at my office."

"Use it for whatever needs improvin' in the town," Bowdre said. "I don't like to earn money like that."

Seldom was such generosity known, and the men who had gathered in the saloon all cheered.

"Drinks are on the house," shouted Orr.

When Sim Bowdre returned to camp, he was leading Paschal's horse.

"What happened to Lefty?" Will Macklin asked.

"He got himself gunned down over a woman," said Bowdre. "It wouldn't have happened if he'd stayed out of town like I told him."

"Who shot him?" Loe wondered.

"I did," said Bowdre. "He drew on me, and he was a mite slow. It wasn't a total loss, though. There's a three-thousand-dollar price on his head."

"The rest of the outlaws looked at one another unbelievingly as Bowdre unsaddled his horse and Paschal's.

"My God," Harve said, "I've known some cold-blooded sons-of-bitches in my time, but Bowdre's got 'em all skinned."

"Now there's only nineteen of us to go after Estrello's load of whiskey," Green Perryman said. "There was just nineteen men in the Barton gang when we attacked Estrello and eleven died. Tarnation, this could be an omen of some kind."

There was little talk in the outlaw camp as the men considered Paschal's death and the cause of it. Paschal wasn't the first man to have died over a woman, but seldom was it at the hand of one who should be tolerant and trusting. Sim Bowdre was neither, his men decided, as they took his measure. Some of the men had split up, talking in twos and threes. The seven remaining men from the old Barton gang had gathered out of earshot of Bowdre's riders.

"I'm sticking with this outfit through the raid on Estrello's wagons," Perryman said, "and then I'm gettin' out. I want me a stake, and that's all."

"I think you got the right idea," said Macklin. "Lefty wasn't a gun-crazy fool. He wasn't all that fast. I think he was pushed into drawing."

And so went the conversation, Paschal's old outfit all but

certain their companion had been forced into a shoot-out. The quiet talk didn't go unnoticed by Bowdre and his men. Blake McSween was the first to speak of it aloud.

"They ain't likin' it 'cause Bowdre gunned down Paschal."

"It does make a man wonder just how far Bowdre will go, when somebody gets on the bad side of him," said Bagwell. "A woman has been the undoing of many a man."

"I wouldn't want Bowdre knowin' it," Winters said, "but I've had enough of the Territory. Once we pull off this raid on Estrello's whiskey wagons, I'm going back to St. Joe and stay there."

"Hell, I'm thinking we should have all headed for parts unknown after that fool attack when Frank was killed," said Weaver. "Now we're stuck with Bowdre, a varmint who kills one of his own men over some damn woman. I got the feeling he'd sell out everyone of us if it was to his advantage."

"Best spread your blankets," Bowdre shouted. "We ride at first light."

"Bowdre," said Wilson Soules, "when you rode off to town after Lefty, you forgot that you were going to send Weaver Upton and Lefty to get ahead of Estrello's wagons, to set up an ambush. Now Lefty's gone."

"I changed my mind," Bowdre said. "Tomorrow morning will be soon enough. Which of you wants to ride with Upton?"

"I will," said Duncan Trevino.

"*Bueno,*" Bowdre said. "The rest of us will allow you a day and a night to get ahead. When you're ready to double back, you'll find us following the wagon ruts. From there we'll take our positions for the ambush. We got to make it good the first time."

Indian Territory. August 28, 1866.

The wagons journeyed on, and to everybody's amusement, the tan-and-white hound ran alongside Ed's wagon.

"He needs a name," Vernon said. "What do you aim to call him?"

"I'm thinking of calling him either Vernon or Clemans," said Ed, "but I haven't decided yet. I'd hate to hurt his feelings."

Estrello had taken to sending a rider to scout ahead for Indian sign, and there seemed to be none.

"That's when you have to look out for Indians, when there's no sign," Bill said.

"Maybe they've all gotten together and are waiting for us at the Washita," said Betsy.

"That's the worst possible thing that could happen," Bill said. "We've been fortunate so far, by them coming after us in smaller numbers. Two or three hundred of them, all of the same mind, and they can take anything we have, including our scalps."

Amanda and Mark were having a discussion of a different nature.

"I'm committed to you," said Amanda, "and all I know of you is what I've experienced while you've been with Estrello's gang."

"That should be enough," Mark said. "I don't know any more about you."

"Oh, but you do," said Amanda. "Betsy and me told you and Bill about us all the way back to when Ma died and old Jake took us in."

"All right," Mark said with a sigh, "what else do you want to know about me?"

"Tell me about the women," said Amanda.

"What women?" Mark asked.

"You're near thirty years old," said Amanda. "There must have been other women. You've never been to a . . . whorehouse?"

"Never. Well, once," Mark said, "but I didn't go in."

"Why not?" Amanda asked. "Afraid?"

"Yes, damn it, I was afraid," said Mark. "I was with some other gents who went on in. They spread it all over the whole damn county that I was feather-legged, afraid of the girls."

"You've never seen a naked woman then," Amanda persisted.

"Once," said Mark, "until I saw you. I was maybe twelve or thirteen, and she was maybe a year older." He refused to look at her.

Amanda laughed delightedly.

"Laugh, damn it," Mark said. "You're the only one I ever told."

"Come on," said Amanda, "I'm not making fun of you. What do you remember most about her?"

"She was barefooted, wearing only a dress," Mark said, "and when she skinned it off, she didn't have . . . anything . . . on her chest. She was as flat as a billiard table."

Amanda laughed until she cried. Mark said nothing, his eyes on the mules' behinds.

"I won't ask you about the rest of her," said Amanda. "At her age, Betsy and me were as flat as you say she was, poor girl. But as you've noticed, we've filled out some over the years. I noticed it didn't bother you all that much when you and Bill first found Betsy and me naked, hiding from Estrello in the woods."

"Well, hell," Mark growled, "I'd growed up some since then."

"And I wasn't flat-chested," said Amanda.

"No," Mark said. "You lived up to everything I expected, and more. Now suppose you tell me how you felt when two strangers found you and Betsy jaybird naked in the woods. As I recall, neither of you seemed in the slightest embarrassed."

"We didn't have so much as a handkerchief to cover ourselves," said Amanda. "Why be embarrassed when there's nothing you can do about it? I'd been scratched and raked by thorns, with so many hurts, I couldn't think of anything else. Besides, after Estrello had stripped us, you and Bill were welcome."

"It's something I'll never forget," Mark said. "I'm just living for the day I can get you back to Texas."

"So am I," said Amanda, "and I can promise you, there'll be no surprises. What you've already seen is what you'll get. Without the scratches from briars and thorns, of course."

The wagons and teamsters had their best day since they had left the steamboats at Fort Smith. Estrello had sent Bideno to scout ahead, and Bideno reported no Indian sign of any kind.

"I figure we're maybe a hundred and twenty-five miles from our old camp," Estrello said during supper. "Ten more days, at the most."

"I hope you have a plan, in case there's three or four hundred Indians waiting there, with plans for taking the whiskey without paying," said Wilder.

"We'll know, well before we get there, what their mood is," Estrello said. "I'll ride on ahead myself, the last day before we reach the Washita."

"You'd better ride ahead three days," Ed said. "A day's travel for a wagon is, at best, twelve miles. A good horse can cover that distance in an hour. All you'll have to do is let that bunch of renegades know they're within riding distance of these wagons and they'll come after us."

"Maybe you got something there, Stackler," said Estrello. "We'll need some time to get ready for whatever they have planned for us. In fact, I think I'll do my own scouting the rest of the way to the Washita."

"Suits me," Tilden said under his breath.

"Me, too," said Worsham. "He don't really trust any of us too far."

Fort Smith. August 29, 1866.

Liz Barton took full advantage of Sim Bowdre's absence, entertaining men in the hotel room after the saloon closed, adding daily to the roll of bills she had begun to accumulate. She had no scruples. Keeping a bottle of whiskey handy, she often got a man dead drunk, rolled him for his money, and then dropped him, unconscious, through her window. Once or twice, Orr warned her, but soon gave it up, for she was bringing in far more patrons than he'd ever had before.

Indian Territory. August 30, 1866.

Upton and Trevino loaded their saddlebags with jerked beef and extra ammunition before riding in search of Estrello's outfit.

"Just be damn sure none of 'em see you," Bowdre warned. "Get far enough ahead so there's not a chance of them suspecting anything, and choose a good place for the ambush. I don't aim for us to get shot all to hell like Frank Barton."

"Hell, we ain't stupid," said Trevino. "If you reckon we ain't got sense enough to do this, then go do it yourself."

"Mount up and ride, damn it," Bowdre said.

Upton and Trevino rode out toward the southwest. Within an hour, they had found the wagon ruts that had resulted from numerous wagon wheels.

"We got to be careful we don't ride right into 'em," Trevino said. "The wind's nearly always out of the west, and that gives us an edge."

"We can't afford not to watch our back trail," Upton said. "You never know when the damn Indians will trail an outfit, just waitin' for a chance to strike. With Estrello's bunch ahead of us, and Indians behind, we're dead."

"We got to make this ambush a success," said Trevino. "I've had the feeling lately that we've about played out our hand. The war's over, and I'm wonderin' how long it'll be until the government decides to clean up Indian Territory. Long as the Indian renegades can hide out here, the Indian problem won't ever be took care of. There'll be sodbusters, schoolma'ams and land grabbers from everywhere. We won't have anywhere to hide."

"I kind of get that feeling myself," Upton said. "If we pull off this raid and the money is as good as Bowdre expects, I aim to take my cut and make myself scarce."

"I hear there's all kinds of good things happening in Missouri," said Trevino. "Them as knows the Territory can get rich leadin' settlers to south central Texas. There's thousands and thousands of acres of land available as grants. There's a wagon train leavin' St. Joseph every week or so."

"Sounds interesting," said Upton, "but there won't nothin' else pay off as big as ridin' the owl-hoot trail."

"No," Trevino admitted, "the money won't be as good, but what there is, you can enjoy it without dodging the law and keeping an eye behind you, so's some bastard don't shoot you in the back. You ever think how it would be, having a place of your own, with a warm bed and a woman beside you?"

"I think of it often," said Upton.

"Then let's make this Estrello raid a success and quit while we're ahead."

Chapter 16

Indian Territory. September 1, 1866.

The wagons were half circled, for the Estrello outfit had made camp for the night. With thirty-two men, Estrello had continued dividing them equally between the first and second watch, and then dividing each watch into two parties. Eight men watched the wagons, while eight others stayed close to the horses and mules. Estrello had assigned each of them to the same watch, so there was no confusion.

"I can't figure Estrello," said Bill to Mark as they began the first watch. "You know he doesn't trust Carl, Lee, Vernon, Todd, Nick, Ed, or either of us out of his sight, yet we're all on the same watch."

"You'll notice the *hombres* you just named are always watching the horses and mules," Mark said. "While Estrello doesn't trust us, he knows we can't afford to lose even one horse or mule. Us being teamsters, he figures we'll watch them more carefully than some of the others might."

"Well, it sure ain't because we're in any hurry to reach the Washita," said Bill. "Betsy spends all her time worrying about what's going to happen when we get there. First, she's afraid we'll all be murdered and scalped by renegade

Indians, and second, she has some real doubts that she and Amanda may not be able to find that stolen gold."

"Well, if we're all scalped and murdered, we won't have to worry about Amanda and Betsy bein' able to find the hidden gold," Mark said.

Bill sighed. "You're a hell of a lot of comfort. Is that what you're telling Amanda?"

"I don't have to tell Amanda what the odds are. She already knows, and we try to talk about other things," said Mark. "It's useless to worry about somethin' you can't change. It was different when we had some hope of reaching Captain Ferguson at Fort Worth. Now we know that's out of the question. I'd be interested in any sensible plan you can suggest."

"If I had any notion as to what we should do, I'd have told you and the others long before now," Bill said. "I had high hopes Ed would reach Fort Smith."

"So did all of us, including Ed," said Mark, "but we can't blame him. He hit a streak of the same bad luck that might have befallen any of the rest of us. Estrello's just too damn suspicious, and he's got too many men."

"Besides Estrello, there's three bastards in this outfit I'd like to gut-shoot," Bill said.

"Suggs, Irvin, and Wilder," said Mark.

"You got it," Bill said. "There's some others I'd like to see gunned down or strung up, but those three are at the head of the list."

Two shadows materialized out of the darkness. It was Ed and his newly acquired hound. "Is this a private conversation, or can anybody join in?" Ed asked.

"The dog can stay," said Bill, "but you'll have to leave."

Ed laughed. "You'll hurt his feelings if you keep calling him 'dog.' His proper name is Arky."

"Arky?" Bill said. "Where in hell did you come up with a handle like that?"

"He found us on the Arkansas near Fort Smith," said Ed. "What would you have named him? Fort Smith?"

Eventually, the rest of their companions joined Bill, Mark, and Ed. They spent the first watch in quiet conversation, frustrated as to what they might do to avoid a disaster that seemed to be coming ever closer.

The following day, while crossing a stream, Nick's wagon was disabled with a broken wheel. The right rear wheel slipped into a deep hole impossible to see in the creek bed.

"Damn your carelessness," Estrello roared. "There's been more trouble this time than we've ever had before."

"It wasn't carelessness on my part," Nick said. "The same thing would have happened if you'd been at the reins. Now get off my back."

"Some of you mule jockeys help him replace that busted wheel," Estrello said, "and get it done before dark. We'll spend the night here."

The teamsters began unharnessing their mules. Todd and Ed freed their teams and waded into the creek to help Nick. With the wagon sagging into several feet of water, it was difficult positioning the wagon jack under the wagon's rear axle. Estrello seated himself beneath a tree and did nothing. Betsy came up with a request while Bill was unharnessing the mules.

"I'd like to go up this creek a ways and wash myself. I'm sure Amanda would, too."

"Too dangerous," said Bill. "There may be Indians about."

"We wouldn't be there very long," Betsy pleaded.

"Not very long where?" Amanda asked, she and Mark having just arrived.

"I want to go upstream and wash myself in this creek," said Betsy, "and Bill won't let me because there may be Indians."

"I'd like to wash, too," Amanda said. "Bill and Mark can go with us."

"We'll have to tell Estrello," said Bill, "and he's on the prod because of Nick's wagon."

"I'll tell him myself," Betsy said. "I'm not afraid of him."

"No," said Mark. "If you're bound and determined to go, I'll tell Estrello."

Estrello watched Mark approach, and when Mark stood before him, the outlaw leader said nothing.

"Amanda and Betsy want to go upstream to wash themselves," Mark said. "Bill and me will go with them."

"Just so you don't get any ideas," Estrello said, "don't take your horses. Go afoot."

Mark nodded. It was what he had expected.

"We have to go far enough so everybody can't see us," said Betsy. "He *could* have let us ride our horses."

"He could have, but he didn't," Bill said, "and I have the feeling that if we're jumped by Indians, we'll be on our own."

Some of the rest of the outlaws watched as the four of them started upstream. Betsy and Amanda had each taken a blanket to use as a towel.

"Hey," Wilder shouted, "what are you *hombres* about to do that needs blankets?"

"Ignore the bastard," said Mark.

"Damned if I will," Bill said. "We ain't aimin' to sleep on 'em, Wilder," he shouted.

Some of the other outlaws who didn't especially like Wilder laughed, while the object of their humor went red in the face. Amanda and Betsy laughed, and that made it worse. They rounded a bend in the creek, where a stand of willows afforded them some privacy.

"This will do," said Betsy. "The water's shallow enough to see the bottom."

"You want Mark and me to turn our backs?" Bill asked.

"Why should you?" said Betsy. "The first time you ever saw us, we were both naked, and we haven't changed any."

"She's right about that," Amanda said, "but that don't include that bunch downstream. Both of you stay right where you are."

Quickly, the girls peeled out of boots, shirts, and Levi's. They stretched out full length in the water, allowing it to flow over them.

"Mark," said Amanda, "why don't you and Bill join us? You're beginning to smell like horse and mule sweat."

"You'll just have to stand us a while longer," Mark said. "I don't aim to take off my britches as long as we're surrounded by outlaws on one side and Indians on the other."

"I'm with Mark," said Bill.

"They're just shy," Betsy teased. "Why, we've seen a hundred naked, drunken Indians. You're no different from them, are you?"

"We're totally different from them," said Mark. "We don't drink. Now the two of you get your washing done, and let's be getting back."

Suddenly, somewhere within the willow thicket, a twig snapped.

"Whoever you are, back off," Bill said. "You're not welcome here."

Irvin and Suggs stepped out of the thicket fifty yards away.

"Turn around and go," said Mark. "The ladies deserve privacy."

"Haw, haw," Suggs cackled. "Privacy, with you two *hombres* lookin' on?"

"They were invited," said Betsy, "and you weren't. Now go away."

"Hell," Irvin said, "what kind of *hombre* would shoot a man over some shirttail gal's naked behind?"

"I would," said Mark. With blinding speed, he drew his Colt and fired. Irvin's hat went flying, and Mark put two more holes in it before it touched the ground.

Irvin retrieved his hat, and without a word the two men went back the way they had come.

"Amanda, you and Betsy had better get out of that creek," Mark said. "There may be some of the others coming to see what the shooting was about."

"It was worth having them show up, just to watch you use that pistol," said Betsy. "Bill, are you as fast as he is?"

"Faster," Bill said.

"He just don't always hit what he's shootin' at," said Mark. "Once, while practicing his draw, the gun sight snagged on his holster, and he shot the toe off one of his boots."

Amanda and Betsy had dressed except for their boots when Estrello arrived. Ignoring everybody except Mark, he spoke. "Every damn Indian within ten miles could have heard them shots."

"They didn't have to hear shots," Mark said coldly. "Every Indian in the Territory has the word on us by now. I could fire a cannon and not put us in any more danger than we are in already."

Indian Territory. September 4, 1866.

Upton and Trevino followed the wagon road cautiously. They found one place where an Indian attack had taken place, for there were several arrows still imbedded in trees.

There were no graves, evidence of the strength of Estrello's gang.

"They've had their problems, I reckon," said Upton, "but they're still makin' good time. What's botherin' me is that we may knock ourselves out findin' a location for an ambush, and then have Bowdre and the rest of the bunch not get here in time to spring it."

"I've thought of that, too," Trevino said. "The whole lot of us should have rode out together. Then a couple of us could have scouted ahead of Estrello's bunch, and we'd have had the men right here, ready for the ambush. Now we got to get maybe fifty miles ahead of Estrello to give our bunch time to get here and set up the ambush. There's something about this that gives me the willies, like it ain't gonna work out the way Bowdre has it all planned."

They rode on, finding the remains of a smashed wagon wheel beside a creek.

"They can't be more than a day or two ahead of us," said Upton. "Then comes the hard part. Suppose we choose a place for an ambush, and they shy away from it? You reckon Bowdre ain't gonna blame it on us?"

"He said follow the old wagon trail," Trevino said. "That's all we got to guide us, and if they go some other way, it ain't our fault. It's gettin' to be more and more temptin' to tell Bowdre it's *his* damn outfit and *his* responsibility to set up these attacks. If something goes wrong and this falls through, he'll be finished."

After dark a cool wind out of the west brought the smell of wood smoke to Trevino and Upton.

"We ought to track them down tonight and find out just how far away they are," said Upton. "Then we can ride far enough to north or south to get around and ahead of them. The Indian situation being what it is, they may be watching their back trail, and in the daytime a little dust could give us away."

"We'd better leave our horses here, then, and go on afoot," Trevino said.

The men on the first watch for Estrello's outfit were speaking softly. Bill, Mark, and their six companions had taken their usual positions, watching the horses and mules. Arky, Ed's dog, got up, and facing their back trail, growled.

"Somebody's out there," said Ed.

"Likely a varmint of some kind," Carl said.

"Maybe not," Ed said, drawing and cocking his Colt. "Come on, Arky."

There was no moon, and by the stars Ed could see nothing. After they had gone a hundred yards, Arky broke into full voice, running on ahead. Ed tried to follow, but caught his foot in some vines and fell headlong. By the time he had regained his feet, the dog had ceased barking. There was nothing to do but return to camp, and there he found Estrello waiting for him.

"I want you to keep that damn dog quiet," said Estrello. "Besides keepin' us awake, he can be heard by any Indians within ten miles."

"He had cause to bark," Ed said. "There was somebody spying on us, and he got away in the dark."

Estrello laughed. "You and the dog are hearing things."

"Go with me at first light," said Ed. "The ground's soft enough, and there'll be tracks. Somebody was out there."

"All right," Estrello agreed, "we'll have a look in the daylight."

Ed made his way back to his companions, expecting to find Arky there waiting for him. But the dog had not returned.

"Somebody was out there," said Ed, "and I have a feeling Arky's trailing him."

The dog was following Upton and Trevino, who had returned to their horses with all possible haste. "We'd better saddle up and get the hell out of here," Upton said. "We didn't count on a dog. The varmint may lead 'em right to us."

Upton and Trevino mounted their horses and rode south far enough to bypass the Estrello camp without being seen. Eventually, they turned back toward the west, paralleling the trail they expected Estrello's wagons to take. At that point, aware that Ed was no longer following him, Arky gave up the chase and returned to camp. Like a silent shadow, he emerged from the brush.

"I don't care a damn what Estrello thinks," Ed said. "There was somebody lookin' in on our camp, and come daylight, I'll prove it."

"I'm with you," said Mark. "I've got more confidence in Arky than I have in Estrello."

Ed was up before first light, awaiting Estrello.

"Damn it, can't you wait until after breakfast?" Estrello growled.

"If that's some varmints with ambush on their minds, we need to know it," said Ed. "Let's go look."

The rest of the outfit looked on with interest as Stackler and Estrello headed in the direction the dog had gone the night before. Carefully avoiding Estrello, whom he did not like, Arky followed Stackler. There were thickets carpeted with fallen dead leaves from years past, with no open ground where they might find tracks. But Arky got into the spirit of the search. He paused, barking. Stackler kicked away some dead leaves, and there was the clearly defined heel print of a boot. Brushing aside leaves, Stackler found another print.

He continued uncovering them until there was no denying the evidence. Arky ran on ahead, barking.

"He knows we're on a trail," Stackler said. "We'll follow him."

Arky got ahead and waited for them. There they found the recent hoofprints of two horses.

"Shod," said Estrello. "They wasn't Indians."

"No," Stackler agreed, "and Indians don't wear boots. This looks like an ambush in the making. Let's follow the horse tracks a ways. If it's what I'm expecting, they'll ride south for a mile or two and then circle wide to the west, getting ahead of us."

"This could be a hell of a walk," said Estrello. "Let's get our horses."

"Not yet," Stackler said. "We'd leave tracks over theirs, and if they ride back this way, they'd know we're on to them. Why don't we leave the wagons where they are for a day? If there's an ambush being planned, we need to know where it is. These two varmints can't pull it off, but they can find a likely place where enough men with Winchesters can."

Stackler and Estrello continued walking, following the trail, until Stackler's prediction proved accurate. The tracks of the two horses turned west.

"By God, Stackler, you called *that* one," said Estrello. "We'll leave the wagons where they are, and some of us will trail that pair of coyotes."

When Stackler and Estrello returned to camp, Estrello explained what they had found.

"Thank God for Ed's dog," Amanda said. "He almost got Ed killed at first, and now he seems to be trying to redeem himself."

After breakfast Estrello called the outfit together.

"We're layin' over here today," said Estrello, "and some of us are goin' to follow these two varmints that was lookin' in on us last night. For a certainty, I want Stackler and his dog to go. Stackler, who do you want to ride with you?"

"Todd Keithley," Stackler said.

"Then saddle up and ride," said Estrello. "Avoid lettin' these varmints see you if you can, and don't follow right on their heels. They'll be ridin' back to report to somebody, and we don't want your tracks followin' theirs. Let them think they've got us where they want us."

"Damn him," Todd said when he and Ed had ridden away, "he thinks we can't follow a trail. A gent that's tracked Comanches can trail *anybody*."

"Let him think what he likes," said Ed. "We're not doin' this to save his bacon, but to save our own. A well-laid ambush in Indian Territory could get us all killed. We'll make it on to the Washita, and that's what's botherin' me."

Occasionally they dismounted and walked the mile or so back to the westbound trail, satisfying themselves their prey were still ahead of them.

"Looks like the rest of their bunch may be three or four days behind," Ed said. "They've got to ride far enough ahead of the wagons for the rest of their outfit to catch up and get ahead of us."

Well ahead of Stackler and Keithley, Upton and Trevino had ridden more than thirty miles before finding what they sought. An upthrust of rock—a stone shelf—stretching north and south and wagon ruts were evidence enough that the wagons had always circled the rough, rocky pinnacles to the south.

"By God, that's what we're lookin' for," said Trevino. "The wagon road comes straight on, not cuttin' away to the south until the wagons and riders are in Winchester range.

All we got to do is hole up behind them rocks and shoot like hell wouldn't have it. The only way they could bust up that ambush is for their outriders to ride north and south, comin' around the rocks and flankin' us in a crossfire."

"If we don't cut down enough of 'em with the first volley," Upton said, "they'll do exactly that. We'd better get back to Bowdre and get our bunch headed this way."

When Stackler and Keithley returned to camp, they found Estrello awaiting a report. In silence Estrello listened as Stackler and Keithley revealed what they had learned.

"You were right, Stackler," Estrello admitted. "First they wanted to know our location, so they'd know how far ahead of us to plan their ambush. Are they followin' wagons ruts, or ridin' somewhere to the north or south of our trail?"

"To the south, a mile or so," said Keithley, "and then they turned west again. We didn't take our horses, so if they come back that way, they won't know we're onto them."

"Estrello, you've been over the trail before," Stackler said. "If you were planning an ambush, you must have some good ideas as to likely places."

"Rocky Point, about thirty miles from here," said Estrello. "It's near a mile long, from north to south, and impossible for a wagon to cross. Some rocks are head high. Once we get there, we'll go around it to the south. It's a near perfect place for an ambush."

"Not if you don't get within rifle range of it," Stackler said. "Anybody planning an ambush will have to assume you'll follow the wagon ruts that lead up to and around the rocks. But suppose, before you reach this Rocky Point— before you're within rifle range—you drive south a mile or two, and then after bypassing the ambush, turn west again?"

Estrello laughed. "That would frustrate the hell out of them. We'll do it."

"Do you know of any other likely places for an ambush?" Keithley asked.

"Nothing the equal of Rocky Point," said Estrello. "Taking us by surprise, a few men with Winchesters could gun us all down once we were within range. There's so many rocks—so much cover—our only defense would be for men to ride north and south, get behind the attackers and catch them in a crossfire."

"That might be something to consider," Keithley said, "once we know they're holed up at this Rocky Point. We can circle the rock formation, staying out of rifle range, but what will stop the same bunch from trying again? Next time, we may not be fortunate enough to know they're there."

"That's an even better idea," Estrello said. "When we're a day away from Rocky Point, we'll divide the outfit, with half riding north and half riding south. We'll circle wide and come up on that bunch of bushwhackers from behind. By God, we'll show 'em how the cow ate the cabbage. I'm obliged, Keithley and Stackler. That was a smart move."

The gang had nothing to do for the rest of the day, except clean and oil their Colts and Winchesters. After Estrello had explained the proposed attack on the bushwhackers, most of the outlaws seemed to regard Stackler and Keithley with some respect.

"Oh, I hope it works out," said Betsy.

"It will," Bill assured her. "All we have to do is give this bunch time to get in position. It's the only sure means of surviving an ambush."

"My God," said Amanda, "how many more times will we have to fight?"

"At least twice," Mark said. "Once at Rocky Point, and again when we reach the old camp on the Washita. But don't worry about Rocky Point. If Estrello knows what he's talking about, we'll win big time at Rocky Point."

"Rocky Point seems so obvious," said Amanda. "Suppose they set up an ambush somewhere else?"

"It's a chance we'll have to take," Mark said. "Ed's goin' to take the lead with his wagon from here on to the Washita. He believes his dog will warn us of bushwhackers on the trail ahead before we get within rifle range."

"Of all the years I've known Estrello," said Amanda, "I've never seen him look with favor on anything or anybody except Ed's dog."

"We owe old Arky plenty," Mark said, "and I just hope Ed can teach him not to bark at the wrong time."

Satisfied they had found the perfect site for an ambush, Upton and Trevino rode back the way they had come. It was suppertime when they reached Bowdre's camp. The outfit gathered around to hear their report, and the pair didn't disappoint them.

"It's a field of stone that runs a mile or more north and south," said Trevino. "Wagon ruts come within just a few yards of it before turning south to go around it. There's so many rocks, you can set, squat, or stand."

"How far from the Estrello camp?" Bowdre asked.

"We figured thirty miles," said Trevino. "Somebody in their outfit's got a dog. He cut loose barking last night, and we had to hightail it."

"Damn," Bowdre said. "They'll see your tracks."

"No," said Upton. "We left the horses near a mile away and went in on foot. When we rode on, looking for a place for the ambush, we rode south a ways before riding west. We didn't follow the wagon ruts."

Wilson Soules laughed. "We didn't know either of you was that smart."

"Shut up, Soules," said Bowdre. "It was the right thing to do. Tomorrow we ride."

Fort Worth, Texas. September 4, 1866.

Lieutenant Wanz, Sergeant Waymont, and Corporal Tewksbury had just returned from Indian Territory and were reporting to Captain Ferguson.

"Sir," said Lieutenant Wanz, "there must be three hundred Indians camped there at the south end of the Washita. Undoubtedly, it's where the smugglers will take the whiskey."

"Then we may not have much time," Captain Ferguson said. "If that friendly Kiowa was telling the truth, Estrello and his outfit are doomed, and there are some men who are on our side who may die with the rest."

"Who are they, sir?" Lieutenant Wanz asked.

"I'm not at liberty to say," said Ferguson. "I want you and two hundred soldiers there before the shooting starts. When you issue your challenge, my men will identify themselves and join you if they're still alive."

"What about the Indians, sir?" Wanz asked.

"They're renegades," said Captain Ferguson. "They get the same treatment as the outlaws. It may be a bloodbath, but there's no help for it. There are some good men with Estrello, and I promised them amnesty for any wrongdoing in exchange for their help in bringing the Estrello gang to justice. They made me a promise, and by the Eternal, I aim to see that they come out of this alive, if I can."

"How many men, sir?" Sergeant Waymont asked.

"Only two of my choosing," said Captain Ferguson, "but

if there are others worthy of amnesty, they will have been told long before now. If you see some men break away from Estrello's ranks, cover them as best you can."

"Sir," said Corporal Tewksbury, "if we're permitted to know, how were you able to learn of the renegade Indians gathering and the arrival of the wagonloads of whiskey?"

"I didn't know for sure about the Indians," Ferguson said, "until you and your men rode into the Territory. The whiskey smugglers made a big mistake in St. Louis. One of them murdered and robbed an illegal whiskey dealer, and his men pursued Estrello's four steamboats. One of Estrello's steamboats had a Gatling gun on the forward deck, and with it they managed to sink the pursuing steamboat. There were six survivors rescued by a commercial steamboat. The survivors talked, and Captain Hailey, commander of the outpost in St. Louis, telegraphed me that the whiskey was on its way."

"My God, how long has this whiskey smuggling been going on, and us unable to stop it?" said Wanz. "I've heard that enlistments are down, and that soldiers are not held in high regard. This should help us."

"I think so," Ferguson said. "Offer them all a chance to surrender, Lieutenant, and be sure every man riding with you has a Henry repeating rifle.* If they choose to fight Indians, outlaws, or both—shoot to kill."

---

*The military did not adopt the Winchester until 1867, although it was available.

Chapter 17

Indian Territory. September 5, 1866.

The day after Upton and Trevino returned, Bowdre ordered the outfit to move out. But they didn't continue following the wagon ruts. Instead, they rode almost five miles to the south and then turned west.

"We can be there by noon," Bowdre said, "and until this bushwhacking's been done, I don't want no fires. We'll be on cold rations. With the wind out of the west, smoke will travel a long ways."

"No smoking, either," said Upton, who didn't smoke.

"No smoking, no fires, no hell-raising of any kind," Bowdre said.

Bowdre's outfit moved on, stopping only to rest the horses. The sun was well past noon high when Bowdre judged they had traveled considerably more than thirty miles.

"Ridin' north from here," said Bowdre, "we ought to come in behind them rocks where we'll set up the ambush. We should be at least two days ahead of Estrello's outfit. All we got to do is load our guns and set behind them rocks until we hear the rattle of wagons."

* * *

Estrello's outfit laying over an extra day allowed Bowdre's band to pass undetected and reach the ambush site.
But that's where Dowdre's luck ran out. At breakfast, before
taking the trail, Estrello had something to say.

"I've decided we ain't takin' the wagons down through
the woods, missin' Rocky Point. If we don't do away with
that bunch, they'll hound the hell out of us. We'll follow
these old wagon tracks to within five miles of Rocky Point,
and that's where we'll leave all the wagons. We'll divide the
outfit, half of us ridin' south, the other half ridin' north.
After we're past Rocky Point, and we know they're waitin'
for us, both halves of our outfit can come together *behind*
Rocky Point. We'll have them in a crossfire, without any
cover."

"I got to hand it to you, Wolf," said Shadley. "That's pure
genius."

"I wouldn't say that," Wilder said. "This whole thing's
bein' set up just on the word of Keithley and Stackler, and I
don't trust either of them."

"That makes us even, Wilder," said Stackler. "I don't
trust you either."

"Neither do I," Keithley said. "I won't be surprised to see
you throw down your gun and run for it if the shooting gets
hot enough."

Furious, Wilder went for his gun, only to find both Stackler and Keithley had their Colts drawn, cocked and ready.

"That's enough, damn it," said Estrello. "By all rights,
you should be dead, Wilder. If you ever pull iron against any
of my men again, I'll kill you myself. If you want to fight,
save it for the bushwhacking. As to trusting the judgment of
Stackler and Keithley, every damn one of you knows there's
no better place for an ambush between here and the old
camp on the Washita than Rocky Point."

The wagons moved on along the rutted trail, not quite three days from Rocky Point.

Bowdrc and his outfit came out three miles west of Rocky Point. There they rode north until they reached the rutted wagon road. They followed the road until it began to curve to the southeast, for they were approaching Rocky Point from the west. When the expanse of stone came into view, they all reined up, staring in admiration.

"By God, I've never seen a better, more natural ambush," Bowdre said. "Upton, you and Trevino told it true."

There was a stream flowing from somewhere out of the massive rock formation, and it provided water for men and horses. The men unsaddled their horses and, taking saddles and Winchesters, found protected positions from which they could see the rutted wagon road approaching Rocky Point. Clouds had obscured the sun, and there was a light wind out of the west. The outlaws stretched out, heads on their saddles, hats over their faces, and dozed.

"Damn it," said Bowdre, his eyes on the gathering clouds, "it'll be raining by tonight. That'll slow down the wagons another two or three days."

Bowdre wasn't the only one watching the darkening sky.

"I had hoped we could reach Rocky Point and get the ambush behind us," Ed said. "Now these ruts will be knee deep in mud. That bunch could change their minds about Rocky Point and come after us while we're bogged down."

"I don't think so," said Todd. "It's as near perfect a place for an ambush as I've ever seen. They know we're headed that way. They'll wait."

"I hope you're right," Mark said. "Guessing wrong on an ambush, you don't get to draw a second card."

Thunder rumbled, sounding far away. Arky, Stackler's hound, took refuge beneath one of the wagons.

"If it has to rain," said Amanda, "maybe it'll quit before dark. If there's lightning, it's always more terrifying in the night. This would be a terrible time for a stampede."

"Hush," Mark said. "Don't even think such thoughts."

But far away, golden shards of lightning swept grandly across the horizon. After the wagons had been semicircled for the night, the first wind-whipped raindrops pattered on wagon canvas.

"Everybody in the saddle," Estrello shouted. "We got to hold the horses and mules if we can."

Amanda and Betsy saddled their own horses, preparing to ride.

"Betsy," said Bill, "we have enough riders."

"Yes," Mark said. "The both of you could be trapped in a stampede."

"Perhaps," said Betsy, "but not likely. We're Texans, you know."

Nothing Bill or Mark could say would change their minds. While thunder rolled, shaking the earth, lightning contented itself by lighting the horizon.

"No lightning striking," Estrello shouted. "We can hold 'em now."

Driven by the west wind, the rain came slashing down in gray sheets, drenching every rider to the skin. Thunder continued to rumble, but the lightning held off. The horses and mules were afraid, but the presence of the riders kept them from running. The rain didn't subside until far into the night, leaving mud and standing water in abundance. Worse, the clouds didn't break up, and there was every evidence there would be even more rain. Thunder slowly faded into the distance, and when the rain started again, there was no thunder or lightning.

"The second watch can handle 'em now," Estrello said. "The rest of you can catch a few winks. Gettin' up early won't make no difference with all the mud and water. We'll be here a while yet."

Bowdre and his men had held the reins of their horses during the worst of the storm. When the rain settled into a steady downpour, they pulled their hat brims down over their shirt collars and turned their backs to the wind.

"Damn," said Kirk Epps, "there ain't nothin' to do except set here and be wet and miserable. It may be a week before them wagons can travel."

"When they get here—however long it takes—we'll be ready," Bowdre said.

The rain didn't subside until almost noon of the next day. The stream ran bank full, and the men remained on the rock ledge, for in places the mud was over their boot tops.

Fort Worth, Texas. September 7, 1866.

Lieutenant Wanz had selected his two hundred men, and they all stood at ease on the parade field. The lieutenant had returned to the post commander's office for a final word with Captain Ferguson.

"The troops are ready, sir," Wanz said. "Do you want to inspect?"

"Not this time, Lieutenant," said Ferguson. "They all have Henry repeaters?"

"Yes, sir," Wanz said. "We had to do some borrowing and horse trading. Each man has been issued a hundred and twenty-four rounds of ammunition, along with enough field rations for ten days."

"Then mount up and ride," said Ferguson, "but don't get there ahead of Estrello and his wagons. We want those renegades, but to go after them before Estrello and his wagons arrive would warn them of trouble. With a west wind, shooting can be heard for miles."

"Yes, sir," Wanz said. "We'll stop a day short of the Washita, and I'll send a scout ahead. We won't make our move until the wagons arrive."

"*Bueno,*" said Captain Ferguson. "Good luck."

Lieutenant Wanz saluted, had it returned, and went to mount his command.

"Prepare to mount," Lieutenant Wanz shouted. "Mount!"

As one, the soldiers swung into their saddles, riding north in a column of fours.

Indian Territory. September 10, 1866.

Two days after the rain ceased, Estrello made the decision to move on. Within less than a mile, four wagons bogged down in mud up to the hubs. It became necessary to harness extra teams of mules to haul out the stranded wagons, and when they tried to move the second four wagons, they, too, became bogged down. Again it required the efforts of extra teams. But that was only one muddy bog. There were others, and three more times the wagons had to be rescued, using extra teams. The mules were exhausted, and the teamsters disgusted and angry. Mark sought out Estrello.

"There's still too much mud and too many bogs," said

Mark. "All we've done is make the men mad as hell and exhaust the mules. We'll have to have another day of sun. Maybe more."

Extrello didn't trust himself to speak. He merely nodded.

"Free those last two wagons, then leave all of them where they are," Mark shouted.

"Thank God Estrello's got sense enough not to fight this mud," Bill said.

"Another two-day delay," said Betsy. "How's that going to affect the ambush we're expecting?"

"Shouldn't affect it at all," Bill said. "If these varmints waitin' for us have the brains God gave a *paisano*,* they won't expect us until the sun sucks up some water and eliminates this mud. It don't take a very bright *hombre* to know a wagon can't travel in hub-deep mud."

"At least we're dry," said Betsy. "I've never been so tired of wet clothes in my life. It's been years since I slept in a warm bed, listening to rain pattering on the roof. There *is* a cabin on that place of yours in Texas, isn't there?"

Bill laughed. "There once was," he teased. "If it's gone, we can always buy us a couple of slickers and sleep out in the brush."

"I'm tired of sleeping in the damn brush," said Betsy, "and I'm tired of sleeping in my shirt, Levi's, and boots. I want to stretch out under blankets, stark naked."

"I might be persuaded to join you," Bill said. "Of course, I'd want to wear my shirt, Levi's, and boots, but I'd take off my hat and my gun belt."

"Oh, don't do that," said Betsy with a straight face. "I don't expect special treatment."

* A *paisano* is a Texas roadrunner.

At suppertime, Stackler fed Arky a decent hunk of bacon, and the dog downed it in a single gulp. He then sought out Amanda and Betsy, where he was fed again.

"We're gettin' almighty low on supplies," Nick said. "That dog's barely gettin' enough to keep him alive. You can see every rib in his carcass."

"Nick," said Ed, "that's a hound. Feed him a haunch of beef, and he'd be just as skinny as he is right now. I'll fatten him up when we get back to Texas."

"*If* we get back to Texas," Carl said. "We still have an ambush ahead of us, God knows how many renegades at the Washita, plus Estrello and his outlaws."

"That reminds me," said Lee. "Suppose there's two or three hundred Indians at the Washita, ready to take the whiskey away from us? You know damn well all of us will be expected to fight the renegades with the rest of Estrello's men. Then, even if we come out of that alive, Estrello's bunch will be more than happy to kill us all."

"Lee," said Vernon, "you're such a cheerful, happy-go-lucky cuss. If you was a doubting kind, I don't believe I could stand you."

They all laughed, but it was short-lived, for the danger ahead of them was very real.

At midmorning of the next day, Estrello's men sprang to their feet, for approaching from the east was a band of twenty-five Indians. Some were armed with lances, some with bows and arrows, and a few with rifles. The leader of the group raised his hand, giving the peace sign. Estrello returned the gesture.

"Want eat," said the Indian. "Grub."

"Sorry," Estrello said, holding out empty hands, "We're almost out of grub."

"No grub, no eat," said the Indian.

But one of his followers had seen Arky lurking under a wagon. Swiftly, he cocked and fired his rifle. Lead screamed off an iron wagon tire, narrowly missing the dog. There was no second shot, for Arky was gone into the brush. Ed had drawn his Colt, and his eyes were on the Indian who had fired at Arky. Others in the gang had their hands near their Colts. Of a single mind, the Indians wheeled their horses, riding back the way they had come.

"Just one damn problem after another," Estrello complained.

"I don't understand," said Amanda. "Why would they want to kill Arky?"

"For food," Ed said.

"My God," said Amanda, "they'd eat a dog?"

"They would," Todd said. "Many Indian camps keep a lot of dogs around, and when the hunters come in empty-handed, they'll just drop a dog in the cooking pot."

To the west time had become wearying for Bowdre's gang. There was nothing to do except wait, and after the rain ceased, the sun bore down with a vengeance.

"Damn it," Perryman complained, "you're wet from bein' rained on, or wet with your own sweat. Why can't we move off these rocks and back a ways, where there's some trees for shade?"

"Because I said no," answered Bowdre irritably. "We're not changing our position until this bushwhacking is over. The rain will have wiped out our tracks, and there's no chance of us bein' discovered until we open fire."

Their only diversion was a dog-eared deck of cards belonging to Blake McSween. Three others had joined McSween in some four-handed poker. McSween had won consistently, infuriating his companions.

"Damn you, McSween," said Kirk Epps, "you got the dog-ears on these cards learned. Anybody winnin' as much as you do has got to be cheatin' somehow."

"Ain't nobody twistin' your arm and forcin' you to play," McSween said defensively. "If you don't like the game, then get out."

"I'll try one more hand," said Epps, "and if you win again, so help me God, I'll shoot you."

"Anybody that pulls a gun, I'll peel his hide off one strip at a time," Bowdre said. "There'll be no shooting until time for the ambush. We've waited this long, and none of you are gonna louse it up now."

The waiting and the boredom continued.

Again Estrello's wagons were moving, the sun having dried up most of the mud. Their first day back on the trail, there was no trouble with any of the wagons. Estrello declared they had traveled twelve miles.

"Another good day like today," Estrello said, "and we'll ride on to Rocky Point and cut down that bunch of bushwhackers. Then it's sixty miles on to the Washita."

During the first watch of the night, Betsy and Amanda approached Bill and Mark. "When you ride in to bust up that ambush," said Betsy, "We want to go."

"No," said Bill and Mark in a single voice.

"Why not?" Amanda asked. "We each have a rifle, and we can shoot."

"You can also get shot," said Mark. "After being without you for five years, you think we're going to risk having either of you gunned down by the outlaws?"

"Damn it," Betsy said, "I'm starting to regret telling them we were promised to them five years ago. They're starting to believe it."

"I remember it like it was yesterday," said Bill.

"It *was* yesterday," Betsy said. "You caught me at a weak moment."

"What in tarnation is this argument about?" Vernon had just joined them.

"They want to ride with us when we go to bust up that ambush," said Bill. "We're telling them they can't. I hate these damn arguments. I feel like we been hitched for twenty years."

The other companions soon joined the discussion. "I'm not doubtin' the two of you can shoot," Nick said, "but this won't be a woman's fight. We'll have an edge, but this bunch will be shootin' back, and if there's enough of them, some of us will be hit before we can finish them. I think the both of you had best listen to Bill and Mark."

"We haven't known either of you for five years," said Todd, "but we still don't want to see you hurt or killed. Can't you understand that?"

"I suppose," Betsy said in resignation, "but what happens when we reach the Washita? Is it right for Amanda and me to hide under a wagon while the rest of you are gunned down?"

"We may need your guns there," said Mark. "We may all end up fighting Indians, and you may be fighting for your lives. But until it comes to that, back off. Do it for Bill and me, if for no other reason."

The second day after the wagons had taken the trail, their progress was as good as the day before.

"As far as we've come today," said Estrello, "we shouldn't be more than half a dozen miles from Rocky Point. Tomorrow we leave the wagons here and bust up that ambush."

Rocky Point. September 12, 1866.

The day dawned clear, the sun already hot by the time Bowdre's bunch finished their meager breakfast.

"I'll look for them sometime today," Bowdre said, "or tomorrow for sure."

"Unless they got wise and passed us somewhere to the south," said McSween.

"Hell, they'd have to cut a new road," Bowdre said. "They've always come this way."

"Then we'll stay here through tomorrow," said Grimes. "If they don't show by then, it means they've run a sandy on us and we've lost 'em. That's when I ride out."

"Yeah," a half a dozen others shouted in a single voice.

Bowdre swallowed hard, controlling his temper. This would be the biggest haul of his life, enough to retire from outlawing forever, and he dared not lose any of his men.

Half a dozen miles to the east, Estrello and his outfit had checked and double-checked their weapons, and were saddling their horses. Mark had taken for his own use the horse and saddle that had belonged to Kendrick, who had been killed. Bill and Mark were about to mount their horses, when Amanda and Betsy came running to them. There was little left to be said, and the girls clung to them in tearful silence.

"Both of you squeeze into one of the wagons," said Mark, "and stay out of sight. If we miss some of those varmints and they escape, the could ride back this way."

"We'll take care," Amanda said. "Come back to us."

The outfit rode out. Including Estrello, they were thirty-one strong. By prior agreement, they divided into two groups. They all reined up, gathering around Estrello for final instructions.

"Those of you in the first group will ride north at least three miles before riding west. I'll lead the second group three miles to the south, and then we'll ride west. Just to be safe, we'll figure Rocky Point is eight miles west of here. Be damn sure you're well to the west of Rocky Point before closing in. Get as close as you can before you start shooting, and nobody fires until I do."

"Wolf," said Wilder, "there's Stackler's dog. He could run on ahead and give us away."

"He's right, Stackler," said Estrello. "Take him back and have one of the women hold him until this is over."

The rest of them waited while Stackler took Arky—much against his will—back to the wagons.

"Come on, Arky," Amanda said. "You're too good a dog to get shot."

When Stackler returned, the outfit separated. The first group rode north an estimated three miles before riding west. The second group, led by Estrello, rode south three miles and then rode west. The first group reined up on a distant ridge, from which they could see the northern end of Rocky Point through the trees and brush.

"We wait here," said Wilder. "The next move is Estrello's."

To the south, Estrello and the rest of the outfit reined up just close enough to see the first outcroppings of rock. A horse nickered, and each man caught the muzzle of his own mount to prevent an answering nicker.

"They're there," Estrello said. "We'll leave the horses here and go on foot."

To the north the rest of the outfit had heard the horse nicker.

"This is as far as the horses go," said Wilder. "We got to get lots closer, and we can't do it mounted."

The men dismounted, using all available cover, making

use of every rock and bush. To the north, the first group had
dismounted and were advancing cautiously. Not until they
were to the very edge of the rock outcroppings did they see
any of the bushwhackers. Then, sounding loud in the stillness, a Winchester roared as Estrello fired. The return fire
was immediate, but the bushwhackers had the stone para-
pets *behind* them, offering no cover. As the outfit opened up
from north and south, the effect was terrible. Bowdre's outlaws dropped their weapons and ran for their horses, but
none of them made it. Two of them had their hands in the air
when they were gunned down. The entire affair didn't last
even two minutes, and when it was over, the would-be bushwhackers were all dead.

"We might as well see who they are," Estrello said, reloading his Winchester.

From the north, the rest of the outfit advanced, meeting
Estrello's bunch.

"Sim Bowdre's bunch," said Estrello as he viewed the
dead outlaw. Bowdre had been hit nine times.

"They should be buried," Lee said. "It would be the decent thing to do."

"The only damn thing we owed them, they already got,"
said Estrello. "The buzzards and the coyotes have to eat,
too. Let's ride. We'll have to circle wide to get past here, or
the mules will go crazy."

"What about their horses? There's nineteen of 'em,"
said McCarty.

"We'll take 'em with us," Estrello said. "Some of you
catch them up on lead ropes and let's get away from here.
We'd better get the wagons by here today. This bunch of
skunks will really be stinking by tomorrow."

They returned triumphant to the wagons, none of them

having so much as a scratch. Amanda and Betsy came running as Bill and Mark dismounted.

"We heard the shooting," Amanda said. "It sounded like a war."

"It was anything but that," said Mark. "I saw men gunned down with their hands in the air, trying to surrender."

"We have Wilder to thank for that," Bill said. "I saw him shoot them."

"How terrible," said Betsy. "They're all dead?"

"To the last man," Bill said. "Estrello wants to circle wide of the area and move all the wagons today. By tomorrow, every buzzard and coyote in Indian Territory will be there."

Quickly, the teamsters harnessed their teams and the wagons moved on. The captured outlaw horses were tied behind the wagons on lead ropes. Estrello led the wagons a good five miles south, and then west, allowing them to avoid the grisly scene of death. But the going was much more difficult than the ruts they had been following, and the left rear wheel of Carl's wagon dropped into an unseen hole. The wagon tilted, with most of the weight thrown to the crippled side, snapping the axle where it passed through the hub.

"Damn it," Estrello bellowed, "seven wagons missed that hole, and you drove right into it."

"I don't care how many passed over it ahead of me," said Carl. "I didn't see it. I have a spare axle."

"Come on, Carl," said Lee. "Vernon and me will help you replace it."

It was impossible to get the wagon jack under the axle near the break. Mark took an axe from one of the wagons and finding an oak tree of the right size, cut it down. With it topped and the limbs trimmed, one end of it was shoved under the broken axle. Eight of the men threw their strength to the pole, raising the sagging rear corner of the wagon high enough to get the wagon jack under the axle.

"We won't lose more than an hour with all of us working," Mark predicted.

"I'm obliged," said Carl. "That bastard, Estrello, acts like he thinks we enjoy replacing axles and wagon wheels."

"No help for it," Bill said. "We had to leave the regular trail and circle down here through the woods with all these dead leaves. We may have another wheel or axle break before we're able to get back to the regular trail."

The axle was replaced in a little more than an hour, and when Estrello judged they were well past Rocky Point and the scene of the killings, he led the wagons north, where they again took the familiar wagon road. They traveled another ten miles before making camp for the night. Betsy was filling a tin cup with coffee when Estrello spoke to her.

"We're two days away from the Washita, little gal. You'd better be refreshing your memory as to where that gold is."

Chapter 18

Again on the rutted wagon road, none of the wagons broke down. Estrello was almost jovial at times as their journey began drawing to a close.

"Tomorrow," said Estrello, "I aim to send a scout close enough to the Washita to see how many Indians are gathered there."

"No use in that," Irvin said. "If there's seventy-five, it'll be trouble for us."

Estrello said nothing, assuring himself that when they had sold the whiskey and had found the gold, he would rid himself of smart mouths like Suggs, Irvin, and Wilder.

Red River. September 12, 1866.

"We can easily reach the Washita in another day," Lieutenant Wanz told his assembled men, "but we're not riding in blind. We know about how many outlaws we'll be facing, but I want some idea as to how many Indians are there. If they decide to fight, they'll be far more dangerous than the outlaws. Sergeant Waymont and Corporal Tewksbury, I want the two of you to ride out immediately, reporting back to me as soon as you can."

The enlisted men saluted and went to saddle their horses.

The Washita. September 12, 1866.

More than two hundred renegade Indians were camped along the Washita River, awaiting the whiskey they knew Estrello's wagons were bringing. But this gathering was unlike previous ones, for none of the Indians had horses, mules, or pelts to trade. Some of the Indians who were not part of the Broken Nose bunch had some doubts.

"No pelt, no horse, no mule," said one Indian. "How we get whiskey?"

"We take whiskey," Broken Nose said. "Kill."

None of those present disagreed with that. Why trade something of value if they could get *all* the whiskey for nothing?

"Otter Tail," Broken Nose said, "come."

Otter Tail, a most trusted friend of Broken Nose, came forth.

"I would have you ride to find the whiskey that comes, so that we may know when it is near," said Broken Nose. "Do not follow the *carro* trail, for they will see your tracks."

Otter Tail nodded and went to his horse.

A day and a half east of the Washita, Estrello was taking similar precautions. He was speaking to Hiram and Odell.

"I want the two of you to ride on ahead. Try to get close enough to the Washita to see how many Indians are waiting for us. If you can, see if there are loads of pelts and extra horses or mules to be traded."

Hiram and Odell went to saddle their horses.

*   *   *

Being only a few miles from the Washita, Sergeant Waymont and Corporal Tewksbury arrived quickly. While it was
risky leaving their horses, they picketed the animals almost
a mile from the river, continuing on foot. Thus they were
able to get close enough to see many of the Indians camped
along the stream. They continued downriver a ways, satisfying themselves that Estrello's whiskey wagons had not
yet arrived.

Otter Tail, following the advice of Broken Nose, did not
follow the wagon road. Riding south for two miles, he then
rode east. He knew of a stream a little more than a day's
drive for a wagon, and that's where he found the Estrello
wagons camped for the night. He counted the number of
wagons and the number of men and rode back to report to
Broken Nose.

Hiram and Odell reached the place where Otter Tail had
wheeled his horse only minutes before. The tracks of the
unshod horse were clear after the recent rain.

"One Indian," said Hiram.

"Yeah," Odell said. "They're wantin' to know how far
away we are with all the whiskey. They've never done this
before. I'd say it means trouble. You reckon there's any use
for us to spy on the Indian camp?"

"That's what Estrello wants," said Hiram, "and I reckon
we need to know how many of the varmints are there waitin'
for us."

Otter Tail returned to the Washita and sought out Broken
Nose. "*Carro* come," Otter Tail said, "two suns."

Broken Nose nodded, saying nothing. They would be ready.

Having seen enough, Sergeant Waymont and Corporal Tewksbury made their way back to their horses and rode south. Reaching the Red River and their camp, they reported to Lieutenant Wanz.

"Two hundred or more," said Wanz. "The question is, have they come to trade for whiskey or fight for it? Did you see any pelts, horses, or mules for trade?"

"No," Waymont said, "but there wasn't enough cover to go any closer, so we couldn't really tell."

Even as Broken Nose questioned his two scouts, Hiram and Odell had found a position in a thicket where they could see most of the Indian camp.

"By the Almighty," Hiram whispered, "there's at least two hundred. Maybe more."

"Yeah," said Odell, "and all I see are Indian horses. They ain't brought a damn thing to trade for whiskey. Broken Nose aims to take it away from us, and by God, he's got the men to do it. We'd better get word back to Estrello."

Quickly, they made their way to their horses, mounted, and rode east at a fast gallop.

"So that's their plan," Estrello said when Hiram and Odell reported. "Well, we won't go all the way to the Washita. I have a better plan."

Estrello called his gang together and told them what he had learned.

"They've gathered at the Washita, aiming to take the whiskey away from us," said the outlaw leader.

"That don't come as no surprise," Wilder said. "What do you aim to do about it?"

"We ain't takin' the whiskey on to the Washita," said Estrello. "We'll take the wagons to within five miles of the Washita, and the Indians can come a few at a time to do their trading."

"I reckon you aim to convince Broken Nose that's a good idea," Suggs said.

"I aim to tell Broken Nose I'll deal with ten of them at a time," said Estrello.

"You're asking for it, Wolf," Wilder said.

Estrello saddled his horse, mounted, and rode toward the Washita. He reined up on a ridge overlooking the Washita and the Indian camp.

"Broken Nose," Estrello shouted, "I want to talk."

Broken Nose mounted his horse and rode toward Estrello. He reined up fifty yards away, saying nothing.

"The whiskey's here," said Estrello, "and we're going to sell it a little different this time. The wagons stay where they are, and your men can ride to them ten at a time." He held up both hands, fingers spread. "Ten at a time," he repeated. "No more."

Estrello turned his horse and rode away without awaiting an answer. Behind him he could hear the voice of Broken Nose. Finally, he was drowned out by a horde of shouting, angry Indians. A chill crept up Estrello's spine, and he kicked his horse into a fast gallop.

"He went down there and blowed the lid off," said Vernon. "Here comes the fight we been dreading."

A horde of screeching Indians swept down the ridge behind Estrello. Those armed with Winchesters were already shooting. Every teamster was bellied down beneath his wagon. Betsy was under the wagon with Bill, while Amanda was under Mark's wagon with him. Both women had their Winchesters blazing. The rest of the outlaws had taken the little cover they could find. Most were bellied down on the ground. The fire was deadly before the Indians were in range with their lances, bows, and arrows. Broken Nose, seeing his men being shot off their horses, shouted an order. He suddenly veered his horse to the north. The Indians knew what he had in mind, and half of them followed Broken Nose, while the others reined up just shy of rifle range.

"Damn it," Wilder shouted, "they're going to surround us."

"Some of you fire at them comin' in behind us," Estrello shouted.

Another band of Indians came over the ridge from the Washita, taking the place of the band that was slowly but surely making its way around behind Estrello's outlaws.

"We don't have a chance, do we?" Betsy asked as lead and arrows struck the wagon box above their heads.

"We always have a chance" said Bill, "as long as our ammunition holds out."

Southwest of the Washita, Lieutenant Wanz and his soldiers heard the distant gunfire.

"It's begun," Wanz shouted. "Ready your weapons and proceed at a fast gallop. Bugler, sound the charge."

As the Indians caught the outlaws in a deadly crossfire, it had a devastating effect. Patton took an arrow in his back and a Winchester slug through his chest. Hiram and Odell were down. Estrello was firing his Winchester as rapidly as he could pump the shells into the firing chamber. An arrow slammed into his shoulder, knocking him backward. He sat on the ground, still firing.

Suddenly, there was the dramatic sound of a bugle as two hundred bluecoats swept across the ridge. Difficult as it was, firing from the back of a running horse, the soldiers had begun firing, catching a large number of the renegade Indians in a crossfire. Those who had ridden beyond the wagons suddenly gave up the idea and galloped their horses away to the east. Broken Nose escaped with them, leaving half of his followers to face the soldiers. They were trapped between the soldiers and the well-armed outlaws. Fifty of their number lay dead. Those remaining saw the cause was lost. Dropping their weapons, they stood with their hands over their heads. The outlaws had ceased firing as the soldiers reined up.

"In the name of the United States of America, all of you are under arrest," Lieutenant Wanz shouted.

But some of the outlaws were wanted for murder. To surrender would mean a firing squad or the rope. The teamsters came out from under their wagons, dropping their Winchesters to show they meant no harm. The rest of the outlaws had dropped Winchesters as well, but they still had their Colts. Suddenly, a dozen of them drew their Colts, charging the surprised soldiers.

"Get 'em," Vernon shouted. Lightning quick, the eight teamsters, joined by Amanda and Betsy, drew their Colts and began firing. They cut down the rebellious outlaws before any of the soldiers were hit.

Estrello had seen the whole thing and wounded though he was, got to his feet. His hate-filled eyes were not on the soldiers, but on the teamsters, who had wiped out almost half of his gang.

"You Judas bastards," he shouted. He tried to raise his Colt, but it suddenly seemed too heavy. His hand went limp, and the weapon dropped to the ground. Then his knees gave way, and Wolf Estrello fell facedown. The outlaw leader was dead.

The soldiers had seen the teamsters cut down the advancing outlaws. They held their fire as Bill, Mark, Carl, Lee, Vernon, Todd, Nick, and Ed walked toward them. Amanda and Betsy held back, as though uncertain as to their reception.

"Lieutenant," said Mark, "Captain Ferguson sent Bill Harder and me. We're teamsters, along with these six other *hombres,* and we've been promised amnesty by Ferguson. The two ladies have been held captives by the outlaws and aren't guilty of anything."

"I'm Lieutenant Wanz," said the officer, "and Captain Ferguson told me about you. I had no idea there were so many of you, and I'm obliged to all of you for helping wipe out this gang. Thanks to your cooperation, we didn't lose a man. Captain Ferguson will be delighted. We'll camp here for the night, and a burial detail will dig graves for the dead. I'll be needing some of you to help me identify the dead outlaws. In my saddlebags I have quite a collection of wanted dodgers. I expect we'll find some familiar faces."

Sixteen of the outlaws were dead. Except for the eight teamsters, only Brice, Graves, McCarty, Schorp, McLean, and Renato were alive. Fifty of the renegade Indians had been captured alive, and they, along with the six surviving outlaws were placed under an armed guard of fifty soldiers. As Lieutenant Wanz had promised, he assigned a burial detail to dig mass graves for the dead. Then he passed out the wanted dodgers to Bill, Mark, and their companions.

"Before we bury this bunch, we need to know who they are. Or were. See how many of them you can identify."

Oddly enough, most of the outlaws were using their own names, and with a reasonably good sketch on the wanted dodgers, every outlaw—alive or dead—was identified.

"My God, what a reward there's goin' to be on this bunch," said Lieutenant Wanz.

"Right now," Bill said, "I'm more anxious to learn how the captain knew when we would be here, and that we were in big trouble."

"You can thank Estrello's bunch for sinking that steamboat," said Lieutenant Wanz. "A commercial steamboat from New Orleans picked up six survivors, and they talked. Captain Ferguson got a telegram from the post commander in St. Louis. Captain Hailey knew that Captain Ferguson was trying to bust up the whiskey smuggling, and he alerted Fort Worth that the whiskey was on its way. A friendly Kiowa at the fort mentioned this gathering of renegades along the Washita, and Captain Ferguson thought he knew why they were here. We camped along the Red and sent a scout to verify the presence of the renegade Indians. When the shooting started, we came to your assistance."

"God bless all of you who had a hand in freeing us," Amanda cried.

"Yes," said Betsy. "Now we can find the gold and return it."

"Gold?" Lieutenant Wanz looked puzzled.

"It's an old story, Lieutenant," said Bill. "Five years ago, Amanda's and Betsy's pa—who was one of the outlaws—hid some stolen gold. When Mark and me joined Estrello's outfit, he was trying to force Amanda and Betsy to take him to the gold."

"But you ladies had nothing to do with the taking of the gold?" Lieutenant Wanz asked.

"No," said Amanda. "We were with Jake Miles when he buried it along the Washita, but we're not even sure we can find the place again."

"I hope you can," Lieutenant Wanz said. "There may be a considerable reward. It could partially repay you for five years of captivity."

"They're going to get their reward," Mark said. "Betsy with Bill, and Amanda with me."

Lieutenant Wanz laughed. "Congratulations to the four of you."

"Do you want us to help your men bury the dead?" Bill asked.

"No," said Lieutenant Wanz, "my men can handle it. However, all of you being teamsters, I'd appreciate your assisting some of my men in manhandling that whiskey off the wagons. It will have to be destroyed."

"What happens to the horses, mules, and wagons?" Ed asked.

"They'll be taken to Fort Worth and confiscated by the government," said Wanz. "Can you teamsters be persuaded to take them there? You'll want to meet with the captain, I'm sure."

"You can count on us, sir," Ed said.

"Lieutenant," Betsy asked, "is there a preacher—a chaplain—at Fort Worth?"

"There is, indeed," said Wanz, "and I'd bet my commission I know why you want him. Now, if you teamsters will help, we'll dispose of that whiskey."

When it came time to get rid of the whiskey, the men simply hacked holes in the kegs with an axe. They started with Ed's wagon. The first two barrels were full of the rotgut whiskey, but all the others were full of water! Less than one third of the load was whiskey. The rest was only water.

"This is one for the record," said Lieutenant Wanz.

Word spread quickly, and the surviving outlaws cursed bitterly. Horses belonging to the dead outlaws were hobbled, along with the mules. The weather was fair, and with the soldiers standing watch, the teamsters had the night free. Since the wagons were no longer loaded, Mark and

Amanda took one, while Bill and Betsy took another. Beneath the wagon canvas, they were comfortable.

"How long will it take us to reach Fort Worth?" Betsy asked.

"Maybe a week," said Bill. "Why? Can't you wait?"

"I suppose I'll have to. I always thought it was men who were in a hurry to find the preacher and take a woman to bed."

"Not really," Bill said with a straight face. "Mark and me . . . well . . . we ain't never done anything like this before, and it might take us a couple of years to get the hang of it. If you and Amanda would kind of . . . help us along. . . ."

Amanda and Mark were also contemplating their arrival at Fort Worth.

"I don't like to think of collecting money for those dead men," said Amanda, "but they were wanted by the law. You already have a ranch. Suppose you suddenly have thousands of dollars in reward money? What will you do with it?"

"I'm going to buy you some dresses and finery, such as silk pantaloons," Mark said. "How long since you and Betsy wore dresses?"

"I don't remember," said Amanda. "Even before Ma died, we dressed like we do now. Don't go buying any pantaloons, unless you plan to wear them yourself."

"A dress with nothing under it but you, and you'll have to learn to sit down all over again," Mark said.

"What do you . . . ?" Suddenly she caught on and laughed. "Be sure that the dresses are extra long, and I won't disgrace you."

The next morning, with the renegade Indians bound and distributed among the wagons, the newly organized caravan

started for Fort Worth. The captured outlaws, their hands
bound behind them, rode their own horses.

Fort Worth, Texas. September 22, 1866.

The arrival of Lieutenant Wanz and his prisoners created
a stir at the fort. Nobody had ever brought so many captives
in from Indian territory. The lieutenant didn't report to Captain Ferguson until all the captives were locked up and under guard.

Lieutenant Wanz knocked on Ferguson's door. Entering,
he saluted.

"Damn the formalities, Lieutenant," said Ferguson. "Tell
me what happened."

Wanz gave him a report in detail, up to and including the
disposal of what was thought to be whiskey but was only
water. Ferguson slammed his fist against the desk in delight
when Lieutenant Wanz told him how the eight teamsters
had turned on the outlaws.

"I'll see there's a pardon for every one of them," said Ferguson. "They've earned it."

"There's one thing more, sir," Lieutenant Wanz said.

He then told Captain Ferguson the little he knew of the
stolen gold, and that possibly Amanda and Betsy might remember how to find it.

"They'd been through so much, so dirty, ragged, and
scared. I didn't have the heart to have them search for that
hidden gold along the Washita," said Wanz.

"You made the right decision, Lieutenant," Ferguson
said. "After a week or two of rest, decent food, and some
new clothing, perhaps they'll go with you and a detail to the
Washita."

"They've promised to do exactly that," said Wanz, "but before they do anything else, they want to talk to the post chaplain. They're wanting to be married."

"Married? To whom?"

"Amanda to Mark Rogers, and Betsy to Bill Harder," Lieutenant Wanz said.

"Well, by God," said Captain Ferguson, "you can't keep a Texan down for long. When this Reconstruction is over, Texas is going to be one hell of a state."

"Do you want to talk to the teamsters, the men who have earned pardons?" Wanz asked.

"I'll talk to them all in the morning," said Ferguson. "I need to study the wanted dodgers you brought back on those outlaws. There's going to be a pile of reward money to be divided among these teamsters. Go to the sutler's store and make arrangements for them all—and especially the ladies—to get anything they need. I'll guarantee payment."

Carl, Lee, Vernon, Todd, Nick, and Ed were assigned bunks in the bachelor officers' quarters, while Mark and Amanda and Bill and Betsy were allowed the privacy of two small cabins. Stackler's dog, Arky, was busy making friends at the mess hall, for his nose had led him there. There was enough time before the evening meal for the eight teamsters and the two women to visit the sutler's store.

"I never had three new dresses all at once in my life," Betsy said as they left the sutler's store, "I just hope we can afford them."

"Lieutenant Wanz says we can," said Mark. "I just hate it they didn't have pantaloons. Now Bill and me will have to teach you and Amanda to sit down properly. Those dresses aren't near as long as I thought they'd be."

"Then you should have bought us both some new Levis," Betsy said, "because I won't ever ride a sidesaddle. The first time I straddle a horse in one of those dresses, everybody's likely to get an eyeful."

"I told Lieutenant Wanz to find the chaplain for us," Bill said, "and he promised to do it right after supper."

"Yeah," said Mark, "it's time to put up or shut up. Damned if I'm sleeping in a bed with my britches on and a female in a new dress beside me."

The evening meal at Fort Worth was a memorable event. The teamsters, including Betsy and Amanda, ate at the officers' mess, where Captain Wanz related the capture of the renegade Indians and the total destruction of the Estrello gang.

"We didn't lose a man," Lieutenant Wanz boasted.

After supper, true to his word, Lieutenant Wanz led Betsy, Amanda, Bill, and Mark to the little post chapel. To their surprise, the place was already packed, and men stood outside the windows, trying to see inside. There was a hushed silence as the two couples went into the chapel, and they weren't surprised to find their six teamster comrades there in a front row. The double ceremony was done quickly, and all six teamsters were on their feet slapping the backs of the embarrassed grooms. Then they began kissing the brides.

"Damn it, just *once*," Bill said when Nick went after Betsy a second time.

Finally, they were allowed to return to their cabins for the night.

"I never dreamed I'd be able to take my clothes off before a man and do it all legal," Betsy said. "What are we going to do if I'm so ignorant I don't know how . . . to. . . ?"

"We'll practice all night," said Bill.

The following morning Stackler's dog was still eating when the teamsters, Amanda, and Betsy left the officers' mess. Lieutenant Wanz escorted them to Captain Ferguson's office. Ferguson shook hands with them all, beaming with pleasure at Amanda and Betsy.

"I've done some calculating," Captain Ferguson said, "and there's more than a hundred thousand dollars in rewards for those outlaws and renegade Indians. It'll take a month or so to get the money, and all of you are welcome to remain here until then."

"We still have to look for that stolen gold," said Lieutenant Wanz.

"I'm almost afraid to go looking for it," Betsy said. "It's been so long, I'm afraid we can't find it."

"You won't be faulted if you can't," said Ferguson, "but we should at least give it a try. Lieutenant Wanz, choose a dozen men to go with you. Of course, Bill and Mark will go, and your teamster friends if they so desire."

The Washita. October 1, 1866.

The thirteen soldiers, eight teamsters, and two women reached the southern portion of the Washita River when the sun was noon high.

"The best I remember," Betsy said, "there was a gnarled old pine tree whose roots had rotted away on the side away from the river. The gold was put in the hole in canvas bags and covered with dirt. Some of the pine's limbs were dead. It may have fallen by now."

They rode for five miles up the Washita and then back down, without finding the old pine. Suddenly, Arky began barking and scratching along the riverbank where it had caved in. One of the soldiers had brought a shovel, and when he drove it into the ground, he brought up a resin-rich pine root. In the same shovelful of dirt was a tarnished but identifiable double eagle.

"The pine rotted down," Ed said, "but I'm bettin' those rich pine roots held the gold right where it was buried."

Fort Worth, Texas. October 4, 1866.

"That gold would never have been recovered, had it not been for Amanda and Betsy," Captain Ferguson said. "I'll do all in my power to see that you each receive a reward. Now that you have your freedom, what do you gentlemen intend to do with your lives? You're not hurting for money."

"If I could get the rest of these *hombres* to throw in with me," said Ed, "I'd buy some wagons and teams and freight goods from St. Louis, St. Joe, and Kansas City, south to Santa Fe. There won't be a railroad there for many years."

"I'll go in with you," Nick said.

"So will I," said Vernon.

Quickly, Todd, Lee, and Carl volunteered. Only Bill and Mark said nothing. Bill looked at Betsy, while Mark looked at Amanda.

"Amanda," said Betsy, "shall we let them grow old and gray driving freight wagons?"

"Why not?" Amanda said. "I'm through sleeping by myself. I'll go with Mark."

"Then I'll go with Bill," said Betsy. "We'll keep the outfit together."

"Maybe you can help solve another government problem," Captain Ferguson said. "We must sell the confiscated freight wagons, mules, and horses, and with Reconstruction playing hell in Texas, nobody's got any money except you folks. How about it? Will you take it all off my hands?"

The teamsters looked at one another and grinned. It was more than they'd ever hoped for.

"We'll do it," they all said in a single voice.

"Good luck," said Captain Ferguson, "and don't be strangers. You'll be hauling to south Texas, and when you do, stop by and eat with us. Stackler's dog is getting fat."

All of them shook hands with Ferguson, saluted him smartly, and stepped out the door. They were on their way to a new life.

National Bestselling Author

RALPH COMPTON

AUTUMN OF THE GUN
THE KILLING SEASON
THE DAWN OF FURY
BULLET CREEK
RIO LARGO
DEADWOOD GULCH
A WOLF IN THE FOLD
TRAIL TO COTTONWOOD FALLS
BLUFF CITY
THE BLOODY TRAIL
SHADOW OF THE GUN
DEATH OF A BAD MAN
RIDE THE HARD TRAIL
BLOOD ON THE GALLOWS
BULLET FOR A BAD MAN
THE CONVICT TRAIL
RAWHIDE FLAT
OUTLAW'S RECKONING
THE BORDER EMPIRE
THE MAN FROM NOWHERE
SIXGUNS AND DOUBLE EAGLES
BOUNTY HUNTER
FATAL JUSTICE
STRYKER'S REVENGE
DEATH OF A HANGMAN
NORTH TO THE SALT FORK
DEATH RIDES A CHESTNUT MARE
RUSTED TIN
THE BURNING RANGE

S543-093010

No other series packs this much heat!

THE TRAILSMAN

Follow the trail of Penguin's Action Westerns at
penguin.com/actionwesterns